THE KEY TO MURDER
An 'Old Maids of Mercer Island' Mystery

By
Lynn Bohart

Dedicated to the fans of Julia and the Old Maids.
You motivate me to keep these stories coming.

Cover Art: Mia Yoshihara-Bradshaw

Published by Lil Dog Communications

Disclaimer: This book is a work of fiction and while many of the businesses, locations, organizations, and historical references in the book are real, some have been created to fit the storyline. I admit I take a fair amount of liberty, while still attempting to capture some of the grandeur of the Pacific Northwest and other locations.

THE KEY TO MURDER

CHAPTER ONE

My uncle was dead before he hit the floor. Not in the literal sense. He would die a minute or so later. But I didn't know that at the time.

It was just after 10:00 a.m. on a dry and sunny August morning. The air was fresh, with the scent of pine carried along by a slight breeze off Lake Washington. Several of the guests at the St. Claire Inn had left for the day. The rest were either in their rooms or out on the back deck, watching the sail boats skim across the lake. It was the kind of idyllic day we savor in the Northwest because we know it won't last long; rain seems always in the forecast.

I was in the main kitchen helping my business partner, April, finish up the breakfast dishes when she turned to me and said, "Can you get the door?"

"Huh?" I replied.

The doorbell rang a second later, and I gave her a mischievous smile.

"Damn! I wish I could do that," I said.

April had what they call a sixth sense. She often heard the phone or the doorbell before they'd even rung. I'd always wondered if her ability came from her ancestors, who were Creole in New Orleans. Not that she'd ever mentioned them sticking pins into dolls or anything. But occasionally, she saw visions that had helped us during our murder investigations.

Wiping my hands on a towel, I hurried to the front door with my two miniature Dachshunds, Mickey and Minnie, running ahead of me, barking. After all, Dachshunds bark at anything, especially a bell.

As I swung the heavy oak door open expecting to find a stranger, I found Carter Davis instead, wearing a buttoned-up shirt under an old army green sweater, hardly necessary on a warm August day. His shoulders were turned looking behind him, as if he was waiting for someone. Then he snapped his head toward me as a green Camaro revved its motor and sped up the street.

"Julia!" he said. "Someone's following…"

A quick inhale cut off the end of his sentence as he lurched across the threshold into the entryway, perspiration covering his forehead. He grabbed me around the waist, nearly pulling me off my feet.

"Uncle Carter," I managed to say, working to extricate myself. I'd known Carter since I was a girl, but we'd never been close enough to, well, fondle each other. "What in the world are you doing?"

He ran his hands down my side as he slid to the hardwood floor, giving Minnie, my little red Doxie the opportunity to move in and begin licking his face.

"Minnie! Stop that," I scolded her, yanking her back.

I shooed her away and stepped out of Carter's reach to stare down at one of my family's oldest and dearest friends. His eyes had closed, and he wheezed with each labored breath. I leaned over and shook his shoulder, calling his name. He didn't respond.

Perhaps he'd just fallen asleep. Carter was a bit of an eccentric, so while unlikely, maybe he had just dozed off.

"Carter!" I said, shaking him again.

Once more—no response. *Was he unconscious?*

I peered closely at his wizened face. His skin had a mottled, reddish tint to it, and there was something white caught in the beard stubble around his mouth. I was about to call for April when his gray eyes popped open, and he grabbed my wrist and yanked me down to his level, scaring the bejesus out of me.

"They killed me, Julia," he said through a slur of spittle. "Tell Ben to look for the—."

His muscles twitched, and his last word got caught in a gag or a gurgle. I wasn't sure which, but I couldn't understand it. He dropped back to the floor and went still, leaving the nasty smell of vomit behind, his gray eyes staring straight ahead.

"Carter?" I yelled. "Carter?"

I shook him again and slapped his face, but this time, my efforts didn't rouse a response. I put two fingers to his neck. When I realized he had no pulse, a wave of shock washed over me.

He was gone. Someone I'd known since childhood was gone. I took a steadying breath as tears flooded my eyes, and I hiccupped a sob, catching it before it became a full-blown wail.

Carter was dead. Funny, quirky Carter.

I cupped my hand across his eyes and gently closed them and then sat back on my heels, feeling a lump the size of a fist close my throat.

What in the world had just happened?

Carter wasn't an uncle by birth. He was my older brother's best friend. The two intellectuals had been inseparable as boys, spending most of their time researching obscure pieces of history or arguing over the many discrepancies found in their high school history books.

I was two years younger than my brother Ben and would often inject myself into their play time when we were young. As a result, we spent hours competing at board games, playing hide and seek, or building forts in our Wisconsin backyard. Ben excelled at the board games, especially if they took any sort of intellectual strategy. I excelled at hide 'n seek because I was small and crafty. And Carter was best at Hold the Fort, because he was big and brawny for his age.

My brain sometimes works like a pressure valve, releasing information little bits at a time. It did that then, forcing me to sit there in shock. In fact, it was a few agonizing seconds before I remembered what Carter had said before he died.

Someone had killed him!

"Oh, my God!" a voice exclaimed behind me.

I turned to find April coming through the breakfast room. It overlooked our deck and the lake beyond. She wore a flour-covered apron pulled tight around her waist, accentuating her rounded hips. She must have used a finger to brush something off her face, because she had a streak of flour splashed across her smooth, espresso skin, looking like a chalk mark on a blackboard.

"Is that Carter?" she asked, hurrying over.

"Yes," I mumbled. I grabbed a tissue from the pocket of the denim vest I'd thrown over my t-shirt that morning and used it to dab at my eyes.

April leaned over Carter's body. "What's wrong with him?"

"Well, he's ... dead."

"Oh, dear." She also searched for a pulse. When she didn't find any, she reached for my hand. "Oh, Julia, I'm so sorry. What happened?"

"I don't know. I just opened the door, and he stepped inside and collapsed. But he said the weirdest thing before he fell to the floor. He said that someone killed him."

Her brows creased. "Oh, dear. I wonder what that means." She looked down at Carter. "Why is his face so red? I mean, maybe a heart attack could do that. But…have you called anyone?"

My brain finally re-engaged. "Oh, no. Of course."

I pulled out my cell phone and dialed 911. I reported the incident and then put in a call to David, my boyfriend, who was also a local police detective.

I hung up, and April asked, "Did he say anything else before he died? Like why he was here?"

"No," I said with a sniffle. "By the time I said hello, he was on his way to the floor. It all happened so fast."

My throat had tightened again, making it difficult to speak. April stood up and put a hand on my shoulder.

"I'm sorry, Julia. I know the two of you were close."

"Yes," I said, lifting myself off the floor. "I just talked to him a few weeks ago. The last time I saw him was at one of his Thanksgiving dinners. You know, I told you about those. Everyone on the guest list came early to take part in preparing the meal. He stopped doing them because he said he just wasn't feeling up to it anymore. I told him I wanted him to join us for Thanksgiving this year." Tears suddenly flooded my eyes.

"Come and sit down," she said, leading me over toward the reception desk.

We were in the Inn's entryway, just in front of our large mahogany reception desk. Our dining room and living room opened off the hallway to our left, while the breakfast room and kitchen were behind us. And the hallway to our right led to the library, a guest bathroom, a single guest room, a service elevator, rear staircase, and my apartment.

April pulled the rolling chair out from our small office that was tucked under the upper landing and brought it over for me.

"Will you be okay?" she asked.

"Yes. Well … no," I said, sniffling. "Carter was quirky, but I was very fond of him."

"I only met him that one time," she said. "When Ben was in town, and they stopped over for an evening of cards."

"He was quirky, you know," I said. "Most people thought Carter had an off-beat sense of humor. And he was persnickety about his immense collection of old books. He didn't like anyone touching them." My eyes rested on his body, thinking how old he looked. "Do you know that at one time he measured over six feet tall? Over the last few years, however, he shrunk considerably, and he's lost a lot of weight. God, I'd love to see those hunched shoulders and crooked smile just one more time."

"It will devastate Ben, don't you think?" April asked. "Where is he these days?"

"Yes, he'll be crushed. He's in London… I think. He's still researching the Lusk letter."

"You mean the one they think Jack the Ripper sent to the police?"

"Yes," I said.

"Do you know how to reach him?"

"I'll text him. He rarely answers if I call. But he's also not very good at returning texts. Unfortunately, Carter has been estranged from his daughter for several years, so I'm not sure who will plan a funeral."

"We can help with that," she said, giving my shoulder a squeeze.

Minnie's sharp bark brought our attention toward the stairs. Curt, the twelve-year-old son of one of our guests, stood halfway down the wide staircase that led to the upstairs guest rooms. His mouth hung open as he stared at Carter's body. Curt was a nasty little thing who had already terrorized my dogs by chasing them around the breakfast-room, threatening them with a stick. They hadn't forgotten that and were both barking and snarling at him from the bottom of the stairs as if they'd like to rip his ankles to shreds. He ignored them, continuing to stare at Carter.

"Is that guy dead?" he asked, his eyes round with shock.

There was no way to sugarcoat it. "Yes. I think you should go back to your room."

I let the dogs continue to bark, hoping it would annoy him. He was unfazed. After all, miniature Dachshunds are, well, miniature. Little did he know how sharp their teeth were.

"No way," he said, descending the stairs. "I've never seen a dead body."

April quickly circled the reception desk, pushing the dogs aside and blocking him from stepping off the landing. "I think it would be best if you went back to your room," she said sternly.

"Yeah, but that guy is toast," he replied, straining to see around April's shoulders.

"Go back to your room now!" I snapped, standing up.

I'm only 5'3", so my stature wouldn't intimidate anyone. But Curt seemed to recognize an order when he heard one and slumped up the stairs.

"Fine. But my dad will want to know what happened."

"We'll let everyone know later. Until then, please stay in your room."

The sound of another door in the guest hallway upstairs showed we needed to do crowd control.

"I'll take care of it," April said. She hustled up the stairs to stop people from coming down.

Mercer Island sits in the middle of Lake Washington and is connected to Seattle and Bellevue by I-90. It isn't a large community, and the police station is only a few minutes away. That's why it didn't surprise me when the distant sound of sirens reached my ears so quickly. There is no hospital on the island, only a primary care center. But we have EMTs and an ambulance, so the ambulance wouldn't be far behind.

I stood up and took a last fond look at Carter before the police took over.

"I'm so sorry, Carter. I'll miss you. Even though you did relegate me to forever setting the table at your Thanksgiving dinners, I won't hold it against you."

In Carter's defense, I did almost kill his cat. In my defense, it wasn't all my fault. Truth be told, his niece had played a role in that one. She bumped into me as I was turning from the kitchen counter one year, making me step back onto the cat's tail. The feline shrieked. I jumped, and then dropped the gravy bowl on its head, sending it to the emergency vet. In the end, the cat was fine, but the following year Carter prohibited me from going near the kitchen. My job going forward, he said, would be to fold napkins and set out the tableware. I smiled at the memory because as I dutifully folded napkins the following year, I knocked over a candle on the dining room table and set fire to the tablecloth. That forced Carter's sprinkler system to go off, sending his guests running for their lives.

I let out a heavy sigh, knowing there would be no more Thanksgiving dinners for us, either at his house or mine.

As the sirens grew closer, I glanced out the door to our small parking lot. The property the Inn sat on slopes from the road down to the water's edge. A police cruiser was just pulling down the drive, so

I quickly rounded up the dogs and got them into my apartment. When I returned, an ambulance had also arrived.

I was careful to step around Carter and out onto the front porch as a uniformed police officer climbed out of his patrol car. He hurried up the steps with a female officer right behind him. I gestured through the open door to the body on the floor.

"It's my uncle. Or, well, not my uncle. He was a family friend," I said.

"Stay here, ma'am," the first officer said and hurried inside.

The EMTs threw open the rear doors of the ambulance and followed with a stretcher, brushing past me. I wandered over to the front porch railing and watched through the open door as they gathered around the body, checking for signs of life. A moment later, April joined me, just as a black SUV arrived. It was David.

"Do you think he ever asks himself what he got himself into when he met me?" I asked, watching David climb out of the car.

April laughed. "I'm sure he asks himself that all the time. But he adores you."

David and I had met when a close friend had died the year before while eating my peach cobbler. Well, that wasn't exactly what happened. She'd been poisoned with arsenic from my pantry. It wasn't my arsenic, and I hadn't poisoned her. Someone else had done that. But she'd died at my dining room table. Anyway, David was a detective with the Mercer Island PD. Shortly after we solved the case, he and I began to date.

My eyes lingered on him as he slammed the car door shut. His crisp blue shirt and dark tie enhanced the color of his eyes, and my pulse quickened. We hadn't seen each other since we'd returned from Chicago, where a foul ball had hit me in the head at Wrigley Field. That had landed me in the hospital for forty-eight hours while they ruled out a concussion. Given a clean bill of health, we flew home, and he'd become engulfed in a string of burglaries on the island.

He climbed the steps, nodded to April, and gazed down at me. I must have looked like a lost puppy because he wrapped his arms around me and pulled me into a hug.

"You okay?" he said into my ear.

"Yes," I replied with a sob.

He squeezed me tight and then released me.

"So, what happened this time?"

The question might seem unusual, even callous. But lately every time I turned around someone in my vicinity was dying under unusual circumstances.

"My uncle. Sorry, he's not my real uncle," I said. "He's a close friend of the family."

"You said something on the phone about someone killing him."

"That's what he told me. I heard the bell and came to answer the door. When I opened it, he just stepped forward and collapsed."

"And he's dead?"

"Yes," I said, a tear slipping down my check.

"There was no pulse," April confirmed.

"All right, wait here," he said, wiping the tear from my cheek. He disappeared inside.

The St. Claire Inn measures almost 6500 square feet with two floors and a large attic. Painted white with a pentagonal tower, a wraparound porch, several modestly ornate gables, and a steeply pitched roof, it was the perfect example of a classic Victorian building, complete with resident ghosts. April and I stood on the wraparound porch and moved over to a wrought-iron bench that sat beneath the living room's bay window. She produced a tissue from her pocket and handed it to me since I'd already shredded mine.

"What do you think Ben will say?" she asked.

"I don't know," I said, drying my face. "He and Carter were in close contact. I think Carter was even helping him do some research. Maybe Ben will know if Carter was ill."

"Carter said nothing about that when you talked to him recently?"

"No. I mean, he told me he was stopping the dinners because he said they were just too much work. But I think he was healthy. I just wonder why he showed up here unannounced."

"Maybe he wanted to talk to you about something. Maybe to tell you he was ill."

"I don't know. It's weird. I opened the door, he reached out and grabbed me around the waist and slid to the floor."

"And he said someone had killed him?"

"Yes. And to tell Ben. Why do people keep dying around me?"

"No idea," she said.

"Wait a minute!" I grasped her hand. "That's not all he said! He said Ben should look for something. But then he kind of gasped or gurgled, and I couldn't understand the last word."

"Try to remember," she encouraged me, her eyes searching mine. "Sound it out."

I paused, thinking back to that moment, and then tried to imitate his sound.

"He said, tell Ben to look for the kaaah," I struggled with the hard sound of the beginning and the gurgle or swallowing sound at the end. "The kuh......ass...stet."

I did it several times, attempting to form the right sounds. A few times, I swear it sounded like I was about to choke, until April suddenly grabbed my arm, stopping me mid-gurgle.

"Julia! I think I know what he was trying to say. He wanted Ben to look for the casket!"

Didn't see that one coming.

CHAPTER TWO

It didn't take long for David to re-emerge and rejoin us. He wore a solemn expression on his handsome, tanned face. I imagine he had steeled himself to tell us something we didn't want to hear. How often did he have to do that as a police officer? Inform families that a parent had died, or their daughter wasn't coming home?

"The EMT's think he died from poisoning," he said.

"What? Oh, my God." Second shock of the day. My heart felt heavy with grief at the thought that this kind man had been poisoned.

"Was there anyone else with him?" David asked.

"No," I said, dropping my head. "He was alone."

"Okay, listen. Several of your guests came down when they heard the sirens. I told them all to go back to their rooms."

"Okay. April told them to stay upstairs. We'll talk to them again shortly."

"And your bird is in there getting wound up."

"Oh no," I said. Ahab, our African Gray Parrot, didn't like crowds or sirens. A loud screech cut through the morning air, making me cringe. "Sorry. We'll have to get in there and move him."

"Wait," David said, glancing around the parking area. "How did your uncle get here? Did he have a car?"

"Oh," I said. "Um, yes, that's his old Range Rover over there." I pointed across the lot.

"Okay, the forensics people will have to go over it. I assume his key is on him."

Another SUV pulled down the drive. I knew before the door opened who it was. Sure enough, the tall and sexy Detective Sean Abrams climbed out, his muscular physique looking ever so much more muscular in his tight jeans and dark Henley pulled tight across his chest.

"He doesn't look like he came from the office," I said, staring at places I had no business staring at.

David glanced down at me. "It's Sunday."

The two men met at the steps and exchanged a few words before going inside. A moment later, a technician from the medical examiner's office arrived. He was a short, bald man who walked with brisk, faltering steps as if he couldn't quite decide whether to go forward or backward. He also disappeared inside.

"You know, if it was poison, this will be a crime scene now," April said. "So at least for a while, we won't be able to use the front door."

The crunch of gravel made us turn to find José, our maintenance man, approaching along the path from the garage. He wore a shop apron over jeans and a tank top, revealing muscular, tattooed arms. He sauntered over as if having a fleet of emergency vehicles in our front yard was a common occurrence. Which, of course, it was.

"I heard the sirens. What happened?" he asked nonchalantly, his dark eyes taking in the full array of cars.

"You heard the sirens but didn't come running?" April asked.

The apron had paint splashes and dark streaks across it. He shrugged. "I was staining that new bench for the back deck and couldn't stop. Anyway, I figured you'd come and get me if you needed me."

I sighed. "It was my uncle. He's dead. From poison. He died just inside the front door." I took a deep gulp of air to calm my insides. I would grieve later in private for Carter.

"I'm so sorry, Ms. Applegate. Anything I can do?"

José had worked for us for almost two years. He was close to finishing his degree in graphic design, which was an accomplishment for a kid who had escaped from the streets of Los Angeles. Before I could answer him, April nudged my elbow and pointed up the driveway to where several neighbors stood on the road pointing and gawking at the activities below.

"We should go inside," she said. "We need to take care of Ahab, anyway."

"I agree. José, guests won't be able to use the front door. We need to make a sign instructing them to use the back stairs and the back door. Can you handle that?"

"Of course," he replied.

"And I need some chocolate. Anyone care to join me?"

"I'll take a rain check," José said. "I'll go make the sign." He turned around and headed back to the garage.

"Let's take the back route," April said.

As we circled the building and came up onto the expansive back deck, there was another loud screech and then a long, high-pitched wail.

"Oh, dear. He's on a tear," April said. "I'll go calm him down." She hurried across the deck and inside a door to the breakfast-room.

In late May, we set out our lounge chairs, filled our large flowerpots and bird feeders, and brought out the birdhouses from the garage. A charming weathervane of a mother dog and her puppy stood as a focal point by our dock. Since it was a beautiful day, a variety of motorboats zoomed around the lake while several sail boats glided lazily across the water.

A young couple visiting from Michigan lounged in two of our Adirondack chairs, wine coolers in hand and ear buds tucked safely in their ears. As April attempted to calm Ahab just inside the breakfast-room door, I tapped the young man named Brett on the shoulder. He removed one of his ear buds.

"There's been an incident inside. Please stay out here for a while."

"What kind of incident?" he asked with a tedious smile. "Did someone die?"

Brett was the kind of guy I usually hate. He was naturally good looking, with a fit but not overly muscular physique, expensive clothes, an easy manner, and just a tad too much attitude. Since he'd rented an expensive car for his vacation and probably wasn't older than 23 or 24, I assumed his parents had money, meaning he'd grown up with the proverbial silver spoon in his mouth.

The woman he was with, Kendra something-or-other, wasn't much better. She looked right off the pages of a tabloid and hadn't said one word to any of us since she'd arrived. Someone had either cut out her tongue or perhaps she just couldn't be bothered with us peons. Either way, I was sure that in her case, silence was golden.

"As a matter of fact, yes," I replied.

"No shit!" he said, suddenly leaning forward to get up.

I stopped him with a raised hand. "Like I said, stay out here."

Another loud screech emanated from the breakfast room, startling us.

"Sorry, that's our parrot." I glanced through the bay window. "April is quieting him down."

April had opened the cage and was attempting to encourage the little bird onto her finger. Brett and Kendra left their Adirondack chairs and moved to the window.

"The police and emergency personnel are in there," I said to them, now irritated to be ignored. "It's a crime scene, so you can't go in. We'll be serving lemonade and snacks out here in a few minutes."

"Crime scene?" Brett blurted. "Whoa. Someone was murdered?"

The blinds inside the breakfast room suddenly unwound and dropped with a snap, blocking Brett's view.

"What the f—?" he exclaimed.

That hadn't been April. She was busy with the bird. It had to be one of our resident ghosts—probably Elizabeth who didn't like rude young men.

"Just stay out here. The police may want to talk to you."

I followed April inside and locked the breakfast-room door behind me, hoping my last statement would make Brett think twice before interfering. I glanced into the entryway, where emergency personnel hovered over Carter's body. Through the open front door, I could see a tow truck backing up to Carter's Range Rover. I was about to head into the kitchen when a high-pitched, siren-like sound from Ahab made me clap my hands to my ears.

I turned. April couldn't get Ahab onto her finger. The poor bird was bouncing around, screaming, and chattering. He didn't like all the people in the entryway. It hadn't dawned on me to move him before the police and EMTs had arrived. I'd rescued him from an estate sale where he had lived with an elderly woman who loved to watch old movies—especially old cop movies. Ahab had learned not only to quote the movies but to mimic the sounds when he got nervous. Like sirens.

April spoke softly to him. He seemed to respond, until he squawked, "Yippee-ki-yay, mother-fu—"

"No! Ahab!" I shouted, stopping him mid-sentence. "My God! He thinks he's Bruce Willis. For heaven's sake, April!"

"Okay! Okay!" she said. "Ahab, it's all right. Everything's alright." She extended a finger again, and this time he climbed onto it while she stroked his head. "It's okay, little boy. It's okay."

"I'll go get snacks started," I told her. "Then I'll have José move Ahab into my apartment."

÷

By the time April joined me a few minutes later, Ahab had quieted down, and I had a tray filled with neatly arranged brownies and lemon cookies ready to set out for guests.

"I temporarily put a towel over his cage," she said. "He was a mess."

"Good thinking."

The kitchen door leading to the deck opened and José came in with a small cardboard sign. "This look okay?" He held up a poster board with the directions on it.

"Perfect. Listen, could you post it at the top of the main staircase and add an arrow pointing to the back staircase?"

"Sure."

"Good. Then, do me a favor and let each of the guests know the police may wish to talk with them. Don't give details. Just that they'll need to remain close by. And I'll set out the refreshments on the deck in a few minutes."

"Yeah, no problem."

"Thanks. Then maybe you can move Ahab to my apartment."

He nodded and disappeared back through the door. I followed him out the door with the tray of snacks, placing them on a long narrow table under the rear window.

"Poor old fart," arrogant Brett said. He'd moved over to peer through the window in the breakfast-room door.

The EMTs had just loaded Carter's body onto a gurney and were carefully rolling him out the front door. A reprimand remained on the tip of my tongue when the first of the other guests came around the other end of the building. April brought out the cannister of lemonade, and the guests clustered around the table to grab plates.

When they began asking questions, I excused myself and stepped away to call the women in my book club. We'd met monthly for over ten years and discussed everything from a murder in the Louisiana Bayou to a woman's trek across the Himalayas. In honor of one of our members who had died the year before, we'd named ourselves the Old Maids of Mercer Island. Not because any of us were old maids, because we weren't. It was because a few moments before our dear friend had died she challenged us to live out our dreams and not to be a bunch of old maids.

Over the years, the four of us had developed an inseparable bond, which now extended to accepting challenges we had avoided earlier in life. Things like horseback riding. Singing Karaoke. Skydiving. And helping to solve several murders.

Only Blair had ever met Carter. She had accompanied me to one of his lectures on the French Revolution after we'd seen Les

Misérables and then flirted with him shamelessly afterwards. Her reaction to the news of his death when I called was so Blair. By that I mean, her first thought was to ask how soon Ben would return to the island. Yes, Blair liked to flirt with any adequately endowed man, including Carter and my brother.

Rudy was on the golf course when I called and was appropriately sympathetic.

"I'm so sorry, Julia. Carter was an intellectual of the first order. We need more of those, not less. I'll stop by as soon as I can."

But it was Doe who responded to the event itself, in other words, the murder. She said, "Dear God. Here we go again."

Besides April, these three women—Doe, Rudy, and Blair—were my closest friends. They knew me better than anyone and knew there wasn't a chance in the world I would ignore the murder of someone so close to me. After all, we'd recently helped to break up a sex trafficking ring, thwarted the murder of my arch enemy, barely escaped being killed by an evil genius, and saved a young girl's life as we fought against a group of murderers on the road trip from hell. So when Doe said, "Here we go again," she wasn't kidding.

"You can't put it off any longer," April said when I returned to the kitchen. "You need to call Ben. And then you'll have to call Angela."

My heart sank thinking of my daughter. "I know. It just makes it so real. Angela loved Carter. He spoiled her rotten. You know, he bought her a new laptop when she got her law degree. I'm sure she still has it." I exhaled. "But you're right. I need to let them both know."

It was time to do what I dreaded the most—inform my brother. I pulled out my phone and sent him a text:

Ben, Carter is dead. Someone poisoned him, and he died here at the Inn. You need to come home to help plan the funeral. Let me know what your flight plans are. José can pick you up. I'm so sorry, Ben. I know how you loved him.

Then I spoke briefly with Angela. She served as an assistant prosecuting attorney in Seattle.

"Oh, Mom, I can't believe it. Carter?" Her voice caught, and I knew she was struggling with the news. "I, um, listen. I'm on my way into court for a big case, so I can't talk, but I'll call you soon. Mom, I am so sorry."

We hung up, and I wondered how long it would be before I heard from my brother. After all, there was an eight-hour time difference with London, and Ben was a bit like the absent-minded professor when he was involved in research. He would get so caught up that I often had to make three or four attempts to contact him before he would grace me with a response. He had once disappeared for six months while hunting artifacts in the Brazilian jungle. Since no one had heard from him, I finally began writing his obituary. I was about to send it to the paper when he called and informed me in a jaunty voice that he was getting married for the third time.

And so, after sending him the text about Carter, I prepared to go about my business, expecting I'd hear from him at earliest the next day.

You can understand my surprise when he replied almost immediately, saying: *I'll be there in fifteen minutes!*

CHAPTER THREE

"He's here in the States!" I exclaimed to April.

April had the electric beaters in her hand stirring coffee cake batter for the next morning's breakfast while I paced back and forth across our black and white tiled kitchen floor.

"Not just here in the States," I continued in a loud voice. "He's in Seattle!"

She had on her reading glasses because she was trying a new recipe and looked over the top of them at me. "I take it he didn't tell you?"

"You think? I had no idea. Last time I heard from him he was in London. The audacity of that man!" I realized my voice was approaching a screech.

"You might want to calm down, Julia. There are not only guests on the patio, but policemen just outside the kitchen door."

"I don't care. I want to know why my brother didn't have the courtesy of telling me he was back in the United States. Who does he think he is?"

"Well," April began, whisking the batter, "he's not your keeper, and you're not his. I'm sure he has an explanation."

"You always take his side," I said petulantly. "You know, he has that effect on women. They all want to take care of him."

"I have no intention of taking care of anyone, especially your brother," she said with a stiff lip.

The kitchen door swung open, and Detective Abrams walked in.

"We're almost done out there," he said. "We'd like to talk to your guests, though, just in case they saw or heard anything."

Standing under the gaze of those piercing blue eyes always made me nervous. I half suspected he would arrest me at any moment. Not that he hadn't had reason to before. So far, I'd been lucky. But thinking about what I might have to do to discover who had killed Carter, I was positive I'd be in his direct line of fire once again.

"Most of the guests are out on the back deck," I told him. "And we asked them to remain available for you."

"I'll also need you to come down to the station later to make a formal statement. Did he have any family?"

"Just a daughter. I don't think they've spoken in years. I'm not even sure where she's living now."

"Do you know her name?"

"Renée…" I stopped to think. "Abernathy. Renée Abernathy. I think she used to live in Detroit, but I'm not sure if she's still there."

He nodded. "Okay. He had his ID and address on him. We'll search his residence. Did he work?"

"Yes. He taught European History in the graduate program at the University of Washington."

Detective Abrams made a note in a small notepad. "Okay. We'll check his office, too. By the way, did he get the poison here?"

"You think I poisoned him?"

He shrugged those broad shoulders. "This wouldn't be the first time someone dropped dead after ingesting poison on your property."

I stared at him for a moment, my jaws clenched. "I have no idea where he got the poison. But he didn't get it here. He showed up at my front door and then died."

Detective Abrams' blue eyes seemed to bore right through me, as if evaluating my truthfulness. I could hardly blame him. He'd been involved in a couple of our investigations. I say that like they were *our* investigations, which, of course, they weren't. But for some reason, we ended up in the middle of each one and were critical to solving them.

The truth was that this good-looking, very intense police officer didn't trust me. Partly because I'd inadvertently assaulted him with a pen during our first interview. That's a story for another time. But also, because he knew me well enough by now to know I wouldn't stay out of this investigation. And then there was the little fact that he was dating Angela. I imagined he was thinking of her right now, wondering how he would navigate the investigation without pissing one or both of us off.

"Right," he said abruptly. "Just get to the station as soon as you can."

He turned on his boot heels and strode back through the swinging door.

"I have a hard time picturing him with Angela," April said, still at the counter. "She's a brainiac, but no less personable than you. On the other hand, he's wound as tight as the underpinnings of a tennis ball."

"Yes," I said with a shake of my head, "but he's…"

"… got to be the best-looking thing on this island!" Blair said as she circled in through the door, her crystal blue eyes still hungering after the retreating detective. Drool may have even been slipping out the side of her crimson lips.

"Did you just walk through an active crime scene?" I asked her.

"They're all finished out there," she said with a flip of her hand. "Besides, I tip-toed through before they could stop me."

Blair had always reminded me of an older version of Marilyn Monroe, if Marilyn had lived to be sixty-three. She had enhanced every important part of her body, and then, through yoga and Pilates, kept the other parts in perfect shape. She also dressed just short of a streetwalker, so you could imagine what she looked like at that moment in her skin-tight, black leggings and emerald-green tank top chosen purposely to accentuate the size of her chest.

"I figured you'd need some consoling," she said, ignoring me and peering into the bowl in which April was stirring the coffee cake batter.

"Sorry, Blair," April said. "It's not sugar-free."

"That's okay," she replied. "It smells divine."

Blair was a diabetic and couldn't enjoy most of what April fixed for the guests. On special occasions, however, April would whip up a batch of sugarless something-or-other just so Blair could join in.

Loud voices on the other side of the door caught our attention, and the three of us pushed through to the breakfast-room and then into the entryway, where my brother was arguing with Detective Abrams.

"I need to know what happened," Ben demanded, staring up at the young officer.

"This is a crime scene," Detective Abrams said. "We'll arrange an interview with you as soon as we can."

Detective Abrams towered over my brother, who was only 5'10". While Detective Abrams looked every bit the ex-Army Ranger he was, Ben looked like a smaller version of Indiana Jones in his khaki cargo pants and loose-fitting beige shirt open at the collar. He even had a canvas bag angled across his chest. All he was missing was the signature hat.

David hovered in the background, clearly letting Detective Abrams take the lead. He and I shared a look as I marched into the entryway.

"Ben!" I blurted. "Let them do their work."

He spun around. "Julia. Where's Carter?"

"They've already taken his body," I replied. "Come into the kitchen."

He hesitated, looking from me to Detective Abrams.

"Now!" I demanded for the second time that afternoon.

I was younger and much smaller than my brother. But I'd always been the more emotionally commanding. He frowned and followed us back into the kitchen, where I turned on him.

"Why didn't you tell me you were back from London?"

His gray-brown eyes grew round at the admonishment. Then he stuttered. "I... I... well, I... Listen, don't mom me," he said, pointing an angry finger in my face. "I don't owe you an explanation. My work takes me all over the world, and sometimes that includes coming back to the States on the spur of the moment."

"Is that what this is? Spur of the moment?"

He shot a guilty look at April, who shrugged.

"Don't look at me. She's your sister," April said.

"Okay, maybe not so spur of the moment," he said. "I've been back since Saturday."

"For three days," I said. "And not even a text to let me know."

"Sorry. I had to stop in New York first and then... look, things have been moving fast, and frankly, I didn't have time."

"What things?"

"You found the Lusk letter!" Blair burst out, bouncing up and placing two manicured fingers on his arm.

"Not the letter," he said, stepping back. "Something else." He expelled a sigh and slumped against the counter like a deflated balloon. "And it might be the reason someone killed Carter."

"What do you mean?" I asked angrily.

"Instead of finding the Lusk letter, I found reference to a box once owned by a man named Sir Archibald Clemency. And I sent, well, I sent something to Carter for safekeeping."

"What?"

He seemed to squirm under my scrutiny. "If you must know, it was the plans for how the box was made."

"Who is Archibald Clemency?" Blair asked, following him to the counter.

He took a step away from her. "A member of a secret society in Britain founded during the late 1800s called 'The Electi.'"

"What are you talking about?" I asked with an edge to my voice. "I thought you were researching Jack the Ripper."

"I was. I *am*. But I stumbled across something explosive."

"Explosive enough to take Carter's life?" Blair asked under her breath.

"Maybe," Ben said.

He dropped his gaze, and for the first time registered some feelings about how Carter's death must have affected him.

"He was your best friend, Ben," I said quietly.

"I know. I feel awful." He shook his head. "This never should have happened. I put him at risk."

"What *has* happened?" I asked. "What's this all about?"

"And where's the box you mentioned?" April asked, pouring the batter into a large pan.

Ben crossed the room and dropped into one of the kitchen chairs. "I only know the box exists. I haven't found it yet. But I was being followed. And when someone broke into my flat in London, I decided I needed to hide the, uh, the plans. So I sent them to Carter."

For the first time, I realized Ben had a fading bruise under a lock of blondish-gray hair on his temple. "You've been in a fight."

His hand fluttered to his face. "Yes. I came home a few days ago to find my flat tossed and some thug waiting for me. He roughed me up, but I got the better of him with a hefty fireplace poker. Anyway, that's when I left the UK. I stopped in New York to interview someone but then got a cryptic text from Carter, which brought me to Seattle. I went to his house in Sammamish, but he wasn't there. In fact, that's where I was when you texted me. The house had been ransacked, and I couldn't find what I'd sent to Carter."

"He was probably on his way here," I said sadly.

"What was the cryptic message?" April asked.

"He just said it was time to come home."

"Nothing else?" I asked.

"No. But when I contacted Carter a few weeks ago, I told him I was looking for the box and that he should find a place to safeguard what I sent him."

"And he didn't tell you where he hid them... the plans?" Blair asked.

Ben flicked his eyes in her direction and back down to the floor. "No. I told him not to. I was afraid whoever was after it... after them... could make me talk if I knew."

"Jeez, sounds like a spy novel," Blair said.

"If it was that important to keep them hidden," I said, "then how did they find out you sent the plans to Carter?"

He shook his head again, causing an errant lock of hair to fall into his eyes. "I don't know. Like I said, I sent him a text. But my phone hasn't been out of my possession since then. And then he sent a telegram back to confirm he'd gotten the packages. So I don't know how anyone could have found out about Carter."

"Are you seeing anyone?" Blair asked, crossing her arms, and forcing her breasts to protrude from the top of her blouse.

He looked up. "No. Why?"

"Have you hooked up with anyone recently?" she prodded.

"My sexual encounters are no business of yours, Blair."

"I think where she's going is—did you sleep with anyone recently?" April asked. "And if so would they have been alone in your apartment for any length of time?"

He stared at April as if she were speaking a foreign language.

"Oh, for heaven's sake," I erupted. "For someone with a high enough IQ to join Mensa, you're an idiot. What she's trying to say is, did you go to the bathroom and leave the telegram out where someone might see it?"

His face blanched, and he shifted his weight as he looked from April to me and then to Blair.

"Oh my God, you did!" I blurted. "Christ, Ben. How could you be so stupid?"

"A man's loins are notoriously devoid of brains," Blair said, leaning her shapely hips against the counter.

"I think we've established that whoever you slept with read the telegram," April said, placing the coffee cake on the top rack of the oven and adjusting the timer.

"Do you even know her name?" I asked.

The sheepish look on his face said it all.

Ben was a hound dog. So, when Blair said men's loins didn't have brains, she was specifically referring to Ben's. He'd been married and divorced three times. In between, there had been a series of brief affairs plus a long string of one-night stands. The only humorous thing about this was that Blair's comment was like the pot calling the kettle black, since she had been married four times and considered every man on the planet a potential candidate to flirt with if not to get intimately acquainted with said loins.

"But why kill Carter for the plans to the box?" Blair asked, bringing my attention back. "If these people have the box, couldn't they just bust it open?" She was twirling the tassel on the gold rope belt tied tightly around her narrow waist.

"First, I don't know who has the box," Ben replied. "But according to the plans, it's a box within a box. And the inner box is made of reinforced steel and protected by a device that would release sulfuric acid if tampered with, destroying the contents. And the documents inside are irreplaceable and probably worth a fortune to the right people."

"Have you seen what's inside?" I asked him.

He exhaled. "No, but I have my suspicions. I found the structural plans. There's a key that opens the outer chamber, which is made of elaborately carved wood with the etching of a serpent wrapped around the sides. Lead lines the inner chamber, however, and it's protected by a 7-digit code. Not only that, but from what I understand, the inner box is booby-trapped. If you break it open without the code, everything inside will be destroyed."

"Wow. Who created it?" Rudy asked.

"A man named Sir Edward Finlay, father of Arthur Finlay. They were both geniuses," Ben said with a defeated sigh. "And members of London's upper, upper class."

"Why did Sir Edward Finlay create such a thing?" I asked.

"For his son, who was a member of The Electi. But I don't believe it was for the society itself, but rather a sub-group of boys who called themselves 'Brothers of the Night.'"

"What in the world are you talking about?" I asked.

"I don't have the complete picture, but from what I can surmise, both Archibald Clemency and Arthur Finlay were members of The Electi when they attended University of London. It was a club created in 1850 for upper-class, wealthy young men who would eventually move into positions of power."

"Kind of like Skull and Bones," Blair said.

Blair may play the dumb blond, but she had a photographic memory and was as smart as a whip. Skull and Bones was the secret society at Yale, which could claim several major U.S. politicians as former members.

"Membership in The Electi was by invitation only, and they forced new members to pass a rigorous initiation that relied not only on their intellect and problem-solving skills, but on their willingness to win the initiation contest at all costs."

"What does that mean?" April asked, removing her apron.

"I mean at all costs," Ben repeated.

"Meaning they'd be willing to kill people?" she asked.

"I couldn't find any record of actual deaths. At least back then," he said, correcting himself. "But in those early years there were reports of some pretty horrific beatings as part of the initiation. Every year they invited fifteen classmen to join for only seven available slots."

"So eight boys had to be eliminated," April said.

"In any way they could. I found records where one boy had an eye put out. Two more in consecutive years ended up with broken legs. There were a couple of open wounds and a broken wrist."

"Why would the school allow such a thing?" I asked.

"Because these men were the cream of the crop. They came from royalty and some of the richest families in England. And their parents were big donors to the school. Besides, the boys had all signed confidentiality agreements. To join the club, they were required to admit to something so embarrassing or so heinous the club could use it against them. If the student hadn't done something that was embarrassing or illegal, I suppose they would just make something up. One way or the other, they had to put their reputations on the line."

"Which kept them quiet," Blair said.

"Right. No harm, no foul. But things changed when women were admitted to the degree programs at the university in 1878. There were reports of sexual harassment and finally rape, one against a member of the society. The school administration forced The Electi to disband. A small group of boys created their own sub-group, calling themselves Brothers of the Night. Their symbol was the serpent. The leader of this sub-group was Archibald Clemency."

"But why do you think the box is so important?" I asked.

"Remember that to belong to The Electi you had to admit to something that might ruin your reputation for life. I assume Brothers of the Night was no different—perhaps worse. And, if members continued to record their indiscretions and/or crimes, well, that might all be in the box. Anyway, I was doing research on the Lusk Letter and interviewed an old cop who got me into the Scotland Yard archives. It was there I discovered that Archibald Clemency's best friend was a boy named Eustice Pembroke. While Clemency went to the University of London, Pembroke attended London Hospital Medical College to become a doctor."

"Don't tell me," I said. "Pembroke was a suspect in the Ripper murders."

"Good guess, Julia. That's how I got into all of this. I followed up on him as part of my research into the Lusk Letter. The police interviewed him after Mary Nichols' murder. It's widely held that she was the first victim of Jack the Ripper. Pembroke was just a student then, but he was interning with a local physician. The night of Nichols' murder, they were attending to a woman in Buck's Row who was in labor. Anyway, the baby came around eleven o'clock, and the family says the attending physician left almost immediately to make another call. But he asked Pembroke to stay until the afterbirth was delivered."

"And then?" I asked.

"Pembroke left sometime after eleven-thirty and returned to his quarters."

"Where's this Buck's Row?" Blair asked.

"In Whitechapel. It's where they found Mary Nichols' body. Anyway, Pembroke said he stopped off at a pub around midnight for a pint and then went straight home."

"What's the problem, then?" Blair wanted to know.

"I don't know there is one. But as soon as I began my research on Clemency and Pembroke, strange things began to happen."

"Like what?" Blair asked, moving over to sit at the table with Ben.

"People started following me. It was always a different person. Pretty much everywhere I went. And then, two men showed up with a camera one day just as I was going into Scotland Yard. While one of them videotaped me, the other one asked if I had anything to do with the murder of a local taxi driver killed a few weeks earlier. Of course, I had nothing to do with it and said so, but they just kept asking questions while everyone around me stopped and stared. Then, a day later, someone stole my trash."

April laughed as she washed the mixing bowl. "Who would want your trash?"

"And how would you even know someone took it?" Blair asked.

"Because I rented a flat on the third floor of a building in Leeds. I had to bag my trash and take it out to a dumpster in the alley.

Anyway, I did it every morning around six o'clock because there were mice in the building. On this day, I'd forgotten to include the box from a Keurig machine I'd just bought. I went out not five minutes later to throw the box away, and the dumpster was empty. I heard a car engine and looked up. Some bald guy with big sideburns right out of the seventies had my trash bag in his hand and was just getting into a Mercedes."

Now we all laughed.

"Seriously?" April scoffed. "Someone driving a Mercedes stole your trash?"

"Yes," he replied. "But that's not all. For two weeks, there was always a black sedan parked across the street from where I lived. A different person was behind the wheel every day, just sitting there, watching the building. I called the police, but there was nothing they could do. When that thug ransacked my flat and attacked me, I left for the states."

The kitchen grew quiet. The only sound was the ticking of the clock above the arched fireplace at one end of the room. Finally, I spoke up.

"But nothing has happened here in the states, right?" I asked. "I mean, besides Carter's death."

Ben's shoulders slumped. "I saw the guy with long sideburns in the alley when I was at Carter's house today. He was just getting into a black sedan."

CHAPTER FOUR

Ben and I went to the police station after lunch to make our statements regarding Carter's death. David and Detective Abrams joined us in their conference room, which held an oblong table, eight chairs, a water cooler, and blackboard attached to one wall, along with a large map of Mercer Island.

There were few formalities. I caught David's eye as we sat down, and he pursed his lips and gave me a solemn nod. It seemed that both David and Detective Abrams realized how difficult this was for us.

"Let's start from the beginning," Detective Abrams said. "And from what it sounds like, this starts across the pond."

Ben was forthcoming about his relationship with Carter, the search for the box, The Electi, and even the attack on him in Leeds. The only awkward moment came when Detective Abrams asked what the London authorities had done about the attack in London.

"Um, I didn't report it," Ben said.

"Why not?" the detective asked.

We were sitting across from them, and Ben's eyes darted over to me and then back again. A sure sign the question made him uncomfortable.

"Because what I'm hunting is a priceless heirloom and something many people don't even know about. I was trying to keep it under wraps."

"Seems like enough people know about it to kill for it," David said pointedly.

Regardless of David's feelings for me, he was every bit the investigator at that moment, and his eyes could have bored holes right through my brother.

I hadn't told David much about Ben in the short time I'd known him. There hadn't been a reason before now since Ben had been out of the country and not an active part of my life. But right then it didn't seem to matter that Ben was my brother. These two men were focused on him as a possible suspect or at least a very important cog in this murder wheel.

"Why is the box so important to you?" Detective Abrams asked.

Ben sat opposite Detective Abrams, and the young cop stared him down, tapping a pencil on the table as we waited for Ben's answer.

Ben sensed the scrutiny he was under and straightened up defensively in his chair.

"I'm a forensic anthropologist. One of things I do is look at old crimes and try to solve them through letters and artifacts. This particular box was at one time in the possession of someone interviewed during the investigation into Jack the Ripper."

"Seriously?" David asked. "You're researching Jack the Ripper?"

"Yes. I started out looking for what they refer to as the 'From Hell' letter that was sent to George Lusk in 1888—also known as the Lusk Letter. Lusk was head of the Whitechapel Vigilance Committee. The letter was accompanied by half a human kidney inside the box. Many people believe the person who wrote the letter could be the real Jack the Ripper."

"Okay, but what happened to the letter?" Detective Abrams asked.

"It disappeared from the Metropolitan Police back in 1888. A few people have speculated it might be in the possession of someone in Canada, and I spent quite a bit of time interviewing neighbors to the north. But no one seems to know where it is. Anyway, a few months ago, I went to London and gained access to the Scotland Yard archives."

"Where you found information about the box instead," David guessed.

"Yes. Because the box, and the secret society that owned it, were all connected to the man I just mentioned who had been interviewed by the police in connection to the Ripper murders. His name was Eustice Pembroke. Since he'd been a suspect, I was hoping this box might contain information that could lead me to the Lusk letter and perhaps to the Ripper's identity."

Ben had pulled his hands off the table and into his lap. Detective Abrams turned his attention to me.

"And you didn't know any of this when your uncle showed up this morning at the Inn?"

"No. I hadn't seen Carter in almost a year. I knew he was helping with Ben's research, though. And I talked to him a few weeks ago about joining us for Thanksgiving this year. But that's the only contact I've had with him."

"And you don't know why he came to you today?"

"Honestly, I don't. He just showed up unannounced and fell to the floor, saying that someone had killed him and that he had a message for Ben. We think he was telling Ben to find the 'casket'. Although, I'm not sure about that. It came out garbled, and he…" My breath caught in a sob, and I searched my purse for a tissue. The men waited until I was ready to continue. With tissue in hand, I said, "He died right after he said that. Anyway, that's when I called you guys."

Detective Abrams leaned back and then stood up. The rest of us followed.

"Okay. We've interviewed all your guests, and they didn't see or hear anything. You can go for now. We'll see what we can find in his car and at his home. We'll also go through his office on campus." He focused his attention on Ben. "Can you think of anyone he might have met recently? Anyone who might have had a reason to hurt him or want him dead?"

Ben shook his head. "No. But you should know that I was at his house when Julia called me. I went inside to see if I could find the plans I sent him, but someone had already been there. The entire house was tossed. I assume they were looking for the same thing."

I glanced at Ben, but he didn't take his eyes off Detective Abrams.

"Okay, thank you. We'll be in touch," Detective Abrams said.

"He was my best friend, Detective," Ben said. "Please let me know if you find anything. I'll be staying with Julia."

÷

The grandfather clock in the Inn's foyer sat in the corner among a smattering of antiques I'd organized to resemble a small reading nook. The clock boomed four times when we stepped inside, reminding me how late in the day it was. The leftover afternoon snacks were strewn across a tray on the sideboard, and I could see a few guests out on the deck. The only guests inside were a group of boys in the breakfast-room playing a board game. Ahab sat quietly in the background staring out at the lake.

Several familiar cars were parked in the lot behind me. I closed the door and texted April quickly, while Ben used the restroom down the hall. I asked her if she wanted to join us. She declined saying she had to go to the store to stock up on supplies.

When Ben returned, we turned for the Inn's living room, where I wasn't surprised to find Blair, Rudy and Doe waiting for us. Because a big part of the Inn's business was the sale of antiques, I often switched out furniture and collectibles in the common rooms. For the summer, I had gone for a beach theme in the living room, bringing in furniture upholstered in whites, light blues, and different shades of reds. Then I accented everything with large conch shells, mariner clocks, and even a restored boat's wheel.

Doe sat on the sofa talking quietly on her phone. Her signature black satchel, which carried much of her business life, sat on the floor by her feet next to an old diving helmet. Rudy was sitting in a chair with her back straight as an arrow reading something on her phone, while Blair sat on the piano bench with her shapely legs extended in front of her picking at one of her manicured nails.

They all stood when we walked in.

"What happened?" Rudy asked.

"Nothing, really. We just reported what we knew," I replied, watching Doe shut off her phone.

Ben flopped into an antique upholstered chair, while I joined Doe on the Queen Anne sofa. Blair and Rudy sat down. My three friends stared at me with concern.

"Are you okay?" Doe asked, placing a hand on my arm. "I know you two were close."

"I'm okay," I said with a nod. "But it's been tough."

"Did you tell them about the box?" Blair asked.

"Yes," Ben said.

"What can we do?" Rudy asked.

They were all staring at Ben, who seemed uncomfortable under their scrutiny.

"I honestly don't know," he said. "I still haven't processed what happened to Carter."

"Do you at least know who is after the box?" she asked.

"I only have a hunch."

"Better than nothing," Blair said. "What's your hunch?"

Ben looked young for 66. A few wrinkles creased his bright, intelligent eyes, and his hair, though still mostly blond, had streaks of gray in it. He's always been slender and still had a muscular physique. He even carried himself with the cocky sort of confidence. Right now, however, he looked his age. The weight of Carter's death had sunk in.

"I think the link to all of this might be the sub-group Pembroke belonged to, Brothers of the Night."

"Wait a minute," Rudy said. "Blair told us the secret society was called Electi something-or-other."

"The Electi," he corrected her. "But as I told Blair and Julia, a group of six boys split off to form their own group called Brothers of the Night when The Electi disbanded in 1888. A journal I found reported their motto as 'quod capit,' which means 'do what it takes' in Latin. I think they were the militant off-shoot of The Electi, willing to do whatever was necessary to get what they wanted. At least initially, the box belonged to them."

"But how do we research that?" Doe asked.

Ben's head snapped around. "*We* don't research anything. This has nothing to do with any of you."

His anger stung, keeping everyone quiet for a moment.

"You seem to forget, dear brother, that Carter was not only my friend, but he died on my entry floor. So whether you like it or not, we're already involved."

"Which might also put you at risk, Julia! I don't want that. I'd much prefer you let me handle this."

"Not a chance. And if you think we're just a bunch of shrinking violets…"

"Or old maids," Rudy added with a sly smile.

"Right," I said, returning her smile. "Then you don't know us very well. We've helped solve three murders in the past several months and had our lives put at risk each time. So don't try to play the big brother card on me."

"Besides," Doe began, "you need us. We have more resources at our disposal than you think. I'm the CEO of a major company. Rudy is an award-winning journalist who knows everyone in the newspaper world here and abroad. And Blair, well, Blair has access to many resources."

Blair smiled at that last comment.

"But what about the police?" Ben asked. "They won't just let you interfere."

The four of us exchanged glances.

"Let's just say we do a lot of asking for forgiveness rather than permission," I replied.

"But you're dating a cop," he retorted.

"I know. And it often makes David uncomfortable."

"More like it puts him in an awkward position," Rudy said.

I sighed. "But this is different. Carter was family. The police will do their thing…"

"And we'll do ours," Blair said, finishing my thought.

"Right. Let's get started," I said, turning to Rudy. "Can you get the whiteboard?"

She got up to leave the room just as young Curt suddenly appeared from the hallway with a frown pulling at the corners of his mouth.

"Hey, we're playing Clue in the other room, and several cards are missing. You shouldn't advertise board games if they aren't complete."

"Um…just a minute. I'll be right there."

I excused myself and followed him into the breakfast-room. As soon as I entered, I noticed a card slip off the corner of the table and fall to the floor. The boys didn't see it happen, but I knew who the culprit was—Chloe, the ghost of the little girl who died when the original house burned down in 1962. Her mother, Elizabeth, her youngest son, and the family dog all succumbed to the fire. Only the older son survived. Although the youngest son had never made himself known to us, we occasionally heard a dog bark and what sounded like panting nearby. And Chloe often made herself known in mischievous ways, mostly to other children and especially to those she didn't like. Apparently, she didn't like young Curt.

I approached the table. "What cards are you missing? I know a group played it just last week, so all the cards should be there."

"Professor Plum and Mrs. Peacock's cards are gone," a freckled-faced boy name Otis said.

"And the candlestick," the other boy said.

"Oh, look." I pointed under the table to where Chloe had stashed the missing items. "They've fallen on the floor."

All three boys whipped their heads around to look underneath the table.

"How the hell did they get down there?" Curt demanded. "I didn't see anything fall off the table."

"I don't know," I responded. "But all seems well." When the leaves of a potted plant in the corner fluttered, I assumed Chloe was still close by. "I have a little friend named Chloe who loves to play this game," I said loudly. "Maybe she dropped them earlier. Anyway, I'm glad you've found them, because I'm sure Chloe would want you to have a good time." I glared toward the potted plant.

Curt leaned down and brought the missing cards and candlestick back to the table. "Okay, fine. You can go now."

What a brat.

"No problem." Leaving them at their game, I wandered over to the plant and pretended to pick off a dead leaf. Under my breath, I said, "Chloe, these are our guests. Please leave them alone to play their game."

I returned to the living room to find Rudy standing next to the whiteboard with a marker in her hand.

"We've put up all the information we have so far," Blair said when I walked in.

"Now, we need to know everything you know," Rudy said to Ben. "And I mean everything. For instance, let's start with what brought you back to the States."

My nickname for Rudy was The Boss. Her demeanor was often brusque and painfully direct, and she was staring at Ben in a way that could make Arnold Schwarzenegger whither under its weight.

"Here's what I know," he said, taking a deep breath. "The Electi was the original group and formally disbanded by the university in 1887. But within a year or so it resurfaced as an independent group not connected to the university."

"What does The Electi mean, anyway?" Doe asked.

"It's Latin for the 'chosen,'" Ben replied.

"Ewww," Blair wheezed with a wrinkled brow. "These guys had the egos of Greek gods."

"That's the point," Ben said. "They believed they were the anointed ones—destined for greatness and above any law. In fact, in several places, I've seen the Latin phrase 'fines non est' associated with them."

"Another motto?" Rudy asked.

"Yes. The loose translation for this one is 'limits don't exist.'"

Rudy sat on the arm of the sofa. "That's a frightening thought. People with influence and power without limits."

"Exactly," Ben replied.

"There were two groups," I said. "The original and larger group called The Electi, and then a spin-off called Brothers of the Night. Right?"

"Right," Ben confirmed. "Anyway, when The Electi resurfaced, they eliminated the severe initiation ritual, I suppose for appearance's sake."

"So fewer eyes put out," Rudy said cynically.

"Yes. But only because they didn't want to draw attention to themselves the way they had in the past. They even adopted a creed of honor. After all, as these young men grew into adults, the few that I could trace moved into powerful positions throughout England. In 1945, or thereabouts, they expanded. First to Germany and France and then to America."

"Wait. You're saying that members of The Electi are now in positions of power here in the States?" Doe asked with a dour expression.

"Again, just like Skull and Bones," Blair said.

"Yes," Ben confirmed. "It's clear these were men who wanted to be in positions of influence. Although, because their membership is secretive, I've only been able to track a few of them and don't have a complete list of American members to work from. I do know, though, that just like in the 1800s, when new members join they must admit to something so personal that it holds them hostage to their pledge of secrecy."

"Damn," I said. "How do we find out more about them, then?"

"Wait a minute. How in the world did you find out that much already?" Doe asked. "I mean if they're so secretive?"

"Dogged research," Ben replied. "I pieced together most of this through letters and documents I found at the University of London and the homes of Eustice Pembroke and Arthur Finlay. For instance, at the university, I found the name of the founder of The Electi, Philip Sallow, and followed him through college to a law degree and then to Parliament. And because he was a member of Parliament, many of his papers were in a museum in London. I got hold of his diary. It names the six boys in Brothers of the Night, including Archibald Clemency, Eustice Pembroke and four others. I then tracked three of *their* heirs to the United States. The most important being Archibald Clemency's great-grandson, who just happens to be a Washington state senator."

"You mean the great grandson of the guy who created Brothers of the Night—the offshoot of The Electi?" Rudy asked.

Ben nodded. "He lives here in Seattle."

The room went silent.

"Wow," Doe finally said with a sigh.

"Wow indeed," I repeated. "But that brings us back to our original question. How do we find out more about The Electi *or* Brothers of the Night?"

"Does Brothers of the Night still exist?" April asked.

"Not officially," Ben said with a raised eyebrow.

"But it's The Electi that expanded to other countries?" I asked.

"Yes. While extremely secretive, they are a known commodity."

"Even to the US government?" Rudy asked.

"Yes. I know someone in Homeland Security who tracks these groups. And while The Electi is on their radar, she told me there was no reason to believe they were dangerous. To her, they're just a group of rich intellectuals. They see themselves as a think tank."

"Who may have committed murder," I said under my breath.

"Does Homeland Security know about Brothers of the Night?" Doe asked.

"Not that I know of," Ben said.

"Then it sounds like someone would have to join The Electi if we're going to find anything useful," Rudy said.

"I don't like the sound of that," Doe said. "We already know these people will kill to get what they want.

"It doesn't matter," Ben said. "Getting in is almost impossible. It not only requires a hefty annual fee but also an IQ of 125 or above *and* a stellar pedigree, by which I mean—family connections or major influence. That's what I was doing in New York, interviewing a former member for the second time. He has terminal lung cancer, and he agreed to talk to me. He's a member of The Electi but knows a fair amount about Brothers of the Night. One thing he told me was that the box remains in the possession of someone they call the Electus, or the chosen *one*."

"Is he their leader?" Doe asked.

"No. Just keeper of the box. The box is handed down from generation to generation through this position. Initially, this person was the seventh member of Brothers of the Night. He was someone who shared their values but wished to remain separate from the group and anonymous. Anyway, seven had a special meaning to Brothers of the Night, and in this case, the seventh member kept to the shadows—literally."

"Why?" Doe asked.

"Not sure. I suppose he wanted to safeguard their secrets. But since he was of such a high rank, he couldn't afford to be openly associated with them. Although the gentleman I spoke to suggested the original Electus did exert influence on the club's behalf. However, once The Electi regenerated itself as a club, then Brothers of the Night went underground. My informant said the Electus then became keeper of *all* the secrets, meaning secrets belonging to members of each group. I believe they used the box to store those secrets along with important documents."

"And this guy you talked to didn't know where the box was?" I asked.

Ben shook his head. "No. But he said it passed from Electus to Electus until 2015 when the 5th Electus died suddenly, and the box disappeared. No one seems to know what happened to it."

"Why was this guy willing to tell you all of this?" Doe asked.

"Apparently, things were changing. And he was unhappy with the direction the club was taking. He implied that Brothers of the Night, or 'BOTiN', as he referred to them, was active again, taking matters into their own hands and carrying out acts not subscribed to nor approved by the larger group."

"Like murder," Doe said.

"I can't say for sure," Ben said with a hunch of his shoulders.

"Wow," I said with an exhale. "This is heavy stuff."

"Okay, but if someone wants to join The Electi, what's the membership fee?" Rudy asked.

"And do they even allow women to join?" I asked.

"Women were allowed to join the club in the early 1900s," Ben said. "But the membership fee is twenty-five thousand a year. I know most of you could probably meet that, and I suppose Julia could meet the pedigree requirement because she's the ex-wife and still a close friend of the current state governor. But that's it."

"Why don't you join?" Rudy asked. "You're certainly smart enough."

"Major problem there. I belong to Mensa. And The Electi see Mensa as its rival and won't admit anyone who has been a member."

"Plus, they probably know who you are by now, anyway. You'd be at risk," I added.

"Agreed," he said.

"Then we have no way forward," Doe said in defeat.

Count to three.

"I could do it."

Four heads swiveled to stare at Blair perched coquettishly on the piano bench.

"What? No," Ben said with a shake of his head. "I don't think so Blair. But thank you."

"Not so fast," I said, raising a hand. "Blair probably *could* qualify."

"Seriously, Julia?" Rudy quipped. "Blair has an almost photographic memory, but by a good pedigree they don't mean that her current husband is a de facto member of the Chicago mob."

Blair glanced over at Rudy and blinked her fake eyelashes twice at the rebuke.

"I'm sorry, Blair," Rudy said. "I'm not trying to be mean. But this is serious stuff."

Blair lifted her chin and took a deep breath. "I'll have you know that I was a member of my college Honor Society for the two years I was at the UW because I held a 4.0 GPA. And I scored at the 99th percentile on the Stanford Binet intelligence test with an IQ of 135. While Mr. Billings is, in fact, loosely connected to the Chicago mob, he is also president of the national import car dealers."

"I had no idea," Ben said appreciatively. "With that IQ, you could join Mensa. But I don't think being president of the national import car dealers is the influence they're looking for. They want influence in politics, big finance, national defense, or a Fortune 500 company."

"Hmph," she managed. "Perhaps being the ex-wife of one of the top NASCAR drivers who was just named the UN goodwill ambassador to Chile would help."

Ben opened his mouth to reply, but Blair cut him off with a wave of her hand.

"*And* Burt, ex-husband number two, is the current CEO of the Geodyne Corporation and holds a Ph.D. in aerodynamics."

"I didn't know Donny got named as a UN Ambassador," I said.

"They won't announce it until next week."

"But what does the Geodyne Corporation do?" I asked.

This time Blair flicked her blond hair in mock petulance, but it was Rudy who responded.

"It's the top aerospace engineering and defense company in the country and works directly with the Pentagon," she said.

Blair smiled. "Yes, Burt has the Secretary of Defense on his speed dial. And as you know, I have *all* my ex-husbands on mine."

The four of us sat in appreciative silence. If Blair played chess, she could have just crowed "checkmate."

"Touché, Blair," Doe said with a sweet smile.

We all turned to Ben.

"Well?" I asked.

He was still staring at Blair. "I admit, you'd be an excellent candidate. But it's still too dangerous, Blair. We can't take a chance like that."

"What if all she does is get the membership list?" Rudy asked. "After all, wouldn't she get to know who else belongs if she becomes a member?"

"I assume so" Ben replied.

"Then, it's a go," I confirmed. "Blair will join The Electi."

Doe ran fingers through her thick salt and pepper hair and took a deep sigh. "Damn, here we go again."

CHAPTER FIVE

"How do I get into the society?" Blair asked.

Ben lifted his brows. "You have to be invited."

"Wait a minute," Doe said. "Didn't you say that Archibald Clemency's grandson is a Washington State senator?"

"Yes. So?"

"What's his name?"

"Wouldn't it be Clemency?" Rudy asked.

"No," Ben replied. "When the family immigrated here, they changed the name to Clements."

My eyes popped open. "Walter Clements! He's the descendent?"

"Do you know him?"

"Not well, but we've met several times. Graham knows him better."

Graham was my ex-husband and the current governor of the state. We met when he was a newly minted lawyer and proud Democrat, which was something that drew us together. As his political ambitions grew, he judged he'd have better luck as a Republican and switched parties. Walter Clements was the current Republican minority leader in the state senate.

"Then Graham would be a good avenue in," Doe said.

"Can you trust Graham with this?" Ben asked me.

Ben had suspected Graham's political motivations since the day I announced we were engaged. The two had squared off several times over the years at dinner parties, arguing over the state of world affairs, the nuances of different religions, and, of course, politics.

"Graham and I are still close," I assured him. "I wouldn't have a problem reaching out to him. But what am I asking him to do?"

"We should probably meet with him in person," Ben said.

"We?"

"Without me, this story will sound like something out of a Dan Brown novel."

"He's right," Rudy said. "The two of you should go."

"Okay, but once again, what are we asking him to do?"

"We just need to find a way to get me in front of Clements," Blair spoke up. "I'll take it from there."

No one laughed at that because it wasn't funny. Blair's talents were gold-medal-worthy when it came to men.

"Okay," I said. "I'll call him tonight and see if we can go down tomorrow. In the meantime, you can stay in my extra bedroom."

"I don't want to put you in further danger," Ben said, furrowing his brows.

Rudy erupted in laughter. "Seriously? Between a house full of guests, two yapping dogs, a very noisy parrot, and a plethora of active ghosts who will scare the hell out of you at the drop of a hat, you're probably safer here than in jail."

÷

Ben shared a pizza with April and me in the kitchen after the girls left while we filled her in on everything. April's husband, Stewart, had been a well-respected surgeon in the area before he succumbed to Alzheimer's only a few months earlier. After he was gone, she had moved into my guest house, giving her 24-hour access to the Inn.

"Are you sure you should do this?" she asked, pulling cheese off the slice of pizza in her hand. "I mean, putting Blair at risk?"

"I'm not sure any of you should be involved," Ben said, with deep concern etched on his tanned face. "But we only want Blair to get the list of members. The list should help us get a handle on who might have killed Carter. Then Blair will be out."

"Clements was also a surgeon before he got into politics," April said.

My eyebrows shot up. "That's right. Do you know him?"

"No. Stewart did, though. They worked together at Swedish Medical Center. I think Clements is a bone guy. As I recall, he and Stewart were pretty good friends at one time. Even went fishing together. I only met him once when he stopped by the house to pick Stewart up for a fishing trip."

"Why don't you come with us?"

"How could I help?"

"Just add more credibility." I looked at Ben. "What do you think?"

He shrugged. "Depending on what Graham says, the least suspicious way to connect with Clements would be through a social situation. In that case, having April there might help."

"Okay, so we make him feel comfortable, and then just let Blair do her thing," April said with a roll of her deep brown eyes. "She's a sight to behold, you know," she said to Ben.

Ben shifted in his chair. "Oh, I know how Blair works. About a year and a half ago, she cornered me in the library. I think one of the ghosts saved me when three books simultaneously flew off a shelf."

April smiled. "That would be Elizabeth. She doesn't like shenanigans."

"Blair does have her talents," I said. "It's funny. You make superb cinnamon rolls," I said to April. "I have an eye for expensive antiques. And, well, Blair has the one talent most women dream about—the art of seduction."

Ben smiled. "I had a colleague who once defined a femme fatale as 'the woman men want but shouldn't have.'"

"He was describing Blair to a T." I wiped my hands on a napkin and stood up. "Okay. Time to call Graham. The dogs need to go out, anyway. I'll let you know what he says."

÷

Mickey and Minnie launched themselves at me the moment I opened the door. Mickey spins in circles when he gets excited, so he kept slamming his little black and tan butt into Minnie, pushing her back and forth as he rotated faster and faster at my feet.

"Okay, you two. Enough!" I commanded, leaning over to give them each a pat. "It's dinnertime, and then I have to make a phone call."

Minnie pushed her way outside when I opened the sliding glass door to my small, fenced yard and rushed over to a metal birdbath in the corner to sniff her way around it. The two dogs did their business and then followed me back inside as I went into my galley kitchen.

The kitchen opened onto a small eating area and the living room. As someone who loved antiques, my apartment fairly overflowed with a variety of antique furniture, old hand tools, wooden boxes, and Tiffany lamps. And then, of course, there was my obsession with The Wizard of Oz.

My collectibles included framed posters, figurines, lunch boxes, and snow globes, and even a welcome mat at the backdoor that had an image of the ruby red slippers with the phrase, "There's no place like home." My favorite, however, was my Wicked Witch of the

West cookie jar that sat prominently on top of a small, wooden bookcase. These were things I loved, and which always brought me great comfort whenever I tucked myself into a chair with a hot cup of tea and the fire going.

I filled the dogs' bowls with kibble and set them on the floor. Mickey, the chowhound, nearly knocked Minnie over, lunging for the bowl.

"Mickey!" I yelled. I pushed his bowl a couple of feet away.

A year earlier, I had bought a dog bowl designed to slow a dog down as he eats. The inside of the bowl looks like a small maze. Mickey circled his bowl, following the kibble around as it moved through the grooves. It made me dizzy to watch.

Leaving them to eat, I pulled my cell phone out of my jacket pocket and went to sit in my recliner. I dialed Graham, feeling my jaw clench at the thought that his wife, Kitty, might answer the phone. Kitty and I didn't have a terrible relationship, but Graham had married her soon after he divorced me, which always left a sour taste in my mouth. Okay, there was that and the fact she was some twenty years younger and a good thirty pounds thinner than me.

Sure enough, Kitty answered the phone.

"Julia," she said. "How's your head? I heard a flyball almost killed you in Chicago."

I felt my jaw muscles tighten. It had been a foul ball, but rather than try to correct her, I decided the easiest thing to do was just to go with the flow and move on.

"Yes. But I'm fine," I said. "Is Graham there?"

"You know, I was surprised when Graham told me about your accident. I mean, how in the world did you get the flyball away from the dog?"

"I'm sorry, um, what?"

I don't have Ben's IQ, but there's no doubt I could cream Kitty in any intelligence competition that involved cognitive thinking.

"I looked it up. Flyball is a dog sport," she said.

In my attempt to move past the incident, I'd made it worse. Feeling I would regret it, I asked, "Okay, Kitty, I'll bite. What dog sport?"

Kitty expelled an impatient breath. "It's called flyball. Dogs carry a ball and jump over things in some sort of competition. I know what it is. I looked it up. I'm not stupid."

The jury was out on that, but she continued.

"I just don't understand how one ball hit you in the head, that's all."

This time, I clamped my lips together to control my reply. I couldn't afford to insult Graham's trophy wife.

"Sorry, Kitty. We were at Wrigley Field in Chicago. It's where they play baseball."

"Oh," she said. "It was a baseball that hit you?"

"That's right."

"I thought it was a flyball."

When I was young, I never tired of Abbott and Costello's "Who's on first?" comedy routine. It feels different in real time.

"Never mind," I told her. "There was no damage done, and I'm fine. Is Graham home?"

"Sure. Just a minute."

A moment later, Graham's velvety smooth voice came on the line.

"Julia, how are you? Any headaches?"

"No. I'm fine. Really."

"I'm glad. I'd hate to have that pretty face of yours marred," he said in a lowered voice.

Like most men, he knew exactly what started my engines. But I ignored the electricity pulsing through my body.

"Listen, Ben is in town. We thought we'd drive down tomorrow to see you. Will you have time?'

"I thought he was in London."

"He was. And now… he isn't. Carter died."

"What? Oh, no. I'm sorry, Julia. You were close. Ben, even closer. What happened?"

"He stopped by the Inn and was poisoned."

"Not again!"

"No. No," I said, shaking my head. "That came out wrong. He died on my doorstep, but someone poisoned him before he got here." *Why did everyone think I poisoned people?* "Anyway, it's a long story. But that's why we wanted to see you. I can't explain it over the phone. But we need your help."

"Of course. Call Yvonne first thing in the morning. I'll tell her to clear a spot on my calendar."

"Okay. Thanks. And Graham… you really need to take Kitty to a Mariners' game."

CHAPTER SIX

Graham's personal secretary, Yvonne, scheduled us to meet with hum at 2:00 p.m. in his office in Olympia the next day. We arrived ten minutes early and sat in the outer office until Yvonne showed us into a small conference room lined with framed head shots of the last ten governors of Washington State. An American flag sat in one corner, while the state flag filled the opposite corner. Against the wall was a bottled water dispenser, and at the center of the table was a tray with a carafe of coffee and paper coffee cups.

"How much will you tell him?" I asked my brother as I poured myself a cup of coffee.

He dropped into a chair and leaned back, resting both elbows on the armrests. Ben hadn't dressed up, even though he was meeting with the governor. He wore a clean pair of cargo pants with a blue linen shirt and a black silk scarf tied around his neck. I smiled inwardly at his purposeful five o'clock shadow, which was popular. I had to admit; it made him look kind of sexy.

"I don't know. What do you think?" he replied, tapping his fingers impatiently on the arm of the chair.

"I trust him," I said. "And besides, it wouldn't hurt to have the governor on our side."

"What do you mean?"

"In case we need him later."

"For what?"

I rolled my eyes before saying, "In case we need a defense. A governor would be a good credibility witness, wouldn't you agree?"

"Why would we need a credibility witness?"

The door opened before I could reply, and Graham strode in. He wore a crisp charcoal gray suit with a royal blue tie. Regardless of my feelings for David, which were strong, my heart skipped the proverbial beat the moment I saw him. He stood almost six feet tall and was still in good shape. While his hair was mostly gray now, his brown eyes still burned with an intensity that I knew women found alluring and men respected.

Even though it wasn't necessary, I stood when he came into the room. To be honest, I secretly hoped he might reach for a hug.

Instead, he smiled at me and crossed to the other side of the table and sat down.

"Good to see you, Julia. And you're looking well, Ben. How long have you been back?"

A sly smile slipped across Ben's face. "Just a few days."

"What brings you into town?"

Graham had never really liked Ben, either. And for basically the same reasons. While Ben had recognized early on how ambitious Graham was and predicted—correctly I might add—that Graham's ambitions would eventually supersede his feelings for me, for his part Graham didn't trust Ben because he was always chasing after the next artifact, regardless of what other people's priorities were. Not that they didn't get along. There was just a constant low-level tension between them.

"We only have thirty minutes, Graham. We should get right to the subject," I interjected.

"Which is what?"

"Jack the Ripper," Ben replied.

Graham's deep-set brown eyes flared. "Really? Okay, catch me up."

Ben launched into a succinct retelling of what he had shared with us, leading to Carter's murder. Graham listened patiently, asking for only a couple of clarifications along the way. When Ben had finished, Graham sat for a moment drumming his fingers on the table, then got up and went to the water cooler to pour himself a glass of water. He took a swig and then said, "What do you need from me?"

He had narrowed his eyes while watching Ben, a sure sign he hadn't decided whether to believe him yet. It was my turn to jump in.

"We need a way to meet Walter Clements."

His eyebrows creased. "You've already met him."

"Walter is a descendent of one of the founding members of the secret society Ben talked about—The Electi. We also believe that he is now a member and want to get Blair inside, but she would need to be invited. That means we need to get Blair in front of Clements, and we thought a social event would be best if..."

"Why do you want to get Blair invited to be part of that group?" Graham interrupted me.

"If she's a member, we think she'll be able to get a copy of the membership list," Ben said. "With that, we hope to find out who else might be connected through their descendants to the original secret society and therefore may kill to keep their secrets secret."

Graham shifted in his seat. He was uncomfortable with this. As a politician, every decision he made was based on a risk-versus-benefit analysis. And I could practically see the wheels in his head turning as he weighed the risk. I say risk because I wasn't sure there was any benefit to him unless he saw how it might tarnish Clements, who everyone knew had his eye on replacing Graham as governor one day.

"But from what you've said, Blair doesn't sound like a qualified candidate," he said.

"Oddly enough," Ben countered, "She just might be the perfect candidate. Apparently, she has a tested IQ of 135, has the requisite influential credentials through her long list of ex-husbands, the money, and her looks would be a plus."

Graham was quiet for another moment, probably contemplating how much he wanted to get involved.

"All you want is an introduction. Nothing else."

"Well, yes, but also a way to put the two of them together," I said. "I mean, they need some time together so that Blair can entice him to invite her to become a member, or at least invite her to talk further."

He sat back. "I suppose I could rearrange the seating at my table," he finally said.

"For what?" I asked.

"The Republican Party fundraiser this weekend."

I released a breath. "That would be perfect. Thank you, Graham. We'll be careful. We won't jeopardize your reputation."

"Look, my ancestors are from Britain, as are many people. And while I'm not fond of the idea of a group of 'quote unquote' upper-class snobs thinking they know better than everyone else, whether they're here or across the pond, all I really care about is finding who killed Carter. He was a good man. A bit of a kook, but a genuinely good man."

Ben rarely showed emotion other than anger or a bristling enthusiasm for ancient artifacts. Not that he didn't have emotion. It's just that historians focused on facts. Right now, however, the tears that glistened at the corners of his eyes told me what Carter's death meant to him.

"Yes," he said. "And while I would give anything to find that box, the priority now is to find who killed my friend."

"Even though you might be on the verge of solving history's most notorious murder case?" Graham asked.

"Even though," Ben said. "Jack the Ripper has eluded everyone for nearly a hundred and fifty years. He can wait a bit longer. Carter's killer can't."

"Well," I said with a nod. "Wouldn't it be sweet though, if said killer turned out to be a direct descendant of Jack the Ripper? Two birds with one stone, as they say."

CHAPTER SEVEN

Ben and I returned home and called the girls to invite them over for an impromptu barbecue on the deck of the guest house, away from prying eyes at the Inn. By seven o'clock, the six of us were situated around April's patio table, beverages in hand and grilled chicken kebabs and rice in front of us. The temperature had flirted with hitting ninety degrees during the day, so the air was warm, accented by a cool breeze off the lake.

"Where is this fundraiser?" Doe asked, pulling vegetables off a skewer.

Doe had always reminded me of Bea Arthur from the hit TV series *Golden Girls*. She was tall and slender with thick, short hair swept off her forehead. Even now, in her mid-sixties, she exhibited an inner strength that served her well as the head of a big company.

"The Grand Hyatt," I replied. "It's $250 a ticket, though."

"Do we all need to go?" Rudy asked.

"I don't think so."

"I'll pay for everyone," Ben said.

I glanced over at him. He was ignoring his food, concentrating instead on the beer in his hand.

"I don't think we all need to be there," I said.

"And frankly, it might be better to keep a couple of us in the background," Doe said. "No need to announce to the world that we're working on this together."

"I agree," Blair said. "We should keep it to a minimum. In fact, Ben, you shouldn't go."

His head came up, and the tension between us rose with it.

"Why not?" he asked.

"Your presence would just raise suspicions," she said.

A water skier zoomed past our dock, bringing waves crashing to the shore before Blair continued.

"What I mean is, if Clements had anything to do with Carter's death, he would know who you are and wonder why you're at the dinner. It would be better if Julia and I went alone."

"We were thinking April should come, too," I added.

"Stewart worked with Clements at Swedish, and I've met him once," April said.

"That's good," Blair said. "I'm also a registered Republican, which will add credibility to me being there. And Julia could say she's there to support Graham. Isn't he about to announce his campaign for reelection?"

"I think so" I replied, shrinking inside at the prospect.

I believed campaigning was probably one of the main reasons Graham had traded me in for Kitty. He needed a willing wife by his side, and I hated the politics involved in politics. Kitty was the picture of a political wife. She was cute and enjoyed mingling with all of Graham's colleagues, where her lack of critical thinking skills benefited her. It made her amusing and almost irresistible.

"So, what's the plan?" Rudy asked.

"Graham has invited us to sit at his table. And we'll make sure Blair sits next to Clements."

"Is he married?" Rudy asked with a lift to her eyebrows. "I mean Clements."

"Recently divorced," I replied. "He should be alone."

"And fair game," Blair said. "I can be as empathetic as the next person."

Doe and Rudy exchanged smiles.

"And you're moving ahead as if I'm not going," Ben stated.

"I agree with Blair," I said. "This must appear as just a normal turn of events, and your appearance would only raise suspicions. Remember, all we're trying to do is get Blair in front of Clements, work her magic, and get him to plan for a follow-up meeting."

"Is Mr. Billings going to be okay with this?" Doe asked Blair.

Blair shrugged her pretty shoulders. "He's out of town this weekend."

For reasons Blair had only shared with me, she referred to her current husband as Mr. Billings instead of his real name, Jacob (Jack) Wentworth. It all had to do with where and how they'd met in Billings, Montana, and their ensuing sexual encounters.

"I guess the question is, if Blair is successful and Clements invites her to join the club, what then?" Ben asked.

"It sounds like you're going into this blind," April said, glancing around the table.

"What else can we do?" I asked. "We don't know where the box is, and we don't know who killed Carter."

"Or, how?" Rudy added. "I mean, do they know yet how he ingested the poison?"

"No," I said. "At least, I haven't heard."

"Well, what else can we do?" Doe asked. "There has to be something else."

I turned to her. "Does your company hold the trash contract for Queen Anne Hill?"

"Is that where Clements lives?"

"Yes."

She scooped some rice onto her fork. "Yes, we do. Their trash day Thursday. Why?"

"Because we could do some more trash diving."

"Looking for what?" Rudy asked.

I was slicing a mushroom. "Anything having to do with The Electi."

"You don't think he'd merely throw stuff like that away, do you?" she said. "He'd shred anything important."

"Maybe not," I said, chewing the mushroom. "People get careless. Plus, there might be random things that would help. Receipts. Bills. Plane tickets. Whatever."

"How about what comes out of his office?" April asked.

"I'm sure that goes into a locked cannister and shipped to a company like Iron Mountain for disposal," Rudy said. "We'd have to break into his office to get anything from there."

"We're not doing that," Doe said.

"I agree." I shifted my attention to Rudy. "Rudy, can you do some research on him?"

"Why?" Ben asked.

"Because we know little about Clements other than his descendants were part of The Electi. We need to know who he does business with, who he socializes with, who he's friends with…"

"And who his enemies are," Rudy said, interrupting me.

"Yes. That, too."

"Okay. I'll get started in the morning," she said.

I turned to Blair. "And once we have a list of business associates and acquaintances, can you find out if Mr. Billings has ever sold cars to any of them?"

Blair's eyes lit up. "Of course. Yeah, good idea. We'll look at this from every angle."

"Right," I said. "I'm thinking that Clements can't be the only local member of this society. There must be others. And most likely, he's close to at least one or two of them, and they might have been in on the murder, or at least be aware of it. We just need to find out who they are."

"And then turn that information over to the police," April said with a stern look at me.

There was a pregnant pause around the table.

When I didn't respond, April said, "You do remember your boyfriend is a detective working on this case."

I nodded. "She's right. We need to play within the rules."

Rudy looked over at Ben. "How many other names from Britain did you track to the U.S.?"

He thought a moment. "About seven, I think. I'll have to go back to my notes."

"Okay. We need those names," I said. "I have a friend who is into genealogy. She can help track these folks. And, before you ask..." I said, as Ben opened his mouth to speak. "... she can definitely be trusted."

"Okay, call her," he said.

"You're not thinking of Aria, are you?" Rudy asked.

I shrugged. "Why not? She was a big help on the trip to Chicago. We wouldn't have been successful without her spyware."

"What?" Ben asked, his brows furrowing.

"Never mind. All you need to know is that if she's in, she's in." I glanced around the table. Each of us seemed energized by the tasks ahead. "You know, Ben, Carter would have loved to have been a part of this quest."

"I agree," he replied with a sigh. "Do you remember when the three of us tracked down Old Man Pendleton's will and saved that big old mansion for his wife? We almost bought the farm on that one."

I chuckled and shook my head. "Of course, I do. You would have thought we were part of the FBI, taking fingerprints and even creating a psychological profile on the thief."

"What are you two talking about?" Blair asked.

Ben and I shared an amused glance.

"Just a case we worked on as kids," I said. "Story for another time. But Carter was the hero back then, with his big brain and his book knowledge. He would have loved this." I lifted my glass of wine. "To Carter."

"To Carter," the rest echoed.

CHAPTER EIGHT

We continued to clarify our plans until almost ten o'clock. After indulging in April's surprise dessert, angel food cake covered in fresh strawberries, the girls left. Ben and I helped April clean up the dishes and then headed back to the Inn. The dogs greeted me with as much enthusiasm as if I'd been gone a week instead of a couple of hours.

"I'm going to bed," Ben said, as I let the dogs out in the backyard. "I still have jet lag." He yawned and stretched his arms over his head.

"No problem. I'll probably read a little. I feel I need to unwind." I put my hand on his arm. "We're going to figure this out, Ben. Someone will pay for what happened to Carter."

He nodded and took a deep breath. "I know. I should have been more careful, though. Remember what Mom used to say... brains aren't the be all and end all..."

"Because it's common sense that will get you over the finish line," I said with a smile, finishing my mother's favorite saying. "I remember. But then, neither one of us has much of that."

He smiled that boyish grin of his, with just the hint of dimples. "I miss her, you know. She was cantankerous, sometimes snotty, and had an opinion about everything."

I cringed inwardly, thinking of the secret I held. Mom had been calling me on her cell phone since our first investigation—even though she was dead. I'd never told Ben. I mean, how could I? Even though he knew about our resident ghosts, he was practical as the day is long and would have thought I was nuts. Sometimes I thought so too. All I said was, "I miss her, too."

He headed down the hall to the guest bedroom, while I took the dogs into the backyard. I glanced up at the clear sky just as a shooting star flashed bright. *Carter, is that you? Were you listening earlier?*

"We're going to do this for you," I murmured to the sky. "You'll see. It's do or die time, Carter. We'll make you proud."

I wiped a tear away at the memory. Do or die had been our motto when we were kids. We'd said it often during our youthful investigation into Mr. Pendleton's missing will. But this time, those three words brought a chill, because this time the 'die' part was real.

I called the dogs in and then made a hot cup of tea. With a heavy heart, I tucked myself into my big recliner with my latest mystery.

It was close to midnight. I stood in the bathroom brushing my teeth. I had taken a shower to release some of the tension in my back, causing the mirror to fog up. After spitting the toothpaste out, I glanced up and stopped short.

The condensation on the mirror was moving as if a finger were trailing through it. My toothbrush dropped into the sink, and I stared at the mirror, my heart hammering. I held my breath, as I always did when these things happened. Two words appeared in the steam.

"Be careful."

"Elizabeth?" I whispered.

Elizabeth often appeared to me, but I never got used to it. She and her husband, John, had built this magnificent home for their family in 1945. John had been in Seattle when the devastating fire started and moved out with his only surviving son immediately after. Since then, the property had been owned by several other families, all of whom reported ghostly occurrences. That had been one thing that had excited me about the property when Graham bought it as a surprise to fulfill my dream of running a bed-and-breakfast.

Elizabeth appeared for the first time when I was home alone one night. She emerged next to me on the sofa, hovering several inches in the air. I nearly had a heart attack and dropped the cup of tea in my hand. I remember stammering, trying to form a sentence.

She had only smiled. Well, at least that's what it looked like. I could see right through her to a picture of Margaret Hamilton as the Wicked Witch of the West on the wall behind her, which, as you can imagine, created a ghastly image.

"Elizabeth?" I whispered again, staring at the mirror.

When Minnie barked and something fluttered behind me, I whirled around. Elizabeth floated beside the shower stall, still wearing the white nightdress she'd died in, with one long, dark braid draped over her shoulder.

"What is it?" I asked her. "What do I have to be careful of?"

She held up three ghostly fingers.

"What does that mean?"

Her image flickered, which always made it difficult to see clearly what she was doing, but it appeared as if she pointed to my arm. I looked down at my left wrist.

"My arm?"

She shook her head. Watching her hazy image oscillate back and forth made me dizzy.

"I'm sorry. I don't know what you mean," I said, feeling a chill settle over me.

She raised three fingers again.

"Three. Yes, I got that part. But…"

Then she was gone, leaving the smell of roses behind. It had been her signature perfume, a gift from her husband when her first child was born. We often smelled it around the Inn, even if she wasn't visible.

I stumbled over to the bed and plopped down to slow my breathing. *What had she meant? Three people? Three more deaths? Three o'clock?*

That could have been it. Maybe she thought something was going to happen at three o'clock the next day. I contemplated what my plans were. I only had usual Inn business to attend to, and so I decided to be extra careful as she had warned. After all, Elizabeth had never been wrong.

÷

I was in the middle of a tantalizing dream about being lost in an underground mine of chocolate and caramel, when Minnie's low, menacing growl woke me with a start. Dachshunds are notorious for burrowing under blankets, and mine were no exception. Their modus operandi was to bury themselves under a large throw I kept on the bed just for that purpose. However, right now, her sharp nose had poked out from underneath the blanket, facing the bedroom door, and her little throat was vibrating.

I reached over and stroked her head. "Shush, girl. It's probably Ben getting up to get a glass of water."

But she was having none of it.

She let out a single, ear-splitting yelp and scrambled off the bed, hurtling toward the bedroom door. She slid to a stop and stuck that long nose of hers along the bottom of the door, sucking in the smell of… what? What was bothering her?

I climbed out of bed and grabbed my robe. Slipping it on and tying it around my waist, I followed her to the door.

"What is it, girl?"

A thud from outside the bedroom gave me a start.

Was that Ben?

I opened the door a crack. Minnie nearly tripped me as she pushed past me into the hallway, racing towards the guest room. In half a second, she was in Ben's room snarling ferociously.

I ran after her, fearing she was about to attack my brother, thinking he was an intruder. I made it inside Ben's bedroom as Minnie lunged at something on the other side of the bed. A deep, scratchy voice let out a cry of pain and a string of expletives.

"Minnie! Come here!" I shouted, thinking she may have gotten hold of Ben.

No such luck.

A figure leapt up onto the bed, rolled across it and came up face to face with me. It wasn't Ben. The only light was from the nightlight in the hallway, so I faced deep-set, dark eyes staring at me from beneath a hoodie.

I whipped around to run, but powerful hands grabbed me and yanked me back.

"Where is it?" he growled into my ear in that husky voice.

I squirmed, trying to get away, but he held me close, his right arm encircling my neck. Minnie was ripping into his ankles by this time, so he kicked at her while he tightened his grip around my neck.

"Get the dog off me!" he snapped.

"I... I can't," I gasped, pulling to get away from him.

A cry emanated from my throat, cut off by his arm, which was squeezing the air out of me. He kicked Minnie's belly, making her squeal in pain, which finally brought Mickey to attention. Before I knew it, both dogs were in the room, barking and making a horrible racket. I hoped that someone would hear them and come running. Meanwhile, while little Minnie kept snatching at the man's feet, Mickey spun in circles. I glanced to the floor where Mickey looked like an eggbeater whipping up breakfast.

I needed to get this guy off balance. I pulled my chin down to see how I could gain some leverage under his arm and saw the dark outline of a turtle tattooed on the back of his left hand. Ignoring that, I grabbed hold of his wrist and lunged to the left with one foot, pulling him with me. That opened his stance and Minnie took advantage of the opportunity.

She jumped and quickly gained purchase where it counts the most. He reacted as if someone had just connected his genitals to an electrical wire and let go of me and spun around. Minnie let go of his… well, you know what… and flew off and hit the bed.

"Shit!" he exclaimed in pain.

While I backed away, he stumbled into the hallway and out the back door. With the threat gone, Mickey finally stopped spinning circles, tilting to one side, clearly disoriented. I dropped onto the bed, massaging my throat, and Minnie jumped up next to me to push her nose under my elbow.

"Thank you, Minnie Mouse. You're a good dog," I praised her.

We sat for a moment, and then I realized... *where the heck was Ben?*

I got up and flipped on the light. The nightstand drawers were open, as was Ben's briefcase. But he was gone.

I went to the hall bathroom, but it was empty. Fearful he might be dead somewhere; I quickly searched the rest of the apartment and the first floor of the Inn.

Where the heck was he?

Confused, I was just coming back into my apartment when he sauntered in through the back door.

"Hey, why was the back door open?"

"Where the heck were you?" I demanded, glancing at my watch. "It's three o'clock in the morning?" I gasped and stared at the watch. "My God! It's three o'clock."

CHAPTER NINE

I called David and told him what happened and asked him to come alone. Since the would-be thief was gone, I didn't think there was a need for sirens and additional police units waking the entire neighborhood. David wasn't happy, but he agreed to my request temporarily.

My antique pendulum clock, which hung opposite a framed photo of the cast of the 1939 movie version of Wizard of Oz, struck 3:30 as Ben and I sat in my small living room waiting. Ben explained to me he'd called an Uber and gone to Carter's home again looking for the papers and had left the back door unlocked so that he could get back in without waking me. I couldn't quite decide if the adrenalin still pulsing through my body was from being choked by the intruder or from my anger at him for leaving the back door open.

"You're an idiot, you know that?" I finally snapped at him. "These people are serious, Ben. How could you be so careless?"

He dropped his gaze to the floor. "I'm so sorry, Julia. Really. I'm horrified he could have hurt you."

"Well," I said, petting Minnie, who sat beside me on the couch. "Thank God for little dogs. By the way, did Carter have a safe deposit box? Maybe he put the plans in there?"

"No. He told me once that he didn't believe in things like that. His parents kept some valuables in a safe deposit box back in Wisconsin. One day someone robbed the bank, and they lost everything."

"I didn't know that."

"He relied on his own inventiveness to hide things that were important to him. For instance, he taped a rare photograph onto the backside of a fan blade that sits in his study because he was afraid someone might steal it."

I chuckled. "That sounds like Carter."

"And he hid an expensive piece of jewelry he inherited from his mother inside the hem of his kitchen curtains. That's why I needed more time to search his house. To look through obscure hiding places. But he could have buried it… I mean them, in his backyard for all I know."

It was another few minutes before I heard a car's tires crunch on the gravel outside my window. I hurried to put the dogs in my bedroom and then opened the back door for David. As soon as he stepped inside, he enveloped me in a hug, and I leaned into the embrace. He had thrown on a sweatshirt over some jeans and smelled of toothpaste.

"My God, Julia. Are you okay?"

"Yes," I said into his shoulder. "I'm fine."

He released me. "Okay, where did this happen?"

We went to Ben's room. "In here."

He walked in and glanced around. "As far as you know, the guy didn't take anything?"

"No. But you'll have to ask Ben. He's in the living room."

He turned and leveled a look at me. "You're sure you're okay?"

"I'm fine," I said, rubbing my neck.

I led him down the hallway to my living room, where Ben sat quietly in my green velvet antique armchair. He stood up when David entered the room. The two men regarded each other for a moment, and then David pulled out a notebook and pen.

"Okay, tell me what happened," he said. "Then I'll decide if we need forensics."

He didn't sit down and hadn't shaved. And there was an edge to his voice that made me uncomfortable.

"Well, Minnie started barking," I began. "Around 3 a.m. And when I opened the bedroom door, she rocketed down the hallway into Ben's room."

"His door was open?" David asked, glancing at Ben.

I snuck a wicked look at my brother. "Yes. Because he wasn't there. But I didn't know that." I shifted my eyes back to David. "Anyway, Minnie ran in and began attacking someone on the other side of the bed. As soon as I came in, the guy jumped up, rolled across the bed, and faced me. I tried to run, but he grabbed me from behind and kept demanding to know where *it* was."

"Wait, first, what did he look like?"

I paused, picturing the guy in my mind. "It was dark. The only light was from the nightlight in the hallway. But he was probably as tall as you. Not heavy, but strong. He had a distinctive voice... kind of like a young Jeremy Irons. And he had dark eyes." I wrapped my arms around myself for warmth as the memory blossomed. "And he smelled like sweat and beer. Oh, and he had a tattoo on the back of his hand."

"What was it?" David asked.

I closed my eyes to picture the guy's hand. "Pretty sure it was a turtle."

David was taking notes. "Okay. Good. What did he keep asking for?"

"I don't know. I kept saying I didn't know, and then I was able to yank him off balance. Minnie... well, Minnie jumped and grabbed hold of his... um, where it hurts."

David glanced up from his notebook with a pained look on his face. We just stared at each other and then he said, "Go on."

"The guy cried out in pain, let go of me, and spun around. That dislodged Minnie, and he ran out the door as fast as he could... holding his crotch, I might add. Not sure if that's relevant. Anyway, I searched the apartment for Ben, thinking he might be hurt, but couldn't find him. Ben walked in a minute later. Then I called you."

"And where were you?" David asked my brother.

Ben shifted his weight but didn't answer.

"I repeat," David said. "Where were you at 3 a.m.?"

Ben inhaled. "I went to Carter's house."

"You what? That's still part of an active crime investigation."

"I was trying to find the plans I'd given him. They're important to my research."

"Once again, this is a murder investigation. You already told us about the plans. So I wouldn't advise withholding information."

"Okay," he said, releasing an impatient breath. "I was looking for a key. It's the key that goes to that box I mentioned at the station."

My eyes grew round. "That thug was looking for a key?" I inhaled. "Wait, a minute! Is that why you said Carter could have buried *it* in the backyard? Dammit, Ben!"

Ben dropped his gaze.

"Why didn't you tell us about this key?" David asked.

David has a moderate temperament and doesn't easily get angry. Right now, however, his eyes could have melted steel.

"I'm sorry. I should have said something."

"Why did Carter have this key in his possession?" David asked.

Now Ben blushed, which he rarely did. Something was wrong.

"Because that's what I sent to him to keep safe for me."

"Wait, a minute!" I said, stomping right up to him. "You said you sent him the plans to the box."

"I know. I know," he repeated, squirming under my gaze. "But I sent him the key."

"And you didn't know about it?" David asked me.

I crossed my arms over my chest. "No."

David turned to Ben, ignoring me for the moment. "And you think this key may have something to do with why your best friend was killed?"

"I believe so" Ben mumbled. He straightened up. "It's the only thing that makes sense. I sent the key to Carter and asked him to hide it when I saw I was being followed. And I told him not to even let me know where he'd hidden it. I think the only reason these people know he had it was the mistake I made with that woman I slept with."

Count to three.

David snapped his notebook shut and reached behind him. "Ben Brouwer, I'm arresting you for entering a crime scene. You have the right to remain silent…"

My hearing must have failed me momentarily as David whipped out his handcuffs and finished reading Ben his Miranda rights, because all I could hear were muffled sounds. Ben threw me a fearful glance, but I was at a loss. As David spun Ben around and slapped the restraints around his wrists, I finally came to attention.

"David, is that really necessary?"

David turned to me, a storm cloud blanketing his face. "I'm done playing games, Julia. This is a murder investigation, not an episode of *Murder She Wrote*."

"I… I… what? David, I…"

"Julia didn't know about the key or my going to Carter's," Ben said. Ben's eyes pleaded with me to just back off.

"Maybe not this time," David said. "But don't push your luck, Julia." He marched Ben down the hallway and stopped at the guest room. "I'll get him down to the station and have a forensics team out here first thing in the morning, so don't touch anything," he demanded. "Including the doorknob."

I floated in a daze down the hallway behind them and watched as David took Ben to the car and left without another word.

÷

Sleep avoided me for the rest of the night. I vacillated between calling the girls and going over to the guest house to tell April. In the end, I just lay on my bed, staring at the ceiling until dawn.

It was 6:15 when April found me in the kitchen, sitting like a zombie with a cup of tea, staring listlessly at the lake. Clouds had moved in overnight, and I thought we might get rain later.

"Boy, you're up early," she said, bringing me to attention. "What's wrong? Did Ben keep you awake?"

She grabbed her favorite apron, dropped it over her head, and tied it around her waist.

"No. Well, yes," I replied.

"What do you mean?"

She opened one of the lower cupboards and pulled out our largest fry pan and got out the ingredients for scrambled eggs. She was extracting a carton of milk from the refrigerator when I said, "Someone attacked me last night in my apartment."

She stopped and turned. "What?"

"In fact, it was a busy night. Someone assaulted me in Ben's bedroom, while he was out searching Carter's house for a key he never told us about. I called David, who came out and arrested Ben and threatened me." I finished with tears blurring my vision.

"Oh, Julia!" She came and sat across from me, putting the fry pan on the table. "What are you talking about? What in the world happened?"

It only took me a few minutes to relate the entire story in between sobs, including Elizabeth's warning. I finished, and April put her hand over mine as I wiped my eyes.

"Wow, I blew that one," she said, gazing past me.

"You mean because you didn't see it?"

She heaved a deep sigh. "Yeah. I had trouble sleeping last night. Just tossed and turned until, well, around 3:00 a.m. I must have sensed something. But that's all. You're okay, though?"

"Yes. I'm fine. Just worried about Ben. And of course, David."

She sat back. "Ben can take care of himself. Why didn't you call me?"

My tea had cooled, so I got up to stick my mug in the microwave. "I almost came running over, but what could you do? If only I'd interpreted Elizabeth's warning better. She must have meant three o'clock in the morning and not this afternoon."

"And now you feel guilty because you didn't somehow prevent it."

"I guess."

"What could you have done?"

The microwave beeped, and I removed the steaming tea. "I might have been able to stop Ben from going to Carter's. And maybe if he'd been here, that guy would have never gotten in."

"How *did* he get in?" she asked.

I sat down again. "Ben left the back door unlocked when he left."

"What an idiot." April got up again and began cracking eggs into a large bowl. "Does this change your plans to have Blair meet Senator Clements?"

"I don't know. Maybe. You know, we've taken so many risks before… but somehow, none of us has ever been arrested. But now Ben is sitting in jail."

"Stop worrying about Ben. Don't forget, this guy could have killed you," she said, eyeing me from across the room. "You do keep putting yourself in danger."

"Well, I didn't actually *put* myself in danger this time."

"No. It seems just the fact you're connected to Ben put you in danger."

"Ben and Carter," I corrected her. "I still don't know why Carter came to me just to die on my doorstep. But apparently there is a key involved. Ben admitted last night to sending a very important key to Carter and not the plans to the box."

"And that's what this guy was looking for last night?"

"Yes. First, he must have looked through Ben's briefcase and the drawers and then kept asking me for it. He must know that Carter came here just before he died and thinks maybe he gave the key to me. Or he thought Ben has it."

"And that's why David arrested Ben? Because he withheld information."

"No. It was because Ben snuck into Carter's house before they'd released it as a crime scene. And David wasn't too nice about it."

She shook her head and started beating the eggs. "Ben has never been very good about playing by the rules," she said. "But maybe Carter came here because he wanted to tell you about the key and where he'd hidden it, but he died before he could."

"Maybe. I assume Ben didn't find it last night when he went back to Carter's, so who knows where it is?"

"I wonder if that thug will be back," she said. "Maybe we need to change the locks."

The door to the kitchen opened and Mr. Muse, one of our guests, popped his head in. "There's a detective out here to see you," he said to me.

"Oh, thank you. Tell him to come in here," I said.

My heart leapt thinking it might be David and that he had cooled down since the night before.

A moment later, the kitchen door swung open, and Detective Abrams walked in, shattering any hope I had of seeing David.

"I have the forensics people with me," he said. "Let's go to your apartment first."

I stood up. "Where's David?"

He leveled a grim gaze at me. "He'll be processing the paperwork from last night. I think it's best that I take over for now."

I swallowed. "I see."

April and I exchanged glances before I led him to my apartment, passing Mr. Muse on the way who sat enjoying the morning view through the breakfast-room window. When we got to my apartment, Detective Abrams ignored the dogs as they launched themselves at his feet.

"Show me the room," he said, pushing Mickey aside with his foot.

I commanded the dogs to go lie down and then took him to Ben's room.

He stopped at the door. "Did you touch the door handle?"

"No. I closed it by wrapping my robe around my hand."

He nodded his approval. "As far as you know, did this guy go anywhere else in the apartment?"

"I'm not sure, but everything else looked undisturbed."

He glanced toward the back door. "And he got in through the back door because it was open?"

"Unlocked," I corrected him. "It wasn't open. But that's how he escaped."

He pulled out his phone and texted someone.

"Okay, I'm bringing the forensics people in. They're waiting out front. I'll let you know when you can have your apartment back. Can you put the dogs somewhere?"

"Of course. I'll take them with me."

I started back down the hallway when he stopped me. "Ms. Applegate... if you knew anything about that key, you could be liable for withholding evidence."

My heart rate went into overdrive. "I didn't know about the key. Honestly." I was ashamed even though I had done nothing wrong. "What about bailing Ben out? Can I do that?"

"Yes. He'll be arraigned this morning at 11:00. You can post bail after that."

I nodded, snapped my fingers to have the dogs follow me, and went back to the Inn's kitchen.

I spent the next half hour helping April finish the scrambled eggs, sausage, and scones and then set everything out in the breakfast room by seven-thirty for the first guests. Mr. Muse was the first in line.

He was a spry octogenarian who was in town for his granddaughter's birthday. He'd already shared that his wife of fifty-two years had died recently and that he often saw her standing over his bed at night. I didn't offer an opinion but thought that if she'd traveled with him to Seattle, she'd be in good company here at the Inn.

"Good morning again, Mr. Muse. I hope you slept well. Would you like me to help you get anything?"

"No," he said with a shake of head. "I can do it. I'm not as young as I used to be, but I'm still kickin'." He laughed and grabbed a plate off the stack at the end of the counter. "I see the police are here again. Did it have anything to do with that man I saw outside last night?"

I sucked in some air. "You saw someone?"

"Sure," he said, spooning eggs onto his plate. "I like to sit up late and watch the lights dance across the lake." His gray eyes twinkled. "I picture my Sarah sometimes when she was young. The first time we met was at Big Sugarbush Lake in Minnesota. The Native Americans named it after the maple trees they used to make syrup from. Anyway, she was the prettiest thing I ever saw."

I smiled as I helped him take a couple of sausages out of the warming pan. "I bet she was. But tell me about what you saw last night."

"Oh, I had my window open to let the breeze in, and I heard a motor. A small fishing boat came up to your dock. There was a full moon last night, so I could see two men in the boat. Only one got out. Maybe you could get me a cup of coffee," he said, pointing to the coffee urn.

"Certainly." I grabbed one of the porcelain cups and filled it as he went to the table. I followed him with the coffee and a couple of packets of sugar and a creamer. "Did you see where the man went?"

"Naw. Just that, he came up towards the building. But then he disappeared into the shadows."

"Do you know what time that was?"

He sat back a moment. "I wake up almost every night around two-thirty. Don't know why other than I usually have to pee. Anyway, after I took care of business, I thought I'd sit a moment with my Sarah. That's why I was at the window."

"Why didn't you tell anyone? Wake me up?"

He chuckled softly. "Hell, I didn't know if someone here was having an affair, you know? Or trading in something illegal." He shook his head. "Didn't want to get mixed up in anything."

"We had a break-in last night," I admitted. "No one was hurt, but this man was looking for something and broke into my apartment. There is a detective here right now. Would you be willing to talk to him?"

"Sure, I'll talk to him," he said. Then his eyes creased in concern. "Gee, I thought I heard your dogs bark last night. I didn't really think it was anything to worry about. You okay?"

"Yes." I paused, remembering back to the moment that thug had grabbed me. This entire thing had shaken me, but I inhaled and said, "Yes, I'm fine. I'll have Detective Abrams come out to speak to you."

"That'd be fine," he said.

I got up to go to my apartment when he stopped me. "By the way, it was an aluminum boat," he said, shoveling scrambled eggs into his mouth.

I turned back. "How do you know that?"

He swallowed and took a sip of coffee. After he wiped his mouth, he said, "I spent my life on the water. Aluminum boats have a different sound to them, you know. When you get in and out. There's a bit of a twang if you know what I mean. Besides, the boat was made by Lund."

I loved this old guy.

"You know who made the boat?"

He laughed again. "It said so on the side of the boat. L. U. N. D."
he said, spelling it out. They're a big maker of fishing boats. Had a
couple of my own." He looked up at me. "You know, you have good
lights on your dock."

"Yes. We do. Because a lot of guests like to walk out onto the
docks at night. Why do you say that?"

"Because she also had a name on her."

"A name?"

"Yeah. Someone painted T. B. on her bow in big letters."

CHAPTER TEN

Detective Abrams interviewed Mr. Muse, along with everyone else at the Inn again. After that, the family with the two boys who had played Clue with Curt decided it would be safer to stay somewhere else and left. Understandable after a murder and a break in. Curt cornered me after breakfast.

"Someone broke into the inn last night. Awesome," he gushed, his beady eyes lit with enthusiasm.

"Actually, just my apartment," I corrected him. "None of you were in danger."

"What were they looking for? A weapon? Do you have weapons in your apartment?"

"Of course not," I replied, thinking I couldn't really describe Minnie as a weapon.

"Well, I could help, you know. I'm pretty good at finding things."

I smiled. There was no way I would let this kid get involved. "That won't be necessary. The police will take care of everything."

His face fell, making me feel sorry for him. I hadn't seen him interact once with his parents since he'd been here, other than at breakfast. His father was in Seattle for a conference most of the time, and his mother spent her time on the back deck or in our library reading. And now the only two kids near his age had left. He was alone.

"But thank you," I said. "Why don't you keep your eyes open? Just in case. You never know when you'll see something important."

You'd think I just gave him a Maserati for his birthday.

"Yeah! Okay. I'll do that. I can be your eyes and ears."

"Exactly. But this is just between you and me. Okay?," I said, placing my hand on his shoulder. This was an innocent enough secret, I thought.

He nodded before joining his mother at the breakfast table. I went back into the kitchen where April was washing the fry pans and told her what Mr. Muse had said.

"Did the police talk to him?" she asked, her arms elbow deep in sudsy water.

"Yes. I'm sure they'll go to all the boat companies now to see if they can find who owns that boat."

"It's a common boat, but it's the initials painted on it that make it stand out. Seems more like a job for someone who lives on the lake and knows everybody's business." She raised her eyebrows in a knowing way.

"Oh, yeah. You're right," I said, my eyes lighting up. "I'll be back. I'm going next door."

Goldie Singleton and her husband lived next door. I didn't consider Goldie a friend necessarily, although we were friendly. I mean, you couldn't help but like her, even though at times she could drive you nuts.

I went out through the breakfast-room door and off the deck to a path that led through some trees along the lake to a small parking lot on the near side of Goldie's property. I veered off the path, heading to her backyard, passing a variety of colorful gnomes set into small vignettes on the way. Goldie loved gnomes and had them positioned in different locations throughout her yard and her home. You could often find them conversing with each other. Well, not really, but Goldie had set them up to look like they were. One of my favorite groupings were three gnomes sitting on a tree stump with a toy picnic basket and fake food laid out in front of them.

I came up through the trees into her backyard and knocked on her sliding glass door. Peering through the door into her rumpus room, my gaze swept across the walls and her collection of mementoes. Being in her house was like being in a very personal museum. She'd accumulated them on her travels as she and her husband had globe trotted over the years.

"Julia!"

I turned to find Goldie coming around the side of the house. She was shorter than me, heavy in the hips, and loved wearing loose-fitting pants that flapped around her legs.

"How 'ya doin', Julia? We haven't talked since you got back from yer trip. I heard about yer head."

My hand went immediately to the spot where the ball had knocked me unconscious. "I'm fine. Really. Just bad luck."

"Humph," she snorted. "You have a lot of that." She stuck her hands into the large pockets of her pants and rolled back on her heels. "Well, I'm glad yer okay. What's up? I heard the police were over there again. Marie from up the street called me. We were away for a few days." She opened the sliding glass door. "C'mon in and have a cup of tea and tell me about it."

This was why I rarely dropped by to see Goldie. It often consumed a sizeable chunk of my day. But I followed her inside and up the stairs to the kitchen, passing framed photographs, small oil paintings, elaborately carved mirrors, and a couple of German clocks on the way. Once in the kitchen, she filled two mugs with water, threw in tea bags, and put them into the microwave.

"Okay," she said. "Let's sit, and you tell me what's been happenin' over at yer place. I see that hunk of a police detective is there again today."

I sighed but sat down. "I don't know how much I can tell you because there's an investigation going on. But my uncle, well, he wasn't my real uncle... Carter Davis... do you remember me telling you about him? He had those big fancy Thanksgiving dinners."

"Oh, oh, yeah," she said hurriedly. "And you got kicked out of 'em."

"Yes," I said, grimacing. "Anyway, I hadn't seen him in over a year, and he just showed up the other day and... died the moment he walked in the door."

Her eyes lit up. "Really? Did he have a heart attack?"

"Um, no. He was poisoned."

"Not again!" she exclaimed.

I exhaled. "It wasn't me this time. I didn't poison him!" *Damn! Why did everyone immediately jump to that conclusion?* "We don't know where he got the poison," I continued. "But Ben is back in town. My Ben. Not yours."

Her husband's name was Ben, too.

"Your brother?"

"Yes. Carter was his best friend. They were working on a project together. It may have been that project that got Carter killed."

The microwave beeped, and she pulled out the two ceramic mugs and put them on the table. After getting a carton of milk and the sugar bowl, she came and sat down. I selected the black mug with the phrase, "Thou shall not try me. Mood 24:7" written in white across the side of it and smiled, thinking, that's kind of how I felt at the moment. Goldie took the mug that was shaped like the udder of a cow. We fixed our tea, took sips, and then sat back.

"Okay," she said, putting the mug down. "So your Ben is caught up in something illegal?"

"Not at all."

Her comment made me pause, but I wasn't about to lay any doubt down in front of Goldie. I didn't really know all that Ben did when he hunted for artifacts. And in this case, all we knew was what he'd told us, and he wasn't always forthcoming with information.

"Well, seems kinda suspicious to me," she said, taking a sip.

"I think my whole life is a little suspicious," I said with a smile. We both chuckled.

"You do have your adventures," she said. "Okay, so how can I help?"

I paused. What I was about to say might make her nervous. After all, she lived less than a hundred yards from me.

"Someone broke into my apartment last night."

"Again?" Her eyes grew big, and she flinched back in her chair. "I take it Carter didn't accidentally die from poison."

"No. Someone murdered him."

"Boy, Julia. You sure know how to suck all the oxygen out of a room. Did this guy… I assume it was a guy… did he hurt you? You know I'm always here with Betsy if you need me."

Betsy was her shotgun, which she fired in my breakfast-room a few months earlier to scare away another intruder.

"No," I assured her. "He restrained me. He was looking for something, and he thought I knew where it was. But the dogs came to my rescue. Or, rather, Minnie did."

She laughed. "That Minnie has a pair of teeth on her."

"Anyway, one of our guests saw two men in a small aluminum boat come up to the dock early this morning. One stayed in the boat, while the other one broke into my apartment. The boat had the letters T. B. stenciled on the bow. I was just wondering if you might know whose boat that could be."

"Hmmm," she murmured and sat back. "T.B. Could be Tom Bateman. He lives on the north shore and does a lot of fishing."

"I suppose it could be a man's initials," I said. "I thought men normally named their boats after the women in their lives, though."

"Well, Tom Bateman's arrogant enough to name an entire fleet of boats after himself. I wouldn't put it past him. But it also might stand for Tobias Boats. You know, they're that big boat maker up by the university." She scrunched up her lips in thought and used her index finger to tap the side of her head. "I'll hafta do some thinkin' about it. And I'll ask Ben. My Ben. Not yours."

"Thanks. Ask around if you can, too. Someone might recognize it."

I got up and put my mug in the sink. I turned to leave and noticed a mist lingering in the hallway. It could only mean one thing—one of the ghosts had followed me to Goldie's. I glanced at Goldie to see if she'd noticed, but she was busy putting her own mug into the sink. I turned back to see the mist floating in front of a colorful framed print in the hallway across from the kitchen. It was a delightful painting of a fairy wielding a sparkling wand that shimmered with glitter. I moved over to it just as the mist evaporated.

I felt a rush of adrenalin. *What did this mean?*

"That's new, isn't it?" I asked, pointing to the picture.

Goldie turned. "Yeah. Ben found it in an antique store in North Carolina when he was there for a conference. He said it reminded him of me." She laughed, snorting through her nose. "As if I was the size of a fairy."

"It's lovely."

I leaned in to get a better look at the picture when it flipped off the wall and onto the floor.

"Oh, dear," I exclaimed. "I'm so sorry." I leaned over to pick it up. "It didn't break," I reported.

Goldie came up behind me. "No problem, Julia. I know how you are."

She meant I could be clumsy. But I hadn't even touched the picture. It had to be Elizabeth or Chloe. The faint aroma of rose water answered that mystery. As I hung the picture back on the wall, I read an inscription printed at the bottom.

"All you need is faith, trust, and a little bit of pixie dust."
— Tinker Bell.

CHAPTER ELEVEN

"It could mean Tinker Bell!" I exclaimed, coming back to the Inn.

April was cleaning off the breakfast bar. She turned to me with a dishcloth in hand. "What are you talking about?"

"The initials on that boat."

"What makes you think that?"

"There's a bar in Shoreline named Tinker Bell's. I looked it up on my phone and remembered that I read about it last week. There was an article about the owner who is a crook or something. Anyway, that would fit. T.B. Tinker Bell."

She stood back and blew out a heavy breath. "That could just be a coincidence. Isn't the dog Doe brought home from your cross-country trip named Tinker Bell, too?"

I frowned. "Oh, yeah. But Doe doesn't have a boat anymore. Anyway, there was a framed picture of a fairy with a wand in her hand at Goldie's. It had a quote by the guy who wrote Peter Pan. You know... Tinker Bell. And Elizabeth knocked the picture off the wall," I said with emphasis.

April's expression remained frozen. "You think Elizabeth followed you to Goldie's?"

"Mist and all. I mean, she followed me to Chicago. Why couldn't she follow me to Goldie's?"

"Okay, maybe Elizabeth was trying to tell you something. But you went there to talk to Goldie. Did *she* have any ideas who the boat might belong to?"

"She mentioned Tobias Boats and Tom Bateman."

"Tom Bateman? Isn't he that idiot who lives up by the bridge and lines the street with political signs every time there's an election?"

"I think so."

"I'd vote for him," she said and turned back to the counter. "No pun intended."

"But the initials *could* mean Tinker Bell."

"Yes, but it could mean any of those names," she said, continuing to work. "The question is... how will you figure out which one?"

"I don't know. But wait," I said, holding up a finger. "I'll be back in a minute."

I went to the office computer and Googled Tobias Boats. They had a very distinctive logo—the letters T.B. with a water spray drawn behind them. I printed it off and went to find Mr. Muse, who was just leaving his room.

"Ms. Applegate," he said, when he saw me. "I was on my way to see my daughter."

"I was wondering if you'd look at this." I held out the Tobias logo. "Does this look like the letters you saw on the boat last night?"

He reached into his shirt pocket and pulled out a pair of glasses. Taking the sheet of paper, he stared at it carefully. Finally, he shook his head.

"No. It wasn't like this. What I saw were just the letters. Nothing behind them. And the letters weren't this heavy. They were, I don't know, more feminine."

My heart skipped a beat. I felt more certain than ever that T.B. meant Tinker Bell.

"Thanks, Mr. Muse. Have a nice time with your family."

I went back to the office and called Blair. "Hey, do you know who owns a bar in Shoreline called Tinker Bell's?"

"I've heard of the bar, but don't know who owns it. Why?"

I quickly explained about the break-in and the boat.

"Wow, Julia. This is getting too close to home."

"I know. But I think I might have a lead on who owns that boat."

"And you think it might be whoever owns the bar?"

"Right."

"You could probably just Google it. Or I could ask Mr. Billings. I'm sure he'd know."

"Call him, okay? I have to bail Ben out of jail."

"I'm sorry, what? You left that part out. Why is Ben in jail?"

"Long story. Just ask Mr. Billings about the bar. I'll call you later. Thanks."

÷

It was noon by the time I had filled out the papers and posted Ben's bail at the county jail. He emerged through a locked glass door, looking angry and disheveled. His shirt and pants were wrinkled, his five o'clock shadow had grown to a 24-hour shadow, and there were dark circles under his eyes. He also smelled like vomit.

"Um… you okay?" I asked, my nose twitching. "You smell awful."

"Never been better," he said, flicking something off his shirt. "Nothing like a night in jail to sharpen your senses."

"Okay, well, let's get you home. I'm sure a shower would feel good."

We rode most of the way home in silence and with the window open. Ben just stared straight ahead. *Was he thinking about Carter? Remembering whoever it was who threw up on him in jail? Or, how he could secretly make life miserable for David as payback.*

We were just pulling down the drive when I said, "By the way, whoever broke in last night came by boat."

That got his attention. "How do you know that?"

"A guest was awake and saw the boat arrive with two men in it. Only one got out and came up to the building. But the guest who saw the boat also saw two letters painted on the bow—T.B."

He turned back to gaze out the window. "Interesting."

I pulled around to the small parking lot next to the back door of my apartment. As we got out, I said, "And we identified three potential names that T.B. might refer to. But I've already eliminated one."

"What are the other two?"

We ambled up to my back door.

"Tom Bateman. He lives here on the island and could own a small boat. But it could also refer to a bar in Shoreline called Tinker Bell's."

He sneered. "There's probably a hundred people or companies in the area with the letters T.B. It could be anyone."

I locked the car with my key fob. "Well, it could also be the bar. Anyway, I'm going to check it out."

"Bateman," he said thoughtfully. "That name sounds familiar. Let me check something first."

As soon as we got inside, he turned left into his room. The dogs ran to greet me, and the three of us followed him over to the bed, where his briefcase still sat open with the contents loosely stacked next to it. Black dust was everywhere from the forensics team's fingerprint powder.

I shooed the dogs away as Ben pressed the button on the front of the case once, twice, three times. And lo-and-behold, the bottom of the briefcase rose about two inches to the gentle hum of a motor.

"What the...?" I said, staring wide-eyed.

He gave me a flicker of a smile. "I live in a world of secrets, Julia. Secrets that some people will go to great lengths to conceal or steal." He slid his fingers underneath the fake bottom and pulled out a small stack of papers. He left a couple of notebooks behind.

"What's all that?"

"My notes," he replied, as we sat side by side on the bed. "Everything I've been researching for the last year."

"Including the plans for the box?" I asked, a knife edge to my voice.

"Those, too."

He pulled out a yellow notepad and flipped through several pages until he found what he was looking for. Seven or eight names, a few dates, and a couple of sentences were scribbled at the bottom. "These are the families I traced from Britain to the United States," he said, pointing to the names. He focused on them and then said, "Just as I thought."

"What?" I asked, leaning in.

His finger rested on the last name on the list. "Alistair Bateman," he said. "He attended the University of London in 1888 and became the Earl of Manchester and served as Lord Chamberlain to Alexandra, Princess of Wales, in 1901." He looked over at me. "His son, Robert, immigrated to the U.S. in 1912."

CHAPTER TWELVE

That afternoon Blair and Rudy met us in my apartment. Doe had a meeting with a client she couldn't miss, so we promised to fill her in later.

"I called Aria," I said as I poured myself a glass of iced tea. "She thinks she'll be able to trace Alistair Bateman's lineage to see if Tom Bateman is his descendent. She said it might take a day or two, though."

"I wonder if there's a way we can find out sooner," Rudy said, sitting on the sofa. "After all, these guys are after this key, and at this point, no one knows where it is."

"And I take it we know no more about the police investigation," Blair said. She was sitting on a bar stool spinning around like a high school girl at the malt shop, wearing a pair of tighter-than-normal jeans (well, tighter-than-normal for the rest of the world) and a colorful, low-cut blouse.

I shrugged. "No. They've been radio silent ever since arresting Ben. And, frankly, I've felt like I should keep my distance."

"Have you talked to David?" Blair asked, catching the counter to stop herself.

"No. He's also been radio silent," I said, a heavy feeling in my stomach.

"Which makes me wonder," Rudy began, "should we be dabbling in this at all? We've been lucky so far. No one has done jail time. I'd kind of like to keep it that way."

"I agree," Ben said, turning to me. "Carter is dead. You've been assaulted. And I was arrested. This is getting too dangerous. I don't want you hurt, Julia. This could even affect your business. I think it's time to leave this to the police."

I looked directly at him. "Oh, don't give me that big brother garbage. I know you. You will not leave this alone because of a little danger. I remember a tribe of natives once took you prisoner in the Brazilian jungle and then you married one of them."

"That is a gross exaggeration. I married a reporter who accompanied us on the excursion."

"Yes, but someone also shot you while you searched for a valuable artifact in Cairo," Blair added.

"And injected you with a slow-acting, lethal poison in Spain when you recovered an Aztec coin for the Mexican government," Rudy said.

Ben had showered and changed into clean clothes. But his hair was still damp, and he exhaled and shook his head, sending an errant lock of hair across his forehead. "I think you're all exaggerating. In Cairo, I was caught in the crossfire between the police and a group of bank robbers. Just the wrong place, wrong time. And when I was in Mexico, I made the mistake of handling a stack of medieval manuscripts that had been bound with arsenic-rich paint. The arsenic had crystallized and got all over my hands. I was never in any real danger. Anyway, none of those situations change the facts here. The fact is that by my being here, you're all in danger. That's why I've booked a room at the Sheraton."

"No," I said. "Carter was family. And we're family. Where you go, I go."

"And where she goes, we go," Rudy said.

He looked at each of us. "You are an amazing group of women; I'll give you that. But you know I'm right. No matter what, we need to be more careful."

"Right. Like not going out in the middle of the night and leaving the back door open," Blair said.

"And not withholding evidence from the police," Rudy added.

"Or, from us," I finished. "Do you remember that time I was in fourth grade and you, me, and Carter hiked through the woods behind our house to explore that old barn up on the hill?"

"Yes. And you tripped on the way back and cut open your knee and went screaming home to mom."

"Right. But remember what she said when you got home?" The sheepish look on his face gave me great satisfaction. "She said that we're better together and that you shouldn't have sent me home alone. Because that's when I fell."

"Well, to be fair," Blair began, "you fall all the time, even if you're with someone."

I grimaced at her.

"The point Julia is making is that we're all better together," Rudy said. "As brother and sister. And as a team," she said, gesturing to Blair. "So where do *we* go from here?"

"Well, we'll have to wait to hear from Aria on Bateman's genealogy. Did Mr. Billings know anything about the bar?" I asked Blair.

"Yeah, sorry." She had just taken a sip of iced tea. "It's owned by a guy named Dave Russo who likes expensive and fast cars. He's bought a couple of Porsches from us. Mr. Billings didn't really know much more about him, other than he once paid in cash."

That got our attention.

"Sheesh! How much was that?" I asked.

She shrugged. "Something like $70,000."

"Well, that doesn't sound legit," Rudy said. "I wonder where he gets that kind of cash?"

I glanced at my watch. "Listen, Doe said she'd be done with her meeting at four. Let me call April and see if she's up for another impromptu dinner at her place. We can plan our strategy to find out more about the bar in Shoreline and Tom Bateman."

÷

We were back at April's, setting the table on her deck at 6:00 p.m. She'd offered to make spaghetti and garlic bread, and Blair and Rudy had helped me make a big green salad to round out the menu.

"You really think Tom Bateman would be arrogant enough to put his own initials on a boat?" Rudy asked.

"Goldie thought so. I only know Bateman by reputation," I said, placing silverware around the table. "He's very active in the state Democratic Party, where he's a bit of a legend."

"What do you mean you haven't met him?" Ben asked. "I thought *you* were active in the Democratic Party."

"I used to be. Not so much anymore. I'm too busy solving crimes," I said, smiling.

Blair snorted as she folded napkins.

"Anyway, I'm told that he dominates the meetings and is loud and abrasive."

"What does he do for a living?" April asked, bringing out the plates.

I had to stop and think. "Not really sure. He lives in an expensive house, though. Right on the water."

"Bateman must have influence somewhere," Ben added. "That is, if he's a member of The Electi."

"He owns Northwest Shipping and is president of Northwest Shipping Alliance," Doe said, stepping onto the deck.

She wore a navy-blue pantsuit with a pale pink blouse and carried the black satchel. She dropped it by the door and slouched into a chair with a sigh.

"Northwest Shipping Alliance is a conglomeration of all the big shipping magnates in the region," she added. "They lobby politicians for laws that favor them. And if you're wondering, the initials on the boat probably belong to his wife, Trina."

We all stopped and turned to her.

"You know them?" Blair asked.

"Yes. Sorry, Julia. I'd like to help with dinner, but I've had back-to-back meetings all day, and I'm beat."

"No problem. You sit tight." I handed her a glass of wine.

"Thanks," she said, taking a large swallow. "Anyway, yes, I know them. Or, I should say I know her. Trina and I used to be in PEO together. I haven't been active for a couple of years. She's currently the membership chair, though."

"What's PEO?" April asked.

"It's a sisterhood that promotes scholarships for young women all over the world."

Blair sat down and poured some wine for herself. "What do you mean a sisterhood?"

"Just that. It's a bit like a sorority. In fact, it was initially founded as a sorority at Iowa Wesleyan University back in the late 1800s."

"Stop right there," April said. "I want to hear this, but dinner is ready."

Everyone helped get the food on the table—well, all except Ben, who was unusually quiet and just sat watching the lake. Once we were ready to eat, Rudy spoke up.

"So, what does PEO stand for?" she asked.

Doe had just shoved a large forkful of spaghetti in her mouth and put up her hand to pause. Wiping her mouth, she said, "Sorry. But, damn, that's good, April. I haven't eaten since breakfast."

April grinned. "I'm glad you like it."

"C'mon, Doe. What does PEO stand for?" Blair asked again.

"I'd have to kill you if I told you," she replied with a smile.

"Very funny," Blair replied. "Just tell us."

"She can't," Ben said. "It's a secret society."

It was the first time Ben had spoken since Doe had arrived, and everyone turned to him.

"They protect what the name stands for," he continued. "Although publicly, they say it stands for Philanthropic Educational Organization. But that's not the true meaning, is it, Doe?"

He was staring at Doe now, who stared back while pulling off a chunk of garlic bread and slipping it into her mouth.

"I'm right, aren't I? Secret initiations and all."

Ben was challenging Doe, which wasn't a good idea. Doe was an intelligent and formidable businesswoman who, frankly, didn't take crap from anyone. She returned Ben's gaze, swallowed, and finally leaned back in her chair, placing her napkin in her lap.

"You're right. It is considered a secret society. Someone must invite you to join, just like The Electi. There is also a secret ritual we go through to initiate new members. And, yes, the real meaning of the initials PEO is kept secret. But the meaning is nothing nefarious. In fact, it's rather nice. Members get a pin when they join and must return the pin if they drop out. Many members, however, ask to be buried with their pin because it means that much to them."

"That's kinda creepy," Blair murmured.

Doe threw Blair an irritated look. "I think it shows commitment," she retorted. She turned her attention back to Ben. "But unlike the societies you're researching, there is no money or intelligence quota needed to join. All that's required is a desire to do good work on behalf of young women. In other words, we don't have to kill anyone or admit to any horrendous personal secret just to become a member. Happy?"

All heads turned to Ben as if we were at a tennis match. He grinned.

"Touché," he said as he lifted his glass in a toast.

We all followed suit, although I didn't know what we were toasting to.

"So," I began. "How do we find out if Tom Bateman is a member of The Electi?"

Rudy turned to Ben. "Would his wife know?"

"Possibly. Although he might not have been truthful with her about it. At least not about the name. If he's the descendant of Alistair Bateman, I would think he'd be proud of it. But if he's a member of the society and attends meetings, he might have called it something else. I have found nothing like this in my research, but it's likely they all have a secondary name for the society so they can tell people, like family members, where they're going when they go to meetings without being honest."

"I know what we need to do to find out more about the Batemans," Doe said, snapping her fingers. She turned to me. "You and I are going to have lunch with Trina."

"What? Why?" I asked, nearly choking on my garlic bread.

"Because I think it's time you joined PEO."

CHAPTER THIRTEEN

David texted me shortly after everyone left, asking if we could get a drink and talk. I hadn't heard from him since he'd arrested Ben and was eager to see him. I'd texted him twice over the course of the last 12 hours and only received terse responses telling me he was busy.

I was getting ready to leave when Angela called.

"Hey, Mom, sorry I've been absent for the last couple of days. How are you doing?"

I sighed. "Okay. I guess. I can't yet wrap my head around the fact that Carter is gone. He doesn't let on, but I think your uncle is taking it very hard."

"I'm sure he is. You know that whenever they were together, they were two peas in a pod. Practically finishing each other's sentences."

"They were brothers-in-arms, so to speak. Very close. Not just in their intellect, but in their interests."

"I know. Remember that time we all went camping? I think I was maybe fifteen. And dad was being dad, you know? All focused on setting up camp. Getting things organized. While Ben and Carter put out camp chairs to finish an argument they'd started in the car. Something called the Secret Gospel of something-or-other."

"The Secret Gospel of Mark," I said, chuckling. "I remember. It started in the car on the way to Mount Rainier, and they argued about it for the entire weekend we were there. I'm not sure they ever got out of those camp chairs. They even ate their meals sitting there."

Angela was laughing on the other end of the phone. "I know, and remember how mad dad got? He stomped around the campsite complaining that there would be questions about Jesus and Christianity for as long as we lived," she said, imitating Graham's voice. "'So why not just set it aside for now and let's get the fishing poles out.'"

"You have a good memory," I said, my laughter subsiding. "In fact, the controversy over the Secret Gospel of Mark has to do with yet another ancient missing letter. They were arguing over if it was a forgery."

"I can't believe Uncle Ben got arrested today, though. Are you okay? I mean, it was David who arrested him, right?"

"Yes," I said with a sigh. "We haven't talked since then. He wants to get together tonight, though."

"It'll be okay, Mom. David is a reasonable guy. How is Uncle Ben?"

"I bailed him out this morning."

"You have to admit, he loves solving mysteries, just like you."

"Listen, has Detective Abrams said anything about what they're doing to find Carter's killer?"

"His name is Sean, Mom."

Her tone reminded me of a teenage Angela.

"I know what his name is, but he's Detective Abrams to me. And the fact that you're sleeping with him doesn't make me feel any less intimidated by him."

"Nor he you," she said.

"He's intimidated by me?"

"You are my mom, after all. I think most men are intimidated by their girlfriend's mothers. But perhaps you should stop getting involved in criminal investigations. Someone attacked you last night. I'd hate to face prosecuting you for obstruction of justice, or even worse, arranging your funeral."

"That won't happen," I said with more bravado than I felt. "And I can't just step aside when it's a question of who killed Carter. He was family, Angie. Or as close as you can get without being family."

"I know. But you've been lucky so far, Mom. And luck tends to run out."

"So, what has *Sean* told you?"

"He plans to call you tomorrow, so I'll let him speak for himself. I just wanted to call and see if you were okay and encourage you to be careful. I'm up to my eyeballs in a big case and won't be able to stop by for a couple of days. Please listen to Sean and do what he says."

"Fine. But, hey, speaking of cases, do you know anything about Tinker Bell's, that dive bar up in Shoreline? I thought I read something several months ago about the owner being arrested."

"Dave Russo" she said. "Yeah. He's a real scumbag. Why?"

I told her about the boat and why I thought the T.B. on its bow might refer to Tinker Bell.

"Well, first, you need to let the police check that out. And I think your theory might be a stretch. I mean, if it really was Elizabeth who clued you into that, then I suppose it could mean something. She's pretty on point with knowing things we don't. But I'm not sure why Russo would be involved in a case linked to Uncle Ben. He has a long history of loan sharking and using muscle to get what he wants. I even prosecuted his son, Spike, for assault and battery a couple of years ago. He's a real piece of work. Not bad looking but has tattoos all the way up his neck. Skulls and chains and stuff. And he's a mean SOB. In fact, neither one of them is a stranger to the inside of a jail cell, so I'd stay clear of those two if I were you."

"He doesn't have the tattoo of a turtle on the back of his hand, does he?"

"I have no idea. But like I said, stay clear of him."

"Well, I want to find out who owns that boat. It could be Tom Bateman. You know he lives on the island. But I'm not ruling out this Dave Russo just yet."

"Mom! You're not listening to me. Let Sean and David do the heavy lifting on this. Stay out of it. Listen, I gotta go. Has the funeral for Carter been scheduled yet?"

"No. The police are trying to locate his daughter."

"Okay, but if you end up planning it, count me in. I'd like to help."

We said our goodbyes, and I finished touching up my makeup, thinking about Dave Russo and his son Spike. Elizabeth had followed me around, even on the road to Chicago. That framed picture of Tinker Bell hadn't flipped off Goldie's wall for no reason. When you live around ghosts, you tend to accept their presence more readily and the messages they try to send. I'd agreed to meet Trina Bateman with Doe, thinking that it couldn't hurt to check the Batemans off the list. But my eye was still on the bar owner.

I was just about to leave to meet David when Ben popped his head into my bedroom.

"I'm leaving. I'll keep in touch."

"Wait. What do you mean?" I asked, coming forward.

"I'm still going to the Sheraton. I didn't want to argue in front of your friends. But it's best if I don't stay here."

"But why? We won't stop working on this case."

"I know. But my gut says that the farther away from you I am, the better. You don't need me when you attend the dinner in Seattle with Graham. You guys have that covered. And Doe has a good way for you to find out more about Tom Bateman. I have a couple of things I want to follow up on myself. Let's touch base tomorrow night." I began to speak, but my brother put a hand up to stop me. "There's no negotiating on this, Julia. I'm a target, which makes you a target. I appreciate everything you're doing. And I know Carter would, too."

His voice caught, and he dropped his head to take a breath. I reached out to place my hand on his shoulder.

"We're going to figure this out, Ben. These people won't get away with it."

He lifted his chin and nodded. "Let's just hope that no one else gets hurt."

He kissed me on the cheek and left.

÷

Twenty minutes later, David and I were sitting across from each other at a table overlooking the Olympic-sized swimming pool at the Mercerwood Shore Club. It was our book club's favorite place to have drinks, and Angela had competed with her high school swim team there. The night was warm and clear, and I'd purposely worn a sleeveless magenta blouse that brought out the color in my eyes and nicely accented my auburn hair. I'd even worn his favorite half-moon dangling earrings.

David arrived but didn't say anything. We just ordered drinks and then sat awkwardly for a few moments as we waited for them to arrive. Finally, he spoke.

"Look, Julia, I haven't... I need to..." He stopped and took a drink from the glass of ice water on the table.

"You're mad at me," I said, cutting to the chase. "Because once again, I'm involved in a murder case. But honestly, David, I don't know anything right now. Yes, I'm hoping to find out more. But anything I..."

"That's the problem," he blurted, stopping me.

I shut my mouth and stared at him. The waitress chose that moment to return with our drinks. She left, and I took a sip of wine to stall for time. He ignored his rum and Coke and watched me silently.

"Listen, I believe you knew nothing about the key. That's not the problem. It's that you keep inserting yourself into my investigations. And not just my investigations, pretty much any police investigation that crosses your path. Case in point was the last one on your road trip. You had no business chasing after those people who abducted that girl. You should have reported it to the authorities. But you didn't. You just forged ahead regardless of the legality of what you were doing or of any danger to yourself or your friends. Julia, I'm a cop. I do things by the book. I get judged on that. And I can't keep making excuses for you or bailing you out of trouble."

My face grew warm, and it wasn't from the wine. I was getting a tongue lashing—one that I probably deserved. But it was especially hurtful coming from the man I loved. I blinked back a tear and gazed out the window, hoping to get my bearings before I responded.

"You know how I feel about you," he continued. "I've been thinking about retiring for a while now and would like to have you in any plans I might make. I even told you I thought we should move in together when we were in Chicago. No response from you on that, by the way. But…"

"Wait, a minute!" I stopped him with a raised hand. "A fast-flying baseball hit me in the head and sent me to the emergency room. You never brought it up again after we returned, and I wasn't sure if I'd heard you correctly. You know, baseball to the head and all."

I sat back, tightening my fingers around my wine glass. I'd wondered for two weeks whether what I'd heard just before I blacked out that day at Wrigley Field was real or not. When David didn't mention it again, I thought perhaps I'd been mistaken. Now, after being soundly chastised for following clues that had so far saved several lives and put bad people behind bars, I was more than a little miffed that he would throw that in my face as one more affront to his manhood. Okay, maybe thinking it was an affront to his manhood was hyperbole. But, at that moment, I was angry and felt the need to defend myself.

"I didn't say anything about moving in together after we came back because I wasn't sure how you felt about it," he said. "You're a very independent woman, Julia. That's something I like about you. And I assumed that since *you* said nothing, you probably weren't interested."

"Did it ever occur to you I hadn't heard you? After all, I had a head injury."

"I knew you heard me because you turned to me when I said it," he replied, his body stiffening. "I just didn't know why you wouldn't mention it again unless you were purposely avoiding giving me an answer. You do that sometimes."

"I'm sorry, what? I avoid things?"

"Yes. You're independent *and* stubborn. And when you're being stubborn, you pretend you don't hear me."

I felt like an errant student being lectured by a teacher. He'd gone out on a limb to suggest moving in together and didn't want to be embarrassed by having to mention it a second time. *Men!* What was it about their egos that they couldn't ask for directions or just openly communicate with personal matters? The baseball sent me to the hospital. And after that, there was only silence from him on the subject.

"Is this about us moving in together or about the investigation? I'm getting a little confused. Because it seems like I'm getting lectured about both."

He pressed his lips together and slowly shook his head back and forth. "Somehow, I knew this would happen. You're so focused on being Mercer Island's resident sleuth that you can't focus on anything else. Why can't you just run your bed-and-breakfast and forget about being Miss Marple? Leave the cops and robbers to the professionals. Then, maybe you and I could have a genuine relationship. That's what I want, Julia. A real relationship with you. You know, something that didn't involve you getting chased by pathological killers, locked in basements, or digging your own grave."

"Excuse me? Just run my bed-and-breakfast? Like I'm not capable of anything else?"

"I didn't mean it that way…"

"And to be clear, we stopped a killer from burying his wife in that grave. No one forced us to dig our own grave. You just made that up."

He slammed an open hand on the table, making me jump. "Stop it! You know what I mean. Stop putting yourself in danger! I'm tired of having to rescue you."

There was an emotion filled pause, as I looked around to see other people staring. I pushed my chair back and stood up. "Good to know. No more rescuing will be needed. Next time, I'll call Triple A." I grabbed the strap of my purse, where it hung over the back of the chair. "Thanks for the wine."

I turned and strode away from the table. I made it to the parking lot before he could pay for the drinks and catch up to me. Just as I reached my Pathfinder, he hurried up behind me and grabbed my arm.

"Julia!" he pleaded. "Please. I didn't mean for things to end this way."

I whipped around to face him. "But you did mean to end it. Consider it done," I said.

I turned back around to unlock my car.

"No… no, I uh… wait. That's not what I meant." He moved next to me and gently put his hand against the door so that I couldn't open it. "Can't we talk about this? Can't you see it from my point of view?"

I looked up at him, tears blurring my vision. "I see your point of view," I said, swiping at the tears. "You're a cop. You want things your way. And you can't have things your way. So my guess is that you were prepared to give me an ultimatum. Either I stop all this sleuthing *stuff,* or we'd have to break up."

He dropped his chin. I'd hit the mark.

"Well, I will not give up sleuthing. At least not now. A lifelong friend just died on my doorstep. My brother has been arrested. Someone assaulted me. And there are real consequences to not solving Carter Davis' murder. You guys are good at what you do. But you'll have to admit that we have helped a lot in these cases." I pulled the car door open. "I'll let you know when we find anything significant."

CHAPTER FOURTEEN

My anger spilled over into my dreams that night, waking me several times and leaving me feeling disoriented. I finally got up at 5:30 and made myself a cup of tea and sat staring at the *Wizard of Oz* poster that hung next to my fireplace.

My head fell back against the chair, and I allowed my mind to wander. I thought about the four travelers in the *Wizard of Oz*: Dorothy, the Cowardly Lion, the Tin Man, and the Scarecrow. They did what they had to do to get Dorothy home. No questions asked. They fought the Wicked Witch of the West and her flying monkeys, and although they weren't any more equipped to succeed than my friends and I were, they defeated her and released everyone from her tyrannical rule.

Was I living in a fantasy to think we were doing the same sort of thing? After all, I had never gone looking for the crimes we investigated; they had somehow found me. For instance, one of my best friends had died at my dining room table, poisoned by something out of my own pantry. Didn't that require a response from me? And then Dana Finkle had come to me demanding that I help her discover who was trying to kill her. How could I refuse? When we discovered a secret room in the attic of my old barn and the possible death of a baby, it nearly screamed at me to get involved. And when I saw a young girl pounding on the back window of a motorhome, as if she were in trouble, didn't I have an obligation to find out if I could help?

Yes, I became a willing partner in all those situations. I admit to that. But I wasn't a busybody. I liked to think that I had risen to the challenge before me, rather than inserting myself into otherwise off-limit police investigations, as David had suggested. And now, a dear friend had practically died in my arms as a victim of foul play. Carter had come to me for a reason. I needed to know what that was. And somehow sitting back and waiting for the police to find the answers just wasn't enough.

÷

Having fallen asleep in the chair, I woke at 7:15 to the ringtone of my phone. I jumped up and ran into the bedroom, grabbing it and swiping it on.

"Hello," I said, stretching my eyes open.

"Julia!" my mother's voice demanded. "What the heck are you involved in now?"

My heart raced as it did whenever any of the ghosts confronted me, but especially when the ghost was my mother. She was a force to be reckoned with in life, and death hadn't diminished that at all.

"What do you mean?" I replied, rubbing my eyes. "You woke me up."

"I keep getting messages," she said. "I don't know what they mean."

I plopped down on the bed. "What kind of messages?"

"Images, really," she said. "Images of you and Ben. And Carter."

"Oh," I whimpered. "Carter's dead, Mom. I thought you'd know that given where you are and all."

"Don't be an idiot, Julia. It's not like I get a text message every time someone I know enters the pearly gates. But that might explain one image I keep seeing."

"What's that?"

She paused before answering. "It's of Ben and Carter sitting out by that big old oak tree in our backyard in Wisconsin. They have a box or something in their hands. Ben keeps talking about an election, and then Carter points to the book and calls out, 'That's it! That's the key!' And then Carter's image disappears, and Ben is alone."

A chill snaked its way down my spine. "And you think that when he disappears, he dies?"

"I don't know. Maybe."

"It wasn't an election they were talking about, but a secret society call The Electi. Could you see what the box looked like?"

"No. But it looked old."

Static on the line interrupted us, and I couldn't understand the next few words from my mother.

"What was that Mom?"

More static.

"Mom, you're breaking up. I can't understand you."

Her voice came and went, and I could only get snippets of words until her last words came out loud and clear. "No one's elected. They're chosen." And the line went dead.

÷

I shared my mother's phone call with April as we made breakfast for the guests. As we cleaned up afterwards, Detective Abrams strode in, his handsome features set into a grim mask.

"The autopsy is back," he stated flatly.

"Good morning to you, too," I said.

"Sorry. Good morning. Is there somewhere we can talk?"

April rolled her eyes, put a last dish in the dishwasher, and wiped her hands on a towel. "You know she's going to tell me anyway."

"We manage the Inn together," I said. "April has a right to hear whatever I hear."

He shrugged those muscular shoulders and gestured to the kitchen table. The three of us sat, Lake Washington glistening in the background. Curt and his mother were in Adirondack chairs on the deck under a bright, blue sky. She was reading something on her Kindle, while it looked like her son was playing video games on a tablet. In the background, the white sails of several sail boats billowed on the lake.

"What did you learn?" I asked, tearing my eyes away from the vista outside.

"The autopsy confirmed that Carter died from arsenic poisoning. A large dose consumed probably the night before he died. He would have had symptoms in the middle of the night. Diarrhea. Excessive sweating. Muscle cramping. He may have thought he just had the flu at that point. But by morning, he would have been vomiting. By noon, he would have known he was going to die. We found a box of See's candy next to a chair in his living room. It was open and half gone. The ME said there was a large amount of chocolate and caramel in his system, and that it was probably the candy that held the poison. We're having it tested now."

My body had gone still, as though I was an inert form of clay stuck on a shelf. I wasn't even sure I was breathing. Then I felt a hand on my wrist.

"You okay?" April whispered.

"Who would do that to him?" I asked quietly. "He was the kindest, most generous man."

Her fingers squeezed my wrist.

"Do you know where he got the box of chocolate?" April asked the young cop.

"We only know that someone delivered the box to him," he replied. "A neighbor saw a kid in a small pickup stop at the curb and deliver a bag of something the afternoon before Carter died. We found the See's bag folded up on the dining room table. We'll be fingerprinting the bag and the box. And we're trying to run down the truck."

"Carter had a weakness for See's chocolates," I said. "I once saw him eat two-thirds of a box in one afternoon. He purposely didn't buy them for himself because he knew he couldn't resist them. But I gave him a box every Christmas." I looked up at the man sitting before me. "Someone knew that Detective. Someone knew that he wouldn't eat just one. That he would consume a large amount all at once."

Detective Abrams looked at me with solemn eyes. "I presume your brother would know that."

My eyes lit up. "No way! My brother did not kill Carter. They were best friends. Don't you dare accuse him of that!"

"I'm just saying," he replied. "If what you say is true, we'll have to look elsewhere for someone who might have known that detail. Can you think of other people who would have been aware of that?"

"Probably any of his closest friends or colleagues. I mean, think of it. There were probably office parties in his department at the university multiple times a year. Someone was bound to bring chocolates to some of those."

"Did you find anything else of value in his home or office?" April asked. "Anything that would point to a reason to kill him?"

"No. But then the killers and your brother all had access to his house before we did. I have to assume that if there was anything important there, one of them would have found it."

"My brother didn't mention anything," I said.

"Where is he, by the way?" he asked.

"He's staying at the Sheraton in Seattle. He felt it would be safer for me if he stayed somewhere else."

Detective Abrams nodded. "Good idea. All right," he said, standing up. "Let him know that we'd like to talk to him again. See what else we can learn about his research. Ask him to call me. We're talking to all the neighbors and many of Carter's fellow professors and students. I'll let you know if we find anything out." He leaned forward a few inches. "I know you won't stay out of this. But be careful. Not just for your own safety. But if you interfere, I will arrest you. And don't forget, there are many people worried about you, including your daughter."

I winced at that, wondering if that included David.

April and I sat quietly for a moment after he left. As much as we'd been through with previous investigations, it was still hard to believe that someone would have been so devious as to hand deliver a death sentence to Carter in a box of See's Candy. It made me sad. Sad to think that something he loved so much, something that he would have found so innocent and delicious, would lead to his death.

"I wonder why he didn't just go to the emergency room," April said. "Why would he risk his life coming here to tell you someone had killed him? He could have called you from the ER to tell you that."

She had a point.

"I don't know. Especially because it's about a thirty-minute drive from his house to here. That was time he couldn't afford."

My cell phone rang. It was Doe telling me would meet Trina Bateman at the Roanoke Inn at noon for lunch.

÷

The Roanoke Inn was the oldest business on Mercer Island. Built in the early 1900s, it sat close to one of the ferry landings, making it a favorite place for weekend getaways back then. There were even rumors of bootleg liquor and dancing girls there at one time. But today, it was just a great place to have a quiet drink or meal with friends.

I met Doe inside the dark interior, and my nose perked up at the tantalizing smell of butter and garlic. We snagged a booth near the door to the outdoor patio and ordered iced teas. As we waited for Trina Bateman, I filled Doe in on what we'd just learned.

"I'm so sorry, Julia," she said. "Sorry for Carter. That had to be a horrible way to go."

"I can't stop thinking about it," I said. "It makes me want to find his killer even more now."

Our beverages arrived, and we each added sweeteners. I was stirring my tea, as I said, "So I have to pretend that I'm interested in joining this PEO group."

95

"Or just seem interested in learning more about it. I was hoping she'd invite us to her home. I figured we might have to be there to find out if her husband is a member of this exclusive club. So I don't know how successful this will be today."

"We'll find a way. Don't worry."

Just then, a tall, slender woman walked in. She had rich gray hair and was wearing a spaghetti strap sundress. She glanced around, removed her large sunglasses, and squinted in the low light. When she saw Doe, she glided over to our booth. Doe got up and gave her a hug.

"So good to see you, Treen," she said.

Treen? That was a nickname?

The woman hugged her back, a Louis Vuitton bag tucked in the crook of her arm.

"You too, Doe. It's been too long."

Doe glanced down at me. "This is Julia Applegate. I thought it was time the two of you met."

I slid out of the seat, but Treen stopped me.

"No need to get up, Julia." She extended a tanned and manicured hand, dressed in a large emerald ring. "It's good to meet you. I've heard a lot about you."

"I hope that's a good thing," I said with a pleasant smile.

"Well, besides being the wife of the governor, you have quite a reputation on the island."

"Ex-wife," I corrected her.

"Of course," she said.

"Please, sit down," Doe said.

Treen slid in next to me, her Shalimar perfume clogging my nostrils. We took some time to peruse the menu and order lunch. I considered going right to the lava cake but settled on a Cobb salad instead. When our orders arrived, Treen turned to me.

"Doe says you might be interested in joining PEO."

I had just taken a drink of tea and almost burped out my response. "Uh… yes. Doe thinks so highly of it."

"Yes, we miss her," she said, giving Doe a wink. "We have a small chapter right here on the island. Of course, there are larger chapters in Seattle and some of the bigger cities around here. But we like to think our little group is richer in friendships and community work."

"What kind of community work do you do?"

"Mostly scholarships for young women. But we also serve as mentors for girls at both the UW and Seattle Pacific University. It's very satisfying."

"How often do you meet?"

"The group meets monthly, usually at someone's home. We sometimes invite speakers in or have members talk about trips they've taken or other work they're doing in the community." She turned to Doe. "In fact, Betty Pearling's daughter just adopted a little girl from China and gave a fascinating talk about their trip to the Hunan Province."

"My, oh, my," Doe began. "Betty Pearling is a proud grandma. I'm happy for her. Who are some of the newer members since I dropped out?"

Trina lifted her chin, thinking. "Oh, let me see. Do you know Candy Dische?"

I choked on my next sip of iced tea. "Her name's Candy Dish?"

Treen chuckled. "Yes. She gets kidded about it a lot. But she spells her last name D.I.S.C.H.E." She went back to thinking. "Anyway, she joined about a year ago. Same time as Lori Greene. Oh, and Henrietta Bentley just moved here and joined."

Doe almost choked. "Wait. I thought she said she'd never set foot on this island again."

"Maybe it's a type of revenge," Treen said. "Move to the place that ended your relationship."

"What does that mean?" I asked.

Treen turned to me. "Henrietta shared a house in Everett for several years with Trudy Clements, Walter Clements' daughter. They were an item," she said with a lift of her perfectly penciled eyebrows. "Not that I have anything against that sort of thing. Love who you want, I say. But Trudy was also involved with someone else at the same time. Some guy who races powerboats. She would sneak down to see him, and Henrietta found out by accident. Right here," she said, looking around the room. "She walked in on the two of them making out in a booth. Created quite the scene, or so I understand. That crack in the mirror is a result of her surprise."

She pointed to an elaborate framed mirror on the other side of the room that had a large crack down the middle. I wasn't sure how I was supposed to react to all of this. But my alarm bells were ringing so loud, it surprised me no one else could hear them. One of my mother's favorite sayings was, "There are no coincidences." I snuck a glance at Doe, and we shared a moment of understanding.

The waitress arrived with our lunch orders, and we spent the next several minutes focused on food.

After Treen had delicately taken two or three bites of her Asian chicken salad, she said, "I have an idea. We have a meeting of the Membership Committee on Monday afternoon at my house. Doe, everyone would love to see you. Why don't you and Julia come? We could all catch up, and Julia could get a sense of what we do."

I don't believe in luck any more than I believe in coincidences. That this woman, who was married to a man we suspected might be involved with Carter's death, had just told us her PEO club included the daughter of Walter Clements made my big-deal-o-meter go off like a train whistle. I mean, I should have been laughing, as if someone was pranking me.

"I'd love to," I said with a sweet and disingenuous smile. "Doe, how 'bout you?"

CHAPTER FIFTEEN

Detective Abrams called Friday morning. "We're releasing Carter's body to his daughter," he said. "We found her in Detroit, just like you said. She'll be flying into Seattle early next week."

"I'm glad."

"We're also releasing Carter's house and office at the university since forensics has been over each of them twice. I believe his daughter will stay at his home."

"Have you found anything helpful?" I asked him.

There was a long pause on the other end of the line. "I'm not obligated to tell you anything," he said. "But I always believe that when a family member dies, the family has a right to know what's going on. I realize you weren't technically family, but from what you and Angela have said, you were close enough. Anyway, we think we know who the kid was who delivered the bag containing the chocolate, but we haven't found him yet. He goes to the U and works for Subway. Unfortunately, he hasn't shown up to work or class the last couple of days."

"Oh, no," I murmured. "I hope he's okay. These people seem ruthless."

"Let's not speculate. He's a kid. He could be with a girlfriend. We'll be asking around."

"What about the candy?"

"We've canvassed all the See's Candies shops in the area, trying to identify who may have bought the chocolate. The store in Kent holds the most promise. A saleswoman remembered a bald man with long sideburns and a British accent when we described him. He bought a pound of dark chocolates the morning Carter died. He paid cash, so we can't get a lead on him that way. And they don't have surveillance cameras in the store. But there is surveillance in the parking lot. We're reviewing that footage now. Unfortunately, we have limited manpower. We had to borrow a detective from Seattle who is working with the airlines to see if we can identify this same guy coming into Seattle from London. That's a long shot, but you never know. We could get lucky."

"What about the boat carrying the two guys who came to the Inn?"

"We're still asking around about that. There are a lot of boats on the lake. We checked with Tobias Boats. That seemed logical. But they said they would never use their initials on a vessel without their full logo."

"That's what I thought," I said, feeling more than a little smug about my prowess. "No other leads on what the T.B. stands for?"

"Just one. There's a company on the lake called Two Brothers. It's a minor operation that rents fishing boats. I have someone going out there right now to check it out."

My heart sank at that news. That could be it. The two men could have just rented the boat. Not that I really cared about being right. I mean, it didn't matter if the bar in Shoreline was behind the break-in at the Inn.

"Anyway," Detective Abrams said. "I'll let you know if we find anything else. I told the daughter—her name is Renée Abernathy—that she could call you. She might want to know more about her father's last moments."

"Of course, I'll talk with her. Thank you."

"Okay. I'll get back to you soon."

We hung up, and I sat back with a sigh. I hadn't asked about David. I figured if he'd wanted to talk to me, he would have been the one to call. But I couldn't stop the profound feeling of sadness that flowed over me.

Dogs are like little barometers that sense your emotions. Mickey jumped up next to me in my recliner and licked my hand.

"It's okay, little boy," I said. "If it's meant to be, it's meant to be. If not, well…"

I had been about to go to the kitchen to help April with breakfast when the detective called, so I wiped my eyes and hefted myself out of the chair. My heart was heavy. Not only because of Carter's death, but the apparent death of my relationship with David. But I kept busy all day and focused on the jobs at hand.

Curt snagged me as I entered the breakfast-room.

"Mrs. Applegate, I have something to tell you."

His green eyes nearly danced with excitement, and I cringed, hoping he hadn't been sleuthing or spying on the guests.

"I found this down by the dock," he said, opening the palm of his hand. In it was a cigarette butt. "I think someone dropped it there recently. It hasn't rained since the break-in, and the paper is still white. And no one staying here smokes. I checked."

He had piqued my interest. "Where did you find it?"

"I heard that Mr. Muse had seen a boat come up to the dock that night. I asked him how far up the dock it tied off. He showed me, and sure enough, it was lying in the dirt at the end of the dock, just in front of where the boat had been. As soon as we found it, Mr. Muse remembered he saw a glow in the boat, as if someone had lit a cigarette. I think whoever stayed behind smoked it while the second guy broke into your apartment."

"Or, it could have been the one who got out. He could have tossed it before coming inside," I said.

I whipped out my phone and dialed David. I stopped. I couldn't call him. Or could I? Maybe if I reported this dispassionately to David, as I should do with any evidence we found, he might see that I was playing by the rules. On the other hand, if I reported it to Detective Abrams because he was in charge, David might feel slighted. I dialed Detective Abrams.

"We may have a piece of evidence for you," I told him.

I explained about the cigarette butt. Detective Abrams asked us to put it into a paper bag, and he would send an officer out immediately. He also asked that Curt show the officer exactly where he'd found it and to ask Curt's mother if they could get a DNA sample from her son just to exclude him.

Once again, I made Curt's day when I told him. Together, we went into the kitchen and found a lunch bag, and he carefully dropped the cigarette butt inside.

"Okay, I'll hold on to it. But can you wait in the breakfast room for the officer? They want you to show them where you found it. I need to help get breakfast ready."

"Sure," he said.

"And Curt, they want your mother's permission to get a DNA sample from you since you've touched the cigarette butt—just to eliminate you."

"Okay, I'll let her know," he said with enthusiasm. "I want to help."

I put my hand on his shoulder. "You've been a big help. Even if this doesn't turn out to be evidence. You did just what I asked you to do—you kept your eyes open."

The grin that spread across his face made my heart swell. This was a kid who just needed some positive attention. I hoped Chloe was nearby, taking notice.

After he left, April said, "You're really good with him, you know?"

She was frying bacon and eyed me over her shoulder.

"He's really not such a bad kid."

"Well, maybe with this his mom will pay a little more attention to him," she said.

"We can only hope." As I got clean plates out for breakfast, I filled her in on what Detective Abrams had said on the call.

"It sounds like the police are being thorough." She eyed me. "How are you doing? I mean, without David?"

A sigh escaped my throat. "I'm sad. I thought our relationship had real promise. But I get it. It's his job, and I keep getting in the way."

She smiled. "You're so mature."

"I just wish he'd see it from my point of view. Carter was family to me. And he died right in front of me. I can't just let that go."

"Well, you could," she said. "You just won't."

I opened my mouth to protest, but she put up a hand. "Don't worry. I'm on your side. I'm just not sure there's going to be a simple answer here."

"I know. Listen, I need to call Ben and fill him in. I'll go outside but be back in a minute to finish setting up the table."

She smiled. "No problem."

I called Ben and told him everything Detective Abrams had reported and what Curt may have found.

"I'm glad Renée is coming into town," he said. "Carter never elaborated on what came between them, but he always seemed deeply sad about it. And now that the police have released his office, I want to go out there. We still might find something. Any chance you'd like to come along?"

His request surprised me. After my falling out with David, I was questioning my involvement in these investigations. But this was my brother. And Carter was his best friend.

"You mean you want your little sister to accompany you?" I asked.

"Yeah. You're fully invested in this. And two Brouwer minds have always been better than one."

My lips spread into a smile. I hadn't thought of myself as a Brouwer since before I got married, other than to consider briefly going back to my maiden name after the divorce. But I saw myself as an Applegate now, unless, of course, I married David.

"Mom would love to hear you say that," I said, pushing thoughts of David into the background. "Yes, of course I want to come. Let me help April get breakfast out, and then I'm free. I could meet you there."

"Let's meet at 10:00. I know the head of the department and can probably get the key to his office. See you then."

÷

As a public research university, the University of Washington has a world-class medical center right on campus. It's also noted for its many collaborations with some of the region's tech giants, including Amazon, Nintendo, Microsoft, and Boeing. The "U-Dub," as it's known locally, also boasts many Nobel Prize laureates and Fulbright Scholars, of which Carter was one.

The campus is on the shores of Union and Portage Bays, with views of the mountains on both sides. Most of the buildings are imposing red brick structures, but during the spring Yoschino cherry trees soften the campus when they are in full bloom. Carter had taught at the university for almost thirty years and had one of the better-situated offices with a view of Portage Bay. Ben had gotten the key from the department chair, and I met him at the door.

"You okay with this?" I asked him. "His office is going to remind you of him. Maybe even more than his house."

"I know," he said. "But I know of a couple of potential places he might have used to hide the key."

I grabbed his forearm. "And you didn't tell the police about those? Ben, do you want to get arrested again?"

"Look, this is all speculation. I have no idea where he kept the key. But remember, we grew up together. I knew him like a brother, and once I'm in there, I might recognize places where he would think to hide something. That's all. If we find anything of use, I promise we'll turn it over to the police."

I didn't believe him. Well, not about turning the key over to the police if we found it. My brother wanted more than anything else to find the key and the box, and then to open it. I felt certain he would risk his life and/or going to prison to do that.

Carter's office was about the size of a kid's bedroom. It smelled like old books, dust, and the faint, woody odor of whiskey. Framed maps, prints, photographs, and awards covered the walls, along with a few antique masks he'd picked up on his travels. Stacks of books and folders stuffed and overflowing with papers filled the corners of the bookcase and layered the tops of the filing cabinet and his desk.

"He wasn't any better at housekeeping here than he was at home," I said, glancing around.

Ben didn't respond, prompting me to glance his way. His expression was distant as he surveyed the room.

"I can't believe he's gone," he murmured. "He was such a giant of an intellect and so full of personality."

"I know. I miss him, too."

He shook his head, as if to get back in the moment. "Well, this could be a treasure trove of information to the right person. After all, he dabbled in lots of research. That entire shelf," he said, pointing to a bookcase against the wall, "holds books he wrote himself or co-authored. Also, he was helping me with the Lusk Letter. If I could find his notes, there may be something in there we could use."

"By the way, you said when you went to the Sheraton that you had a couple of things to follow up on. Did you find anything?"

He was moving toward the old cast iron heater against the wall. "No. The police took his laptop, but I took several of his research folders back to the hotel to go through them. There was no reference to the key or the Lusk Letter." Ben stuck his hand behind the heater, felt around, and pulled it out again. "Listen, why don't you flip through the pages of some of his books? He might have hidden something in there."

I dropped my purse on a large wooden armchair and moved to the bookcase. While I thumbed through book after book, Ben lowered the blinds on the only window in the room and checked each slat. Then he crawled under Carter's desk to look underneath, pulled out the drawers and flipped them over, and finally began pulling all the framed prints and masks off the walls.

After almost an hour of searching, we came up empty.

I flopped into the armchair, pulling my purse into my lap. "Sorry, Ben. This trip may have been a bust."

While Ben continued to rummage through Carter's file drawers, my eyes roamed across some mementos on Carter's bookshelf.

"Look at that shelf of toys," I said, gesturing to a collection of antique cars, small tin airplanes, and a few wind-up toys. There was even a small teddy bear sitting in the corner of one shelf. "Are they from his childhood?"

Ben looked up. "Some. But many he collected over the years. Others were given to him. I gave him that little Teddy Bear back in high school. Remember, we were the Bears! And that one," Ben said, his voice catching as he pointed to an elaborate antique carriage drawn by two small, white horses, "is a replica of the hearse that carried Abraham Lincoln to his final resting place in Oak Ridge Cemetery in Springfield, Illinois."

I peered at the lacquered black hearse, gilded around the edges, with gold and silver adornments and topped with eight plumes of black ostrich feathers.

"It looks almost real," I said.

"He received it in return for a talk he gave at the annual meeting of the Abraham Lincoln Association."

"Sad," I said. "I wonder if Renée will want to keep any of those kinds of things."

Ben closed the file drawer and slumped into Carter's office chair. "There's nothing here. I thought maybe he'd leave me some sort of message."

My ears perked up. "Wait, a minute. A message." My mind rewound to the day Carter died and his garbled last sentence. "He did, Ben. Just before he died. Remember?" I turned my head toward the shelf of toys and zeroed in on Abraham Lincoln's hearse. Jumping out of the chair, I hurried to the bookcase and picked up the carriage, knocking the horses over. Holding it up to my eyes, I peered through the back windows. "Ben, look!"

"What is it?" he said, rushing over.

I gave Ben a triumphant grin. "Don't you remember what Carter said just before he died?"

"Yeah. You thought it was something about finding a casket."

I turned the hearse so that Ben could look in through the back windows of the small figurine.

"Holy shit," he exclaimed.

He took it from me and set it on the desk and then carefully opened the back doors of the hearse. Inside was a small replica of the ornate casket that had carried the sixteenth president. The black leather casket had four silver handles, with tiny silver tacks adorning the sides in a sweeping, curved line. Ben took it out and set it down reverently, staring at it for a moment.

"Did you know that a gang of counterfeiters were going to steal Lincoln's coffin and hold it for ransom when the police arrested their top engraver and threw him in prison?" he asked. "The gang was going to ask for $200,000 in gold and the release of their engraver. Fortunately, the police foiled their plot. Carter told me that story once."

Ben got lost, staring at the small casket.

"Do you actually think that's what he wanted you to find?" I asked, nodding toward the casket.

"I wouldn't put it past him. Only one way to find out."

My skin tingled at the prospect we could be close to finding the key.

Ben used his thumb to lift the lid on the small black casket. Inside, the makers had lined it with white satin, but instead of a tiny replica of the dead president, it held a folded piece of paper. He pulled that out and put the casket on the desk next to the hearse. When he unfolded the paper, he read:

Ben, my magician friend. I know you'll find this. You were always good at hiding things and following clues. I think we're both in trouble now, so I'm taking the key to Julia. Have heart, my friend. If you've found my notes, you'll know that you are very close to the truth. Carter.

CHAPTER SIXTEEN

Ben was good at his word and turned the note over to Detective Abrams. He told me later, however, that he had not found Carter's notes. That was one mystery still to be solved. Plus, if Carter said he was giving the key to me—where was it?

"I have to assume that whoever broke into his house found the notes first," he said. "They could be lost forever."

We were back at the Inn, and most of the guests were out for the afternoon. Ben and I were sitting in the main kitchen, having an afternoon glass of wine to celebrate our finding the message from Carter. April had joined us.

"Wouldn't all of his research be on his computer?" she asked.

Ben shook his head. "Not for something this sensitive. Anyway, the police took both his laptop and his office computer. I'm sure they've gone through them by now."

"From the note, it sounds like he found something important, though," I said. "Didn't he mention it to you?"

"He and I met at the St. Regis Hotel in Toronto in March. I was trying to track down that Canadian lead on the letter I mentioned. That's when I told him about The Electi. He wanted to help, so we decided he would investigate their presence here in the States. To be honest, I've only talked to him twice since then. But I think he would have told me if he found something definitive."

"Was he researching Walter Clements?" I asked.

"Probably."

"Maybe that's why they thought he had to die," April speculated. "He was getting too close to the truth."

"I wish I knew. He sent me a weird text a couple of weeks ago, though. He said, 'The key to all of this isn't the key, although you won't find anything without it.'"

"What the heck did that mean?" I asked. "The key leads to something even more important?"

Ben threw up his hands. "I don't know. It was right at that time I noticed I was being followed, and my attention got diverted."

"I wonder if that's what Carter meant when he said in the note that he thought both of you were in trouble now. Maybe he was being followed, too."

"You know, that's a good point, Julia," Ben said. "Before I got that weird message about the key, I talked to him briefly on the phone. But he cut me off and said he had to go. When I texted him about it later, he only said that he thought he saw someone outside his window. I thought nothing of it at the time. I wasn't being followed yet." Ben shook his head. "Why didn't I check back with him on that? He was in real danger, and I didn't even know it."

"You can't blame yourself," April said. "You both knew you were dabbling in some pretty risky stuff."

Voices from the breakfast room brought us to attention. I got up just as the kitchen door swung open and Goldie and Aria Stottlemeyer waltzed in.

Aria was tall and bone-thin, with sharp edges everywhere, including her personality. She was someone who enjoyed making other people uncomfortable. She not only liked to comment in public on the few extra pounds I carried but had once interjected the need for the mayor to trim his nose hairs at a City Council meeting. *How does someone do that?*

Aria held the position of postmistress on the island and was very smart and a member of the National Genealogical Society. That's why I'd reached out to her to see if she could track down Tom Bateman's ancestry.

I introduced both women to Ben, who knew very few of my neighbors.

"I'm sorry about your uncle," Aria said to me. "It's all over the island how he was poisoned and dropped dead at your feet, Julia."

And… there was one of those sharp edges.

"Um, thanks, Aria. Can I get you guys a glass of wine?" I reached for the bottle.

"No," Goldie said, waving me away. "We're gonna have dinner at Panera's and then go to bingo. We just wanted to stop by so Aria here could tell ya what she's learned."

"Let's go into the breakfast room where we can be more comfortable," I said.

They followed me through the door to a table against the wall. Curt and his mother were on the deck again. Curt was standing next to the weathervane. There was a brisk afternoon breeze coming off the lake, turning it, delighting Curt to the point he was laughing.

Ahab was bouncing happily around his cage, watching two birds at the closest bird feeder. Once we invaded his space, however, he stopped and said, "Hello. Hello. I see dead people. I see dead people."

Goldie laughed. "That's a good one." She turned to me. "Is he talkin' about Elizabeth?"

I opened my mouth to respond, but Aria cut me off.

"Goldie! There are no such things as ghosts. How many times do I have to tell you that?" she said, pulling out a chair to sit down. "Julia just made that up as a marketing ploy, didn't you, Julia?"

She began to lower herself into the chair when it flew out from under her, making her land unceremoniously on the floor. There were gasps all around as I rushed in to help her up.

"I'm sorry, Aria. Are you okay?"

I retrieved her chair, but the scent of rosewater put me on alert. Elizabeth didn't have a sense of humor, but this type of behavior belonged more to her daughter, Chloe.

"I see dead people!" Ahab squawked again.

"Humph!" Aria grunted.

I placed the chair beside Aria, and she clenched her Groucho Marx eyebrows together as Goldie giggled in the background.

"Was that you, Julia?" Aria asked angrily.

I put my hands up as if I were surrendering to the FBI. "No way. I was a good three feet away from you."

I stepped back and sat at the end of the table. She eyed every corner of the room. I suppose she imagined I had hired someone to play a trick on her. Satisfied no one was there, she puffed up her skinny chest and sat down.

Once we were all seated, April said with a suppressed smile, "Goldie said you were here to report on what you found."

"Right," Aria said in a clipped voice. "Okay, here's what I know. First, I'm sorry I didn't have time to research some of the other names you gave me, but you indicated Bateman was the priority. Anyway, you probably already know that Alistair Bateman was the Earl of Manchester and served as Lord Chamberlain to Alexandra, Princess of Wales, in 1893."

"That's as far as I got in my research," Ben said.

"Yes, that much is well-recorded," she said with her pointed nose in the air.

I suppose she thought she was a better researcher than Ben. Truth be told, he could have found it just as easily had he had the time and not overwhelmed with Carter's murder.

"Anyway," Aria continued. "I won't bore you with the years, because it doesn't matter," she said. "I'll just give you the rundown of who's who. Alistair Bateman did, in fact, attend University of London. He married Imogene Rollinberry, and they had two children: Ruth and Robert. In 1911, Robert, who would have succeeded his father as Earl, suffered a terrible scandal at 18. He also attended the University of London and was in some sort of fraternity or men's club that challenged him to drug a young woman and have sex with her. Turns out she was only fifteen."

"Oh, dear," April said.

Ben and I exchanged glances. *It sounded as if Robert Bateman could have also been an early member of The Electi.*

"Young Robert would have been thrown in jail," Aria said, "except that the young woman in question had a reputation of sorts. Rather than drag her name through the courts, her parents dropped the charges. However, the scandal stuck."

"And he escaped to America," Ben surmised.

"In 1912, his parents sent him to live with a relative in Boston where he finished his schooling at Harvard. He married Wendy Stuart, and they had a daughter, Rosemary. Rosemary Bateman married John Ellison and had a child, Vincent. When she divorced Ellison, she took back her maiden name of Bateman and raised Vincent as a Bateman. He grew up and married Eleanor Doone. They had three boys—Gregory, Timothy, and..."

"Thomas," I said, finishing her sentence.

"Yes," Aria said, giving me the evil eye for having interrupted her. "Thomas was the youngest. He was born in 1958. His brother Greg went to MIT. Tim Bateman went to Northeastern University, and..."

"Tom Bateman went to Harvard," Ben said.

Aria huffed out a breath. "Shall I tell this story, or shall you?"

"Sorry," Ben said. "Please, go ahead."

She settled back in the chair and continued. "Anyway, you are correct. Tom Bateman got a graduate degree in business from Harvard. He came to Seattle and started a shipping company and married a divorcee, Katrina Franklin."

"And now's she's Trina Bateman," April said.

"Yes."

"So he *is* a direct descendent of Alistair Bateman," I said.

"Right again," she said. "Through his mother."

There was a moment of silence around the table until Goldie said, "Hope that helps, Julia."

"I bet you didn't know that Aria is related to the duke of something-or-other," Goldie blurted.

"It's the Duke of Norfolk," Aria said with a slight twitch to her upper lip.

"Really?" I murmured, glancing toward Aria.

That explained her imperious attitude.

She stood up. "We've got to get going."

We all stood. Ben reached out a hand to Aria.

"Thank you, Aria," he said. "You did a fine job, and you've been a big help."

She inhaled through her nose and gave him a broad smile. Ben had clearly filled her with pride.

"I'm glad to help. Let me know if I can do anything else." She turned to me. "And if you're going to solve your uncle's murder, remember what's in the back of my camper."

After the two women had left, Ben asked, "What the heck is in the back of her camper?"

"You don't want to know," I replied. "Genealogy isn't her only hobby. She's a member of something called the Spy Academy, and they conduct weekend spy games."

His eyebrows creased. "You mean like the people who reenact the Revolutionary War?"

I shrugged. "I suppose."

"Now that we know Tom Bateman is a descendent of Alistair Bateman, what next?" April asked.

"Well," I began, "at least we don't have to hunt for that information at his home on Monday. I guess the main thing we need to find out now is if he's a current member of The Electi."

CHAPTER SEVENTEEN

It was the night of the Republican fundraiser and just after seven o'clock when Blair, April, and I entered the Grand Hyatt Hotel on the corner of 7th and Pine in downtown Seattle. The lobby was unremarkable, as expensive hotel lobbies go. A stream of people headed toward the ballroom, where the event would be held. As we moved with the crowd, I felt my face grow warm as we passed the restaurant, remembering a minor incident I had suffered almost a decade earlier.

Graham and I had been there for dinner in October, and I carried an umbrella. As I swept past a table of four, the tip of my umbrella hooked the strap of a woman's purse hanging over the back of her chair. Without knowing it, I walked off with her red leather Gucci bag swinging from my umbrella. Her husband, a small man wearing an ill-fitting toupee, jumped up with a loud cry and brought the entire room's attention around as he chased after me.

Graham is no slouch when it comes to being physical if the situation calls for it. He once clocked a guy who dared to suggest that I be prohibited from going out in public just because I tripped on a carpet at a cocktail party and threw a couple of stuffed mushrooms in his face. The incident at the Hyatt, however, was different. Graham had just announced his candidacy for the state senate and couldn't afford a public fistfight. So, as the man with the toupee reached for my umbrella, Graham pulled me behind him, resulting in a tense standoff between them. Finally, a nice lady at a nearby table tapped me on the shoulder and pointed to the purse I'd taken hostage by mistake. Story of my life.

This time, I passed the restaurant without incident. Since this was a political fundraiser and not a black-tie affair, April and I had dressed up, but weren't fancy. Not so with Blair, who wore a short, low-cut, black sequined dress, with four-inch patent leather heels and dangly crystal earrings that caught the light perfectly. She had pulled her hair back into a chignon which accentuated her long, graceful neck. Blair knew how to stand out in a crowd, and the lingering stares she got from both men and women as we entered the ballroom proved it.

I missed not having David with me. Watching couples chat up other couples with glasses of champagne balanced in their hands brought a lump to my throat. I had purposely focused on finding Carter's killer over the last forty-eight hours rather than thinking about David. But with each passing hour he didn't call, my hopes of a quick reconciliation were fading.

"There's Graham," Blair said.

Blair was naturally taller by about three inches, and with four-inch heels, it was easy for her to find Graham in the crowd. We weaved our way through the packed room to where Graham was leaning forward, talking with a heavy-set woman in a black pantsuit.

"Oh, man," April said with a sigh. "That's Marjorie Warner. I sure hope she's not at our table."

Marjorie Warner was the State Republican Committee Chair and well known in baking circles as the owner of a popular bakery in Seattle that had expanded to four other locations throughout the state. She also had a reputation for her churlish personality and getting into arguments with judges at baking competitions, complaining about competitors' ingredients. Her complaints usually accused someone of some sort of deception.

She and April had squared off one year at the state fair. And while April won a blue ribbon for her double chocolate mint brownies, Marjorie took the cookie competition with her pumpkin crisps. April was certain, however, that Marjorie had won by sabotaging her pecan sandies. Only minutes before the judging took place, April swears she saw Marjorie lean back against the table with a water bottle in her hand. Moments later, April found her pecan sandies flooded with water, turning the cookies to mush.

"Well, it wouldn't surprise me if she's seated at our table," I said. "After all, she is the committee chair, and Graham has to kiss up to her."

"Yeah, well, if she sits anywhere near me, don't be surprised if something spills all over that pedestrian looking pantsuit she's wearing."

I stifled a laugh because April wasn't usually snarky or vindictive.

Kitty was standing next to Graham and noticed us. As usual, she looked amazing in a tight, low-cut dark blue dress that not only brought out the color of her eyes but her best asset, her chest. She waved, leaving Graham alone with Marjorie Warner.

"Hey, Julia," Kitty crowed, coming through the crowd. "I was glad to hear you were coming tonight."

She pulled me into a feather-light hug, the scent of orange blossoms enveloping me in a scented fog.

"You smell divine," I said, stepping back, feeling a little lightheaded.

"Oh, yes. Jo Malone's Orange Blossom cologne," she said, her eyes alight with pride. She pulled me in close to whisper, "It's Kate Middleton's favorite."

There was a moment when we all smiled without saying a word, and then Blair stepped in.

"It's a delightful scent. But I prefer the perfume of American royalty," she said, eying Kitty. "I'm wearing Jackie O's favorite... Joy by Jean Patou."

Kitty's eyes nearly popped open. "Isn't that considered the most expensive perfume in the world?"

Blair merely proffered her hand and said, "Nice to meet you. I'm Blair Wentworth."

I didn't know if Blair was really wearing such an expensive perfume. I wouldn't put it past her, though. She liked to change up her perfumes, so I had stopped asking her long ago which one she had on. Given her task for the evening, however, it seemed in character for her to wear something that would get attention.

"Sorry, Blair," I said. "This is Kitty... um, Applegate." I always stumbled when I said Kitty's full name. It was just hard to acknowledge that she was not only married to my ex-husband, but that we shared the same last name. "Washington State's first lady," I finished.

Kitty had never met Blair and had only met April once. Kitty was petite, with bright blue eyes and a curvy yet trim figure. But she was several inches shorter than Blair, and of course a couple of decades younger. And yet, she seemed to wither as she took in Blair's appearance.

"Well, I'm glad you could all come. We're at table three, right in the center up front," she said, gesturing over her shoulder. "The program will begin shortly."

Kitty disappeared into the crowd, I suppose, feeling outgunned by Blair. Before we could head for the table, though, I felt a hand on my arm.

"Well, if it isn't the *former* Mrs. Applegate."

I turned to find probably the only person in the room besides Graham I actually liked. In fact, it was a woman I adored.

"Mae Beth Battenberg," I said, giving her a hug. "God, I haven't seen you in ages."

"It's been far too long," she said with a slight Kentucky accent. "But you look wonderful. What in the world are you doing here, though? This isn't your normal cup of tea."

"Uh, I'm here to support Graham."

"Of course," she said. "Who are these lovely ladies with you?"

Mae Beth had been out as a lesbian for over twenty years, and although she was now married, she was an unapologetic flirt. Her green eyes almost danced across Blair.

"Sorry. Let me introduce you. This is April Jackson, my business partner."

She grasped one of April's hands in both of hers. "Oh, of course, I've heard so much about you. Perhaps the best culinary baker in the Northwest."

With April's dark skin, it was usually hard to tell when she blushed. But her cheeks blossomed at Mae Beth's compliment.

"Um... thank you," April said.

"And this is Blair Wentworth," I said, turning to Blair.

Mae Beth's eyes flared. "Not married to Jacob Wentworth, who owns Wentworth Motors?"

"The same," Blair said, using her left hand to whisk an invisible hair out of her eyes while showing off the giant diamond on her ring finger.

Mae Beth smiled. "Oh, I know your husband well," she said, catching hold of Blair's hand and turning it so that she could study the ring. "I bought both my BMW and my current Porsche from him. This is just the sort of trophy I'd expect him to give his wife."

Blair just stared at Mae Beth a moment before pulling her hand back. *Had Blair met her match?*

Mae Beth was tall and athletic, with short, dark hair cut in a bob tucked behind her ears. Her vivid green eyes seemed to always search the room, perhaps for people she knew or for people she wanted to know. Although striking, she didn't have Blair's looks. She was a match for Blair's sense of confidence, however, and Blair knew it, making Blair uncharacteristically quiet.

I had met Mae Beth several years earlier when she was wooing Graham to join the Republican Party. Even though I didn't change parties along with Graham, Mae Beth and I became instant friends. She was one of the most successful corporate lawyers in the area, specializing in tax fraud, and had an office in the 929 Office Tower in Bellevue. She was smart and completely irreverent. Something I loved about her.

"But why are you here, flanked by two beautiful women?" she asked me. "I heard a rumor that you were stepping out with a very handsome police officer."

I inhaled before replying, "He's very busy with a murder investigation right now."

"Oh, my stars," she said, putting her hand on my forearm. "Of course. I read about that in the paper. A man died at the Inn. How silly of me. Was it someone you knew?"

I felt a tear forming and steeled myself for the answer. "Yes. He was an old and dear family friend."

"I'm sorry, Julia. I didn't mean to be so callous. You let me know if you need anything. Truly. Even if it's just a shoulder to cry on."

"Thanks, Mae Beth."

Her wife, Donna, a short, stocky woman with shoulder-length blonde hair, appeared behind her and touched her shoulder. Mae Beth turned and then quickly excused herself. A moment later, a short, bald man appeared at the podium and tapped the microphone. The room quieted.

"They will serve dinner momentarily. Please take your seats."

"I hope they have wine at the table," Blair said. "Because so far we're dry."

We moved in a single file through the crowd to our table. Small white place cards at each plate showed where we were to sit. Blair was seated in between Graham and Senator Clements.

Leave it to Graham.

Ten chairs circled the table. Unfortunately, April would have to sit on the other side of Clements, but next to Marjorie Warner. I was directly across from Blair, with Graham on my right and an empty seat to my left. April glanced across the table when she realized Marjorie was next to her and nodded at me as if to say, "Don't blame me if something happens."

As hostess, Kitty sat across the table from Graham, next to Mae Beth and Donna. The empty seat next to me remained open until the salads were removed and the main course plated. As I reached for my water glass, a tall, elegant woman, probably in her early fifties, swooped in and sat down next to me.

She had deep red hair piled on top of her head in loose curls and wore sharp black pants and a white lace tank top covered by a flowing embroidered silk caftan.

Once she settled into her seat, she leaned over and said, "Sorry I'm late. I'm Alex Janssen."

"No problem. I'm Julia Applegate."

"Oh!" she said with a smile. "Graham's ex. How lovely. It's nice to meet you."

Her open and welcoming smile disappeared the moment Walter Clements noticed her. His face twisted into a scowl as he glared across the table. She let out a dismissive "tsk" and grabbed her fork.

"Well, he doesn't look happy to see you," I whispered to her.

"That's probably because I'm *his* ex," she said with an evil chuckle. "And I just took him to the cleaners."

CHAPTER EIGHTEEN

Dinner was uneventful, unless you include the moment April clumsily knocked over her water glass, drenching Marjorie Warner's dessert plate so that she had to go without the raspberry chocolate cake everyone else inhaled. Or, that Kitty got a teensy-weensy bit tipsy so that when she laughed at someone's joke, she literally blew snot out of her nose. Glad it wasn't me.

Other than that, I mostly kept my eye on Blair and Walter Clements, trying desperately to catch what they were saying. Watching Blair flirt, though, was like watching Roger Federer play tennis. They were both in a class all their own—highly skilled, blindingly fast, and so good at what they did they made it look effortless. After all, like Federer, Blair had put in long hours of practice which paid off in spades; she had three ex-husbands, one current husband, and a big bank account to prove it. And like tennis, if winning point combinations is the key, Blair could win her shots from an offensive or a defensive position. She was that good.

Since I couldn't hear what they were saying, I could only watch the two of them laughing and giggling. At one point, Blair looked up and gave me a brief, conspiratorial smile. I glanced at April, who was close enough to overhear their conversation. She grabbed her wineglass with her thumb up. I got the message. Blair had succeeded. In what, I wasn't sure. But I could hardly wait to hear the blow-by-blow account on the way home.

The program began, and I braced myself for a bunch of boring political speeches, and I wasn't disappointed. Several people droned on and on about how the Republican party was changing, and people had to 'get on board' if they wanted to see their agenda implemented. As a Democrat, some of it grated on me, but I'm pretty good at staying neutral in social situations. After all, I run a business, and you never know who might need a place to stay. I couldn't miss the look Graham gave me a couple of times, though. He knew my position on many of the topics that night and might have worried that I would take exception. But for once I was comfortable keeping my mouth shut.

About forty-five minutes into the program, Clements left the table to introduce Graham. As Graham strode to the podium, a nervous flutter tickled my stomach. After all, it would be dishonest of me to say I wasn't still attracted to him. He had been the love of my life and was father to our adopted daughter. He was wicked smart, funny, charming, and shrewd. It made him a talented lawyer and an even better politician.

As suspected, after giving a brief state-of-the-state address, he announced his candidacy for a second term. There was a loud round of applause, and Alex poked me in the ribs.

"He still has it, doesn't he?"

"Yes," I said with a sigh. "Depending on who runs against him, he's probably a shoo-in."

She glanced at me. "You still in love with him?"

"No. But we're close, and I'm very fond of him," I said.

She sighed. "You guys are lucky to have such a good relationship. If you don't mind me asking, why did you separate?"

I laughed and flitted my eyes toward Kitty. "You're looking at her."

"Really? She's cute and all, but I would have thought he'd want someone sharp as a pencil next to him."

"Well, it's the old story. She's significantly younger than him, great looking, doesn't challenge him, and has the right cup size."

"She also has a brother who is the top Republican fundraiser in Arizona and a cousin who is the Republican Attorney General in Missouri. She comes from the right political stock," Alex said with a shrug.

"Interesting. I didn't know that." I sighed and shook my head. "I hate to think Graham is so transparently conniving, but I suppose if you're as ambitious as he is, you'd have to be."

"Why are you here tonight? Just to support him?" she asked.

"Um... yeah, of course. We're still close, like I said."

She shrugged and took a sip of wine. "I just wondered because I saw you watching your very blonde friend over there flirt openly with Walter. It doesn't matter to me. She can have him. But I was just wondering if that's why you guys came... so she could get her hooks into Walter."

"Oh, no. Blair is married. I mean, yes, she's a flirt, but..." I stopped, realizing I didn't know how to respond. Alex was watching me with a quietude that made me uncomfortable. "It's her thing," I finally said. "She flirts the way I eat chocolate."

That brought a smile to her face. "I see." She glanced over at Blair, who had her perfectly manicured hand on Clements' arm. "She's good. I'll hand her that."

"Why are you here?" I asked her. "I mean, clearly you two don't get along, and yet you're seated at the same table."

She smiled. "Good point." She nodded toward the podium, where Graham was still talking. "Graham asked me to chair his re-election campaign."

My eyes opened wide. "Really? Oh, well... that's fantastic. Is that what you do? I mean, are you normally a political operative?"

This time, she chuckled. "You make it sound like I work for the CIA. No. But I own a marketing and public relations firm. And, clearly after living with Walter for the past twelve years, I'm known in state Republican circles. Graham thinks I can be an asset. Plus, I think it's a way for Graham to get a dig in at Walter."

I liked this woman.

"Do you want to have lunch sometime? I bet we'd have a lot in common... ex-husbands and all."

"You're not going to try to bring me over to the dark side, are you?"

This time, I laughed. "You make the Democratic Party sound like some secret society or something."

As soon as the words left my mouth, my heart rate jumped. *Did I just say that?*

"You mean like Scientology," she said. "No. I don't think liberals are like that. But don't get me started on secret societies."

Now my heart *was* racing. "You say that like you have experience."

She sighed and leaned into me. "My sister belongs to Scientology. And has all but cut herself off from the rest of the family."

"Oh, I see." Bells were going off in my head. *Would she know if her ex-husband was a member of The Electi?* "Yeah, I've never understood the allure of belonging to a group like that. I didn't even join a sorority when I was in college."

"Neither did I. But Walter belongs to some group I've never heard of. He's very secretive about it." She laughed. "I guess that's why they call them secret societies."

If I was still breathing, I couldn't feel it. "Oh?" I kind of squeaked out. "He doesn't seem the type. I mean a joiner."

"Well, what is the type? He's as ambitious as Graham and surrounds himself with just the right people."

"And this club… does that for him?"

"I suppose. He goes to meetings once a month, always dressed the same and wearing some weird pin. It's called the Benevolent Society." She leaned in and bumped my shoulder. "I bet they even have some goofy secret handshake when they get there."

"Ha!" I laughed too loudly.

Calm down Julia. Don't seem too eager.

Alex didn't seem to notice. She was enjoying making fun of her ex-husband. The Benevolent Society, I thought to myself. With the initials B.S., I wondered if that was an inside joke to the members.

"Is that why you guys split up?" I asked as innocently as I could. "Because of the secret society?"

"Oh, God no! We split up because he's a selfish, narcissistic, power-hungry politician who paid to have his competition eliminated."

CHAPTER NINETEEN

The audience erupted in a standing ovation when Graham wrapped up his speech. Alex and I rose from the table with the others, but I felt the adrenaline flooding my bloodstream. *Had Alex just suggested that Walter Clements killed someone? Or had he just made a shrewd business decision?* Either could be true, and I had to be careful. Jumping to conclusions could spell disaster. After all, he was a sitting state senator.

Before I could ask a follow-up question, though, Alex left the table to find her way to Graham's side. Everyone else began picking up purses, getting ready to leave.

April glanced across the table and nodded toward Clements, who was writing something on the back of a business card. He handed it to Blair.

Bingo!

As people left the table, I grabbed Mae Beth's hand.

"Hey," I said. "Quick question." I flicked my gaze behind me to make sure Alex was out of hearing and Senator Clements was busy with Blair. "What's the scuttlebutt on why Alex and Walter got divorced? He was shooting poisonous darts at her all night."

Mae Beth pulled me a few steps away from the table and leaned in. "He's as ambitious as Graham. Everyone knows Graham's eye is on the White House. Walter wants to follow Graham into the Governor's mansion."

"So, what's the problem?"

"He's also one of the most arrogant SOBs on the planet. Good-looking, I'll hand you that. But he also thinks he's God's gift to everyone. And that puts him in competition with everyone around him."

"You mean he competes with Alex," I said.

"Yes. She's a powerhouse in her own right and really doesn't want to play second fiddle to anyone."

"And that's why she left him? She said something about him eliminating the competition."

Mae Beth smiled. "Oh, he didn't just try... he succeeded."

When my eyes grew wide, she placed a hand on my arm. "It's not what you think. Once he got into politics, he retired from his medical practice and bought into Apollo's Steakhouse. At the time, The

Prime was the most popular restaurant in Seattle and was just about to open another restaurant in Olympia. Walter hired their top chef away with a financial bonus that would make your head spin. And the chef brought the recipe for The Prime's secret steak sauce with him, tweaked it just enough to be legal, and then they did a big launch at Apollo's. It buried the Prime. Clements is a cutthroat businessman and politician," she said with a roll of her eyes. "People don't get in his way."

"I get it," I said. "Well, Alex impressed me."

"You know she's going to run Graham's campaign?"

"Yes, she told me. I think he's probably in excellent hands. Hey, listen, call me. It's been way too long."

"I agree," Mae Beth said.

The two of us separated, and I met up with Blair and April as we joined the horde of people heading for the exits. Blair nudged my shoulder.

"We'll talk in the car," she said. "I think tonight was highly successful."

"You have no idea," I said with a lift to my eyebrows.

÷

Blair could be a demon behind the wheel, especially if she was in her sports car. But tonight, she had borrowed her husband's Mercedes for the evening and seemed content to melt into the line of cars leaving the car park.

"So," April began, "spit it out, Blair."

April was in the back seat, and Blair looked up at her in the rearview mirror. "You heard most of it."

"Yes, but Julia didn't."

"Walter clearly gave you his phone number or something," I said.

"More than that," Blair replied. "He invited me to a barbecue he's having on Sunday and gave me his address."

"He knows you're married, right?" April asked.

"Yes. But I don't think he cares."

She yanked the steering wheel, swerving to cut someone off who was trying to slip in ahead of us.

"Did you talk at all about The Electi?" I asked, settling back into my seat.

"Not directly. No."

"What do you mean?"

"We talked about Ben."

I shot an alarmed look at her. "What? You didn't tell him anything, did you?"

"Of course not. But he seemed very interested in why you were at the dinner since you and Graham are divorced. I explained how close you and Graham are, especially because of Angela. He knows Angela by reputation and commented on how smart she is. That opened an entire conversation about your family, which included Ben."

"Did he know who Ben is?"

"No. Or at least he said he didn't. But since we were talking about how smart people are, it gave me the perfect opportunity to mention that Ben belongs to Mensa."

"And?"

Blair had to slam on the brakes as a man stepped in front of the car.

"Damn," she exclaimed. "Why don't people look where they're going?"

The man glared at us through the window and continued to the other side of the parking lot.

"He doesn't have a very high opinion of Mensa," Blair finally continued.

"If Walter belongs to The Electi, then he wouldn't," April said from the back seat.

"Exactly," Blair agreed.

"Could you tell if he was grilling you?" I asked. "Because if he was involved in Carter's death, I assume he'd know that someone broke into the Inn and tried to steal the key from Ben."

"Which means he *would* know who Ben is, and that Ben is here in Seattle," April interjected.

"Right," I agreed.

"It didn't seem like he was grilling me at all. He was totally into the flirtation, maybe because his ex-wife was sitting across from us. The conversation about Mensa came up naturally." Blair glanced over at me. "What did you want to report?"

"Well, if he doesn't belong to The Electi, he belongs to some other secret society."

"What do you mean?" April asked.

"Alex told me. Somehow we got off on Scientology, which, by the way, her sister is involved with. That prompted her to mention that Walter also belongs a secret group he called the Benevolent Society. She even joked that he goes out to meetings wearing the same clothes each time and a club pin. But apparently he's never shared with her what the group is or what it does."

"We need to ask Ben about that," Blair said. "He hasn't mentioned a pin, but maybe he knows if there is one."

"If Ben doesn't know, I wonder how we'll find out," I murmured.

"At the barbecue," Blair said with a flair. "You're going with me."

"What? Why?"

"He initially invited me and my husband. Although it was clear he didn't want Mr. Billings there. When I told him Jack would be out of town, he encouraged me to come alone. Then he rubbed his knee against mine under the table. I suggested bringing you for appearances' sake."

"Good idea," I said. "You *are* one smart cookie."

She smiled. "Yes, but if we're going to do some sleuthing while we're there, we'll have to come up with some sort of strategy."

"Like me finding a way into the house alone while you keep him occupied elsewhere."

"Yes."

I sat back with a smug smile. "Leave that up to me."

CHAPTER TWENTY

The next day, I sent a text to David, hoping for a response. All I said was, "*Miss you. Hope you're well.*" All I got back was, "*Miss you, too. Very busy.*"

"That's positive," April said when I told her. She had her hands submerged in sticky dough that would soon become her very popular cinnamon rolls. "At least he responded," she offered, trying to be encouraging.

"I suppose," I said with a sigh. "It would be nice if we could just get together and talk."

April's eyes lit up, and she nodded toward the front door. "Can you get that?"

"What? I didn't hear anything."

The bell at the front desk jingled.

I smiled. "I should've known." It was April's sixth sense again. "But I wonder who that is," I said, glancing at my watch. "It's so early."

I hurried out to the reception desk. It was only 6:30 in the morning, and my front desk help wasn't due until seven. A tall, thin man stood at the desk with a leather satchel on the floor next to him.

"May I help you?"

"Yes. I'm sorry to be here this early, but I was hoping you had a room available. Just for one night."

He had intense golden-brown eyes that reminded me of the glass eyes taxidermists put into the animals that hunters mount on their walls. There was also the unmistakable odor of cigar smoke that seemed to waft around him.

"Yes. We have two rooms," I said, stepping to the computer, trying to hold my breath. "One by our back staircase. It has a partial view of the lake. The other is at the top of the stairs and to the right," I said, gesturing behind me. "It has a full view of the lake."

"The one with the partial view would be fine," he said, removing his wallet.

He dressed casually in denim jeans and a crisp Seahawks jersey. But nothing about this man felt casual. He had perfect posture, to the point of being rigid. And then there were those eyes that seemed to follow my every movement.

"Wonderful," I said. "That will be $210 for the night. If you'll just fill this out." I slid a clipboard and a pen across the counter. "We'll also need your license plate."

"I came by Uber," he said, pulling a roll of cash from his pocket.

"Oh, that's fine, then. I see you're a Seahawks fan. Did you get to visit the Virginia Mason Athletic Center over in Renton?"

He looked up. "Who's Virginia Mason?"

"Um… it's a medical center."

His eyes narrowed. "What does a medical center have to do with football?"

His tone was surly, and I didn't want to irritate him, so I skipped the explanation that the Seahawks headquarters had been thusly named because of a partnership with the medical center. "Never mind. It doesn't matter," I said. "Were you just driving around looking for a place to stay? It's early in the day to be out and about."

He extended his hand to grab the pen lying on the counter but paused at my question.

"No," he said, watching me.

The pen rolled away, and I quickly slapped my hand on top of it. *Chloe!*

"I was staying at the Hilton in Bellevue and was on my way to the airport when my boss called to say I had to stay another day. We were just passing Mercer Island, and I asked the driver about places here instead of going back to the hotel. He mentioned this place. It seems you have an excellent reputation."

I handed him the pen, and he focused on the registration form.

Even though I felt a rush of pride at being recommended by an Uber driver, there was something about this guy I didn't like. People rarely pay in cash. Nor do they just show up on our doorstep since we're in a residential neighborhood. But sometimes things aren't usual. He finished filling out the form, and I turned it around and read, "Mr. Robert Clavis. Well, it's nice to have you. By the way, we have a no-smoking policy," I said, gesturing to a sign behind the desk.

"That won't be a problem," he said with a slight sneer.

"Great. Let me show you to your room."

÷

Ben and the girls came over for a late lunch to report back and discuss strategy. Rudy hauled out the whiteboard again and brought it to my apartment. I kept lunch simple by ordering sandwiches from Subway and then made a big pitcher of iced tea. April surprised us with lemon bars.

"Who wants to go first?" Rudy asked.

She was at the whiteboard, poised and ready to write.

"I will," Doe said, unwrapping her sandwich. "I don't have much to report, other than I have a bunch of trash and recycling in the back of my SUV. We not only picked up Walter Clements' but Tom Bateman's. Can José unload it?" she asked me.

"Yes," I said. "I'll text him now. Anyone care to join me in the garage later?"

Rudy and Blair put up their hands as I pulled out my phone to send a text to José, asking him to empty Doe's car and put it all into the garage.

"Sorry, I have a contractor coming over at three," Doe said. "I'm remodeling the guest bathroom."

"No problem. Ben, can you join us?"

He hesitated. "Maybe. I have a lead on something I want to check out."

"What lead?" I inquired.

He shrugged. "Just let me see if it pans out. I'll fill you in later."

"Okay, why don't we get started, then? Blair and I can report on what happened at the dinner last night."

"Did you meet Clements?" Ben asked.

"Yes," Blair said with a broad smile.

Blair related the results of her flirtations with Clements. Ben sat forward in his chair, listening intently.

"You'll be at his house tomorrow?" he asked.

"Yes. Along with Julia."

He turned his gaze on me. "I'm not sure how I feel about that."

"There will be dozens of people there," I argued. "And we're just going to do some sleuthing. Not putting ourselves in harm's way. In fact, I know one thing I'll be looking for."

I told them about my conversation with Alex Janssen, Clements' ex-wife, and my subsequent conversation with Mae Beth about his business dealings and his super arrogant personality.

"And you're hoping to find the pin at his home?" Doe asked.

"Yes." I turned to Ben. "Did you ever hear about a club pin?"

"No. But that doesn't mean they don't have one. I'm worried, though. To find something like a pin, you'd probably have to go into his bedroom."

"Maybe. I'll be careful. Don't worry."

"This all can't be a coincidence," Doe said. "I think we've got him. At least as far as the secret society goes."

"Wait a minute," Rudy interrupted. "We have information. But that information doesn't yet point the finger at anyone for Carter's murder."

"You're right," Ben agreed. "But frankly, I didn't think we'd get this close. You guys have done a great job. We've established that Tom Bateman is a direct descendent of Alistair Bateman, who was a major player in the original Electi group and Brothers of the Night back in the 1800s. And we've established that not only is Walter Clements related to one of the members, but he could be a current member of the society."

"Do you think Bateman and Clements could be working together?" April asked.

"We don't even know if they know each other," Blair said. "I mean, isn't Bateman a Democrat?"

Rudy spoke up. "Let me put that to rest." She pulled some notes from her purse. "I had a friend help me, and we did a thorough internet search, along with an article search through past newspapers and business journals. And not only do they know each other, they're business partners."

"You're kidding?" I asked in surprise. "But Blair is right. Bateman is a Democrat."

"That wouldn't matter in business," April said.

"Anyway," Rudy continued. "Both Bateman and Clements bought into Apollo's Steakhouse, and they're shareholders in First Northwest Enterprises. It's an investment company that has offices throughout the Puget Sound area and does very well, I might add."

Everyone was silent for several seconds, processing.

"This is like putting a jigsaw puzzle together," April said.

"You also wanted to know who Clements' enemies are. He has a lot," she said, referring to her notes. "Not only the guy who used to own The Prime, but several other restaurant owners and, of course, any politician he's run against and beaten. Plus, he was written up in the newspaper for a couple of rather public arguments, but I don't think any of these names are important to our research."

"Don't throw them away, though," I told her.

She nodded. "I found a list of some of his biggest political donors," Rudy added. "It might be helpful. Names like Jeremiah Corning, Dr. Rodney Pollock, and Judge Henry Wicker."

"All well-known Seattle names," Doe said. "No surprise they'd donate to his campaigns."

"What's next?" April asked. "I mean, we know some things. But not enough to hand anything over to the police."

"I guess we'd need to know if the guy with the long sideburns was seen with either Bateman or Clements recently. That would be a big clue since he's directly related to both the break-in at my London flat and he was at Carter's house," Ben said. "But he seems to have disappeared."

"We also still have to find out who owns the boat," April said. Her eyes suddenly opened wide. "Wait a minute. That reminds me of something Walter said last night. He and I were talking about Stewart, who he knew when they both performed surgery at Swedish Medical Center. He told me some of his fondest memories of Stewart were when they went fishing up in Kenmore. They liked to go up there to find largemouth bass near the mouth of the Sammamish River."

"So, you're thinking… what?" Blair asked.

"Just that they would have had to rent a boat, and they would have rented it up there."

"Unless Clements owns a boat," Rudy said. "That's always possible."

I pulled a piece of paper and a pencil from the drawer in the side table next to me. "Okay," I said, taking a note. "We need to look for evidence of The Electi at the barbecue, the pin, and whether Clements owns a boat."

"I'd pay attention to any photographs he has displayed. Look for the friends he's pictured with," Ben said. "It would be good to know more about who he's close to."

"Yeah, that would be good," Rudy said. "Because I have a list of people he's done business with, people who have sued him, even people he went to college with. But I have nothing to compare it to."

I wrote as Rudy talked.

Ben reached out his hand. "Let me look at your notes," he said to Rudy.

She handed over the sheet of paper. Ben skimmed through it. "I see a few names that look familiar." He pulled out his phone and took a photo. "I'll check these names against some ones I've collected."

Just then, my phone rang. "It's Detective Abrams," I said, as I clicked it on. "This is Julia," I said.

"Sorry to bother you," he said. "But we have some news I thought you should hear. We found the kid who delivered the candy to your uncle."

"Oh? What did he have to say?"

"I'm afraid he's dead. An overdose of heroin."

My heart sank. "Did he have a history of drugs?" I asked, staring at my friends.

"No. In fact, his parents said his brother had OD'd on heroin and so it scared him. Which leads us to believe it wasn't accidental. You need to be careful, Mrs. Applegate. Whatever is going on, these people are serious."

"Yes, of course. I know," I said more dismissively than I felt.

"No. You don't. That's what I mean. We'll be positioning a patrol car at the Inn for the next few nights, and our patrol boat will swing by there as well."

"Why?"

"Because when we searched this kid's truck, he had your address written on a slip of paper."

CHAPTER TWENTY-ONE

The afternoon sun filtered through a large oak tree outside my window, casting strands of soft light across the carpet and furniture in my living room. It was a beautiful day in the Northwest, and yet the air in the room felt suddenly oppressive.

"What is it, Julia?" Doe asked quietly.

I put the phone back in my pocket and dropped my gaze to the carpet, thinking it was time to shampoo it. Finally, I inhaled and said, "They found the body of the kid who delivered the See's Candy to Carter. He's dead… from an overdose of heroin."

"Oh, God," Doe murmured.

"Was it accidental?" Rudy asked in a restrained voice.

I raised my eyes to hers. "They don't believe so since he was terrified of it. But that's not all. He had my address written on a piece of paper in his truck."

"Shit," Blair murmured.

Everyone was quiet for a moment. Then Rudy asked, "Do they think he was supposed to deliver candy to you, too?"

"It doesn't matter," Ben said. He looked over at me, his features set in a stern mask. "Once again, I don't think you should be involved in this."

"I already am," I said. "Remember that note we found that said Carter was delivering the key to me? These people might know that—or think they do. That's why they came here looking for it. There's nothing I can do about that now. I'm involved in this whether I like it or not. Detective Abrams said they're going to put a patrol car out front for the next few nights."

Ben didn't look convinced. "Maybe I should stay in the guest room again, just in case."

"That might actually put her more at risk," Doe said. "You have a big target on your back."

"I'll stay tonight," Blair said.

"No. No one needs to stay tonight," I assured them. "I'll have two dogs, several resident ghosts, and a cop right outside my door. I'll be fine. So unless there is anything else to report, we have a mountain of trash to go through." I stood up. "Who's going to join me?"

"That's my cue," Doe said. She got up and leaned over to give me a kiss on the cheek. "I'll check in with you tomorrow. Stay safe."

"I will."

"And I have to get refreshments ready for guests," April said. "But you'd better have me on speed dial tonight, just in case."

Ben gave me a hug and whispered in my ear, "If anything happened to you, Mom would never forgive me. I'm not sure I could live with that." He gave me a quick kiss on the cheek and released me.

The three of them left, while Blair, Rudy, and I went to the garage and donned rubber gloves. We spent the next hour and a half going through Walter Clements' and Tom Bateman's trash and recycling one empty envelope, cereal box, and receipt at a time.

The only things of interest in the Bateman trash were two empty prescription pill bottles for Lithium with the name scratched off. Doctors prescribe Lithium for mood disorders, which raised a bit of a red flag, but we couldn't tell who the prescription was for. In Clements' trash, besides the usual things, there were several empty envelopes from his attorney's office, an empty box of some man-boosting formula, and an empty manila envelope from an address in London. That seemed the most interesting, and I wondered out loud if we could trace the address.

"Leave it to me," Rudy said.

"Be sure to keep your gloves on when you handle it. Just in case it's important."

She nodded and slipped it into a large zip-lock bag.

Blair and I made plans to meet for Clements' barbecue at one o'clock the next day, and then she and Rudy left. I returned to the Inn exhausted.

As I came through the breakfast-room, several of the guests, including the new guy, Mr. Clavis, were helping themselves to mint brownies and lemon bars. Ahab was bouncing around in his cage, repeating, "Say goodnight to the bad guy. Say goodnight to the bad guy. Squawk!"

Mr. Clavis stared at Ahab and then muttered, "Someone should shut that bird up."

"I'll put him in my apartment," I said.

He wheeled around, surprised I was behind him. "I'm sorry. He's just kind of annoying."

Curt was just putting a second brownie on his plate. "I think he's cool," he said, glancing at Ahab. "He quotes a lot of old movies. That's a quote from *Scarface*. I watched it once with my dad."

The small paper plate Mr. Clavis held suddenly flipped sideways, sending the plate with his lemon bar to the floor.

"What the fu—?" he snapped.

Curt stifled a laugh, rolled his eyes, and then moved over to where his mother was sitting. I bent down to retrieve the dessert.

"Don't worry about it. Accidents happen," I said.

"That was no accident," the man said angrily, turning toward Curt. "That kid did it."

I slid the squished lemon bar onto the paper plate, along with some crumbs, and straightened back up. "It wasn't Kurt. He was too far away. Like I said. Don't worry about it. There's plenty more.

I knew it hadn't been Curt's fault. It was most likely Chloe. In this case, however, I wasn't going to scold her. I had decided I really didn't like this guy.

I threw the small paper plate and lemon bar into the big trash can at the end of the table and then said, "By the way, we have a washer and dryer in the back if you'd like to get rid of that cigar smell."

Those steely eyes glared at me. I returned his gaze with a sweet smile and pushed my way through the swinging door into the kitchen, where I found April pouring a giant can of lemonade into our big dispenser filled with ice.

"What's Ahab so wound up about?" I asked her.

She put the empty can down and screwed the top onto the dispenser. "I don't know. But he's been repeating that same phrase for the last several minutes."

"Well, he pissed off our new guest, Mr. Clavis. But I think Mr. Clavis pissed off Chloe."

"Why is that?"

"She just flipped his lemon bar onto the floor," I said with a broad smile.

April laughed, her espresso eyes dancing. "That's our ghosts," she said. "I have to get this out there."

She took the lemonade into the breakfast room, while I texted José to ask him to move Ahab into my apartment again.

÷

It was almost eleven o'clock, and I had just finished putting a drape over Ahab's cage before getting ready for bed. My energy was spent, and I felt like I could sleep for a week. But my phone rang, making me wince, thinking I didn't really want to talk with anyone. When there was no caller ID or phone number visible, pin pricks raced across my skin.

It had to be my mother.

I swiped the phone on and said a tentative, "Hello?"

"Julia, what's going on now? I can sense you're in danger. Can't you just live a normal life like the rest of the world?"

"Hi, Mom," I said with a churlish edge to my voice. "Nice to hear from you, too."

"Seriously? That's all you have to say?"

"Look Mom, there are some heavy things going on right now that involve Ben. To be honest, I thought you would be better informed. You being dead and all."

Sometimes my mother's insensitivity just got on my nerves.

"Why would I know anything? You two never told me anything when I was alive."

"Yes, but I told you that Carter Davis had been murdered. Ben is here now, and we're trying to find out who killed him."

"That must be it. I could feel the negative energy around you, like the electricity in a light socket if I stuck my finger in it."

"If you did that, you'd be electrocuted."

"Not my problem anymore."

I sighed. "Look, someone poisoned Carter with See's chocolates, and it seems they may have been planning on sending me some of that chocolate, too."

"That's a blasphemous use of See's Candy. But I remember how much Carter liked his chocolate. What does this have to do with Ben, though?"

"They were doing some research together on Jack the Ripper and stumbled onto some secret society. We think they got too close to the truth."

"And now you're involved, too."

"Yes, so anything you could do in that regard would be greatly appreciated," I said, feeling impatient.

"You know that's not how things work."

"How *do* things work, Mom? You've never actually explained that to me."

"Can't. There are rules. You'll know soon enough."

"What's that supposed to mean?"

"No. No. Sorry. I just meant… time is different here. Things that take years to happen where you are feel like they happen in a flash here. That's all I meant. Anyway, I gotta go. Just be careful. I see a shadow around you. It makes me feel like someone close to you isn't what they seem. I don't know how else to describe it. You need to watch your step. As much as I love you, I really don't want to see you over here soon."

And then she was gone.

It was always like that. She somehow always knew when I might be in trouble and could warn me, but with no specifics. I had decided that once I got to the other side, I would investigate how to change some of those rules she kept harping about.

Anyway, I needed to heed her warning. She'd always been right. But I wasn't sure what having a shadow around me meant. Or that it was someone close to me.

I went to my window and pulled back the curtain to check on the patrol car out front. It gave me peace of mind knowing the officer was there. His presence might even scare someone away. Mom could sense danger, but I doubted she could sense protection.

I let the curtain fall back into place and then grabbed a steak knife from the kitchen and put it next to my bed, just in case.

÷

Somewhere around 2 a.m., a lot of yelling yanked me out of a deep sleep. The dogs started barking, and I heard thunderous footsteps on the staircase near the registration desk. I was already out of bed when I heard the word 'Fire!'

I grabbed my phone and robe, and rushed into the hallway, leaving the dogs in the apartment. Rounding the corner to the foyer, I nearly knocked Mr. Muse off his feet as he hurried off the last step of the staircase.

"What's going on?" I yelled, pulling on my robe.

"There's a fire outside," he said, pointing to our back deck.

I ran to the breakfast-room windows and saw flames leaping from our dock. Several of the guests stood on the deck, watching.

"Get out front!" I yelled through the open door.

Reluctantly, they followed me through the breakfast-room and through the front door to the safety of the front parking lot, where most of the guests were huddled. Curt stayed at my side.

"You need to stay out here," I told him. "I'll call 911."

"My dad already called it in," he said.

I glanced back at the building, noticing several lights on upstairs.

"We need to make sure everyone is outside," I said, moving toward the front door again.

Curt grabbed my arm. "I checked all the other rooms." He glanced around. "Everyone is out here."

"You're a good kid, Curt," I said, placing my hand on his arm. "Is it just the dock?"

"So far. We could see it from our window."

"Wait! I have to get my dogs and Ahab! Stay here."

I yanked my hand away and hurried back to my apartment alone, thinking about the dogs and the bird. The door wasn't locked, and I pushed it open, feeling something heavy on the other side. Ahab was muttering inside his draped cage, but the dogs were silent. *Why weren't the dogs barking?* They would normally bark their heads off.

I gave a final push on the door and slipped through the opening into the apartment. I glanced down the hallway and called their names. Nothing. My left foot pushed up against something, and I glanced down. Both dogs lay motionless on the floor at my feet.

I dropped to shake them, feeling a sense of panic mount inside me. *They couldn't be dead. They just couldn't be.*

Mickey was closest, but as hard as I shook him, his entire body was as limp as a noodle. My eyes teared up. That's when a hand grabbed the collar of my robe and lifted me off the floor.

"Tell me where it is. Now!"

The smell of cigar smoke washed over me as Mr. Clavis' arm wrapped around my throat.

"Where is that damn key?"

"I… I… don't know," I said, struggling to get away from him.

"You're lying. We know you have it."

Clavis nearly broke my neck when he yanked his arm up toward my chin. I tried to loosen his grip by getting my fingers under his elbow, but no luck. I gasped for air.

Where was the officer watching the house?

A deep voice growled behind us, "Get away from her!"

Someone suddenly yanked Clavis away, releasing me against the wall. A struggle went on behind me as I slid to my knees. I heard grunts and groans and wondered who had followed me to my apartment. I struggled to my feet just as there was a loud thud.

I turned to find Mr. Clavis out cold near my bedroom door. Standing over him was a hulk of a man in a plaid shirt. I didn't know if this was friend or foe until he straightened up and turned around.

"Do you have anything to tie his hands?" he asked.

I sucked in a deep breath and stood for a moment in utter shock, staring at Jake Weatherly, a man I had met a few weeks earlier on our cross-country trip.

"What are you doing here?" I croaked, my hand massaging my throat.

"My niece is in the hospital here in Seattle," he said. "I checked in this afternoon, but you were in a meeting. Now, what do you have that I can tie his hands with?"

I shook my head to make sense of the situation and then turned for a drawer in the kitchen. I pulled out a ball of heavy twine and handed it to him. He flipped Clavis over and secured his wrists. He finished and turned back to find me staring at my dogs with tears running down my cheeks.

"I think he killed my dogs," I whispered.

"Wait. Let's see," he said, bending over. He picked Mickey up with one hand and cradled his little body to his face. "He's breathing. Barely." He handed the dog to me and grabbed Minnie, doing the same thing. "She's breathing too. Most likely, they've been drugged."

"Oh…" I sobbed. "Oh, thank God."

While holding Minnie cradled in his left arm, he reached out and put his right hand on my shoulder. "Julia, you need to get them to an emergency vet. Just in case."

"But… the fire…" I said, gesturing weakly toward the lake.

The blaring of sirens announced the fire department as April appeared at my door in pajamas and slippers.

"Julia! Are you okay?" She took one look at Jake and said, "Who the heck are you?"

"A friend," I said. "Don't worry about him. We need to get the dogs to the vet. They've been drugged." I was still holding a limp Mickey in my arms and nodded towards Minnie.

"Isn't that one of our guests?" April said, glancing down at the body on the floor.

"Yes. Mr. Clavis. He just tried to kill me. Now can we go to the vet?"

"Everyone needs to get out of the house," a voice shouted from behind April. A firefighter in full gear appeared, gesturing to the front of the Inn.

"We're on our way," Jake said to him. He turned to me. "Go. I'll take care of things here."

"I'll drive," April said. "Give me the dog," she said to Jake.

He handed over Minnie, while I ran to grab my purse. I stopped at the door, glancing back at Jake.

"Thank you," I said. "I... I don't know what..."

"Just go," he said.

April and I hustled out the door as Jake turned to the firefighter and said, "Can you get a police officer? I think we caught the guy who started the fire."

CHAPTER TWENTY-TWO

"Who was that guy?"

April and I were sitting at the emergency vet, still dressed in our pajamas, waiting while the doctor examined the dogs. April knew all about the harrowing experiences we had had on the trip to Wisconsin when we delivered a motorhome to a friend of Rudy's and stopped at Jake's Deli in Minnesota for sandwiches. Not only were we chasing a group of killers, but Jake saved us that day from a couple of bikers that Aria had pissed off (a story for another time).

Now here he was, coming to my rescue once again.

"I told you about Jake, right? The guy at the little country store?"

Her dark eyebrows rose in question. "Seems to me like he keeps coming to your aid."

"Yeah, I guess so," I said, blushing. "He fended off some bikers with a shot gun back then. Who knew he'd show up here?"

"And from the way he looked at you, he's interested, if you know what I mean."

My phone jingled, and my muscles clenched when I saw David's name.

I swiped on the phone and said, "Hey."

"Are you okay? I heard about the fire."

"I'm fine. I'm at the vet, though. The guy who started the fire drugged the dogs."

"Oh, Julia, I'm sorry. Will they be okay?"

I felt myself tear up again but swallowed to control my emotions. "I think so. The doctor is with them now. April and I are just waiting."

"I'm glad. I called the officer on duty at the station, and he said they caught the guy who started the fire."

I flinched at the word they. *Should I tell him about Jake?*

"Yes. I'm sure he's in custody."

"Well, I'm told he also drugged the cop who was assigned to watch your place. He came out of the Inn with a steaming cup of coffee and delivered it to him."

"That's probably because he was a guest."

"Damn! He didn't hurt you, did he?"

A part of me wanted to downplay what had happened. On the other hand, David had ignored me for the better part of two days. Perhaps if he'd been a bit more attentive, this wouldn't have happened. So…

"I'm fine. He had me by the throat, but a friend came to my rescue and knocked him out."

"What friend?"

"Someone who came to visit."

The door to the examination room opened, and the doctor poked his head out.

"Julia, who's this friend?" David repeated.

"Someone I met on our road trip. You remember. I'm sure I mentioned Jake. Listen, I have to go. The doctor wants to talk to us."

I clicked off the phone and stood up. The doctor was a tiny, Asian man whose dark-rimmed glasses kept slipping down his nose.

"Ms. Applegate?"

"Yes, that's me."

He smiled and pushed his glasses back, coming forward. "Your dogs will be fine. Someone gave them a small dose of chloroform. Probably pressed up against their noses, just enough to knock them out. You can take them home. Just keep them quiet for a while."

I dropped my head and released a breath. "Thank you."

With a huge amount of relief, we took the dogs home. The firetruck was still there, but the firefighters were reloading the hoses and getting ready to leave. Jake loomed large outside, talking to one of the police officers. He turned to me and smiled, and once again, my heart fluttered.

"I'll take the dogs inside," April said, nodding toward Jake. "You can handle matters out here."

"Thanks. I'll be in soon, and we can survey the damage."

She hefted a sleepy dog under each arm and skirted the firefighters and police officers as she went inside. All the guests must have been back in their rooms or perhaps on the back deck. Jake caught my eye and excused himself.

"Everything okay?" he asked, his gaze following April inside.

Jake was over six feet tall, with short, curly dark hair graying at the temples and deep-set dark eyes. The timbre of his voice reminded me of the cello I tried to learn in junior high. But it was the warmth of his smile that I found most attractive.

"Yes, thanks. The dogs will be fine. Listen, can I get you a cup of coffee?"

He grinned. "Any of those minty chocolate brownies left over from this afternoon? I checked in when there was only one left."

"If not, I'm sure April has something in the kitchen we can steal."

He followed me into the breakfast-room, where we passed a surly-looking Brett, along with his ever-mute Kendra. They were heading for the staircase. Brett stopped.

"You know, you ought to put a sign out front that warns people of the risk if they stay here. I should have taken out travel insurance before we left."

With a mean sneer, he followed his girlfriend up the stairs.

"Just ignore him," Curt said.

He and Mr. Muse had just returned from the back deck.

"Never a dull moment around here," Mr. Muse said with a smile. "I'll have lots to tell my granddaughter."

"I'm sorry about that," I replied.

"No problem, Ms. Applegate," he said with a wink. "I was up anyway. Unfortunately, not looking out the window this time."

He passed us and went upstairs. Curt stopped and looked up at Jake.

"Good job getting that shithead who started the fire."

Jake arched his brows and looked at me. He seemed uncomfortable with the foul language. "Thanks. Just glad I was here."

"I knew there was something about that guy," Curt said to me. "FYI, the police cleaned out his room. I showed them which one it was."

"Thank you, Curt. You've been a big help."

"Curt!" his mother snapped. She was standing at the bottom of the staircase. "Back to bed."

He slumped away, and Jake and I pushed through to the kitchen. I found the mint brownies and put a couple on a plate.

"Are you a milk and brownie guy?" I asked him. "Otherwise, I could make coffee or tea."

"Definitely cold milk," he said. "Let me help."

While I pulled a couple of glasses down from the cupboard, he found the milk carton in the refrigerator. We met at the table.

Once we were situated, I said, "So what brings you to Seattle?"

"As I said, my niece is in the hospital. She was in an accident. Someone T-boned her in the middle of an intersection."

"Oh, my God. Is she going to be okay?"

"The doctors are optimistic. She has a bunch of broken bones and a collapsed lung, but she's strong. So fingers crossed," he said, holding up two crossed fingers.

"I'm glad. But why didn't you call and make a reservation?"

"I got a call from my brother and hopped a plane. As soon as I landed, I went directly to the hospital. I just took a chance that you'd have an opening. And if not, at least I thought maybe I'd get to see you."

My face grew warm, and I studied my brownie as if it had something to say. It remained quiet, and I looked up again.

"Well, I'm glad you're here," I said. "I'm just sorry I didn't see you earlier."

He smiled. "Curt filled me in on all the goings on around here. The old man was right—never a dull moment."

I shook my head. "My life isn't always like this."

"Really? I seem to remember sitting with you at the front of my store watching a road race you referred to as the Keystone Cops. You said you were chasing someone who had abducted a young girl. I read about that, by the way. The article said a group of women on a cross-country trip found her in the wilderness not too far from there. Sound familiar?"

I chuckled. "We rescued her from a small home up by Lake Cleary. Her kidnappers drugged her and held her hostage."

"My God, woman. You're fearless. What's the story this time? Who was that guy tonight?"

In between brownie bites, I told Jake the entire story of Carter's death, Ben's research, even the note in the mini hearse. When I finished, he just shook his head.

"I think 'never a dull moment' is an understatement," he said. "Someone has broken into your apartment not once, but twice, and each time the intruder attacked you. Someone died on your doorstep, and someone else set a fire on your property. Sounds to me like you need a personal bodyguard."

Our eyes met, and I smiled mischievously. "Have anyone in mind?"

He grinned. "As a matter of fact, I do."

Jake and I talked for another thirty or forty minutes. Turns out, we had a lot in common, including a love of animals, art, music, and books. Jake was politically more independent than me, perhaps even a little conservative, but I didn't hold that against him. He was open-minded, thoughtful, and amusing. And I appreciate anyone who can make me laugh.

It was after four o'clock when I finally made it back to my apartment. I found several drawers and cupboard doors pulled open, with some contents tossed onto the floor. Obviously, Mr. Clavis had tossed my apartment looking for the key while everyone else was running from the fire. Deciding to leave the clean up until the morning, I went to bed. I was just about to turn out the light when a text came in from Ben.

The lead I mentioned looks promising. I don't think Carter brought the key to you but came to tell you where he hid it. I'm going back to Carter's tomorrow to check it out. Talk soon.

Just like Ben to be cryptic. I'm sure he wouldn't tell me what the lead was until he'd seen it through. But the fact he thought Carter hadn't brought the key to me made me feel slightly better. If only we could somehow get the word out to the bad guys, maybe people would stop attacking me because they thought I had it.

As I got under the covers I gave each dog an extra hug, thinking how lucky I was that nothing had happened to them. My thoughts drifted to the upcoming barbecue at Walter Clements'. My role was to snoop around while Blair kept Walter busy and, hopefully, wrangle an invitation out of him to join the secret society. I didn't know how she planned on doing that, but she had told me she had an idea. I hoped that didn't mean I'd find her in a compromising situation while I did my snooping. Although I enjoyed watching Roger Federer do what he did best on the field of play, I couldn't say the same about Blair. That would be a bridge too far.

÷

After only a couple hours of sleep, both April and I met in the kitchen to make breakfast. I didn't see Jake at all that morning. He'd told me earlier that he would be at the hospital with his brother and family. I spent the morning paying bills and saying goodbye to Mr.

Muse, who checked out to return home to the memories of his dear wife.

Curt and his parents left to sightsee in Seattle, which made me happy he'd finally get some quality time with them. I suggested not only the Space Needle but Pike Place Market as must-sees, as well as a few lesser-known spots. Around ten o'clock, a couple in town for a family reunion checked in.

About the same time, the claims adjuster from our insurance company showed up. I spent the next forty-five minutes showing him what remained of our dock and referred him to the police station to get a copy of the police report. And, finally, Brett and his silent girlfriend stopped by the front desk to demand a refund.

"I talked with my father," snotty Brett said, holding our brochure in his hand. "This brochure claims the Inn is a restful and relaxing retreat. A murder, two break-ins, and a fire can hardly be described as restful or relaxing. Since we paid in advance, we expect a full refund when we check out."

I stared into his selfish green eyes a moment, thinking how different he was from Mr. Muse, who had thanked me for a thoroughly entertaining stay. But I guess I couldn't blame young Brett. When you're as shallow as a cookie sheet, you can hardly be expected to accept life on its own terms rather than looking for a way to capitalize on it.

"Fine," I said to him. "I'll be glad to sign you out now, and we'll mail you a check once we've deducted taxes, food, cleaning, and laundry costs. After all, what you consumed, you pay for."

His mouth opened and closed. "How much will that be?"

I smiled and glanced at Kendra standing beside him, picking at a bronze fingernail. "I'd guess more than what your girlfriend here pays every two weeks for the chrome mani-pedi she gets, but much less than the cost of the BMW you drive."

"It's a Lexus," he said.

"Exactly. Shall I make the check out to you or your father?"

"Well, we're not leaving yet. Let's hope nothing else happens while we're here."

They left the reception desk, and I momentarily regretted my sarcasm since they'd be there for another forty-eight hours. As the saying goes, who knows what tomorrow would bring, especially when you're investigating a murder?

CHAPTER TWENTY-THREE

Blair arrived at 12:30 wearing her version of barbecue attire, which meant ice-blue skin-tight capris, black wedge espadrilles that tied around her ankles with a cute bow, and a sparkling cross-wrap halter top that made her breasts look like melons held against their will.

We were in my apartment, and I was just putting on small hoop earrings to complement my washed denim jeans, loafers, and short-sleeved, floral peasant blouse.

"Are you nervous?" I asked her.

"No. Why would I be?"

"Well, we may have only one shot at this. We have to make it count."

"I will," she said with confidence. "Just don't get caught snooping. You tend to… uh, well, sometimes get noticed for the wrong reasons."

I narrowed my eyes and pursed my lips as I eyed her boobs. "Not like you, I suppose."

She raised a bare shoulder. "Depends on the reason you want to be noticed; I suppose."

Blair had a new black Audi R8, which she told me boasted a V10 engine, whatever that was. It was just a black sports car to me. But I suppose it was appropriate for the task that lay ahead that afternoon.

Clements lived on Queen Anne Hill, which sits northwest of downtown Seattle. It's an affluent neighborhood with a mixture of ultra-modern and majestic Victorian homes, with more modest homes thrown in for good measure.

Clements lived in a huge Victorian home that sat at the top of the hill and took up the entire corner. The exterior colors of the building represented the time-period in which it was built, slate blue offset with golden brown. Not my color choice, but it had been popular during that era, and it didn't surprise me that Clements would want to be authentic. The home included a broad front staircase, wraparound porch with a gingerbread trim, a wrought-iron fence that ran the entire perimeter, and a corner turret.

"Understated," I murmured, gazing up at the turret.

Blair laughed. "It's no less grand than the St. Claire Inn."

"At least the Inn looks comfy cozy. This is so formal; it looks like everyone would be expected to dress for dinner each night."

Parked cars lined each side of the street, but Clements had anticipated this by having valet parking. We pulled up to a marked-off area and got out. Blair handed the keys to a studly young man in uniform and said, "I know every inch of this car like I know every mole, scar, and blemish on my husband's behind. So... do not put a scratch on it."

His eyes opened in surprise, but he accepted the challenge with a nod and took the keys.

Another young man opened the iron gate for us, and we sauntered up the long front path. A small, calligraphed sign at the foot of the front staircase read, "Come to the back" with an arrow pointing to the right.

"Damn," I said. "I hoped we'd be able to go through the house."

"That would have been easier to get a fix on the layout," Blair said, starting off on the path. "I guess you'll have to find another excuse to get inside."

Two young girls ran past us going the opposite direction as we rounded the building. Music floated through the air, and I marveled at the perfect view of the Space Needle in the distance as we came around to the backyard. It was a crystal blue day, and so we had a clear view of the Seattle cityscape.

The house sat on a hill, and the backyard sloped down to the house below it. An arched gate led to a large redwood deck that stretched the width of the house and then descended to a flat yard by a series of stairs. Towering pines surrounded the yard and rustled in the afternoon breeze, throwing shadows across a winding rock path, set off by strategically placed rocks, boulders, Pampas Grass and other flowers and shrubs. The path led from the deck to a large, outdoor kitchen, where smoke billowed up from the grill, and the tantalizing smell of cooked meat wafted in our direction.

Swimming pools aren't common in the Northwest because of the rain, but Clements had one. It sat in the far corner of the yard and looked more like a large wilderness pond surrounded by a two-foot wall made from river rock. More pine trees flanked the pool, along with a manmade waterfall cascading into the far end. Just beyond that was a squat building made of marble.

"What do you suppose that is?" I asked Blair, pointing at the small building.

"Looks like a mausoleum or something," she said. "This is an old home. I suppose in the early days of Seattle, they might have buried people on the property."

My gaze flitted over to where clusters of patio furniture sat in front of a Tuscany-y-looking fireplace. This was bordered by a four-foot, semi-circular rock-faced counter that held a stainless-steel sink, workstation, and outdoor gas grill. Two men in chef's aprons manned the grill, handing out plates of food.

"Man-oh-man," Blair said. "I have to admit, I like the way he lives."

"Not me," I said, cringing at a fountain made from a Roman column that rose from the middle of the only green lawn in the yard. "Too much for my taste."

"How many people do you think are here?"

I skimmed the area. "Forty. Maybe more. Not including the band," I said, gesturing to the string quartet stationed under the shade of the pines.

Blair was wearing sunglasses, so I couldn't see her eyes. But it appeared she was looking for someone.

"There's Clements," she said, nodding toward the far side of the upper deck.

He wore crisp gray slacks and a loose-fitting black polo shirt, which set off his perfectly tanned muscular arms and thick gray hair. Two women hovered next to him.

"Are you going to talk to him now?"

"No. I'll let him come to me. Let's get a drink."

Guests had a choice of two bars: one close to us on the next level down and one by the pool. We made our way to the closer one. With drinks in hand, we moved off to the side to gaze down on the yard, in the direct line of sight of Clements on the deck above us. I watched him, but Blair never once looked his way, choosing instead to concentrate on the guests below.

"Is Tom Bateman here?" I asked, scanning the crowd.

"I don't see him," she replied. "But that doesn't mean he's not here. Oh, wait. Isn't that him down by the grill?" She nodded in that direction. "I think he's talking to your friend, Mae Beth."

Sure enough, Tom Bateman stood in the yard below, huddled up with Mae Beth, their heads almost close enough to touch.

"I wonder what they're talking about."

"How well do you know Mae Beth?" she asked.

"Not that well, I guess," I said with a shrug. "I mean, I met her many years ago. It was back when Graham was only flirting with switching parties. Mae Beth is one of the party's biggest fundraisers. She convinced him that with his good looks and personality, he'd be a shoo-in for the party nominee and had a real shot at winning."

"And he won."

"Right. She tried to get me to come along, too, but I just couldn't. In the end, she and I became friends. We had lunch and went out for drinks a few times. But I hardly ever see her anymore since I dropped out of politics."

"Is that Bateman's wife?" Blair pointed to a hard-looking woman to Bateman's left. She appeared uninterested in the conversation as her head swiveled to watch the people around her.

"Yes. Treen, as Doe calls her," I said with a grin.

A heavy waft of cologne announced Clements' arrival before I saw him.

"Was that an Audi R8 I saw you drive up in?"

Walter Clements stood at Blair's elbow with a glass of wine in his left hand.

"Yes, it was," Blair purred. "Your home is lovely," she said, pulling off her sunglasses to stare into his eyes. "Your wife has exquisite taste. Sorry, ex-wife."

I wasn't sure why Blair mentioned Alex, other than to remind Clements that she was aware of his divorce. Or perhaps to set up a comparison. Regardless, his reaction surprised me.

"You're right. Alex does have exquisite taste." He glanced around. "She did all of this. She enjoyed making a statement." His gaze dropped to Blair's breasts and then down to her ankles. "Much like you."

Count to three.

Feeling like the proverbial third wheel, I spoke up. "What's that small building I see through the trees?"

I nodded toward what Blair had described as a mausoleum. It had a wrought-iron gate set into the middle of it and accessed by two steps leading down to a little patio on the other side of the pool.

"Is that your man cave?" I said with a stupid grin.

His eyes met mine, but the smile he displayed was disquieting.

"It's actually a mausoleum left over from the Paddington family who built the home back in the late 1800s."

My eyebrows arched. "Oh, so there are people buried on the property."

"Not buried," he corrected me.

"Sorry. Right. Just interred."

His head pivoted to Blair. "Would you care to join me on the upper deck? There are hors d'oeuvres and wine up there and a cozy place to relax."

Still feeling like the third wheel, the three of us climbed the short flight of stairs back to the main deck, where there was a large bronze fire pit with an open flame brewing. A four-foot railing with a heavy, black fabric netting surrounded the entire deck.

"What's the netting for?" I asked him.

"The builders left too much space between the deck floor and that first crossbar. My grandchildren like to play out here. It's too dangerous. They could fall through. I installed the netting as a safety measure."

"Good idea," I said.

Two Adirondack chairs flanked the fire pit, a zero-gravity chair, and an elaborately carved wooden bench. I was familiar with zero gravity chairs because Doe had one on her patio. They were outdoor recliners designed to swing back and suspend your body with your feet elevated above your heart. Good for circulation. I'd always wanted to try one, and so chose that, while Clements and Blair took the Adirondack chairs.

The moment I sat down, I realized I was too short for the chair. I couldn't get my butt all the way to the back. But since I'm not someone who gives up easily, I stood up again and threw my backside into the deepest part of the chair.

And that's when it happened.

My butt hit the sweet spot, and my momentum backwards slid the chair about four inches so that the lower rear bar skimmed right off the edge of the deck, getting caught in the netting. The chair collapsed in on itself, trapping me inside. I screamed. My wine ended up in my lap, splashing all over my blouse, but fortunately, the deck netting held tight.

However, I was stuck!

Blair and Clements jumped up. He tried to help. But when I say I was stuck, I mean stuck. Gravity had me firmly planted at the lowest point of the chair, while the back of the chair had folded over the top of me. I'm sure I looked a little like an oyster. Only the crossbar of the railing and the net held me in place. Otherwise, I pictured myself sliding through to fall to my death.

While Clements grasped my hand and tried to pull me out, two other men appeared and attempted to pull the chair forward. After a few hefty tries, they yanked the chair out of the railing, freeing me, and throwing me forward. The wine glass rolled free, while I landed on my hands and knees gasping for air, my face nearly in the fire pit.

"My God, Julia, are you okay?" Blair said, as she and Clements helped me to my feet.

Truth be told, I was on the verge of tears. And not just from the embarrassment. After a lifetime of pratfalls and mishaps, I was used to becoming the center of attention for all the wrong reasons. But this time, I could have been seriously hurt or killed.

"I… I need to clean up," I said to Clements, shaking wine off my hands. "Maybe even lie down for a minute."

My voice was shaking, and I was pretty sure that everyone on the top deck was staring at me. All I could think of was getting somewhere where I could hide.

"Of course," Clements said. "Come inside."

I followed him to the sliding glass doors. As I passed Blair, she winked at me as if I'd planned the entire thing just to get into the house alone. I shot her an incredulous look.

Clements took me into the large kitchen, where a team of caterers were busy filling trays, washing dishes, or chopping produce. He motioned for a small, stocky woman with short black hair and buggy eyes to come over.

"This is DeeDee, my housekeeper. DeeDee, please take care of Mrs. Applegate. She's had an accident. I'm sure there's something upstairs in what's left of my wife's things that she could wear."

DeeDee's dark eyes swept across my wardrobe disaster. "I'll be happy to," she said.

Clements went back to the party, while I followed DeeDee all the way upstairs to a guest bedroom and bathroom.

"You can freshen up in here," she said. "And some of the former Mrs. Clements' clothes have been moved to this closet if you'd like to change your blouse." She opened a closet door and showed me a full rack of clothes that Alex had apparently left behind.

"Thank you. I think I need a few minutes to just decompress, if you don't mind," I said, angling for more time. "Please let the senator know I'll be down in a little while."

"Happy to," she said again.

She nodded and left.

I couldn't believe my luck. Well, not luck. It's never lucky to almost kill yourself. But my clumsiness had placed me right where I wanted to be.

It took me only a few minutes to wet a washcloth and clean off my neck and arms. I dried myself off and then checked the closet and found a cute animal print tunic top I thought would fit. I slipped out of my peasant blouse and pulled the tunic over my head. It was too long, but otherwise looked pretty good. I then rolled up my wet blouse and stuffed it into my bag, took a deep breath, and went looking for trouble.

CHAPTER TWENTY-FOUR

I had no trouble finding the master bedroom. It looked like something out of a *Better Homes and Gardens* magazine. White carpet. White Curtains. White wallpaper flecked with silver. Antiqued white furniture. A king-sized bed with a tufted white comforter, accented by a silver duvet. And over the white fur (yes, I said fur) covered headboard was an enormous, framed print of the inside of a giant flower that, had I been in mixed company (or any company), would have made me blush. I'm not an art aficionado, but I knew a Georgia O'Keeffe painting when I saw it, and this one resembled the intimate part of a woman's body.

Leaving any thoughts regarding why Walter Clements had this print above his bed for later, I did a fast search of the room, even though I doubted he would leave anything out in the open related to The Electi. I did my due diligence, however, and pulled out a few drawers, hoping to find the club pin. Sifting through a man's underwear and socks drawer felt too intrusive, so I did a cursory look and then found the walk-in closet, thinking he might have a jewelry box in there. When I saw nothing, my courage failed me, and I skedaddled out of there.

Descending the stairs, I landed in the broad entryway to the home, staring through the intricately designed stained glass window in the front door to the street. To my left was the dining room, which led into the kitchen at the back of the house. I could see the caterers busily working away with DeeDee supervising.

Not where I wanted to go.

The living room sat to my right, and I stopped two feet inside the elegant French doors. Alex had designed it beautifully, with rich burgundy walls accented by dark wood trim and high-paned windows framed with heavy velvet drapes. An elaborate circular Asian rug commanded the center of the room, laid over a highly polished wood plank floor. A mahogany Regency table stood in the center of the carpet, anchored with a large, porcelain Chinese vase holding fresh flowers. The vase alone had probably set Clements back a couple of grand.

I moved further into the room where a large, carved white fireplace sat against the far wall, set off by two tufted, green antique chairs. I ran my hands over the silk fabric of the chairs, wishing I could make an offer and take them home with me.

What surprised me wasn't the décor, however, but something else.

Above the fireplace was an enormous, heavy, gold-leaf-framed painting of the senator, complete with a brass plate at the bottom—Senator Walter Clements, 2019. It was the year, I thought, that he had become minority leader of the State Senate. His pose reminded me of Napoleon, just without his hand tucked inside his shirt.

The painting was regal and yet smug, all at the same time. The artist had softened the lines in his face to make him look distinguished instead of the mature age of 56 that he was. And the artist had added a cream-colored dot to his eyes to give his expression a fresh, inspired appearance. The painting commanded the room the way, I suppose, Clements felt he commanded others.

A line of expensively framed photos stretched across the mantle just below it, showing him with various Republican VIPs, such as President George W. Bush, Senator Mitch McConnell, and football star Tom Brady. Dozens of frames covered the adjoining walls. I saw framed copies of bills he'd passed in the senate, awards he'd received in the community for one thing or another, and more photos of him with notable personalities. And then under the window was perhaps the most pretentious piece of all—a sculpted marble bust of the senator.

A small chuckle erupted from my throat at the arrogance. But as I gazed around me, I realized the entire living room was an homage to him. Perhaps that's one reason Alex had left. It had to be suffocating living here.

I took a few minutes and studied some photographs, mementoes, and artwork, just in case I'd find something important. The only thing that caught my attention was a framed photo of Clements, Tom Bateman, Mae Beth, and Dr. Rodney Pollock, one of the top cardiac surgeons in the area. I remembered that Pollock's name was on Rudy's list of Clements' donors. The photo looked like it was at a fancy dinner. I took a quick photo for consideration later.

I went back to the hallway and turned toward the rear of the house. An older gentleman came out of the downstairs bathroom just as I was passing, and we nearly bumped into each other.

"It's a lovely house, isn't it?" he said.

"It is. I was just looking around."

He smiled and turned for another set of French doors that led to the back deck. I paused, not sure which way to go. A long hallway to my left led along the back of the house to a door that looked like it might go outside. I scooted down the hallway, passing a couple of other doors on my way. I ignored those because I was conscious of the fact that I was passing in front of several windows to my right that opened onto the deck. Clements was probably still out there, and I didn't want to be seen.

When I got to the door at the end of the hallway, I put my hand on the doorknob and glanced back to make sure I was alone. Feeling a sense of relief, I turned the knob and stepped into an enormous garage filled with several expensive cars... and a boat!

Glancing around once more to make sure no one was looking through the windows, I closed the door and moved further into the garage, weaving my way past a sky-blue Lexus and a vintage Mustang to where the boat sat on a trailer.

It wasn't the small LUND boat that had brought my attacker to the Inn. This was a Master Craft ski boat, complete with an inboard motor and swim platform on the back. At least we could check that box, I thought to myself.

I returned to the hallway and back to the main staircase. So far, my search had turned up bupkis. A door to my right beckoned me, and so I eased it open and slipped inside. This room felt heavy, with its luxurious leather furniture, deep green walls, and imposing executive desk that sat before another fireplace. This had to be Clements' office.

A finely carved lion's head fronted the magnificent mahogany desk, with four more hand-carved lions on either side, with their teeth barred. In my monthly *Antique Register* magazine, I had seen photos of a desk just like this. Named after Lord Thomas Raffles, whoever he was, they referred to it as the Raffles Lion's desk. It made the same statement as the painting in the living room. A clear picture of the depth and breadth of this man's ego formed in my mind.

Circling the desk, I tried all the drawers, but they were locked. I racked my brain trying to remember if the Lion's Desk had any secret compartments but couldn't think of any, and so switched my focus to the glass top. It was immaculate, graced only with a smart phone and video display, a decorative antique clock, and a framed photo of Clements with what looked like his late father. I glanced at some of the speed dial tags on the phone, but only saw numbers, no names.

An elaborate, 18th Century German 8-day grandfather clock stood in the corner. There was a hood with half-columns and turned finials. It drew me toward it like a piece of Godiva chocolate and had to be worth upwards of $10,000. Saliva flooded my mouth, as I imagined it sitting in the foyer to the Inn. It was about to chime the hour, but I had no time to wait for the privilege of hearing it. I had to keep looking.

Behind the desk and above the fireplace was a huge, gilded framed painting of Mt. Rainier. To the left of that was a wall-to-ceiling cherry-wood bookcase filled with law books, a framed copy of Clements' MBA from Harvard, and a photo of Clements and Bateman on the golf course with Judge Henry Wicker, who had gained notoriety for having been the judge in a very public discrimination case against the City of Seattle. They shared the photo with Jeremiah Corning, who had made a couple of unsuccessful runs for Seattle Mayor. Both names were also on Rudy's donor list.

What really caught my eye, however, was an old, polished ebony box that was the size of a large picture book. An intricately carved serpent, complete with rubies for eyes, encircled the box so that its fangs met his tail just above the keyhole on the front panel. I glanced at the top of the box and released an involuntary gasp. Set right into the center was a large *E* carved in a very heavy script.

Damn! This had to be the box that belonged to The Electi.

If it was the box Ben sought, then it seemed surprising Clements would leave it out in the open. But then The Electi wasn't a known quantity like Skull and Bones and nobody but someone like me would recognize it for what it was.

Once again, I made sure I was alone and then reached into my purse for my phone. I quickly snapped two photos, wondering if I should try to open it. Then I remembered Ben had said there would be a second box inside that required a code, so I decided against it.

"You look like you're feeling better."

I whipped around, pulling the hand holding my phone behind me. Clements was standing at the door, one hand on the doorknob. *Damn! Why hadn't I closed the door?*

"Yes, sorry. I've been looking around and admiring your beautiful home." As I stepped away from the bookcase, I hoped honesty would be the best policy. "My side business is collecting antiques, so I'm especially impressed with the quality of the pieces you have. And I love that painting of you in the living room," I said, folding my arms across my chest to hide the phone beneath my left hand. "And when did you get to meet George Bush?"

I knew I was blabbing, but I hoped that by focusing on what he loved best, himself, it might throw him off. The slow smile that spread across his face, though, wasn't comforting.

"I was at the White House just before he left office in 2009," he said, stepping into the room.

"Alex must have been thrilled."

"She wasn't with me," he said with a probing look. "You didn't always travel with Graham, did you?"

His eyes remained trained on me, and I thought perhaps he was challenging me. It made me nervous, but there wasn't much I could do but attempt to bluff my way out of this.

"No. Of course not." I glanced around and stepped away from him. "But you've certainly had an illustrious career," I said, gesturing to the photos and mementoes. "And this room is so…"

The deep resonance of the grandfather clock chiming the hour camouflaged the moment my breath caught, cutting my sentence short. I had just turned to face a large, framed oil painting which took up most of the wall directly across from the desk. The painting was of a sprawling gothic-looking building with the letter E emblazoned in gold on a huge purple banner hanging off the second-story balcony. This time it was the letter that was encircled by a serpent. A curved stone wall in the foreground identified the building as the University of London.

My expression must have prompted Clements to turn toward his treasure. I say treasure because he obviously loved it; it was something he would see every time he sat at the desk.

"You like it?" he purred.

I inhaled and bit my lip, trying valiantly to control my breathing. I dropped my phone back into my purse while he faced the other way.

"I… uh… it's striking." I took a breath. "Um… but you didn't attend the University of London, did you?"

He laughed lightly. "Oh, no. Harvard. My ancestors are from the UK, though." He tilted his head to look down at me. "Aren't we all from somewhere else?"

"I suppose. What does the E stand for?" I asked, purposely moving closer to gesture to the banner.

He laughed again. "It stands for Elektro—part of Swiss Electric, a giant energy company headquartered in Switzerland. I'm a major stockholder."

He came up behind me, sending a creepy-crawly feeling down my spine. I moved a step to the side.

"If the company is in Switzerland, though, why would the company logo be painted into a banner at the University of London?"

"A friend from college had the painting commissioned. He used to accuse me of trying to take over the world and gave it to me as a joke."

I felt he'd practiced that answer a hundred times. And it seemed ridiculous, considering what I knew. Well, other than the part about taking over the world.

Our eyes locked momentarily as both of us stood stock-still. The undercurrent of his expression left me breathless; there was no mirth in his dark eyes. In fact, it felt as if there was no life in them, either. They were just two black orbs set in a face that presently looked as frightening as a theatrical mask from a Greek tragedy.

I felt sweat develop under my armpits. My ruse was fraying around the edges, and I was entering dangerous waters.

"There you are!"

Blair's voice cut through the tension, and Clements and I moved apart. She came up beside me.

I took a gulp of air before saying, "Yes, the senator was nice enough to let me borrow one of Alex's blouses," I said with the most diplomatic smile I could muster, gesturing to the blouse. "And then I took a self-guided tour of the house. Listen," I said, putting a hand on Blair's forearm, "I'm starving. I think I'll go down and get a burger. Want anything?"

She peered at me as if trying to read my thoughts, but then just smiled. "No. I'll be fine. You go ahead."

I didn't dare look at Clements before departing. I wasn't sure what I'd see, so I just left. Bursting through the French doors on the upper deck, I exhaled and then refilled my lungs with the warm afternoon air. I hadn't even realized I'd been holding my breath. But it felt good to be outside.

CHAPTER TWENTY-FIVE

"You okay?" a voice said.

It was one of the men who had come to my aid earlier.

"Yes. I'm all cleaned up, and I'm ready to eat," I said with a smile.

"Good to know," he responded. "The burgers are amazing."

I left him and descended the stairs, heading straight for the outdoor kitchen. I didn't really feel like eating a juicy hamburger right then and detoured to the bar. This time, I got a Diet Pepsi, took a big swig, and turned, bumping into Mae Beth, spilling most of the Pepsi down the front of my borrowed blouse.

"Oh, Julia, I'm sorry," she said. She reached out a hand with a napkin and attempted to blot the mess, but I stopped her.

"Don't worry. It's my second mess of the day," I said with a strained chuckle. "It's not even my blouse this time."

"You okay? You seem a little rattled?"

I nodded toward a garden bench. "Can we sit down?"

We sat under the spreading branches of a large pine tree, and I relaxed back against the bench.

"Sorry," I said. "I had an accident up on the deck earlier and went inside to change." I looked down at the animal print blouse. "This is one of Alex's old blouses."

"It suits you," she said. "Even saturated in Pepsi." She smiled.

My gaze wandered across the yard, taking in the mixture of faces.

"Walter knows a lot of important people, doesn't he?"

She followed my gaze. "Of course. He's not only a senator but a very successful businessman."

"Well, this is a lovely spot," I said. "I also took a turn around the house. I mean, the house is really something."

"Yes, it is."

"Have you seen that painting of Clements in the living room?"

She chuckled. "Of course. Everyone's seen it. I think that's the point."

As my breathing slowed down, I relaxed. "Well, I continued my self-tour and ended up in his office. I was looking at some things in his bookcase when he walked in. I'm sure he thought I was snooping."

She leaned in with her shoulder. "Well, weren't you... just a little?"

"Ha," I laughed. "Yes. Well, I guess. I mean, there's a lot of stuff to look at. He's met a ton of important people and won more awards than Meryl Streep."

I wasn't about to admit to the real snooping I was doing. But I hoped that Mae Beth might just mention the situation to Clements and portray my interest in his bookcase as just that: interest.

"Yes, he can't get enough of himself," she said with a chuckle. "But although he's his number one fan, he is a good senator."

"I suppose," I said with little conviction. I took another gulp of Pepsi, enjoying the cold fizz as it went down my throat.

"Hey, the Republicans have done a lot for the state," she said.

"Well, he sure has a lot of framed awards and certificates to prove it," I said. "A bunch of mementoes, too. I suppose when you're a politician, people give you a lot of interesting things. In fact, he's got a crazy-looking box with a snake carved around it. I'm not terribly fond of snakes."

Mae Beth didn't take my bait, and instead quietly sipped her wine. I tried a different tack.

"I didn't know you knew Tom Bateman so well. I saw you talking to him earlier. He's not a popular resident on the island, you know."

"Oh, he's not bad. Another one who probably spends a little too much time looking at himself in the mirror, but he's donated a lot to charity. He and I sit on the ballet board together."

"Really? So he's into the arts."

She smiled. "I wouldn't say that exactly. I think it's a board he believes he *should* be on. From what I can tell, he knows nothing about ballet. But frankly, if he writes us a big check every year, the rest of us can take care of the important business."

"Can I ask you a question, Mae Beth?"

Her green eyes lit up. "Of course. Anything."

"Do you trust these guys?"

She tilted her head. "Who do you mean?"

Blair and Clements had emerged from the house and stood together on the upper deck. A gray-haired man in an expensive cut of clothes leaned in close to Tom Bateman, while several more conclaves of heavy hitters seemed to share secrets all their own.

"All of them," I said, nodding toward the crowd. "I mean, I trust Graham mostly. I don't think he'd do anything illegal. But what about the others? These are all powerful, ruthless men who, like most four-year-olds want what they want and don't care how they get it."

She chuckled softly. "And that's why politics would eat you alive."

"I don't understand."

"It's a cutthroat business. Maybe as cutthroat as it comes. There is no middle ground. Only winners and losers. And, no, I probably don't trust anyone but myself in the long run. But why do you ask? Why this sudden sense of cynicism?"

I heaved a sigh. "It's just that one of the most gentle, intelligent, and kind human beings was murdered because he had something someone else wanted. Something that apparently could embarrass, maybe even be career-ending for someone. But not something worth killing over."

Her eyes opened wide. "And you think someone here might be the killer? Or at least someone in my political circle?"

I leaned back against the seat again. "I don't know. All I know is that my mother taught me to believe there are no coincidences. And yet, it seems as if I keep running into people who may be connected to my uncle's murder in ways they shouldn't be." I turned to her. "You get a kick out of all of this, though, don't you? I mean, all the hobnobbing and political theater."

She leaned back and gazed out at the yard. "I guess I do. I grew up with it, you know. My father owned Alleghany Pharmaceuticals."

"No kidding?" I said, my eyebrows reaching to my hairline. "I didn't know."

"I don't make a big thing of it, although I don't hide it. Anyway, my dad was quite the mover and shaker in politics. He funded some of the biggest political races *and* some of the most controversial political bills in Kentucky. I'm an only child, and I grew up not only sitting in on discussions about political issues but also attending countless teas, luncheons, and fundraisers with either my mom or my dad. I guess it was natural for me to follow in my father's footsteps."

"I admire you," I said. "Besides being a kick ass legal mind, you're a kick ass political operative. What I don't get is how charming you can be. You seem to turn the political crap on and off whenever you want."

Her green eyes sparkled with mirth. "It's a gift. But when you're the only child of a wealthy, hard-nosed capitalist, you must be light on your feet because one moment you're swinging with the big boys, and the next you're persuading a wealthy old woman to invest in a candidate she's never heard of based on the strength of your personality."

I shook my head. "And I just like you because you have a wicked sense of humor."

"Oh, Julia," she said, smiling. "You are a treasure. I have no doubt that Graham sometimes wonders if he made the right choice when he left you behind. You'd be an asset to anyone." She leaned a shoulder into mine. "But you're probably better off where you are. In the world I live in, you need more than a wicked sense of humor to thrive, or even to survive."

Another woman approached and tapped Mae Beth on the shoulder. She excused herself, and the two moved off to the bar. It was nice sitting alone for the moment and to allow my nerves to unwind. The last few days had felt like a road race, and I ruminated for a moment on how difficult it was becoming to identify Carter's killer. There were so many possibilities. And unlike other investigations, this one seemed to have more moving parts, making it hard to focus on one person or one thing.

There was the key, the box, the secret society, the unidentified boat owner, the guy Minnie had clamped onto, the guy with the sideburns, the kid who had delivered the candy, and the mystery man who had set the fire at the Inn and attacked me. *Who was Mr. Clavis, after all?* I felt the box I'd seen in Clements' study had to be the one Ben was looking for. I only had to show him the picture.

Laughter interrupted my thoughts, and I turned to find two young men by the pool yukking it up as they ogled a very attractive woman who stood nearby. Both men wore jeans and t-shirts with artwork splashed across the front. The guy with stringy dark hair had a ring of keys dangling from his belt, like a maintenance man would, while the other guy, who was decent looking, had the tattoo of a skull on his neck and silver rings across all four fingers of his right hand. The men had to be in their thirties in a crowd of seasoned professional businesspeople and politicians, making their demeanor too casual and their behavior crass for this group. It made me wonder why they were there.

My stomach rumbled, and the alluring aroma of the barbecue enticed me to get up and make a beeline for the food table. I put my drink down, grabbed a plate, and built myself a burger. Add a little potato salad and a pickle on the side, and I was ready to dig in.

I was just about to return to the bench when a familiar voice behind me said, "Dude, I'm outta here."

I whirled around and smashed into the young man with the rings and tattoos who had been by the pool. Once again, my food hit the deck, and I splashed my Chardonnay all over Alex's animal print tunic.

"Oh, damn!" I muttered.

"Hey, man, sorry," he said.

My muscles tensed at the sound of his gravelly voice. We both bent down to retrieve my plate. I quickly grabbed my burger, onion, and lettuce while he scooped the potato salad back onto the plate.

"I'm sorry," I said.

"Shit happens," he replied.

He reached over to grab the pickle, and I inhaled quickly at the sight of a tattooed turtle on the back of his hand.

We straightened up. I paused, staring at him. The voice. The tattoo. This was the man who had attacked me in my apartment—the first time, when Ben had left the back door unlocked.

He slowly handed me the plate as his eyes locked on mine. The wolfish expression in those eyes made me think of Little Red Riding Hood, and I was the grandmother who was about to be eaten.

"There you go," he said. "Be more careful next time."

"Thank you," I said, short of breath.

He wheeled away with his friend, leaving me rooted to the spot. I couldn't take my eyes off him as he sauntered back to the food table.

"Julia, you okay?"

It was Blair, bringing me out of my petrified state. I grabbed her arm to steady myself.

"Julia, seriously, are you okay? Come and sit down."

She guided me back to the bench, my limbs moving like a robot.

"Here, let me take care of this." She took the plate of food and threw it into a nearby trash can, grabbed a couple of napkins from the table and came back to wipe me down. "What happened? I got here just as you were picking stuff up from the ground. Did that guy hurt you?"

I shook my head, but still couldn't get a word out. My hands were trembling, and she placed her hand over mine to calm me down.

"I bumped into him," I finally said.

"So?" she said. "You do that all the time. Why are you upset?"

I took a deep breath. "Because he's the guy who attacked me in my apartment. Not Clavis. The first one. Why is he here at Clements' party?"

Blair shifted her gaze to the two men who had returned to the pool with their food. "Should we do anything?" she asked.

"Not here. I don't want to make a scene."

"Why are you sure it's him?"

"He has a distinctive voice. Plus, he has a turtle tattooed on the back of his hand."

"Shit," she said, sitting next to me. "We should still tell the police."

"Yes, but not now. This is Clements' home. It would end up in the newspapers. And it would alert whoever is behind this."

As I eyed him, he seemed to say goodbye to his friends and put his empty glass on a nearby table. Just then, Mae Beth startled me.

"Julia, you look pale. Are you okay?"

"I'm fine," I said, standing up. "Mae Beth, who is that blond guy in the long-sleeved black t-shirt over by the pool?"

"Oh, that's Spike Russo. A rather distasteful young man. Why?"

Russo turned toward us and glared at me as he made his way toward a side gate.

"Remember when I said someone had killed Carter because they thought he had something they wanted? Well, Spike Russo attacked me in my home because he thought Carter had given that something to me."

"Wait a minute, Julia," Mae Beth countered. "Spike is a brat and probably a bit of a thug. But he wouldn't attack you. I mean, why would he?"

"We need to go," Blair said, looping her hand through my elbow. "I'm sorry, Mae Beth, but it's been a long day."

"Um, sure. No problem. Listen, Julia, I'm sure you're wrong about Spike. He's just a spoiled rich kid."

"I hope so. But wasn't his father arrested for money laundering or something?"

"Well, yes, but how would Spike or his father be connected to the death of your family friend?"

Blair had grasped onto my arm now and was pulling me toward the same gate. I stopped and turned back to Mae Beth.

"Through a ruthless secret society that I intend to make public," I said, the anger flaring inside me.

"Oh, Julia," Blair laughed. "What are you talking about? C'mon, we need to go," she said, yanking me to get my attention. "Let's get you home. Mae Beth," Blair said before we turned away. "I hope we can depend on your discretion. Julia is upset right now. Death of her friend, and all."

"Of course," she said. "Julia, I'll call you, and we'll do lunch."

Blair guided me out the gate to the street, and we climbed the hill to get her car. Just as the car was brought up by the attendant, a green Camaro sped past.

"Oh, shit!" I exclaimed. "That was Spike Russo."

"Okay," Blair said, getting into the car. "He drives a green Camaro. So what?"

Once inside, I said, "I forgot all about it, but when Carter came to my door that day, he was looking back at the street just as a green Camaro sped away. Then he stepped inside and collapsed."

"So you think Spike Russo killed Carter?"

"I don't know. Maybe. Or maybe he was following Carter. Because the first words out of Carter's mouth were, 'Julia, someone's following...' and then he collapsed. I think he was going to say that someone was following him. I must've blanked it out because the next thing he said was that someone killed him, and that Ben should look for the casket. And then, of course, he died. But the person following him was Spike Russo."

Blair started the car. "Well, now you'll have two things to tell Detective Abrams."

I turned to her. "I'm sorry about back there."

"No need to apologize," Blair said as she pulled away from the curb.

"But I shouldn't have said so much in front of Mae Beth. It just made me so angry to see Russo so cavalier."

She snuck a glance at me while she drove. "You have a perfect right to be pissed off. It looks like if he didn't kill Carter, someone he knows did, and then that someone got *him* to break into your apartment to look for the key. But tipping your hand to people, even if they're friends, isn't a good idea. As soon as we get back, we're calling the police about Russo."

"I agree. At least they might take him in for questioning." I pulled out my phone. "I want to tell Ben." I dialed his number, but it went to voicemail, so I left him a message to call me. "I wonder where the heck he is."

"Sounds like Ben is being Ben. I wonder sometimes if we even share the same goals," Blair said.

"What do you mean?"

She hunched her shoulders. "I just sometimes think he's more interested in finding the key and the box."

I nearly jumped out of my seat. "The box! I forgot to tell you. I think I found it."

CHAPTER TWENTY-SIX

On the way back to the Inn, I described the intricately carved box to Blair and showed her the picture while we waited for a light to change. We called Doe and Rudy and asked them to meet us at the Inn. Then I called Detective Abrams to tell him about Spike Russo.

When we returned to the Inn, Jake was in our library. Blair excused herself to go get April while I talked with Jake.

"Hey," I said.

His eyes lit up, and he put down the book he was reading. I glanced down and saw that he'd been glancing through *Crime and Punishment*.

"Dostoevsky," I said. "A little light reading?"

He smiled. "Oh, I've read it several times. I'm a big fan. Did you know that in 1956, Russia printed a postage stamp with Dostoevsky's face on it? Only 1,000 were printed, and a friend of mine has one." His eyebrows lifted in a mock salute.

"Well, that has to be worth something."

"No kidding," he said.

"How's your niece?" I asked.

"Doing well. She's awake and smiling."

"That's wonderful."

"It's a great relief. And my brother is trying to talk me into staying awhile."

"Really? That would be nice," I said, blushing.

"Would it?" he asked. "Does that mean I'd get to see more of you?"

My face grew even warmer. "Maybe," I said with a coquettish smile.

"Then I'll stick around a bit. Hey, listen, what's going on with your investigation?"

I told him about running into Spike Russo and finding the box and painting. He sat forward with his elbows on his knees.

"Wow, you had a productive afternoon. You feel okay about running into the guy who attacked you?"

I crossed my arms as if to hug myself. "Not really. But I'm glad to know who it was. Trouble is, now he knows I know."

"Which means you might not be safe again."

"Right. I've asked my friends to come over so we can talk about it."

He zeroed in on me. "Want me to join you?"

"Would you? I mean, I don't want to get you all wrapped up in my troubles."

"I'm happy to help. Maybe an unbiased ear will help. And, frankly, I'll sleep by your door tonight just in case. I'd like to know that you're safe."

I laughed. "You don't have to do that. I have a guest bedroom."

His eyes lit up again. "Fine. I'll just move downstairs." He leaned into me. "You're not worried about rumors?"

"Not in the least."

"What does your brother say about all of this?"

"I don't know. He's not returning my calls or texts. I'm sure he's hunting down clues somewhere. Listen, the girls will be here in about a half hour. I'll meet you in my apartment then."

We split up, and I went to the apartment. I let the dogs out and was about to change my top when my back door opened. Mickey and Minnie left me to race down the hallway, barking all the way. A giant black-and-white harlequin Great Dane named Lucy lumbered through the door, followed by Angela. The Dachshunds went into a frenzy, bouncing around Lucy's feet. As big as she was, she bristled with enthusiasm and the three dogs nearly knocked me over as they ran into the living room.

I reached out for Angela and pulled her into a hug. "What are you doing here?"

"Our case went to the jury today," she said, as we walked into the living room with my arm around her. "I had some time and wanted to come over. This is for you."

She handed me a card and a bouquet of roses.

"Thank you," I said, giving her another hug.

"I tried calling Uncle Ben, but no answer," she said. "How are you doing?"

We went into the kitchen, and I found a vase to hold the flowers.

"Let me do that," she said, taking the vase from me.

While I watched, she filled it with water and unwrapped the flowers.

Graham and I had adopted Angela from China when she was just a baby. She was about the same height as me, but slender. She had pushed her long black hair up carelessly in the back and secured it with a big barrette and wore jeans and a t-shirt instead of her usual corporate navy-blue skirt and blazer. I purposely hadn't told Angela about the latest break-in since she was so busy, but figured she'd probably heard about it from Sean.

"Well, now that you're here, I'm better. You and this big lug of a dog," I said, reaching down to give Lucy a hug. Lucy slobbered all over my arm while the doxies bobbed around her feet.

Angela put the flowers on the counter and glanced around the room. "I thought Uncle Ben would be here."

"He's staying at the Sheraton. But I can't get hold of him, either."

She smiled. "That's so him. Sean said he's staying there because someone broke into your apartment, and he felt he was putting you in danger. Sean assured me you were okay, or I would have been over here in a flash."

"Well, not only that, but someone else set fire to our dock last night just to get everyone outside so they could search my apartment for this dumb key. It's been a busy few days."

She shook her head. "I worry about you, mom. This is getting dangerous. Maybe you should hire someone to stay with you."

My eyes brightened. "Funny you should say that. Do you remember me telling you about a guy named Jake that I met on our trip to Wisconsin?"

"He owned that little store, right?" When I nodded, she said, "And he loved architecture and seemed really smart, you said."

"Yes. Well, he's here. In fact, he saved me from the second thug who had me by the throat."

Her eyes opened wide. "Well, isn't that fortuitous?"

"Not really. His brother lives in the area, and his niece was in a terrible accident. He came out to be with his family and checked into the Inn yesterday afternoon. I didn't even know he was here until he threw the guy to the ground."

"Sounds very chivalrous," she said, giving me a little wink.

I'm sure I blushed. "Well, David and I broke up."

The light in her eyes dulled. "I know, Mom. Sean mentioned something about that. I'm so sorry."

"Me, too. He just can't accept my getting involved in these investigations."

"Well, you know…" she began. "You really shouldn't be involved. If you'll remember, it was only last year that Lucy saved you from some guy who had broken into your bedroom."

I glanced over to where Lucy had sprawled in front of the fireplace with the wiener dogs pulling on her ears.

"I know. I keep getting saved by dogs or handsome men."

"Listen, I can't stay long," she said. "I have a bunch of research to do on a new case I just pulled. Do you know when there will be a service for Uncle Carter?"

"No. His daughter is supposed to fly in soon, though. I'm sure we'll discuss it."

"Okay, I want to help. I can't stop thinking about him. Sean has shared with me everything Uncle Ben told him about the secret society and the reason they think someone killed Carter. It still feels so random. I mean, what threat could someone like Carter have been to anyone?"

I went to the refrigerator and pulled out a bottle of Diet Pepsi. "I don't know, other than I know he was helping Ben do some research. Then, there's this business about the key itself."

"Well, that's what I mean, though," she said, climbing onto one of the bar stools. "Why would they kill him before they got the key? It doesn't make sense. Does Uncle Ben know what Carter's research uncovered? Maybe Carter learned something that put him in danger."

"First, can I get you a Pepsi or some iced tea?"

"No, I'm good. Like I said, I can't stay long. I'm just bummed Uncle Ben isn't here. I really wanted to talk to him about all of this."

"He'll probably call later tonight. Anyway, in answer to your question, no, Ben doesn't have Carter's research. Carter's house was ransacked, and Ben thinks his notes were stolen."

Lucy, who stood almost as tall as the counter, came over and planted herself next to Angela, her harlequin marked head high enough to allow her to gaze over the counter. The Dachshunds milled around her feet again, trying to get her attention.

"I wish you'd called me when that guy broke into your apartment."

"I didn't want to worry you. And I knew Sean would tell you. But unfortunately, I ran into him at the party I just came from."

Her eyes popped open. "You did?"

"Yes. I recognized his voice and a tattoo he has on the back of his hand. It was none other than Spike Russo." I took a big chug of Pepsi and sat in a chair at the table.

She slid off the bar stool and joined me. Lucy pushed her nose under my elbow and poked her enormous head through my arm so that I could pet her.

"That little twit. And you've already told Sean?"

"Yes. I called him when we were on our way home."

She leaned back in her chair and released a sigh. "Well, I have something to tell you, and it will make it even more interesting. After I talked to you, I did some research on Dave Russo his dad. And since you're such a believer in 'there are no coincidences,' here's a big coincidence for you."

I swallowed quickly. "What?"

"The name Tom Bateman rang a bell when you mentioned it the other day. I went back through all my notes on the cases against both Russo and his son, Spike. I don't know if this means anything, but Dave Russo's first wife was Trina Russo... now Trina Bateman."

"Really? And..."

"And yes... Trina Bateman is Spike Russo's mother."

"Oh my God! Aria told us that Tom Bateman married Trina as a divorcee. But Aria must have given us her maiden name, Franklin. You'll tell Detective... uh, Sean, won't you?"

"Already did."

"It feels like that changes a lot," I said. "Doe and I are supposed to go to Trina Bateman's tomorrow for a PEO meeting. It's a philanthropic group Doe used to belong to, and we're pretending that I might want to join just so we can get into her house."

"To snoop around," she said cynically.

"Well, yes. To see if there's anything there that would show that her husband, Tom, is a member of that Electi group? I mean, Walter Clements has a giant painting on his wall of the University of London with a big E painted onto a banner."

"And you think that stands for The Electi?"

"Don't you?"

She shrugged. "Could be. You know, Mom, you shouldn't be doing all of this. Uncle Ben has already been arrested. Frankly, if you weren't dating David, and weren't my mother, I think Sean would have arrested you by now for interfering."

My chin came up. "But what have I actually done? I've been attacked in my home. Twice. Gone to a Republican fundraising dinner. Attended a barbecue at the home of a prominent state senator. And tomorrow I'll be discussing a national philanthropic group with a group of older women. Tell me what about any of that is interfering in the police investigation?"

Voices interrupted us. Mickey and Minnie raced down the hallway a second time, and a moment later Doe's voice rang out, "Hello wieners!" I got up and met Doe as she appeared with two bottles of wine in her hands.

"I brought the wine," she announced.

"And I brought jalapeno hushpuppies and jerk chicken skewers from Marjorie's," Rudy said, coming in behind her, carrying a couple of bags from the popular Seattle restaurant. "Hello, Angie," she said. "How many corporate influencers have you put behind bars this week?"

Angela smiled. "Not as many as I'd like."

"Here, let me help," I said, taking the bags from Rudy.

Rudy, Doe, and I crowded into my little kitchen. I opened a drawer and pulled out a stack of paper plates and napkins while they put everything on the counter.

"Has Lucy eaten?" I asked my daughter.

Lucy had her nose in the air as food came out of the bags.

"No. But I've got to get going, anyway."

"Don't leave on our account," Doe said. "We rarely get to see you."

Angela smiled. "Thanks. But I have a ton of work at home."

"You working on that case against Puget Chemicals?" Rudy asked.

Angela rolled her eyes. "Yeah. It's a big one. Just went to the jury today."

"No kidding," Rudy said. "I've been following it in the news. They have a lot to explain when they're caught red-handed dumping chemical waste onto tribal lands."

"And with any luck, they'll pay through the nose," Angela said.

She came around the end of the counter and gave me a hug. "Be careful, Mom. And tell Uncle Ben to call me."

"I will. I'll call you tomorrow."

She and Lucy left, while Rudy and Doe arranged the food and wine on the counter. There was a quick rap on the door and then April, Blair, and Jake sauntered in from the Inn side. Seeing Jake, Rudy lifted her eyebrows at me and then pulled me to the side.

"Are you sure you want him in on these discussions?"

"Why shouldn't he be? He saved me from that guy, Clavis, and will stay in my guest room to give me some protection."

She shrugged. "Okay. I just think the fewer people involved in this, the better."

"I understand. But we can trust him."

"What about David? How's he going to feel having this guy staying with you?"

My eyes shifted to where Jake was leaning over to greet the dogs. "I haven't heard from David. I assume we are no longer an item."

She put a hand on my shoulder. "Okay. But don't throw a good thing away just because a shiny new bauble showed up."

"Got it." I was just about to tell people to eat when my phone jingled. It was Detective Abrams again. "What is it, detective?"

Everyone turned their attention toward me as I put my phone on speaker mode.

"We put a rush on the cigarette butt that kid found at the end of your dock to see if it had any traceable DNA. It belongs to Spike Russo. We're on our way to bring him in for questioning."

I don't know what I expected to feel. Happy? Relieved? Triumphant? All I knew was that I was glad we had at least made some headway and identified someone in this case.

"Thank you, detective," I said with relief.

I hung up and April put her arms around me and gave me a hug.

"I'm glad," she said. "One down."

I eyed Jake over her shoulder. He was sitting at the end of the sofa and gave me a quick nod.

"Okay," I said. "Everyone, get some food and wine, and we'll fill you in on the rest of what happened today."

÷

We spent the rest of the evening going over what I'd learned at Clements' house, namely that he didn't own the boat we were looking for but did have the box Ben was searching for. I also described the painting of the University of London and the banner with the initial E. And I told them about my encounter with Spike Russo.

"Wow," Rudy said. "That seems to nail Spike Russo and Clements."

"But didn't Ben say that one of the guys he was researching went to the University of London?" April asked, biting into a hush puppy.

"Not exactly," Blair said. "He said that a group of upper-class twits created The Electi *at* the University of London. Then the university disbanded them."

"That's right," April said.

"Wait a minute," Rudy interrupted us. "Aria said that Robert Bateman, son of Alistair Bateman, also attended the University of London."

I nodded. "You're right. It was obviously a hotbed for these guys. Listen, Angela had a bit of a bombshell to report. Turns out that Trina Bateman used to be married to Dave Russo."

"Let me guess," Rudy said. "Trina is Spike Russo's mother."

"Bingo," I replied.

"Aria told us that Tom Bateman had married a divorcee."

"The plot thickens, as they say," Doe said.

"Yes," Rudy agreed. "So far, we've established that Bateman and Clements are business partners, and we connected Bateman and Russo through Trina Bateman and her son Spike. And just happens to be the guy who broke into the Inn demanding that Julia turn over the key."

"And I forgot all about this until today, but he was following Carter on the day Carter came to the Inn."

I explained what Carter had said and about Russo's green Camaro.

"I guess this proves, at least to us, that there's no way these people aren't connected to Carter's death," Blair said.

"Okay, tell us how you did with Clements," Rudy said to Blair.

Blair took up the rest of the story and described how Clements brought up a club he thought she might like to join and invited her to dinner with two other members the following Wednesday night.

"Did he mention who that would be?" Rudy asked.

"No. But I eased into the discussion after Julia left the room by asking him about the university painting."

"Did he tell you the E stood for a big tech company in Switzerland? That's what he told me."

"No. But then, I didn't ask. I focused on the motto."

"What's the motto?" Jake asked, wiping his hands on a napkin.

"Limits don't exist," Blair replied.

Jake's eyebrows arched. "Really? Sounds like the British monarchy."

"What do you mean?" Blair asked.

"Their motto is… God and my right shall defend me."

"In other words, it's all about them," she said.

He shrugged. "They're the monarchy. They're above it all."

"Just like The Electi," I added. "That's the point. They think they're destined to rule the world."

Jake got up to refill his wineglass. "Well, mottos have a specific purpose. They're designed to motivate a group of like-minded people. But not necessarily to rule the world."

"Like a club," Blair said.

"A club. Sports teams. Even countries," Jake said. "They originally related mottos to rank and a family's pedigree. And in war, mottos were emblazoned on the shield above or below the family crest."

"To act as an inspiration going into battle," Doe said.

"Right."

"And that's obviously what this motto does," I added. "To inspire them in their quest for power."

"And the motto implies that basically they have a right to it all," April said.

"Whatever 'all' is," Rudy added.

I looked over at Blair. "How do you feel about going to this dinner on Wednesday night?"

She was sitting in my wingback chair with her legs crossed at the ankles. "Fine, I guess. I mean, nothing's going to happen in a public place like a restaurant."

"Are you sure you'll be going to a restaurant?" Rudy asked.

"He didn't say. He just said dinner."

"I bet it won't be at a restaurant," Rudy said. "Not for something so secretive. I'll lay odds it will be at someone's home."

"But whose?" April asked.

"I don't know," Blair replied. "He said he'd call me on Tuesday."

"What did he say about this club?" Jake asked. "Did he give you any details?"

She thought for a moment. "We were talking about the motto and how he finds it inspiring. He mentioned he grew up in an environment where a lot was expected of him. Not just good grades. His father had insisted he run for student body president in high school and in college. He lost the campaign in high school, something his father never let him forget. Instead, he became president of the Key Club and Future Business Leaders of America instead."

"And then he won student body president in college," April speculated.

"Actually, at Harvard. But he didn't stop there. He became president of the Porcellian Club at Harvard. He talked about how elite it is and that they don't allow nonmembers beyond the bike room."

"Jeez, these people are arrogant," Doe said.

"Tom Bateman went to Harvard, too," I said.

"Yeah, I wonder if he belonged to this Porcellian Club," April said.

"Well, Clements seemed very proud of the fact that Teddy Roosevelt and the Winklevoss twins had been members."

"The internet boy wonders," Jake said with a smirk.

"Didn't they sue Mark Zuckerberg over Facebook?" Doe said.

"Yes. But they lost," Jake said. "Never fear, though. They still became bitcoin billionaires."

"Of course, they did," I murmured. "What else did Clements say?"

"He talked about the concept of elitism. I mean, I felt like he was quoting Wikipedia or something the way he rattled off his belief system. According to him, people who come from high-value backgrounds…"

"Like him," Rudy muttered.

"Exactly, like him. He said these people have an intrinsic quality that makes them constructive, rather than destructive to society." She shook her head. "Seriously. It was like a recitation from a brochure. He said that because of that, they deserve positions of influence and power more than the rest of us."

"God, that had to be difficult to listen to," Rudy quipped.

"How did you convince him you should be a candidate for his club?" Jake asked.

Jake didn't know Blair and didn't know what her secret weapons were.

She smiled seductively. "I challenged him to a duel."

"What?" April asked.

"He bragged that the members of the Porcellian Club are smarter, cleverer, and more accomplished than others. Since we had just come from his living room where there is an entire wall of framed photographs, awards, and bills he's signed into law in the state senate…"

"Yes, I saw that wall. There had to be at least thirty perfectly organized frames up there."

"Actually, thirty-three," she said.

"And that's what you challenged him to?" Rudy asked.

"A little more complicated than that. I asked him what percentage of the frames on the wall had over two people in them?"

Jake laughed. "You've got to be kidding? Did you know the answer?"

"Of course. I studied the wall because I was mapping who his friends were."

"What did he say?"

She grinned. "He had no idea. So I gave him the answer, and then we returned to the living room, where he confirmed it."

"Remind me never to play poker with you," Jake said with a grin.

"At that point," she continued. "I shyly told him I'd always been smart but didn't get tested until a guy I was dating in college challenged my IQ. And then he stopped dating me when it turned out I was much smarter than he was. Clements got a kick out of that and immediately said there were some people he wanted me to meet."

"How did you pass the influence test, though?" Rudy asked.

"That was easy. One picture on his wall is of him with the CEO of the Geodyne Corporation."

"But wait," I said. "You told us your ex-husband is the CEO."

She shrugged. "Exactly."

Rudy nearly choked. "You mean he has a picture on his wall of him and your ex-husband?" When Blair nodded, Rudy shook her head and said, "Damn, you can't make this stuff up. By the way, I forgot to mention that I did some research on that envelope. You know the one from London? It belongs to an old church building that is now owned by a corporation called Hours of Darkness."

"That's a weird name," Doe said.

Rudy shrugged. "Yeah, it is. I couldn't find out much about it. And what little I did made me think it's a shell corporation."

"Meaning it's a sham for something else," I said.

"Right. It could just be a vehicle through which someone launders money. Or it could be the London version of The Electi for all I know."

"Hours of Darkness," Blair mused. "Sounds a lot like Brothers of the Night."

Rudy nodded. "You're right. It does. But we'd need a lot more time to pin down what it might have to do with Carter's death."

"Where does all of this leave us?" Doe asked.

"I don't know," I said. "I wish I could talk with Ben."

"Why don't we go see him at the hotel tomorrow morning?" Blair said. "We can drag him out of bed."

I laughed. "Not the best way to get on his good side," I said. "He's just being Ben. I'll hear from him soon."

"Don't forget our meeting at Trina Bateman's tomorrow," Doe said.

"Do you think we should still go? Especially now that her son is being picked up by the police?"

"We should if we don't want them to know what we know," she said.

"Okay, but it will take every ounce of restraint I have not to clock her for what her son did to me."

"We can't let on that we know anything about him," Doe warned.

I blew out a breath. "I know. Okay, maybe we'll learn something valuable."

"That's the plan. Okay, I've got to run," she said. "I have another early meeting tomorrow."

"And she's my ride," Rudy added.

The two of them left while the rest of us began cleaning up.

"If you need me for anything tomorrow," Jake said, taking his plate to the kitchen. "Remember that I promised to be your knight in shining armor for the duration of this."

That stopped everyone in their tracks. Blair and April turned to me. I blushed and got very busy throwing things in the trash.

CHAPTER TWENTY-SEVEN

Doe and I were on our way to the Bateman home when I finally received a text from Ben. All it said was:

Onto something important. I'll be in touch soon.

I sighed loudly.

"What was that?" Doe asked, nodding toward my phone.

"Ben. There's nothing to report yet on his end. He's still following up on something. I'm just glad he finally got back to me. You know, he's so damned stubborn, just like my mother. And he always feels he has to go it alone. You'd never know the rest of us were even involved."

She smiled. "You carry some of that stubbornness, too, you know."

I twisted my mouth into a grimace. "Maybe."

"I hear Jake stayed in your guest room last night," she said, changing the subject. "Anything you want to tell me?"

I shifted in the seat. "It's not what you think. There's some flirting going on, but I still don't know how I feel about what's happening with David. I'm invested in that relationship… in him… but he's ignoring me right now," I said, my voice catching. I took a deep breath. "Anyway, Jake offered to camp out in my guest room as protection. He's a friend helping a friend, that's all."

"Okay," she said. "I don't want you to get hurt."

"Thanks. I still have hope David and I can salvage things."

It was just after one o'clock when we pulled down the long, winding drive to Trina Bateman's home. The house was an ultra-modern cube style architecture that looked like someone had stacked four or five huge white stucco blocks in a random configuration, with one block hanging over the water. To me, it felt more like a stucco prison rather than a comfortable home.

Doe pulled up behind someone's Mercedes. A crisp breeze rustled the pines that surrounded the house but did nothing for the knots in my stomach. Before Doe could get her door open, I stopped her with a hand on her arm.

"Wait a minute, Doe," I said. "Do you think this is a good idea? I mean, now that we know Trina is Spike Russo's mother, the likelihood she's involved, or at least is aware of what is going on, is high, don't you think? Especially because her son has at least been questioned by the police if not arrested."

She sat back, gazing at the house. A face at the window showed someone had noticed our arrival.

"Maybe. But we can't leave now. Her housekeeper saw us," she said with a nod toward the window. "Besides, there will be other PEO members here who I'm sure aren't involved. If we were going to back out, we should have done it before we got here. We're just trying to see if there is anything in the house that screams Electi. Let's just keep it casual and focused on PEO. I've been here before, so I'll get up to use the restroom. That way I can make a quick check of the ground floor."

"And after that?"

She thought a moment, her eyes shifting to the second floor. "The house is amazing. Since it's built on a cliff, the master bedroom hangs out over the water. Why don't I suggest she take you on a tour after the meeting breaks up? That way, you'll get to check out the second floor."

"Okay. But let's not be here too long." My gaze swept across the two Mercedes and one Lexus in the driveway, along with the BMW coupe in the garage. "I just have a bad feeling about this."

A slender, middle-aged woman in black slacks and a long-sleeved, black blouse answered the door. She led us down a long hallway and through a great room. To the left was the family room with an enormous river rock fireplace. To the right was an open floor plan kitchen with multi-colored modern lights hanging over a marble topped island. The great room opened onto the patio, where we found Trina and three other women at a large, round glass table.

The house sat right on the water with a dock and an expensive ski boat tied up. The patio extended some 100 feet away from the building and past a large pond with lilies floating on the surface. There was also an enormous hot tub that looked large enough to fit the entire cast of Hamilton, and a lap pool, along with two working fountains. The yard ended in a small stand of pine trees, giving them privacy from the neighbors.

Trina's outdoor décor was as minimal as the embellishments to the exterior of the house. There were several giant earthen pots filled with ferns, a few flowerpots, and a rustic potting bench set against the wall of the house, looking out of place in such modern surroundings.

Trina got up when we emerged from the house and gave Doe a brief hug, as did a plump woman wearing a heavy gold neck chain, several gem-encrusted rings, and big diamond stud earrings.

"Let me introduce you, Julia. This is Meghan Reynolds," Trina said, gesturing to her left. "She lives in Bellevue now but has made her home on the island for many years. Her husband is the top plastic surgeon in Seattle."

I smiled, thinking her husband must have used her as his working canvas. Her entire face looked molded out of plastic and then surrounded by cringe-worthy red hair.

I merely smiled and acknowledged the introduction with a nod.

"And this is Jeanne Pepper," Trina said. "She lives on West Mercer Way. Her husband owns Pepper Electric Company, with stores all over the Seattle area."

This was the plump woman who had hugged Doe. I wasn't sure why it was important to know what everyone's husbands did, but I assumed prestige mattered even if they earned it through their spouse.

"I've shopped at your store many times," I said with a smile.

"Nice to meet you, Julia," Jeanne said. "We miss our Doe. Any friend of hers is a friend of ours."

"Thank you."

"And last but not least is Liz Corning," Trina said, nodding toward a petite woman who had to be in her eighties. My eyes skimmed across her jacket with its fine detailing, thinking it was made of Sea Island cotton, the most expensive cotton in the world. Mae Beth had worn a blouse made from it when we'd lunched one day and had waxed eloquently about the rarity and quality of the fabric.

Trina continued. "Liz lives off Island Crest Way at the top of the hill, with a perfect view of the Space Needle."

The older woman leaned forward in her chair and glared at me. My skin tingled as if her milky blue eyes were lasers, leaving blisters on my skin. Then a smile flickered into place, and she reached out a withered hand to clasp mine across the table.

"It's so nice to meet you, Mrs. Applegate," she said in a husky voice. "We're all fans of your husband."

"Ex-husband," I corrected her.

"Of course," she agreed, pulling back her hand.

Doe and I sat next to each other, facing the house.

"Would you like some wine or iced tea?" Trina offered, gesturing to a tray in the middle of the table.

Doe took the wine, and I took an iced tea. After I'd put lemon and sweetener into it, Trina added, "Help yourself to one of Meghan's oatmeal raisin cookies." She pointed to a decorative tin sitting next to the tray.

Since a protein bar had been my main course for lunch, I reached for a cookie. I'm not a snob when it comes to baked goods—okay, maybe I am because of April—but I took a large bite of the cookie, and the dry, chalky taste almost gagged me.

"They're vegan *and* gluten-free," Meghan said with pride. "Pretty good, don't you think?"

The cookie was stuck to the top of my mouth, so that all I could do was give her a closed-mouth smile and a thumbs up. When Trina spoke, I reached for my iced tea to wash it down.

"As I mentioned at lunch, Julia, we're a small club. Only fifteen members here on the island. And of course, Meghan, who lives in Bellevue. But we're always open to new members. Especially those whose hearts are in the right place and who have the time to make a difference in the lives of young women."

Still trying to swallow the cookie, I only managed to nod again. That was enough to keep her going.

"Last year, we gave away $5,000 in scholarships to two young women who will attend Gonzaga this fall," she said.

"One wants to become a doctor and the other hopes to open her own business," Jeanne said proudly.

"I understand you run a business out of your home," Liz Corning said. "Don't you find that intrusive?"

"Um…" I began, but the cookie had gummed up my mouth. I had to swallow again to get rid of it. "Um, no. Not intrusive at all. I run a bed-and-breakfast and sell antiques there, along with a small variety of baked goods. But I also have my own private apartment."

Meghan's eyes lit up. "Oh, maybe I could offer some of my cookies for sale there. I've often thought I'd like to own a bakery."

I put my hand up to say, "Just a moment," and then I took another sip of my iced tea to give myself time to think of a response. After I swallowed, I said, "I'm afraid our business license only allows us to sell things made by my business partner on the premises. Quality control and all."

"Didn't I read that someone was poisoned at your establishment last year?" Liz inquired with a stiff lip. "Speaking of quality control."

This woman didn't like me, although I didn't know why. Trina hadn't rattled off Liz's pedigree because she didn't have to. The Corning name was well known in the Seattle area. Her husband, who had died several years earlier, had owned Corning Lumber & Shipping, which bragged big mills as far south as Oregon and as far north as Bellingham. Rumor had it that Mrs. Corning had stepped in to help her two sons run the company when her husband died. I remembered the picture in Walter Clements' house of him and Jeremiah Corning and thought this was not a woman to trifle with.

I returned her hard stare, hoping I was leaving behind little blisters of my own. "Yes, there was a very unfortunate incident at the Inn about a year ago. One of my best friends was poisoned by a neighbor who, by the way, ran a sex-trafficking ring. My friend got in the way," I said pointedly. "It was one of the most heart-wrenching moments of my life to watch her die right in front of me."

"I was there when it happened." Doe put her hand over mine. "Julia's right. The woman who died was one of the kindest and most generous women I've ever known. But Julia had nothing to do with her death. She did, however, help bring her killer to justice."

I glowed at Doe's praise. But Liz Corning was like the crone witch without her broomstick.

"Still, doesn't make for a good reputation," she said, sitting back in her chair.

"Didn't I read that someone else had died at your inn recently?" Jeanne asked. "A family member or something?"

This was not at all where I wanted the conversation to go—a litany of all the people who might or might not have died at the Inn.

"It was a very close family friend," I said.

"The paper said he was also poisoned," Meghan added with concern.

Damn!

"Yes, but also not by me."

Jeanne leaned in. "Do the police have any leads?"

Maybe the son of your PEO membership chair, I thought to myself.

"Ladies," Trina interrupted us. "This is not what we're here to talk about. We're here to answer questions Julia might have about joining PEO."

I gave Trina a somewhat grateful smile. "Um, thank you, Trina. I think your organization sounds amazing. But I was wondering how you raise money for the scholarships?"

"Excuse me, I need to use the ladies' room," Doe said. "I'll be right back." She got up and disappeared inside.

While Doe was gone, the other women talked about their annual fashion show and silent auction fundraisers. Trina never took her eyes off me, and I wondered if she knew about her son's late-night visit to my apartment. The sweat growing under my arms suggested her gaze was making me nervous, and I rested my forearms on the table in hopes the breeze would help dry me out.

"Perhaps we could hold an event at the Inn," Trina suddenly suggested to the others. Her eyes flashed back to me. "Maybe around Halloween. Don't you use ghosts at the Inn as a marketing ploy?"

A stack of decorative ceramic pots chose that moment to fall off the potting bench, breaking into little pieces on the natural stone pavers that made up the patio. Everyone jumped and looked over at the mess. Well, all except me. I took a breath and pressed my lips together. *Dammit, Elizabeth!*

"Was that one of your ghosts?" Meghan asked with an anxious giggle.

Trina glanced at the pots and then at me, her expression a mixture of suspicion and irritation. Liz Corning just openly stared at me.

"Excuse me a moment," Trina said, dragging her eyes away from me as she got up to go inside.

Trina slipped through the sliding glass door as Liz Corning said, "You are an interesting woman, Mrs. Applegate."

"I will take that as a compliment," I said in a cool tone.

"I guess we'll have to see," she replied. Even though she smiled, the smile didn't reach her eyes.

Without Doe there as my security blanket, I felt I had been dropped into the middle of a viper pit. I inhaled, wondering if it was indeed Elizabeth or perhaps Chloe who had accompanied me to the meeting. It seemed more like a reaction by Chloe and the faint sound of a child's giggle a moment later gave me my answer.

"I didn't know Trina had children living nearby," Jeanne said, glancing around.

"Could be someone's grandkids," Meghan suggested, grabbing another cookie from the tin.

Trina returned with the housekeeper who carried a dustpan and small handheld broom and went to work cleaning up the mess. Doe came back out and must have sensed the tension. She glanced at the woman cleaning up the pots.

"What happened?" she asked.

"Seems one of Julia's ghosts may have joined our little meeting," Trina said with a tight smile.

Doe gave me a quizzical look as Trina sat back down at the table.

"There *is* a brisk breeze. Perhaps the pots were too close to the edge," I offered.

My reasoning was ridiculous, but what could I say? I glared toward the pond, hoping to signal Chloe, and thinking this meeting was going downhill fast.

"How often do you meet?" I asked to distract everyone's attention.

"As I told you at the restaurant, we meet once a month," Trina said pointedly. "Fourth Wednesday from 6 to 8 at night. We rotate houses and whoever is the hostess provides a light meal."

"Do you have much volunteer experience?" Liz Corning asked, almost cutting Trina off.

"I do."

I listed several organizations I had supported over the years, including the library, the museum, and the domestic abuse center, and then described my volunteer positions and tasks.

Meanwhile, Trina's housekeeper went back inside. Through the sliding glass doors, I watched her go into the kitchen and dump the dustpan into the trash. A moment later, she disappeared. A minute later, she appeared again with a bald man. I continued talking until the housekeep appeared at the door motioning for Trina.

"Mrs. Bateman, someone wants to talk to you."

Trina glanced behind her. "Excuse me a moment," she said and followed the woman inside.

I continued talking about the library when the bald guy turned from looking out the side window to Trina. I stuttered, losing my train of thought.

"I...uh...I..."

Doe saved me. "Julia has always been very active in charitable work, Liz," she said to Mrs. Corning. "Trust me, she'd make a great PEO member."

I covered my momentary freeze by reaching for my iced tea again. Meghan used the moment to describe progress on a cookbook she hoped to use as a fundraiser for the organization. That got the rest of the women chatting privately about how to collect recipes. Once I regained my composure, I put a hand on Doe's arm.

"Doe let's go have a look at the pond. You remember how I was thinking of creating one in the backyard."

Before she could respond, I got up and walked over to the small water feature, noticing that Liz Corning had followed my departure. Doe joined me with a curious expression.

"I never heard you mention a pond," she said quietly.

"Oh, sure I did. Oh, look at the Koi fish," I said, pointing into the water.

She followed my gaze, but I leaned into her and whispered, "I don't want to talk about the pond or the fish. Did you see the man Trina is talking to?"

We had our backs to the house, and she turned.

"Don't look!" I snapped, grabbing her wrist. "I swear, it's the guy with the old-fashioned mutton chops. The one who attacked Ben in London."

"Are you sure?" she whispered; her brows crinkled.

"I couldn't see him very well, but I'm pretty sure it's him. He's bald, with long black sideburns."

"Okay, hold on." She stepped around to the other side of the pond so that she was facing the house. "Look at this one, Julia," she said, pointing into the pond. "It's beautiful." She glanced up at the den, and her face went pale. She quickly returned to my side. "Shit, Julia. If he doesn't have long sideburns, he has a very dirty face. What should we do?"

"Nothing right now. We don't want to call attention to ourselves here. We can call the police as soon as we leave, which needs to be soon. But let's stay here a moment. I don't want him to see me. If it is him, he probably knows I'm Ben's sister."

We feigned interest in the pond until Trina came back outside.

"I apologize," she said. "Where were we?"

Doe and I returned to the table, while I checked to make sure Sideburns was gone.

"Excuse me. But I need to use the facilities, too," I said, already heading for the sliding glass doors.

"Just inside the front door," Trina said, gesturing behind her.

Inside, I hurried to the front window and watched Sideburns pull away from the house in a dark sedan. I caught the last three numbers of his license plate and stepped into the bathroom to call Detective Abrams. When I finished, I stepped back into the entryway and almost bumped into Trina.

"Is there a problem?" she asked, her eyes flicking to the phone in my hand. She glanced up, staring at me with lifeless eyes. She knew I knew.

"No," I said, dropping the phone into my pocket. "Everything's fine."

A Cheshire Cat smile played across her lips. "I know you're not in politics anymore, Julia. If you were, you'd know better how to play the game."

"I'm not sure what you mean."

She placed her hand on my shoulder, squeezed it, and then guided me back down the hallway.

"Oh, I think you know what I mean. Playing the game is important but winning is everything." She led me through the family room to the sliding door and slid it open. Before we stepped out, she leaned in and said, "And you shouldn't join a game you don't know how to win." With that, she almost pushed me onto the patio.

"Ladies, I think we'll call it a day," she said. "Tom will be home soon, and I need to figure out what I'll be doing for dinner." She still had her hand on my shoulder, digging her fingernails into my flesh until it hurt. "I think Julia needs some time to think about joining PEO." She finally released her grip. "It is a big decision, don't you think?"

I was done and wanted to go home. I didn't need to know any more about Trina, her disgusting son Spike, or her arrogant husband Tom. They were all involved, and it took everything I had not to grab *Treen* by the throat in front of all her posh friends and choke the life out of her.

"She's right," I said, turning to the group. "You've all been very helpful." With a self-satisfied smile, I turned back to our hostess and said, "Thanks, Trina. I think I know exactly where I stand."

CHAPTER TWENTY-EIGHT

My body thrummed with adrenalin as we headed back to the Inn from Trina Bateman's. I briefly told Doe about my encounter with Trina in the front hallway, sharing that I felt openly threatened.

"Damn," Doe exclaimed. "I've known that woman for years. I thought her husband was the scumbag. To be honest, it hurts to know she's involved up to her fake eyelashes in all of this."

My phone rang. It was Blair.

"What's up?" I asked her.

"I heard from Clements," she replied. "Just as we thought, we're not meeting at a restaurant. He wants to meet at his home."

"I don't like it," I said. "You're too vulnerable. And now that we know Spike Russo is a friend of his, it's too dangerous. Plus, we just left Trina Bateman's house and guess who showed up to talk with her? The guy who broke into Ben's flat in London."

"Oh, jeez. Did you call the police?"

"I was just about to. I got the last three numbers of his license plate, too. Listen, Blair. I'm worried they know more than we think. I don't want you going there. This could all be a setup."

"But why? If Clements suspects we're fishing for information, he just wouldn't invite me to join the club."

"But remember, this is all about the key. They need it to open that box without destroying everything that's inside, and they think that either Ben or I have it. So while we're fishing, they're fishing. I just think they have a bigger hook."

"That's just the thing, though. If what's inside the box is incriminating evidence and something they don't want made public, wouldn't they *want* it destroyed?"

"Maybe. But Ben doesn't know exactly what's in the box. He suspects it's highly valuable. Which could mean it's potentially damning evidence or highly valuable in terms of money. It could even jewels."

"Don't go without a safety net, Blair," Doe called out.

"I agree," I said. "I'm calling Aria. If you go, you need protection."

"Not tonight. We're entertaining one of Mr. Billing's customers. Let's meet with Aria tomorrow night."

"Okay, that will work. Plus, who knows what else we'll learn by then?"

We hung up as Doe pulled into my driveway.

"Want me to stay?" she asked.

"No. I'm going to call Aria to see if she can come over tomorrow night and then get something to eat."

"Where's Jake?"

I shrugged. "He was gone when I got up. He said last night that he'd be going back to the hospital."

She smiled. "You may have to decide soon, you know."

"What do you mean?"

"You have two very attractive men leaning into you."

"Well, David, not so much."

"Oh, don't count him out so easily, Julia. He just needs some time. Anyway, get April to come over if Jake isn't back yet. I don't want you to be alone. And call me if you need me."

"I will. And thanks for today. I'm sorry that one of your PEO sisters is probably a crook."

Once in my apartment, I tried Ben's number again, hoping to learn more about what he was doing. The call went to voicemail, and I shook my head. *Damn him!*

There was a knock at my door when I was in the kitchen getting some Pepsi. It was April. I let her in, but it was apparent something was wrong. Her entire body seemed unusually tense, and she was wincing as if she had a headache.

"April, what is it?" I asked. "You look worried."

We moved into the dining area and sat on bar stools.

"I… didn't sleep well last night," she said, rubbing her temples. "And so, I took a brief nap this afternoon before we put out snacks. But…"

"April, what is it? I'd say you look like you saw a ghost, but then, it happens to all of us."

She took a deep breath. "You need to call Ben. I think he may be in trouble."

My solar plexus tightened. "What do you mean? He sent me a text earlier today. Did you see something?"

April's visions were often just random images she had to interpret. At other times, she heard voices. Although sometimes those were obscure and hard to understand, as well. She heaved a sigh.

"I had an image of him somewhere very dark. He was injured and alone. And scared. That's all I know."

Jake walked in with a McDonald's bag in his hand. He was sucking on the straw of a large drink and stopped when he saw us.

"What's up? You two don't look good."

"We think Ben is in trouble." I grabbed my purse from the end of the counter and pulled out my keys. "I'm going to the Sheraton."

"Not without me," he said. He put the bag of food in the refrigerator.

"Should I go with you?" April asked, a pained look on her face.

"No. But call Angela and tell her what you saw. She can decide whether to tell Detective Abrams."

She nodded. "I'll hold the fort down here." She came around the counter and placed her hand on my shoulder. "He's okay for now, Julia. I'm sure you'll find him."

Jake and I left through the back door and climbed into my Pathfinder. I filled him in on April's special talent and what she'd seen. As we pulled up the road, he just shook his head.

"You and your friends get curiouser and curiouser."

"Do you believe in psychic abilities?"

"Oh, yeah," he said. "My aunt was a practicing psychic for a while. But Minnesota isn't into that sort of thing much, so eventually she stopped giving readings and only did them for family and friends. She predicted I would marry a woman who would divorce me for another woman named Rebecca, and that I wouldn't have kids." He glanced out the window.

"I presume she was right."

"Down to the color of Rebecca's hair." He gave a short laugh. "Life sure throws you some curves, doesn't it?"

"I thought I'd be with Graham until we were old and gray. I guess he had other plans."

"But you have a daughter. Is she still close to her dad?"

"Yes. They don't spend a lot of time together, but she followed him into law and is a workaholic like him."

"I come from a family of workaholics, too. My grandfather was quite wealthy and used to preach to me about how hard work beats talent any day. He forced my father to follow him into the business…"

"Which was what?" I asked.

Jake turned with a surprised look. "Oh, uh, steel, actually."

"Oh my. Your family is wealthy?"

"Yeah. Me, not so much. I didn't choose to follow in the old man's footsteps, other than going to Yale, I guess."

"Yale. That's impressive."

"I suppose."

"And you used your degree from Yale to buy a country store?" I smiled at him.

"No. I used some of the inheritance from when my dad died."

"Oh, sorry."

"No problem. By the way, does your daughter support your amateur sleuthing? After all, she's a lawyer."

I let out a laugh. "Absolutely not. She's as black-and-white about those things as David is. But we're very close, and she understands my need to do these things, so she's more forgiving."

"And that's why you told April to call her?"

"That, and because Angela is aware of April's ability and trusts it just like I do. Detective Abrams… well, let's just say he's more skeptical, although he's had his fair share of ghostly encounters at the Inn. Anyway, depending on what we find at the hotel, April's vision might be all we have to go on. Which isn't much."

"I get it," he said, nodding.

Traffic was unusually light on I-90 as we crossed the floating bridge into Seattle, so it only took twenty-five minutes to arrive at the Sheraton. Ben had texted me his room number the night he checked in. We took the elevator to the third floor, where I pounded on the door to 315. No answer.

"What do we do?" Jake asked. "Want to check the restaurant?"

I pulled out my phone and dialed his number. "Let me try to call him again."

Our ears perked up at the sound of the theme from *Ghostbusters* from inside the room. Jake stared at me.

"That's my brother's phone," I said.

"Now what?" he replied. "Can we get someone up here to let us in?"

"I doubt it. But let me try."

I dialed the front desk and put the phone on speaker. I explained that my brother might be in trouble, and as Ben's sister, I hoped they would let me into his room. They refused.

I hung up as Jake lifted his leg and slammed his foot into the door.

"Jake!" I exclaimed.

"I'll pay for the door," he said.

He did it again, and the door splintered, making me jump. Adrenalin flooded my body as I glanced around to see if someone had noticed. We were alone in the hallway.

Jake pushed his way in. I followed, but when I saw the room, my heart sank. Someone had knocked the lamp next to the bed onto the floor, as well as a glass from the nightstand. There was a wet spot on the carpet, probably white wine from the open bottle that also lay on the floor. A small round table had been turned on its side, and Ben's phone lay on the floor next to his bed. The bed was fully made, meaning Ben hadn't slept in it. I felt my muscles tighten as full-blown fear threatened to make me faint.

"Where is he?" I asked, barely above a whisper.

Jake put his arm around me. "Deep breath. Let's see what we can find."

We searched the room, but there was nothing to indicate who had taken him or where.

"Wherever he is, he didn't go willingly," Jake said.

I dropped into a small armchair. "Someone has abducted my brother," I said, tears forming. "Who *are* these people?"

In all our investigations, nothing like this had ever happened. Well, that's not exactly true. A psychopath had once held Doe and me captive in the basement room of an old house on Camano Island. And the leader of a sex trafficking ring had abducted and held me captive in a church. Oh, and then there was the time Blair, Rudy, and I thought we had the upper hand on a killer in a cemetery one night, only to be told we had to dig our own grave.

But nothing exactly like this. And it left me feeling defeated.

Ben was my brother and a fearless relic hunter. Who had gotten the drop on him? And where had they taken him?

"What about this?" Jake asked, pulling Ben's empty briefcase forward from where it sat open on the bed.

A few papers were scattered across the floor, along with a notebook, a map of London, and his passport.

"It must be someone who wants the key and whatever else Ben has found on The Electi," I said.

Jake picked up the stray papers and thumbed through them. "These aren't anything but random notes about train schedules and people he wanted to interview," he said, tossing them onto the bed.

"Wait!" I exclaimed. I grabbed the briefcase.

"What are you going to do?" he asked. "It's empty."

"Maybe not." I pressed the button on the front of the case three times, just as I had seen Ben do the night Spike Russo had attacked me. A low-pitched motor whirred, and the bottom popped up, revealing a stack of papers underneath. "These were his most confidential notes."

"Damn," Jake exclaimed. "This is like living in a James Bond movie."

I removed the sheaf of papers and two notebooks and handed one notebook to Jake, while keeping the other one.

"I hope this tells us how to find who's behind all of this," he said.

"I think it's also time to call the police," I said. "We need to get them involved if we're going to find him."

"But they'll confiscate all of his," he said, gesturing to the notebooks and papers.

I let out a heavy sigh. "I've already gotten into deep trouble with them. We need to play this by the book. I promised my daughter. And Ben's life could be at stake."

"I just don't want them to take this stuff before we can find something useful."

"Then we'll have to work fast."

With mixed feelings, I put a call in to Detective Abrams and filled him in.

"And you're sure he's been abducted?" he asked.

"Yes, Detective. There has clearly been a struggle here, and his phone is here, but no Ben."

"Okay, we're on our way. I'll also have to let Seattle PD know. And since you've now contaminated the scene, perhaps you could stop touching things."

"I deserve that," I said. "His room is number 315. I'm also going to let Angela know."

"Angela called me earlier to tell me about April's vision," he said. "We're on our way."

I hung up with a sigh. "They'll be here soon. Meanwhile, let's see what else we can find."

I plowed through Ben's notes and scribblings. Ben's penmanship had never been good, so it was difficult to decipher some of his notes. I started with the loose-leaf papers and tore a blank sheet out of one of the notebooks to make my own notes.

"I think this has some interview notes," Jake said, skimming a page from the notebook I'd given him. "And this page is headed by the name Eustice Pembroke."

"That was the med student who was a suspect briefly in the Ripper murders," I told him.

He lifted his eyebrows at that but kept reading.

My stack comprised of a large sheet of paper folded in fourths that appeared to be the plans to the box, plus copies of deeds to a couple of London properties. There was also a folder entitled 'Walter Clements,' which held Ben's notes on Clements' heritage, as well as a few photographs of some of his descendants, notes on positions they had held both here and in London, and copies of deeds to more properties.

"I wonder why there are so many property deeds," I said, studying one. "This is weird."

"Why is that?" Jake asked.

"It's the deed to the Seven Seas Building here in Seattle."

"Is that significant?"

"I don't know," I admitted. "It's a historical building that's been vacant for some time. It was in the news last year because some big hotel company wanted to buy it, but the deal fizzled out. Here's a picture." I held it up. In the photo, modern buildings towered over an old building, six or seven stories high.

"And Clements owns it?" Jake asked.

"I guess So" I said, thumbing through several other sheets. "It appears he owns several buildings, including one in Olympia, one in Portland, and... this is weird." I glanced up at Jake. "He owns one in the East End of London."

Jake put his hand out to have me pass over the paper. "That is strange."

"Well, it says Walter Clements and partners," I said. "It doesn't say who the partners are. But we found an envelope from London in Clements' trash, and..."

"You went through his trash?"

"Hey, I'm not above anything when it comes to finding who killed Carter. So yes, we went through his trash. And Rudy found this envelope connects to an old church building now owned by a company called Hours of Darkness."

Jake's eyebrows lifted in surprise. "You guys really know how to do your homework. But, yes, I remember Rudy mentioning that earlier."

"I wonder if it's the same building," I said.

I picked up the other small notebook and started skimming through it. My ringtone went off, and I pulled my phone from my purse. When David's name appeared on the screen, my heart leapt.

"Hello," I said.

"We're on our way up," he said.

"Okay." I hung up. "They're downstairs," I said, thinking this could be awkward.

A minute or two later, Detective Abrams and David appeared on the other side of the broken door. They stepped in, studying the shattered doorjamb, and glanced around the small room.

"You're right," Detective Abrams said, eying the lamp on the floor. "It looks like something happened here. Was the door kicked in when you got here?"

"Uh, no. We did that," Jake said.

He expelled a frustrated sigh. "We'll have to let the manager know. Perhaps you two could wait for us in the lounge." He gestured to the hallway.

"Wait. Let me tell you a few things," I said quickly. "First, this is my friend, Jake Weatherly. He's been helping me," I said, gesturing to Jake. "And this is Detectives Abrams and Franks," I said, pointing the two men out to Jake.

They all nodded to each other while David glared at Jake.

"Is that it?" Detective Abrams asked.

"No. We've been going through the contents of Ben's briefcase, and here's something interesting," I said. "There's a note from an interview Ben had with a guy in New York who was dying. Ben told us about him. He's a member of The Electi and was willing to talk since he only had a short time to live."

"Is he really credible, though?" Jake said, leaning over to see what I was reading.

"I don't know. But Ben believed him. In fact, he mentions the Seven Seas Building here, which just happens to be their U.S. headquarters."

Detective Abrams leaned over and glanced at what I was reading. "Why would their headquarters be in a place like Seattle and not New York or Washington, DC?"

"Why not? This is a metropolitan city. But I also found the deed to the building," I said, holding up the document. "You know the building I'm talking about, don't you? It's in downtown Seattle. Well, it turns out that Walter Clements owns it." I realized my voice was rising, but I couldn't help it. "If I had to guess where they might have taken Ben, it would be there."

"Is this common knowledge, though?" David asked. "That this is their headquarters? I mean, is it like a place hundreds of people might visit in a day?"

"I doubt it," Jake said. "Everything these people do seems to be highly secretive."

"We found all of this," I said, gesturing over the bed, "in a secret compartment in Ben's briefcase. My guess is that *had* they found it, this would all be gone, too. The good thing is they didn't know Ben had it, or they would have taken the whole briefcase. Which also means they don't know *we* have it. This all has to do with The Electi, Detective," I said to Abrams. "And if their headquarters are here in Seattle, it's likely that's where they took Ben."

Detective Abrams sat in one chair next to the bed with his elbows on his knees, sleeves rolled up, exposing the Army Ranger tattoo on his forearm. Jake noticed it and glanced over at me and cocked an eyebrow.

"We have no evidence of that, though," he said. "We don't even know yet if he's missing."

My heart rate sped up as my anxiety rose. "Listen. Ben texted me this afternoon and said he was onto something and that he'd get back to me soon. Here," I said, pulling out my phone and finding the text. I showed it to Detective Abrams. "I've called him several times over the last couple of days, but it always goes to voicemail. I felt relieved when I got the text. But now I wonder if that text really came from him."

"And he hasn't left you any messages?" David asked. "Any voice mail?"

"No," I replied, glancing at my phone. "No messages... oh wait." My gaze had drifted to the icons at the bottom of the phone. One showed a missed call.

"What is it?" David asked.

"There *is* a message here. I hadn't noticed it before. I left my phone in the kitchen when..."

"Click on it and see who it's from," David snapped.

Jake's eyes shifted in David's direction for a moment before I clicked open my voicemails. "It is from Ben," I said, my breath catching. I hit the play button and turned up the volume.

"We have your brother," a woman's voice said. "We want the key and will call you at five o'clock tomorrow night to tell you where to bring it. Tell anyone, and your brother dies."

The call went dead.

It's hard to describe what listening to that message felt like. Perhaps like someone squeezing my chest or like an asthmatic without my nebulizer. Besides that, the voice had sounded vaguely familiar, although I couldn't identify it.

"I've heard that voice before," I said, my throat tightening. "I just don't know where from. What do we do now?"

"Once again, there is no 'we' here," Detective Abrams said. "You need to let us do this."

"And just how are you going to do that?" I shot back, standing up. "We don't know who took him, or who the voice on the message belongs to, or where he might be. What exactly are you going to do to find him?"

My anger and frustration overflowed as tears threatened. David stared at me with a pained expression.

"First, now we have his phone," he said, gesturing to Ben's phone where I'd put it on the bed. "We'll track any calls he's made within the past few days. And we'll need to take all this stuff with us."

"But..." Jake began.

"I think what Detective Abrams means is that we *will* take this stuff with us," David snapped at Jake.

Jake and David stared at each other, and I feared it might escalate.

"It's okay," I said with a nod to Jake. Turning to Detective Abrams, I said, "But you'd better get a search warrant for the Seven Seas Building ASAP."

Detective Abrams nodded. "I agree. On it now."

He stood up and stepped into the hallway.

"And just what is your role in all of this?" David asked Jake.

I was afraid this would happen.

Jake shrugged. "Just being a friend."

"But where exactly did you come from?"

Jake's eyes shifted to me and then back to David. "Minnesota. I met Julia during her road trip a few weeks ago."

"And you're here in Seattle because....?"

Jake shrugged his massive shoulders. "My niece was in an accident." He stood up as if to leave. "Look, I'm not trying to cause any trouble. Just trying to help."

I stepped in between them. "David, you have no reason to be mad at Jake. He really is trying to help. And frankly, he's been a great comfort to me."

I finished that sentence a bit like the snap of a wet towel, and David flinched.

"Fine. But you'll have to put all of that back into the briefcase," he said, gesturing to the papers and notebooks.

"No problem," I said.

Jake and I put everything back and handed the briefcase to David.

Detective Abrams came back. "I hope to have a search warrant by tomorrow morning, if not sooner."

"Tomorrow morning?" I nearly shouted.

"Look, we can't go barging in there. Clements is a sitting state senator," he said firmly. "And the building is in Seattle, not on Mercer Island. Besides that, we don't have a lot to convince a judge for the order. But the person working on the search warrant has an in with the judge. Plus, she has a vested interest in getting it as quickly as possible."

"And just who would that be?" I demanded.

"Your daughter."

CHAPTER TWENTY-NINE

There was nothing more we could do that night, so Jake and I returned to the Inn. April came over, and we brought her up to date.

"Dear God," she murmured. "I was right." She had her hands clasped in her lap.

I put my arm around her. "And thank God you told me. At least we had the chance to find Ben's notes."

"Any chance you can see where he is?" Jake asked her. "Maybe recreate the vision?"

She let out a heavy sigh. "It doesn't work like that. At least not for me. I can't just call up the visions."

"Yes, but what did you see just before you told me Ben was in trouble?" I asked her. "Can you remember any details?'

She closed her eyes and went still as she thought back to the moment she'd had the vision. Thirty seconds passed, and then she opened her eyes again,

"Dark," she said. "Just very dark, and I smelled cigar smoke." She shook her head. "Sorry, that's all."

"Cigar smoke. Like Clavis. But he's in jail." I sat back, thinking. "I wonder if that's somewhere in the Seven Seas Building. That's where they're searching. I'm sure they've had meetings there when men smoke cigars."

I picked up my phone and called Angela again to tell her.

"Thanks," Angela replied, after I told her. "We'll find him, Mom. I'll let you know as soon as we have anything. By the way, what's up with this Jake guy?"

Jake was too close, so I turned away and lowered my voice.

"I don't know. But David broke up with me because I can't stay out of his investigations. So…"

"And here you go again," she said. "You really need to trust the detectives, you know?"

"I do. But I trust Jake, you, and the rest of my friends, too. You all know how much Ben means to me, and I know you'll do anything to help me find him."

"Okay, Mom. I'll call you."

I hung up, and Jake asked, "You okay?"

"Fine," I replied.

"I'm going back to the guest house," April said. "Let me know if you hear anything."

I nodded. "Thanks, April."

After she left, I mentioned dinner to Jake. My mind couldn't cope with cooking, so we ordered a pizza and shared it at my small dining room table with some white wine.

"Feel like telling me what happened with David?" he asked between bites.

I took a moment to consider my answer before swallowing. "We had a falling out. Obviously, he's a police officer. And, as you know, I keep getting mired in murder investigations. I don't go looking for them. They just seem to find me. Like that girl in the RV who was abducted." I pulled off a string of cheese. "It's weird. I can't seem to stop myself. When there's a wrong, I have to right it. No matter how much danger it puts me in."

"And that's what he was upset about?"

"That, and the fact he can't keep saving me. Although I think he's only come to my aid once. But he and Detective Abrams feel we're interfering in their work. Like tonight. I'm sure they're all pissed off because we trampled all over the crime scene before they got there."

"But when we went in, we didn't know it was a crime scene."

"Exactly. I'm sure David will tell me the moment we realized there had been a fight in there, though, that we should have stopped, backed out and called them."

"Doesn't seem like the natural thing to do, especially when it's your brother."

"I know. But like I said, he's a cop. He sees things in black and white."

He reached out and placed his hand over mine, completely enveloping it.

"I have a good feeling about this, Julia. I don't think this will end in tragedy. And I'm here to make sure it doesn't."

"Oh, God, don't tell me you're psychic, too?"

He chuckled. "Not at all. I just listen to my gut. You have a lot of people working on your behalf. And on Ben's. I just choose to stay positive."

Jake helped me clean up the dishes and then said good night and went to the guest room. No fanfare or awkward moments. I retired to my bedroom; my stomach tied in knots. What if something did happen to Ben? My mother would never forgive me. And I would never forgive myself.

I lay on my bed and glanced over at the wall above my dresser. Hanging there was a collage of family photos. One was of the whole family at the state capital in Madison, Wisconsin when Ben and I were teenagers. In another one, Ben was jumping off a cliff into the river at the Wisconsin Dells. He was probably only seven or eight at the time. In one photo, I was fishing from the dock in Sturgeon Bay with my dad right behind me, his arms reaching around to help me hold the pole. A photo at the bottom of the collage included Carter. Tall, gangly Carter, with black-framed glasses and knobby knees. Ben was standing next to him, holding the skull of a fox they'd found in the hills behind our home. Ben already dressed himself like Indiana Jones and had a light in his eyes that betrayed his future love for hunting artifacts.

Tears made me reach for a tissue in the drawer next to my bed. *How could this be happening? And how could Carter be gone, and Ben be missing? Abducted by arrogant, crazy people intent on preserving what they thought was their legacy to rule the world.*

Minnie's head popped up from underneath the blanket, ears alert. A voice drifted down the hallway.

"Just a minute, Minnie," I said to her.

Without putting on my robe this time, I went to my bedroom door and quietly opened it, poking my head out. From the guest bedroom, I could hear Jake's voice. I wondered who he was talking to this late, but then shrugged. His brother probably. Or maybe a girlfriend somewhere. After all, I didn't really know him that well and had never asked about other female relationships. I'd assumed a lot over the last few days. Closing the door, I went back to bed.

"It's okay, girl," I said to Minnie, giving her a pat.

My phone jingled, and I grabbed it off my side table, hoping it might be Detective Abrams. It wasn't.

"Hi, Mom," I said. "I think I know why you're calling. It's Ben, isn't it?"

"He's in trouble," she said.

"Yes. Someone's abducted him."

"What? Why?"

The crackling on the other end of the phone always unnerved me.

"I wish I knew, Mom. I mean, I know why they took him. They want a key they think one of us has. But we don't. And if we don't give them the key by tomorrow night, they'll kill him."

"These are the people who killed Carter," she said.

"Yes."

She was silent for a moment, and all I heard was a faint hum of static.

"Is there anything you can do?" I asked her hopefully.

"I'm not supposed to interfere. You know that. In fact, I got chewed out for helping you with that electric light show a while back."

"You mean at the barn? But you helped to save our lives and the life of that young girl."

"I know. But life is supposed to play itself out. I just wish that if I'm not allowed to help, I wouldn't know when you're in trouble."

"What's a mother to do, huh?" I said with a half-hearted chuckle.

"Yeah," she said, sighing. "My Bennie. I'd like to wring the neck of whoever has him. But I can't see where he is, although what I see is a lot of darkness around him."

"April saw that, too. She said she smelled cigar smoke."

"Hmmm, no. I don't smell cigar smoke. I smell decay. Musty decay."

"That sounds awful."

"I feel death around him, Julia. Death and water."

"You hear water?"

"Not so much hear it as feel it. There is definitely a body of water nearby."

"Anything else?"

She'd gotten my hopes up. Between her and April, I thought we might get enough clues to start a search.

"I see the wings of an angel."

"Does that mean you need to go?"

She chuckled. "No. The angel's not here. There. There's an angel close to Ben."

"Oh my God. Does that mean he's…"

"No. He's not dead. Yet. It makes me think he's in a graveyard, though."

"Really? That might help. Thanks. I'd say I'll call you back if we get any news, but then I don't know how to do that."

The deep rumble of her chuckle reminded me of when we were kids. My mom was tough on us, something that grated on me as I got older. But she loved us both to death.

I called Angela after I hung up even though it was late, hoping that Sean might be there. I told her what my mother had said about seeing Ben around death, water, and an angel. Maybe a graveyard.

"Okay, I'll pass it along, Mom. I know you're worried about Uncle Ben. You're not going to go looking for him, are you? I mean, things are getting dangerous."

"I know that. And I'm sure Ben knows that. But honestly, I don't know where I'd look. There's probably a hundred graveyards in the area if that's even where he's being held." I felt myself tear up at the thought of Ben tied up somewhere, beaten and bleeding.

"We'll find him, Mom. Don't lose hope."

Deep sigh. "I won't."

After we said goodbye, I silently thanked my mom and just hoped that whatever she'd seen, it didn't mean she would be seeing either of her kids in person soon.

CHAPTER THIRTY

The sun was just barely up when Angela called back.

"We got the warrant," she said. "They're on their way to the Seven Seas Building now."

"Thank God," I said. "I'll keep my phone with me."

"Mom, it's going to be okay," she said. "Uncle Ben will be okay."

"I hope you're right. He's a pain in the ass, but I don't know what I'd do if I lost him." My voice caught as I held back a sob.

"You won't. I'll let you know if I hear something."

As I hung up, a storm of emotions coursed through my body. I was furious over Ben's abduction and the arrogance of the people who had taken him. I not only feared for his safety, but still felt a deep grief at Carter's loss.

Despite the hour, I called to let Blair know the news. She said she'd call Doe and Rudy to fill them in.

I got dressed and went to my kitchen, the anxiety of the past few days wearing on me. It had been almost midnight when we went to bed, so I purposely didn't disturb Jake. Keeping busy seemed like a natural calming tonic. I began making a big breakfast: a vegetable frittata, biscuits, and sausage. I finished setting the table and was just getting the frittata out of the oven when I heard his door open and his footsteps going down the hallway and into the guest bathroom. A few minutes later, he appeared fully dressed.

"Good morning," I said, a little shyly.

Even though he'd spent the night before in the guest room, we'd each left without seeing each other in the morning, so it felt weird having him in my apartment.

"Good morning." He stretched his arms over his head, his hands almost touching the ceiling. "Something smells good."

"I thought I'd make breakfast."

"Did you hear anything about your brother?"

"My daughter called about forty-five minutes ago. They got the warrant and were on their way to search the building."

He smiled. "Good. Fingers crossed." He eyed the frittata. "I see that cooking keeps your mind occupied."

"Exactly. I don't have coffee, but would you like some hot tea?"

"That would be perfect," he said.

Mickey and Minnie wiggled around his feet, looking for attention, and he finally reached down to greet them. I made his tea and then put everything on the table.

"Sit down and eat," I said. "By the way, I heard you on the phone last night. Or I should say, Minnie heard you. Everything all right?"

He gave Minnie a last pat on her butt. "That was my brother. My niece had some breathing problems, and they had to take her back into surgery."

"Oh, I'm so sorry. Will she be okay?"

He sat down at the table. "I think so. I talked to him when I got up this morning, and she's doing better. He's worried though. I might have to go over there today at some point."

"Of course. Family first. Help yourself," I said, gesturing to the plate.

He scooped up a slice of frittata and then took a couple of sausages and a biscuit.

"It's tough, you know," he said. "She's the light of his life."

"I don't doubt it. What's his wife like?"

Jake glanced up with a sad expression. "She died a few years back. Breast cancer. It's just him and Sierra."

"I'm sorry."

We shared a rather quiet breakfast after that. My mind drifted to Ben, while I'm sure Jake's thoughts were on his brother. It was nice to respect the solitude and not try to fill the empty spaces with idle chatter. We were just clearing the table when Angela called again.

"They didn't find anything," she said. "They took a large team, but there wasn't any sign that Ben had even been there. It's just a big empty building."

My body slumped. "Not even cigar smoke?"

"I don't know," she said. "But even if they smelled cigar smoke, it wouldn't mean much. It's an old hotel and plenty of people probably smoked in there. It would have seeped into the carpet and wallpaper."

"I see. Nothing to suggest The Electi was there?"

"Not recently."

"Maybe they moved him."

"It's just an empty shell, Mom. I'm sorry. We'll keep looking."

"What about a search warrant for Clements' house?"

She sighed. "He's a state senator, Mom. It would be all over the news. We'd have to have more evidence."

My heart sank. "Of course."

"Don't give up hope, Mom. We still have options. By the way, Sean wants to come by and set up a tape recorder."

"What for?"

"Aren't the kidnappers supposed to call you back this afternoon to tell you where to meet?"

"Oh, yes," I said, my heart rate speeding up.

"The police want to record the call. He'll be by soon. And they have an idea of how to handle the key. Don't lose hope. I'll talk to you later."

We hung up, and I filled Jake in on what Angela had said. It was only fifteen minutes later when David showed up with a taping device. We were doing the dishes, and although David offered a diplomatic smile, his facial muscles stiffened at the sight of Jake planted in my kitchen.

"I've… uh… stopped by to plug this into your phone," he said, holding up something that looked like a memory stick. "It's a Bluetooth recorder. It will record both your voice and whoever is on the other end. Where's your phone?"

His eyes kept flitting to Jake as I grabbed my phone off the counter and handed it to him. "Angela called and said you found nothing."

He plugged the device in and then looked at me. "No. We searched every square inch of the place. Ben was never there as far as we can tell."

"Does Clements know you searched his building?" Jake asked, wiping his hands on a towel.

David scowled at him. "He owns the building. He had to be informed. What exactly are you doing here?"

Jake was a good three inches taller than David and yet, in a fight, I thought the two of them would be evenly matched. The tension in the air was palpable, and I stepped in.

"Jake offered to stay in my guest room just until all of this is over."

David's eyebrows arched, and the two men locked eyes; I felt helpless. Fortunately, Jake relented.

"I'm here as a friend only," he said. "To do what I can to help. That's all."

David's muscles relaxed, and he stepped back. "Okay. Hopefully, this will all be resolved shortly, and you can go back to your store in Minnesota."

"Do you really think so?" I asked him. "I mean, that it will be over soon?"

He turned to me, his gray eyes softening. "We called in the FBI, Julia. We're doing everything we can to find your brother." He put a hand on my shoulder. "I know you're worried. You have a right to be. We're sending an agent over shortly to stay with you. She'll coach you on answering the call. Agent Glass specializes in abductions and will be right here with you. Have you thought anymore about where that key might be? They'll be expecting it at five o'clock when you meet with them."

"I thought about it most of the night. But I really don't know. Carter never made it past the front door. And he certainly didn't hand it to me."

"Okay. We're building a strategy about how to handle that and the meeting at five o'clock." He glanced at Jake and then left.

÷

Agent Stephanie Glass showed up about thirty minutes later. Probably in her late twenties, she was a small powerhouse of a woman who couldn't have been over 5' 4" of curvy muscle accented with luminous brown eyes and a dark brown ponytail. She reminded me of Sandra Bullock in *Miss Congeniality*, minus the pratfalls.

"Take a deep breath, Mrs. Applegate. I'll walk you through this."

The corners of her mouth flickered into a brief smile, which then disappeared quickly. She was attempting to put me at ease, but I wasn't sure anyone or anything could do that. Even Sandra Bullock.

"I just want my brother back safe and sound."

"I know," she said. "We've already checked the data from the first call you received from his abductors, and it appears to have come from a burner phone."

"These people have unlimited resources," I said. "I doubt there's any way they'd be stupid enough not to hide who they are."

"You're right. But we'll record the call, so I want you to keep them on as long as possible."

"Because you want to trace the call," I said.

"No. That's just in the movies," she said. "We'll be able to pull the metadata off your phone unless they use a VPN or an encrypted voice app. They could even use another burner phone."

"What's a VPN?"

"It refers to a virtual private network. They can use a phone connected to a computer located almost anywhere in the world, and it will look like the call is coming from there," she explained. "Anyway, the details aren't important. What is important is that you ask for proof of life. Say that you need to speak to your brother before you agree to do anything."

My stomach was in knots, and I wondered if I was going to be able to pull this off. Even though I'd faced several murderers, I didn't have regular conversations with them. And the idea I would have to listen to my brother's panicked or pained voice while I pictured him beat up and bloodied sent shivers down my spine.

"The longer you keep the woman on the line, the better," Agent Glass said. "You never know if sounds in the background will help us locate them, or if the person calling will slip up in some way. Get chatty with her if you can."

"I recognized her voice," I told the agent. "I just can't remember where from."

"That's good, though. Maybe the more you listen to her, the greater chance you'll remember."

I nodded. "Okay, anything else?"

"Any possibility you and your brother used code words as kids? Something you could use to prompt him to give up something that would help us?"

"Like what?"

She shrugged. "I don't know. Maybe something you used when you played hide and seek or some other game. Some way to get him, in code, to suggest where he is or who is holding him."

"I don't know. I'll have to think about it," I said.

"All right. Here's a list of reasonable questions you can ask to keep this woman talking," she said, handing me a sheet of paper. "The longer she talks, the likelier she might divulge something useful."

I gave her a fearful look, and she reached out and put a reassuring hand on my arm. "You'll be fine, Ms. Applegate. I've heard stories about you and your friends. This should be a walk in the park."

"Somehow, coming face to face with killers and kidnappers doesn't sound like a walk in the park."

"No. I'm sorry. I made that sound too simple. I know this isn't easy for you, nor will it be completely safe. You're probably going to have to meet them somewhere, but we'll set you up with a hidden wire, and we'll be close by. Nothing will happen to you. You'll be safe. I promise."

I stared into her eyes, wondering how confident she really was.

"Aren't you supposed to never promise anything in situations like this?" I asked her.

She merely stared back.

÷

An hour later, while April was in the kitchen, Doe, Blair, Rudy, Jake, and I were sitting around one of the big tables in the breakfast room. Agent Glass was on her phone in the hallway.

"So, you have to sit here and wait until they call?" Rudy asked. "There's nothing we can do?"

I shrugged. "What can we do? The police are going through Ben's phone and all his notes."

"What about his computer?" Doe asked.

"It wasn't in his room. I assume whoever took Ben took his computer."

"By the way, what happened at Trina Bateman's house yesterday?" Rudy asked. "Doe said she threatened you."

Jake's eyes lit up, but he kept quiet while Doe and I filled them in on Chloe's antics, the guy with the sideburns, and the details of how Trina had threatened me. As we talked, Jake rested his elbows on his knees, wringing his hands together.

"What's bothering you?" I asked him.

"Just that if that Bateman woman openly threatened you, I think you're getting too close. They've already kidnapped your brother and attacked you. What's next?"

"I agree with Jake," Rudy said. "This whole thing makes me nervous."

"I'll be okay. The FBI is going to outfit me with a wire, so the police will listen in, and they'll be close by."

"Haven't you ever watched those movies though, where the FBI's best laid plans go haywire?" Blair said. "These guys could use decoys to distract the Feds. They could even drive up in a van and throw you in and be gone."

"Okay," Jake said with a raised hand. "It won't help to get Julia all wound up." Jake's phone rang, and he glanced at the read-out. "Excuse me. It's my brother." He left the table.

"When's Aria supposed to get here?" Blair asked.

I glanced at my watch. "Soon."

"By the way, you're not going through with the meeting with Clements, are you?" Rudy asked Blair. "Not after Ben's abduction."

Blair shrugged. "I'm not canceling anything yet. We need to work all the angles."

My text ringtone chimed. It was Aria.

"Meet me at your back door. Just you. No one else."

"Listen," I said. "I need to let the dogs out. I'll be back in about ten minutes."

I slipped past Agent Glass, who was in deep discussion with someone, and met Aria at the back door to my apartment. She wore a hoodie with the hood up and came in as if she were sneaking into the White House.

"C'mon," she said, glancing around. "Let's go to your bedroom."

I took her into my bedroom, and she stopped me in front of my dresser.

"Okay, you said when you texted me this morning that your brother had been abducted and that you would have to deliver something to these folks later today. Is that right?"

"Yes. I doubt Blair is going to go through with her plans to join the society now. It's me that needs your help."

"Got it. Here," she said, holding out a small rectangular plastic sleeve no bigger than the tip of my pinky finger with something inside made of dark plastic.

"What is it?"

"It's a GPS tracking device. It's smaller than anything the FBI will have. A friend of mine in the Academy is an IT guy. He developed it and is selling it to the government."

"Our government, I hope," I said cynically.

"Yes. He's a good guy. Anyway…"

"Anyway, what?" Blair said, walking in. "What do you have, Aria?"

"Dammit, Blair. You need to keep your mouth shut about this," Aria snapped.

"I can do that," Blair said with a petulant jerk of her head.

I closed the door behind her. "Things have changed, Blair. I told Aria about Ben, and she's brought something for me when I go to meet these people."

"Good idea," Blair said. "So, what is it?"

Reluctantly, Aria showed her what she had in her hand.

"What's that?" Blair asked, peering at it.

"It's a wafer-thin tracking device," Aria said. "It weighs under 2.5 grams and is smaller than the Micro Hornet GPS chip, which is currently the smallest in the world. And yet it has an integrated antenna, filters, and radio frequency shields. I have the tracking unit here," she said, holding up a small box with an adjustable antenna.

Blair's perfectly arched brows lifted approvingly. "I'm impressed, Aria. You know a lot about this."

Aria's caterpillar eyebrows scrunched together as if she questioned Blair's sincerity. "Well, yes. It's all part of the Spy Academy. Anyway, we just need to figure out where Julia could put it."

Blair took it and flipped it over. "The tracking device is that tiny rectangular thing inside this plastic sleeve?"

"Yes," Aria said.

Blair held it up and stared at it. "The whole thing is paper thin."

"Just what I said," Aria impatiently replied.

"Can it stay in the sleeve and still work?" Blair asked.

"Yes."

"Easy-peasy," she said, turning to me. "Julia, we're going to do your nails."

"Huh? Okay, but wait." I took out my phone and texted Rudy, letting her know I'd be another few minutes because I was feeding the dogs.

It took only five minutes for Blair to seal the GPS chip under two layers of nail polish on my left thumb and then polish the rest of my nails.

"Let's test it," Aria said. "Why don't you go into your parking lot, Julia?"

I did as she suggested, while Aria turned on the receiver. Sure enough, Aria found me in the far corner of the parking lot behind our shed.

"Thanks," I said to Aria, when I returned. "This makes me feel better." I turned to Blair. "Will you be the keeper of the tracking unit?"

"Uh…I'd prefer that I do it," Aria said with an arch to her neck.

Blair and I exchanged a look. Finally, I shrugged. "Sure. I don't know why not."

"But don't tell anyone else. Not even the FBI," Aria said with emphasis. "This will just be between the three of us in the extreme case you need it."

"Why? Is it illegal?" Blair asked.

"No," she said. "The technology just belongs to someone else, and he doesn't know I'm loaning it to you."

Blair turned to me. "You okay with that? You're already crosswise with David."

"Yes. For once, I want a backup plan. Let's face it, we usually go into these things without a lot of forethought. We act on emotion. And we've been lucky so far. Look, neither you nor Aria are in any danger, nor are you subject to interference by the police. Having you act as my backup comforts me. I don't know what's going to happen, but I trust you guys to have my back."

"Always," Blair said, her face set in a grim expression. "Speaking of that. I also plan to be there when you drop off the briefcase. Somewhere."

"Are you going to let the FBI know that?" I asked her.

"Nope. Don't worry. No one will see us. We'll stay well away from you—but watching. Nothing wrong with a few extra sets of eyes."

"We?" I asked.

"You don't think we're going to let you go out there by yourself, do you?"

"Do you think that's wise?" Aria asked. "You could blow the entire operation."

"We won't. We have a plan, too. I called Grant, Mr. Billings' nephew," she said with a wink at me.

"Doesn't he work at the Seattle Rep?" I asked.

"Yes. He's the theater's makeup director. Trust me, even *you* won't recognize us. Look, Julia. Things are getting squirrelly. These people have already kidnapped Ben. If he really doesn't know where the key is, then Jake is right. They're likely to come after you. We can't let that happen."

"I agree," Aria said. "Count me in with your makeup guy. However, if it's that dangerous, I have one more thing for you, Julia," she said. "But first, we'll have to remove the sole of one of your shoes."

CHAPTER THIRTY-ONE

The three of us finished up just as there was a knock at my front door. I turned around to warn Aria, but she'd already slipped into the hallway and out the back door. *Damn! That spy academy stuff really paid off.* Blair and I answered the door to find Detective Abrams, David, Agent Glass, and Angela.

My eyebrows arched. "Is anyone left at the station to answer a burglary call?"

"Funny, Mom," Angela said. "We're here until you get the phone call." Angela's nose twitched. "Were you in here doing your nails?"

"Uh…" I started.

"It was me," Blair said, blowing on the fingernails of her right hand.

Since that was completely believable, Angela just rolled her eyes and moved into the living room. Before I could object, the rest of them stepped past me as well. Detective Abrams eyed Blair.

"It's best if your friends aren't here," he said. "For once, you need to leave it to the professionals."

I objected, but Blair stopped me with a raised hand.

"It's okay, Julia. We'll be waiting to hear from you," she said with a conspiratorial nod of her head.

"Okay," I replied. "Thanks. I'll walk you out."

I accompanied her to the front door and waved the others to join us. I explained my apartment was now filled with law enforcement, and everyone said their goodbyes.

Blair leaned into me to whisper in my ear. "Let your fingernails dry." She gave me a quick hug and darted out the door.

"Listen, do you want me to stay with you?" Jake asked, as the girls' cars pulled up the driveway.

I was so focused on the meeting with the kidnappers, I'd almost forgotten him.

"Yes. You're with me."

We returned to the apartment. Jake's presence raised some eyebrows, but I held up my hand. "Jake is part of this."

"Are you sure that's wise?" David asked. His eyes narrowed as he snuck a glance toward Jake.

"He's been intimately involved since the fire on my dock."

From their reactions, you'd have thought I had just bared my breasts.

"Sorry. That didn't come out right. He's just been helpful since he saved me from Mr. Clavis on the night of the fire." I climbed onto one of the bar stools. "How is this going to work?"

It was 4:15. We had forty-five minutes.

"We'll have several FBI agents there, plus us," David said.

"And we've reviewed all of Ben's materials," Detective Abrams said. "It appears no one knows what this key looks like."

"We brought you this," David said, holding up an antique bronze key.

"What if they *do* know what it looks like?" Jake asked. "That could put her in danger," he said with a nod toward the fake key.

Once again, the two men glared at each other, and the tension in the room rose.

"Julia sent us the picture of the box in Clements' study," Agent Glass cut in. "If that's the box Ben is looking for, we studied the size and configuration of the keyhole and then studied keys made in the 1800s. We had to work quickly, but the one Detective Franks is holding is consistent with the type of key made for a box that size during that time."

I took the key in my hand and felt it, wondering if this would work. "What if they don't buy it?"

"You'll have to sound credible when they call. Tell them you found the key somewhere Carter might have dropped it."

I glanced up at her, my mind racing. "How about under the antique clock near the door? It could have been kicked over there by mistake. I could say we found it when we were cleaning."

"That would work," she said. "Then we'll just have to wait and see what they do. There's no way to guess their response."

"What if they take it?" Jake asked.

"We had this one specially made with a tracking device embedded in it and then had it artificially aged. It looks like the real deal, so we hope they'll take it to wherever the box is to try it out. We'll be close behind."

"The box is at Clements' house. I can't imagine they'll all just drive up there," I said.

"They could also have the box with them," Jake said. "They might just try it right there. Then what?"

"We'll be on site to monitor what happens and to take immediate and necessary action. Our top priority is to keep you safe and then to find Ben," Agent Glass said.

"They'll obviously know the police are involved since you searched the Seven Seas Building," I said. "I just don't think we're going to fool anyone."

"What if they try to get Julia to go with them?" Jake asked.

"You are not to go with them under any circumstances," Detective Abrams said.

"But if it helps find Ben…" I began.

"No!" David snapped, standing up. "Do not go with them, Julia. There is no earthly reason you should have to go. Remember, if you can identify them, they will kill you."

It felt like someone had suddenly thrown a cold blanket around me, and I shivered. Jake stepped in close.

"They won't let anything happen to you," he said. He leaned into my ear. "And neither will I."

Setting the key on the counter, I said, "Excuse me."

I pulled away from Jake and left them staring after me as I escaped to my bedroom; the dogs close at my heels. I sat on the end of the bed, lifting the dogs up to sit beside me. It felt like tears would come, but I took several deep breaths and controlled my emotions. All I could think about was what if I screwed up, and Ben died. I couldn't let that happen. I had to be strong for him.

The door opened, and Angela poked her head in. "You okay, Mom?"

I motioned her to come in and close the door. She sat beside me on the bed, and I reached out and grabbed her hand. The warmth of her grasp comforted me.

"We can't lose Ben," I said.

"I know, Mom."

"He can be a bastard sometimes," I said. "Distant. Arrogant. Even self-absorbed. But he's our Ben."

She squeezed my hand. "I want him back as much as you do. He's the only uncle I have. Besides, he's the one person who agreed I should go into law, like Dad."

I smiled. "You're right. I didn't think we needed another lawyer or politician in the family. But Ben understood how sharp your mind was and how you had the potential to be an even better lawyer than your father. He adores you. Ben does. Do you remember when you were little, and he bought you that giant panda because pandas come from China?"

She smiled. "Of course. It was bigger than I was. You kept it, didn't you?"

"It's up in the attic. He was proud of that. Do you know he carries a picture of you hugging that damn panda in his wallet?"

Her hand flew to her chest. "No. I didn't know that." She swallowed and shook her head, as if to shake away the tears. "We'll find him, Mom. We have to."

I gave her a weak smile. "Yeah, we do."

The door opened to reveal Agent Glass. "Your phone is ringing."

I jumped up and ran into the kitchen. My phone sat on the counter with the recording device plugged in. All eyes were on me. David gave me an encouraging nod. I picked up the phone and swiped it on.

"Hello."

"Do you have the key?" the female voice said.

I took a deep breath to calm my nerves. "Yes, I do. We found it under my grandfather clock I keep by the front door. Carter must have dropped it when he collapsed, and it got shoved over there."

"Okay, then. Your brother just might make it out of this alive. It's five o'clock," she said. "Be at the International Fountain next to the Space Needle by 5:45 with the key. Put it in your brother's briefcase and leave the briefcase with everything in it on the wall of the fountain and walk away. Come alone. If we see any police or FBI, or any of your little friends, your brother dies."

"Wait!" I said, but the line went dead.

So much for proof of life.

÷

I left my apartment and approached my Pathfinder at 5:10 for a trip I dreaded. Jake was on the phone as I was about to climb in. He hung up and rushed over, pulling me aside.

"I… I'm sorry I can't be there. That was my brother, and my niece has taken a turn for the worse. I must go."

He wrapped his powerful arms around me and whispered in my ear. "Stay strong. You can do this." With a kiss on the cheek, he left for his car.

The trip to Seattle was the longest of my life. The police had gone on ahead to position themselves close enough to watch from a secure location. By the time I parked the car, I could feel the tension in my back and a headache was crawling up the side of my head.

At 5:32, I trudged toward the base of the International Fountain, lugging the briefcase with me. Although it couldn't have weighed more than a few pounds, it felt heavy enough to be filled with rocks.

It was a hot August day, and tourists filled the area around the fountain. Hundreds of people were there enjoying the weather. The fountain basin is probably a hundred yards across and surrounded by a two-foot cement wall. Inside the wall, the pavement slopes down to a flat circle, at the center of which is a large, silver half dome. Dozens of nozzles set into the dome spray water in graceful arcs high into the air. Since the entire floor around the fountain is embedded with water jets, the pavement is always wet.

Dozens of people milled about inside the fountain. Two women with baby carriages. Four boys playing frisbee. Several kids skateboarding. A group of Japanese students all taking selfies and photos of the fountain. And perhaps twenty or thirty young people and a couple of dogs playing in the water jets. I scanned the crowd, feeling weak and slightly nauseous.

The police had purposely not told me where they would be stationed so that I couldn't accidentally acknowledge them. And I didn't know where Blair and the others were. I'd seen what Blair's nephew could do with stage makeup and knew she was right; they would be unrecognizable.

I checked my watch. The minutes ticked by as sweat formed once again under my armpits. At 5:43, I glanced around one more time and set the briefcase on the wall surrounding the fountain. It took everything I had to walk away, but I left the briefcase behind, not knowing if my brother was even still alive.

With my heart pounding and tears threatening to explode, I purposely didn't look back as I worked my way toward a bank of trees that stood between the fountain and the Space Needle. When I reached the trees, my curiosity got the better of me, and I turned around. The briefcase sat alone on the wall, until a tall young man dressed in a black hoodie zoomed past on a skateboard.

He reached out a hand, and the briefcase was gone!

My throat constricted as the skateboarder disappeared up a walkway and over a hill. *Had I just said goodbye to my brother?*

I left the park with a heavy heart and a feeling of dread. My instructions were to meet David and the others in the parking lot behind the Pacific Science Center. As I retraced my steps and approached the Space Needle, I noticed a heavy-set woman with very shapely legs sitting on a bench.

"Blair?"

She hefted herself off the bench and smiled, her now milky blue eyes filled with compassion. "You're safe. That's all I care about."

I squinted up at her, stopping when I zeroed in on her eyes. "What in the world did he do to make your eyes look like you have cataracts?"

She grinned. "Contact lenses."

"Amazing. Listen, I'm supposed to meet up with Agent Glass and the detectives. Do you want to join us?"

"No," she said. "Better they don't even know we were here." She placed a hand on my arm, and I noticed that even though she had used makeup to age the back of her hands so that her veins protruded, she'd left her perfectly manicured red nails intact. "Keep your spirits up. It may seem like that kid got away with the briefcase, but the FBI is tracking it."

"I hope so. Thanks. I'll see you back at the Inn."

I passed by the Space Needle and came up on the back side of the Pacific Science Center. The FBI had a white van parked there, where they were monitoring my movements. I knocked on the door and David slid it open. He reached out a hand to help me climb in. Detective Abrams, Agent Glass, and an FBI technician were inside, focused on two monitors.

"What is all of this?" I asked, looking at the monitors and an array of equipment strewn across the floor.

"We had people with highly sensitive, long-range cameras and microphones hidden close by," Agent Glass said. "Just in case you had the chance to engage with whoever was going to pick up the briefcase. That's why we wanted you to wear a lapel mic. Unfortunately, the kid just whizzed by and disappeared."

"So nothing," I said, feeling my stomach clench.

Agent Glass glanced at the detectives before looking back at me. "No sound. But we obviously got a video of the kid." She nodded toward the technician, who was busy at the monitor. "We're going through it frame by frame and will continue to study it to see if we can identify the kid or anyone else within the vicinity."

I had a momentary start, thinking they may end up identifying a bunch of old women who were there only to protect me.

"And the tracking device?" I asked, looking at the monitors. "Can you tell where they're taking the briefcase?"

"No," Detective Abrams said, his face devoid of all emotion. "We could track the key to the perimeter of the park, and then it disappeared."

"What?"

David put a hand on my arm. "Julia, they probably had a lead-lined box of some sort. If they put the briefcase in that, we can't track it."

I felt like I couldn't catch my breath. "So... so there's no way to track the damn thing? No way to find Ben?"

My voice filled the small confines of the van, and I could feel the officers lean away from the force of my outburst.

"We're not giving up," Detective Abrams said. "They might slip up and take it out of the box when they get where they're going. At that point, we can track it again."

I bent over from the waist and put a hand on my thigh, trying to control my breathing.

"Julia, we're doing everything we can," David pleaded.

Once again, I'd had enough. I'd played by the rules and gotten nowhere. With a rather dramatic flourish, I ripped off the wire and the lapel mic they'd planted on me and threw them on the floor.

"These people have been one step ahead of us the entire time. They already know the FBI is involved, so I doubt they're going to let themselves slip up, as you say. Nor will they let you track them." I reached out and slid open the door and jumped out.

David followed me. "Wait! Julia, where are you going?"

I rounded on him, my anger and frustration boiling over. "I'm going home. Hopefully not to just to wait to hear that my brother is dead."

CHAPTER THIRTY-TWO

I had parked my car parked on Denny Way, across from the Pacific Science Center, and hoped I could get away before Detective Abrams or David stopped me. Once in the car, I called Blair.

"They screwed up. Not the kidnappers, the FBI."

"What?"

"It doesn't matter. They can't track the key. And I need to do more than just go home and wait to hear that Ben is dead. The only thing I know how to do is to network. And I want to talk to someone who knows more about these sicko people than I do. I'm going to Mae Beth's. I want you and Aria to track me. If you don't hear from me within an hour, come find me."

Before Blair could talk me out of it, I hung up and called Mae Beth and asked if I could stop by. I didn't know exactly how she could help, but she was one of the smartest people I knew, and she knew all these people intimately. Not only that, but she also had influence in this circle. At the very least, maybe she could offer some advice on how we could stop them or stall them. We just needed leverage, and she'd probably know what that was.

It took me twenty minutes to get to Newcastle, a swanky town in between Renton and Bellevue on the Eastside of I-405. Mae Beth had chosen a home there because it gave her quick access to the freeway that would take her into her Bellevue law office or south to Olympia when she had to meet with politicians.

She lived in a large multi-level brick home that sat on a hill. I pulled up the drive a few minutes after 6:30 feeling emotionally drained and yet weirdly on edge. The police and FBI had few options, and neither did I. This might be a Hail Mary pass, but it's all I had.

Mae Beth met me at the door with a concerned look on her face. By that time, my resolve had finally broken, and I broke down in tears.

"Julia! What's the matter?"

She guided me into the kitchen and poured me a glass of wine. We sat at her big marble kitchen island.

"What in the world is going on? You seemed anxious on the phone."

I wiped my eyes and took a swig of wine. After a deep breath, I said, "Is Donna home?"

"Yes, but she's upstairs. She won't disturb us."

"Okay, because what I'm about to tell you must stay between us. And only us."

Her eyes grew round with concern, but she nodded. "Of course." She held out her hand. "Give me a dollar."

"What?"

"Just do it."

I reached into my purse, grabbed my wallet, and found a single dollar bill. "Here you go. Do I get a Pepsi or something in return?"

She smiled. "I'm an attorney, and you are now officially my client." She slapped the dollar bill onto the counter. "Now, what do you need to tell me?"

I relaxed a little, thinking it had been a good idea to come here. Putting my purse next to the dollar bill, I launched into a quick and disjointed recounting of everything that had happened since Carter's death, including the boat, the two break-ins at the Inn, the guy with the sideburns at Trina Bateman's, Ben's abduction, Spike Russo and his mother, and my visit to the International Fountain. When I was done, she blew out a breath.

"We need something stronger than wine. Go sit in one of those comfy chairs, and I'll grab us some Scotch."

She got up and went to a liquor cabinet at the end of the kitchen counter and pulled out a bottle of Lagavulin's single malt Scotch whisky. I'm not a big drinker, but even I knew that was the good stuff.

She came back to the center island and reached into a cupboard to bring out two gold-banded, finely cut crystal glasses. I left her to pour the liquor and crossed over to a tufted leather club chair, stopping to stare out the window. A minute later, she came up behind me.

"Here you go," she said, handing me a glass filled with two fingers of scotch. "Relax, take a swig, and then tell me how I can help."

Mae Beth sat across from me in a large leather armchair flanked by a side table that looked like something out of an Art déco magazine. I dropped into the tufted club chair and took a drink, feeling the Scotch burn my throat. The warmth expanded into my chest, and I took another sip, just allowing myself a moment to get centered.

"Better?" she said.

I nodded.

"Okay. I'm not sure what I can do in a situation like this but tell me how you think I can help."

I took a final, comforting sip of Scotch and put the glass down. After a deep breath, I said, "You know everybody who is anybody in this town, including all the players I just mentioned. Clements. The Russos. The Batemans. For instance, Trina Bateman threatened me at her home yesterday."

She flinched back. "Really? What in the world did she say?"

"She told me I shouldn't play the game if I didn't know how to win. That's why I'm here. I don't know anyone who knows these people—or how to play their games—better than you. I can't lose my brother, Mae Beth..." My voice cracked, and I stopped to get control.

She watched me for a moment. "Well," she said, sitting back and swirling the scotch in her glass. "I'm not sure I can be of any help. I know nothing about this Elec... what did you call it?"

"The Electi."

"I've never heard of the group. And you're sure all these people belong? I mean, I can believe that Clements might. But Tom and Trina Bateman? That's a stretch."

"I don't know for sure who does and who doesn't belong. But somehow they are all connected to Carter's death."

"And by default, to Ben's abduction," she said.

"Yes."

She blew out a breath. "Okay, let me think a minute."

She took a sip of her drink and leaned her head back, thinking.

I took another drink, feeling the burn calm my insides. It was as if the alcohol was releasing the tension on a tightly wound spring.

While she contemplated my request, my gaze fell on the bookcase behind her, where there were several historical books, a novel by Bill O'Reilly, and a lineup of Disney books along with a few Disney collectibles, including a Peter Pan snow globe. I smiled as the alcohol lightened my mood, and I wondered how a hard-nosed political operative like Mae Beth got into Disney stories. But then, I was a *Wizard of Oz* fan.

My eyes came to rest on a beautiful figurine of Peter Pan, the Lost Boys, and…

Donna's voice rang out over the house intercom, "Hey, Tink. What about having sushi for dinner?"

Mae Beth's head dropped back into place as my eyes flicked away from the image of Tinker Bell sitting on a toadstool next to Peter Pan.

"Tink?" I asked her.

A long pause stretched between us as we stared at each other without moving.

"Donna's nickname for me," she finally said in a monotone.

"Short for Tinker Bell," I said.

I stood up and turned for the counter, a wave of dizziness almost tipping me over. I steadied myself and headed for my purse.

"Don't, Julia," she said, coming up behind me.

My hand was halfway to my purse when she circled around in front of me, a small pistol pointed at me.

"Damn! You're a magician, too? Where did that come from?" I asked, staring at the gun.

"A hidden drawer in the table next to me. I'm sorry about this, Julia. I always liked you."

"Funny," I said, now feeling more than woozy. "You never struck me as someone who would use a cliché like that. But then I never pegged you as a killer, either."

She smiled a lethal smile. "You told me once that your mother used to say there were no coincidences. Well, mine told me never to assume anything."

I faltered to the side and had to catch myself on the counter, my head swimming.

"What are you going to do with her?" a voice asked.

It was Donna. She was standing at the bottom of the stairs.

"Help me get her into the car. She won't be able to walk in a minute."

I threw out a well-placed insult, but my words slurred together. Which didn't matter now. They grasped me by each elbow and guided me to a door that led to the garage. Down two steps. The world tilting at odd angles.

"Get the door open," one of them said.

They pushed me up and into the back seat of a large car and closed the door. My brain screamed, "Aren't you going to put the seat belt on me?" Apparently, they didn't care.

I turned my head, wondering if I had the wherewithal to get out and make a run for it. But the engine started, and we moved. As we pulled out of the garage, my eyes came to rest on the last piece of the puzzle— a small, silver fishing boat sitting on its trailer in the garage with the letters T.B. stenciled on the bow.

A moment later, my world went dark.

CHAPTER THIRTY-THREE

I didn't know how long I was out, but I woke up feeling groggy, disoriented, and a little queasy. It took me a minute to get my bearings.

My surroundings were dark and dank, and I felt grit on whatever I was sitting on. The surface was also cold and hard, and the sound of water splashing came from behind me. As the brain fog slowly lifted, a voice whispered, "Julia?"

It was Ben.

"Ben, where are you?"

My voice echoed, making me wonder where we were.

"Across from you. Give yourself another couple of minutes, and your eyes will adjust."

I turned too quickly, got dizzy, and almost fell off whatever I was sitting on.

"Careful," he said.

"Damn, what did they drug me with?" I said, grabbing my forehead. I closed my eyes again as the world spun around me.

"Something powerful. They did it to me, too."

I scooted around and pried my eyes open. Ben was on the floor, leaning against a wall. As my eyes adjusted to the dark, I realized there was a shaft of light coming through a wrought-iron gate next to me. The gate led to the outside. I reached out and grabbed the gate and pulled myself to my feet. Walking my hands over gate rung by gate rung, I made it to a large, ancient padlock. I peered through the gate into a small patio surrounded by trees.

"We must be in the mausoleum at Clements' place," I murmured.

The trickling sound of the water feature by the pool sounded like something out of a fantasy. But even though it was only a few steps away, a yank on the padlock told me I had no way to reach it. My mother had been right. Ben was close to death and water.

I turned around and leaned against the gate. The moonlight cast a golden hue across Ben's face. He was in awful shape. His head lolled to the left, he had a badly swollen eye, and he was holding his arm across his ribs.

"You don't look so good," I said, shuffling across the dirt floor, kicking up dust as I went.

"Been better. I think they broke a rib, fractured a tooth, and maybe ruptured my spleen."

I swayed and had to reach out for the nearest thing to save myself from falling. My fingers wrapped around the smooth stone wing of an angel perched on top of a sarcophagus. I glanced at it and shook my head.

"Mom said there would be an angel."

"What are you talking about? Sit back down. Give yourself some time," he said.

"We don't have time," I replied. "We have to get out of here."

"And just how do you propose we do that?"

I shook my head and leaned against the sarcophagus, trying to displace the cobwebs in my brain.

"Blair will come for us."

"She can't help. These people are too powerful."

"Hey, where's that Indiana Jones spirit?" I said, with a manufactured chuckle.

It was chilly inside the vault, and I sucked in a deep, dusty breath and closed my eyes, willing the world to stop spinning. When I opened them, things were stationary, at least for the moment.

We were in a small space filled with two stone sarcophagi, large enough for two adults, and a small one, which must have held a child. I made a mental note to do some research on the Paddington family, the original owners, when I got out of there.

As my eyes traveled across the space, I said, "Damn, this reminds me of every B horror movie I've ever seen."

"Except this is real," my brother said through gritted teeth.

"No kidding." I went back to the bench and sat down again. "Okay, we have to get out of here." I lifted my left foot.

"What are you doing?" Ben asked.

"Getting the only weapon I have on me."

After removing the heel of my shoe, I pulled out the small switchblade Aria had hidden there. It was only two inches long, but when I pressed a button, a very lethal-looking slender blade popped out.

The blade glistened in the moonlight, and Ben said, "If you're going to use that, you'll have to cut an artery. Are you prepared to do that?"

I gave Ben a resolute look. "If I have to."

A noise alerted us that someone was approaching. I quickly closed the blade and dropped it into the pocket of my jacket, and then secured the heel of my shoe again. Voices sounded on the other side of a door tucked into the shadows at the back corner of the mausoleum. A metal grating alerted us to a key turning, and the door squeaked open.

"I see you're awake," the now familiar voice of DeeDee, Clements' housekeeper, said. She emerged into the shallow light with a gun held tightly in her right hand.

"Are you really the housekeeper?" I asked. "Or the ringleader of this little group?"

She laughed mirthlessly. "Just the very well-paid help."

A bulky guy with a shaved head and the tattoo of an eagle outlined on his neck stood behind her.

"Get her brother up," she said with a yank of her head. "Bring him with us."

"You must be the muscle," I said to him.

"Just get up so we don't have to hurt you, too," DeeDee ordered me.

The muscle, as I now referred to him in my head, leaned over to lift Ben up, while DeeDee gestured to me with the gun.

"Let's go. They want to meet with you."

"They?"

"You'll see. You first," she said, gesturing with the gun,

I stepped through the door and stumbled down some stairs into a tunnel, with her henchman practically carrying Ben behind us. If the mausoleum was chilly, the tunnel was biting cold. We were surrounded by rock and hard-packed earth. The only light was the bouncing beam of DeeDee's flashlight, which made me nauseous. That and the uneven ground had me struggling to keep upright.

The tunnel curved to the left and sloped upwards. We approached more stairs, and I had to put my hand on the wall to steady myself. At the top of the stairs, we continued for another 100 feet until we climbed three more steps. By the time we stopped at an arched wooden door, I was exhausted.

Once again, a set of keys jingled, and DeeDee opened the door. A rush of warm air greeted us, and we stepped into the long hallway at the back of Clements' big Victorian house. To our right was the door to the garage. Following close on DeeDee's heels, we turned left down the paneled hallway. I contemplated whether this would be a good time to use the knife. But with the muscle behind us, and in my current condition, I decided against it. I needed to wait for a better opportunity.

DeeDee stopped and pressed a square panel in the wall, and a secret door opened. The bright light from the room on the other side nearly blinded me.

"In here," she said, pushing me inside.

I stumbled forward into a small but elaborately decorated room with no windows. Squinting at the light, I could see rich leather furniture, hanging tapestries, colorful glass sculptures, and a large banner hanging on one wall with the letter E encircled by the now familiar ruby-eyed snake. Seated around an oval table were five people I recognized. Senator Clements, Mae Beth, Liz Corning, Trina Bateman... and Jake.

My entire body stiffened at the sight of Jake, and my breath caught as our eyes met. We stared at each other, and a flame of anger rose in my belly.

"You bastard," I whispered. "That's how they kept one step ahead of us."

"Sit down," he said, standing up and gesturing to a chair. "No one wants to harm you. Least of all me."

"You don't get to be polite to me!" I snapped. "So no niece, I suppose. Do you even have a brother? And is that why drawers and cupboards were open when I got back from the emergency vet that night? It wasn't Clavis who did that—it was you?"

He stared at me as mixed emotions played across his face.

"How did they recruit you? Promises of big money?"

"I've been a member for many years. Recruited right out of college, as a matter of fact. By my grandfather."

"Sit down, Julia!" Mae Beth ordered me.

As my eyes roamed across the table, I noticed each of them wore a small gold pin with an enameled letter E in the middle of it. Jake was near the end of the table. Mae Beth was to my left. The muscle pushed me into a chair across from her. My purse sat on the table between us. Jake winced at the man's forcefulness, but he remained silent and just sat back down. The muscle man shoved Ben into a chair next to me.

Muscle moved to the far wall, which held a large bookcase. He pressed something, and the bookcase swiveled open, revealing

Clements' study on the other side. He and DeeDee stepped through, and the bookcase closed.

"Well, now that we're alone," I said. "What do you want with us? Why won't you believe we don't have your damn key?"

"Because you do have the key," Liz Corning said in her withered voice. "We know because the note Carter left your brother said so."

My eyes sought Jake again. "Was there anything you didn't tell them?"

"My goal was always to protect you while furthering the mission of The Electi."

"But they killed an innocent man," I pleaded.

He glanced at Mae Beth. "I told them it wasn't necessary. But BOTiN does what it wants."

"BOTiN? Ah! Brothers of the Night," I said.

I glanced around the table. "So that's what this is." I turned back to Liz Corning and steeled my spine for the conversation yet to come. "Well, too bad for you. I don't have the key. If Carter meant to give it to me, he didn't. He might have dropped it. Or more likely he meant to tell me where it was but succumbed to the poison you nitwits gave him before he could. And now, because of your heavy-handedness, it's lost forever."

Corning arched a brow. "You're a formidable woman, I'll give you that."

"Not looking for compliments," I shot back.

"No, I don't suppose you are. But you'd be an asset to our cause."

"Seriously? To do what? Rule the world?"

"That's not what we're about. We work to influence change. Change that will benefit our country and continue to secure America as leader of the free world."

"Sounds noble."

"It is. We are not evil people, despite what you think."

"But you kill to get what you want."

"Only when it's necessary. As in any war, there is always collateral damage. And I'm truly sorry your friend had to die."

"Why don't I believe you?"

"You live in a bubble, Julia. Most of America lives in the same bubble. We've had it good for a long time. But the world is changing. Other countries are vying for position and would like nothing more than to see the United States forced into submission. We won't allow that."

"But your society was founded in Britain, not the United States. I thought you were a global group."

Corning paused and snuck a glance at Mae Beth.

"That's true to a large extent. But we're on the forefront of change."

"We? As in the people around this table," I said.

"You don't need to know the details. Just know that our intent is honorable."

As I stared at the old witch, it occurred to me she really believed what she was saying.

"And finding the key is your protection," I said.

"There is information in the box that cannot become public."

There was a long, tense pause before Mae Beth spoke up.

"We never wanted to involve you in this, Julia. But frankly, you're better at this than I ever thought you would be. And your brother just wouldn't give up the chase."

I glanced at Ben, who looked like a shadow of himself. "He's always been tenacious like that—a dog with a bone, so to speak. I suppose we both are."

"But it doesn't have to end badly," Corning said. "I'm impressed with you. You have not only the intellect we seek, but a tenacity that few people possess. We could use someone like you. Think about all the good you could do by joining us."

"You want me to join you?"

"Like I said, you'd be an asset. You could help make a real difference. You live in a small world at your inn. Just think of how it could expand."

I scoffed. "You must be kidding."

"I never kid," she said with a straight face.

I smiled. "I bet you don't. You must be a kick to have at parties."

The others remained silent.

"Look, I get it," I said, glancing at each one. "You're the ringleader of this rag-tag group. A woman in the lead seat. Not bad."

"I see you can appreciate the modernization of a century-old men's club," she said with a half-baked smile. "But don't underestimate the power in this room and throughout The Electi. We command influence in the world of politics, law enforcement, finance, government, and business that would make your head spin."

"Frankly, my head is still spinning," I said, sneaking a glance at Jake. He averted his eyes.

In my mind, I was hoping to stall long enough that Blair could alert the others and come after me. But I realized that both Ben and I were in a very dire situation.

"And what about you, Mae Beth?" I asked, shifting my gaze to the woman I had called a friend. "How did you get mixed up in this?"

She held my gaze. "My father was a member. He introduced me to The Electi when I was in grade school."

I risked a smile and nodded. "I guess it was only natural for you to graduate from lawyer to killer."

Her face darkened, and the corners of her mouth turned down. "Be careful, Julia. You are among friends here if you choose to be. But challenge us and loyalties go out the window."

"Good to know."

"What will it be, Ms. Applegate?" Corning asked. "Are you with us? Or against us? I do believe we could use you."

"What's the initiation fee for the two of us?" I asked, nodding toward Ben.

Eyes darted around the room.

"What?" I asked.

"I'm afraid the invitation only extends to you," Corning said. "Your brother is not welcome."

Anger welled in my breast, but Ben hardly registered this revelation. He sat slumped over. Bruises stood out on his face and arms. And in several places, whatever they'd used to beat him with had lacerated his skin and made him bleed. The anger inside me welled brighter. I had both hands stuffed into the pockets of my jacket, my fingers toying with the small knife. Looking around the room, it seemed ridiculous to think I had a chance of getting both of us out of there, especially with such a small weapon. And my hopes of rescue were fading.

Until I smelled the scent of rosewater.

A book flew off the bookshelf and hit Corning in the side of the head, nearly knocking her out of her chair. My heart leapt! Second to go was a beautiful glass sculpture of a water lily. It whizzed through the air, hitting Jake in the back of the neck. Simultaneously, a book and a heavy clock flew across the room. One hit Treen in the chest, the other slammed into Clements. Then all hell broke loose.

Anything that wasn't nailed down took flight. People were out of their chairs, ducking and holding up their hands to protect their heads. A trophy clipped Jake in the jaw as he was standing up, knocking him to the floor. Trina attempted to shield Corning, while Clements had backed up against the wall, his eyes wide with fear.

Only Mae Beth seemed unfazed as she locked eyes with me. The small pistol she'd held earlier suddenly reappeared, and she jumped up, circled the table, and pointed the gun at Ben.

"Enough!" she shouted. "Call off your stupid ghosts, Julia, or I'll shoot him right here and now."

I stood. "You wouldn't."

"God, you're right out of a storybook," she seethed. "Who do you think killed Carter?" She pressed the gun barrel to Ben's temple. "I'll count to three," she said. "One. Two."

"Elizabeth, stop!" I screamed.

All activity in the room came to a halt as a book held mid-air fell to the floor.

The room looked like a tornado had passed through. Jake's jaw was bleeding. Clements' lip was swelling, and Trina was attending to Liz Corning, who had fallen from getting out of her chair, twisting her ankle.

Mae Beth still glared at me from across Ben; the gun still pushed against his temple. She shook her head. "I told them you'd never join us. Too righteous. Too goody-two shoes. We almost had Graham; you know. He's the one we really wanted."

I sucked in a quick breath.

"Don't worry, though. He wouldn't bite. I thought when he left you, we might recruit him, but he's more like you than I realized."

"I'm glad," I said, lifting my chin.

"Yes, but now we'll have to kill you both."

Jake stood up. "That's unnecessary. There's been enough killing!"

"What do you care?" I snapped at him. "I was just a means to an end for you."

"Not true," he said, coming around the table.

"Sure, it is. It was you who warned them about the warrant to search the Seven Seas Building, so they had time to move Ben and clean it out. You told them about the fake key and the tracking device. You told them about the note. You were their inside man the entire time."

He came up to the other side of the table and loomed over me. "I purposely came to Seattle to protect you."

"Just for the record, though, how did you get from a small store in Minnesota to here? I mean, were you plotting this when we sat together on your front porch?"

"Of course not. I've been a member for many years. What we do is important work, and your brother was getting in the way. Most of us knew about Ben and his search for the box and the key. What I didn't know was that he was *your* brother. You do have different last names, after all. Applegate and Brouwer. But then he came to Seattle, and you got involved."

"And they recruited you."

"I *offered* to come and help because I wanted to keep you safe, Julia. Sitting with you in Minnesota, I knew how determined you could be. I'd seen it." He turned to Corning, who was leaning on Trina on the other side of the table. "There must be another solution. The Electi isn't about killing people."

"And what would that solution be?" Corning said stiffly.

My ringtone jingled from inside my purse, which was still on the table.

"Ignore it," Mae Beth said. "It's probably just one of her silly book club friends."

Well, that pissed me off.

"It could be my mother," I said.

Ben's head came up, and he turned to me.

"Your mother is dead," Mae Beth said.

My mind was racing, trying to figure out how I might get them to let me answer the phone. If it was my mother, she might help.

"You're right. She is dead. But if there's anyone who might know where the key is, it would be her. She sees all when it comes to me. And Ben."

Ben's eyes, though swollen, were staring at me with a curious light. Trina got up and grabbed the purse.

"Don't give in to her," Mae Beth snarled. "She's just stalling for time."

"Clearly, you don't know how ghosts work," I said. Of course, I didn't either. But Mae Beth was right, and I was stalling for time.

Liz Corning's eyes lit up. "We can't afford to be wrong on this. We need that key."

"Here's the deal," I said to Trina. "Look at my phone. If there's no name on the screen, it's my mother."

There was a long silence in the room. Finally, Jake reached across the table and snatched the purse away from Trina. He reached in and pulled out my phone, stared at the screen and then at me.

"There's no name, is there?" I asked him.

"No," he said.

Hope springs eternal! I reached out, and he handed me the phone.

"Put it on speaker," Clements said, the fear in his eyes still clear.

I swiped the phone on and put it on speaker. "Mom?"

"Julia! Is Bennie there?"

Her voice boomed loud and clear, making Ben sit forward.

"He's right here, but he's hurt. I hope you can help him, Mom."

Mae Beth's hand shot out and grabbed the phone from me. "Who is this?" she demanded.

"Who the hell are you?" my mother said in her Lauren Bacall voice.

"She's the one holding a gun to Ben's head," I said loudly enough for my mother to hear.

Mae Beth and I locked eyes as if we were in the middle of an arm-wrestling match, and then suddenly she cried out in pain and flipped the phone in the air. The phone landed on the table, the metal rim of the safety case glowing red. Thank God I'd never gotten a plastic case for it.

"Dammit, Julia!" Mae Beth growled, waving her beet red hand in the air.

She came around Ben toward me. I backed up as she pointed the gun at my face, still shaking her hand painfully.

For a big man, Jake can move fast. In a heartbeat, he pushed me behind him, coming face to face with Mae Beth.

"You will not hurt her," he demanded.

"You're an idiot," she said to him in a low tone.

"Perhaps, but you'll have to come through me."

She pulled the trigger, hitting him in the stomach. The gun shot shocked everyone in the room. Jake doubled over and crumpled to the floor at my feet. His compassion must have struck Mae Beth as humorous because she laughed.

"Remember our motto, Jake? Limits don't exist," she taunted him.

My heart thumped wildly. She'd just shot a member of their inner group. I'd like to say I felt sorry for Jake, but I didn't. I didn't believe for one minute that he was there to help me. And I would not help him. But then, I didn't need to because the lights suddenly went off, throwing the entire room into pitch black. Once again, Mom was breaking the rules.

The room erupted in motion. Voices rose in alarm. Chairs got knocked over. Someone bumped into me, nearly knocking me over.

"Stay calm," Clements called out.

But people were in motion, and chairs were scraping against the floor. I reached out for Ben and pulled him out of the chair, knowing that Mae Beth was close by. In the background, I heard the lumbering noise of the bookcase moving again. Someone was coming in or going out. Perhaps in the mayhem, Ben and I could sneak out unnoticed. But Clements' voice rang out a second time.

"Stop. Everyone!"

The lights clicked back on, catching everyone by surprise and freezing their movement. *Dang!*

Clements had his hand next to a metal panel on the wall. "I told you before, we have a backup system for this room."

I held Ben up with my arm around his back, but we were only a few feet from the chair he'd been in.

"Go back and sit down, Julia," Mae Beth said, waving the gun toward the chair.

She pushed Ben away, forcing him to stumble back against the wall. I watched him helplessly as he steadied himself, a resigned expression seated on his face. He knew we were doomed.

"Stop where you are!" a female voice commanded.

With shocked expressions, everyone spun around to where four decrepit old women stood just inside the open bookcase. The one with the big boobs held DeeDee's gun. Two had spread out on either side of her with baseball bats raised and ready to whack someone. And the third one held a taser.

The cavalry had arrived! But my relief was short-lived.

In a whirlwind of movement, Mae Beth grabbed me, flipped me around, and put me in a chokehold, the gun now pressed against the back of my head.

"Put the weapons down, or I'll shoot her," Mae Beth commanded.

Blair hesitated and glanced at the others. "Sorry, Julia," she said, lowering the gun. "I'm afraid *Omar* would be really disappointed."

Omar? A light bulb went off in my head!

What Mae Beth didn't know was that on the road trip from hell, a guy named Omar had taught the four of us how to get out of chokeholds. I took a deep breath to steady my nerves and made my move.

In a single motion, I brought the switchblade out, turned my head and tucked my chin. I shoved Mae Beth's elbow up and came out with the blade in my right hand, slicing it hard across the underside of her wrist. She cried out in pain as blood spurt out and into my face. She grabbed her wrist, which began surging blood. I'd cut the radial artery. Her gun dropped to the floor and Trina made a move for the gun, but I stopped her with the raised blade.

"Don't even think about it." Then I leaned down and picked up the gun.

Doe and Rudy moved further into the room with the bats raised again, one above Trina and one above Corning. Blair aimed her gun at Jake on the floor while Aria approached Mae Beth.

"I should've known you were too good to be true," Blair said to Jake.

He was no threat at this point. His stomach was bleeding profusely, and he looked ready to pass out.

The sound of banging somewhere out in Clements' house brought us all to attention, and I braced myself for an army of Electi minions, but it was David, Detective Abrams, and Agent Glass who crowded through the bookcase with their weapons drawn. David's eyes grew wide at the sight of Jake, but he rushed toward me, while Detective Abrams and Agent Glass began putting people in flex-cuffs.

"You okay?" David asked, grabbing me into a hug.

"Yes," I replied. "But Ben needs an ambulance. Never mind about these two." I pointed to Mae Beth and Jake.

Jake appeared to be bleeding out near my feet, and Mae Beth was desperately pressing her hand over the blood-pumping wound.

"Where's Clements?" Blair asked.

The door that led to the hallway stood open. Clements had disappeared.

"There's a tunnel at the end of that hallway," I said. "It leads to the mausoleum in the backyard."

David nodded to Agent Glass, who disappeared out the door and down the hallway in hot pursuit. I turned to help Ben, who had slumped onto the floor. David joined Detective Abrams in securing the rest of the room, allowing the girls to come and help me.

We got Ben into Clements' study and lowered him into the desk chair behind the Lion's desk. He faced the open bookcase and the box. His eyes lit up like neon lights when he saw it, and he struggled to get out of the chair.

"Wait. Let me," I said. It was the first time in days that I could draw a calming breath. I reached out and took the box off the shelf and placed it on the desk as Ben sat back down. "Is this it? Is this the box?"

With tears in his eyes, he nodded. "After all this time," he said in a weak voice. "Now, if only we could open it."

CHAPTER THIRTY-FOUR

The next day, Detective Abrams called for a debriefing at the MIPD and asked that we all be present. April stayed behind to take care of things at the Inn, while the rest of us converged on the police station around 10:00 a.m. I hadn't slept well, lying awake most of the night thinking about Jake and how he'd been able to fool me. Ben had spent some time in the ER. They admitted him overnight, and when I picked him up, he looked like a racoon with dark circles under his eyes along with bandages everywhere.

"You doing okay?" I asked.

We were heading toward the conference room, my arm around him to help take pressure off his ribs.

"The painkillers wore off around 3 a.m., and then my mind took over, thinking about everything that's happened since I first learned about that damned box."

"Well, it's all over now, and perhaps we'll get some closure today."

"I wouldn't count on it," he said.

"You don't think all these people will go to jail?"

He shrugged as I opened the conference room door. "I don't know. Maybe. But they're all very well-connected. I suppose Mae Beth will, if there's proof she killed Carter."

"I'll swear to that, at least," I responded. "She told me she was responsible."

He flicked his eyebrows up in skepticism. "I hope you're right."

Blair, Rudy, Doe, and Aria sat together at one end of the small room and made a beeline for us when we stepped in.

"Here, let me help," Doe said, pulling out a chair for Ben.

"Have they said anything yet?" I asked.

"No," Rudy replied. "We just got here, and they told us to wait in here."

The door opened and Sean, David, and Agent Glass came in. I remembered that Agent Glass had told me she be there one more day to help wrap things up.

David gave my shoulder a squeeze as he passed me. Everyone spread out around the oval table.

"Where's the box?" Ben asked Detective Abrams. "I hope you're safeguarding it."

He nodded. "Of course. It's in our evidence room. We don't really know what to do with it since we can't open it. We've checked with the FBI, and they don't want it. I put in a call to the Governor to see if he wanted to weigh in, and he wasn't interested either."

I flinched at that news he'd called Graham. I had wanted a chance to be the one to tell Graham about the events of the night before.

"Anyway," Detective Abrams continued, settling into his chair, "we wanted to update you on some details and have you help fill us in on the rest. First, we found the guy with the sideburns. His name was on the flight manifesto from London a couple of days before Carter's death. His name is Jack Raines, and he is a hired thug. From what we can tell, he knows nothing about the secret society or why they wanted the key. He was just hired to get rid of Carter and to find the key, whatever it took."

"Who hired him?" I asked.

"He hasn't said yet. He lawyered up immediately."

"Did he even know why he was looking for it?" Rudy asked.

"No. He was just told to find an old key. Remember, no one in The Electi knew what the key looked like."

"Was he the one who killed the kid who delivered the candy to Carter?" Ben asked.

"According to him, he had nothing to do with that. He bought the candy, though. He admitted to that much. Then he asked for a lawyer. But we also interviewed a colleague at the university who said someone who matched Raines' description was in the department break room one day talking about buying Carter a present. Apparently, people were all too willing to share about how much he liked See's Candy."

I blew out a defeated breath. "Carter didn't have a chance."

"Who injected it with the poison, though?" Doe asked.

"That would be Mae Beth," I said. "She admitted that to me last night. Which means, she's also probably the one who killed that poor kid."

The detective nodded. "We'll follow up."

"She lost a lot of blood," David said. "You hit an artery. That was a fancy bit of slicing you did. Where'd you get the knife?"

I couldn't help a glance at Aria. "A friend," I said. The corners of Aria's mouth flitted into a smile.

"We also found Clements," David added. "He got caught crossing the border into Canada. How did you end up in Clements' secret room, by the way?" he asked me. "You said you were going home after you left the Space Needle. Was Jake there? Did he drug you?"

"No. I went to Mae Beth's, hoping to find out more about that entire group of people because she knows them so well. I was so upset though, that I spilled everything. She gave me Scotch to calm me down, but with an extra kick to it," I said with a rueful smile. "Little did I know she was one of the leaders of the group. Anyway, she drugged me and carted me off to Clements' mausoleum, where they'd also stashed Ben."

David was sitting next to me and squeezed my knee. "I'm just glad you're okay."

"I take it you weren't able to follow that guy on the skateboard," Rudy said to Detective Abrams.

He shook his head. "No. He disappeared, and they put the briefcase into a box lined with lead so that we couldn't trace it. We found the box in a van outside of Clements' house."

"What we don't know is how they knew we'd wired the key," Agent Glass said, eyeing me suspiciously.

"Don't look at me," I said. "I'm sure that was Jake. Just about the time I was supposed to leave for the Space Needle, he supposedly got a call from his brother and said he was going to the hospital. He must have immediately called Mae Beth or one of the others. I'm sure he also told them about the secret compartment in Ben's briefcase. That's why they wanted me to bring it along with the key." I turned mournful eyes at David. "I trusted him. It never occurred to me that someone I met in a small grocery store in Minnesota would end up being part of this gang."

"Don't feel bad. He did a lot of talking once we got him to the hospital. I guess his grandfather was a big poohbah in The Electi and always wanted Jake to join when he came of age," David said. "He comes from a lot of money and ran that small store you stopped at only because he loved it and not because he had to."

"He told me about some of that the other night, never mentioning that he knew all about The Electi. He did try to save me, though," I said.

"He made a point of telling us that repeatedly," Detective Abrams said. "Once he realized you were Ben's sister, his entire goal in coming to Seattle was to make sure you were safe. He wanted to find that key as much as anyone, but not at your expense. And I guess there's more to why they were willing to kill to get the key."

Ben perked up at that. "What?"

"You know how the name of the society stands for 'the chosen.'" We all nodded.

"When Brothers of the Night was first created, there was a single silent partner whose name doesn't show up anywhere, except in the box. This individual was part of the original larger society but said he couldn't afford to have his name associated with Brothers of the Night. Jake said that there is a gem encrusted pin with a serpent that signifies Brothers of the Night. It was given to this individual. Apparently, he was so high in the nobility back then that he had widespread influence, and even helped to guide the investigations into Jack the Ripper in the wrong direction."

"That sounds like something out of a Marvel comic book," Rudy said.

"I know," Detective Abrams agreed. "But he said that the direct descendants of this individual have remained the keepers of that pin and the group's secrets for over a century."

"And that pin has been passed down from generation to generation," David added.

"And the box holds that pin as well," Ben offered.

"Yes," Detective Abrams said.

"We need to open that box and find the name of that person," I said. "Who knows how he or she is influencing world events?"

"Agreed," Detective Abrams said. "But I suppose it would depend on what position they hold today."

"By the way, Jake lost a lot of blood, but he'll survive," David said, patting my hand. "He'll be charged with accessory or conspiracy, though, and will probably spend time in jail."

"Okay, by me," I said.

"I wonder why they went to all the trouble of kidnapping Julia, though?" Doe said. "If they knew the key was a fake, why didn't they just call your bluff?"

"Because then we might have figured out that they had someone on the inside," Agent Glass said. "And that would have compromised Jake. You're what foiled their plan," she said to me. "They didn't count on you showing up at Mae Beth's."

"And they still had Ben and hoped to get the actual key," David said.

I shook my head. "Who knew I'd foil anything? But it turns out that Mae Beth is Tinker Bell."

"You mean the boat?" Blair asked.

I nodded. "It was Donna's nickname for her. And you'll probably want to pick up Donna since she helped Mae Beth get me into the car," I said to David.

"What's her last name?" he asked, taking notes.

"Olney, I think. Something like that. My guess is she's long gone. But the boat should be in Mae Beth's garage. I saw it through blurry eyes as we were leaving."

"I'll send someone out there now," Detective Abrams said. He pulled out his phone and excused himself, stepping into the hallway to make the call. David took the cue.

"We found some notes that might be Carter's," he said to Ben. Ben sat forward expectantly. "They're hard to decipher because his handwriting was atrocious. But I guess he was working with some of his colleagues in the UK and pieced together more about what's in the box. Apparently, it contains notebooks from the original Electi group *and* Brothers of the Night. The notebooks not only name names but also identify their very personal secrets."

"Did Carter discover what any of those secrets were?" Ben asked.

"Not that we could tell. But he got names, and we believe it may be one reason they killed him. After all, we could never figure out why they would kill him before they'd found the key. But clearly, he may have been able to identify someone involved today."

"Which makes me think that maybe one of those colleagues he talked to in the UK might also be a member, and that's who tipped off the group here in Seattle," Rudy said.

David nodded. "We'll follow up as much as we can, but the fact that whoever he talked to is in another country might make that difficult."

"But that could mean they'll go scot-free," Ben said.

"Perhaps," David said with a shrug. "But if we get any verifiable information, we'll share it with Scotland Yard. Which is probably also who will ultimately take possession of the box."

"Out of curiosity, why did the room look like a war zone when we got there?" Blair asked. "Had you already attempted to escape?"

"No. That was Elizabeth," I replied. "But Mae Beth wasn't having it and threatened to kill Ben if I didn't call her off. I thought we were goners until my mom cut the lights."

Ben turned to me but said nothing.

"No, that was us," Blair admitted as Detective Abrams came back into the room.

"Someone is on the way to Mae Beth's home now to confiscate the boat and see if her wife is still there," he said. "But please, don't let me interrupt you. You were about to tell us how many laws you broke by storming the house last night," he said to Blair.

"Hilarious," Blair said with a flip of her head. "But we didn't break any laws. When we got there, the back door was wide open. Just as we got to the hallway outside the study, the housekeeper and the guy Julia calls 'the muscle' came through the secret bookcase. DeeDee put the gun down while she got herself a drink, and I picked it up."

"I might have knocked the muscle guy out with a baseball bat," Doe said, sheepishly putting her hand up. "It had to be me because I was the only one tall enough to do it."

I held back a chuckle.

"We didn't know what was happening on the other side of the bookcase," Blair continued. "But we saw how they activated the bookcase. Muscle guy pushed a large glass bowl back into place. It sat on a metal stand wired into the bookcase. Anyway, we figured the best thing to do was to cut the power before going in."

"I did that," Rudy said, holding her hand up.

"When you called us, though," David said to Blair, "you didn't tell us how you knew Julia was at Clements. I mean, she just said that she went to Mae Beth's."

Aria, who had been sitting quietly, finally spoke up. "That would be me," she said. She came around the table and reached for my hand. Pulling a matching switchblade from her pocket, she flipped it open and peeled the GPS chip off my thumbnail and held it up. "We gave this to Julia before she went to the Space Needle. Blair and I had the receiver."

"And thank God, it's the one thing Jake didn't know about," Blair said.

Detective Abrams got up and took the chip from her, turning it over in his hand. "Where'd you get this?"

"I belong to the Spy Academy," Aria said with her pointy chin in the air. "Our members are very tech-oriented."

"I'd bet that's where you got the knife you used on Mae Beth, too," David said, giving me the side eye.

Detective Abrams gave the GPS chip back to Aria. "Just out of curiosity, was there a reason all of you dressed up for Halloween last night? I wasn't sure who to arrest."

The smirk on his face told me he was playing with them now, and David laughed.

"Blair's nephew is a makeup artist," Rudy said. "It must have worked because we were at the fountain the entire time Julia was there, and you didn't notice us."

"We have Julia's back," Blair said proudly. "Never forget that."

"We never do," Abrams said with a smile. "Maybe I'll have to deputize all of you in the future." This time, a pleasant smile graced his handsome face.

"Hey, by the way," I said. "When April had the vision about Ben's abduction, she smelled cigar smoke. Were you ever at the Seven Seas Building?" I asked, turning to Ben.

Ben winced as he shifted in his seat but shook his head. His entire demeanor had changed. Gone was the arrogance and bravado he often showed when in pursuit of a precious artifact. He was pale and broken.

"I was there. But they moved me that night to the mausoleum."

"Jake, again," I said with a sting of remorse. "I heard him on the phone in the guest room that night. He was probably reporting in. What a fool I was. He probably doesn't even have a niece."

"Don't be too hard on yourself," David said, grabbing my hand.

"Do you know any more about the box itself, though?" Ben asked, with a hopeful glint in his eye.

"No," the detective said. "You warned us not to open it, and the FBI didn't have a clue what to do with it. Like I said, it's just sitting in our evidence room for now. I guess your quest for the key continues." He stood up and gathered his notes. "Listen, I think we're good for now. We'll let you know if we find out any more information."

Detective Abrams and Agent Glass disappeared into another office while the group of us converged on the parking lot. As the girls got into their cars and left, I helped Ben back into my SUV.

David lingered as I crossed around to the driver's side door.

"I'm sorry about Jake," he said, shifting from one foot to the other. "He seemed like a good guy. Maybe a little too good."

"Until he wasn't," I said, resting my hand on the door handle.

"Well, one thing I like best about you is your trusting nature," David said. "Listen, can we have dinner? I think I have some apologizing to do."

Those dreamy eyes made my heart melt. "How about an intimate dinner in my apartment? After you wrap things up on the case."

"Sounds like a plan." He gave me a peck on the cheek, squeezed my hand, and returned to the station.

÷

Later that afternoon, while Ben recuperated in my recliner with his ribs wrapped, I helped April deep clean the main kitchen and then did some inventory on my antiques. The focus on work allowed me to decompress.

It was close to dinnertime when I took a break to do some personal laundry, something I hadn't done since Carter's death. I loaded the washer but stopped when I got to the denim vest I had been wearing the day Carter died and held it up, feeling a lump in my throat.

"I'm so sorry, Carter," I said, staring at the vest. "At least we brought your killer to justice."

I let out a deep sigh, threw the vest into the washer, added detergent, and pushed the start button. Back in the kitchen, April knocked as I was making a cup of tea.

"How's Ben?" she asked, stepping inside.

"He's sore, but the doctors told him everything will heal."

"Good. Just thought I'd let you know that Brett and his girlfriend checked out and didn't demand a refund after all. They let their full payment stand. Something about a conversation with Curt."

"I wonder what that was about."

April shook her head. "Don't know, but Curt has been waiting to talk to you. His family is also getting ready to check out."

I followed April to the registration desk, where Curt and his mother were waiting. His dad was already on the front porch. Curt's eyes lit up when he saw me.

"Hey, Mrs. Applegate, I heard you figured out who that boat belonged to."

"Yes," I said. "It was the person who killed my friend. Thank you for your help."

"I'm just glad the guy didn't get away."

I didn't correct him in his assumption of gender.

"Listen," he continued, "I heard that numb-nut Brett complaining about everything that's happened here—you know, the fire and all. He was bragging to someone on the phone about getting a full refund." Curt pulled me a few feet away from his mother, who was tapping away on her phone. "I know this place is haunted," he said.

"Well, our brochure says that."

"I know. So I told Brett I'd sic Chloe on him if he didn't pay up," Curt said with a glint in his eye.

"I'm sorry, what? How do you know about Chloe?"

"The brochure mentions she died here, along with her mom and brother. I figured that's who was playing tricks on us that day that we were in the breakfast room and the cards fell on the floor."

This kid was smart. "Why didn't you say anything?"

He shrugged. "Cuz, let's face it, I was being a brat. I do that sometimes. But Chloe and I have hung out a bit. I can't see her or anything, but I know when she's there. Anyway, as soon as I told Brett that I'd sic Chloe on him, she ruffled his hair and snapped his belt. He almost peed his pants," Curt said, laughing.

"So you're the reason he paid his bill in full," I said.

"Yeah. I guess." Curt was grinning from ear to ear. "I'll never forget this trip. Will you friend me on social media?"

That took me by surprise. "Um, I guess. Sure. I'm not on Facebook a lot, but you also have the Inn's email address. Why don't you email me sometime?"

"Curt," his mother said. "The Uber is here."

"Okay." He turned and threw his arms around my waist. "Take care of Chloe for me."

He released me and ran out the front door. I stood on the porch and waved goodbye as they drove away, thinking how funny life can be. I had been so critical of Curt in the beginning, and he turned out to be a smart, nice kid. On the other hand, I had pegged Brett and his mute girlfriend perfectly. And Jake... well, I wouldn't dwell on that.

÷

I was finishing up the dinner dishes when I realized I had forgotten to put my clothes in the dryer. I contemplated running them through again, but just stuffed everything into the dryer, added a couple of dryer sheets, and turned it on. As I was putting dishes away, Renée Abernathy, Carter's daughter, called.

"How are you doing, Renée?"

"I'm okay, I'm staying at my dad's. It's difficult to get my head around all of this."

"I haven't quite accepted it yet, either. Do you need any help there?"

"I don't know. The place is a mess."

"I'm just glad you're here," I finally said.

"We hadn't talked in so long," she said, sniffling. "Over some stupid argument."

"If you don't mind me asking, what was it about? He never said."

She took a deep breath. "When I got married, my husband and I kept our own last names. I've published several nonfiction self-help books and am well known on the speakers' circuit. I wanted to keep Davis as my last name."

"Seems reasonable."

"Yes, but when I got pregnant, we didn't know what to do about the last name for the baby. We decided that if it was a boy, it would carry my husband's last name, Abernathy, with Davis as the middle name. If it was a girl, she would carry my last name with Abernathy as the middle name."

"And it was a boy," I said.

"Yes. Dad was old-school, and I was his only child. He wanted a grandchild, especially a grandson, to carry on his last name. But we'd made our decision, and we got in a big argument about it. I'm afraid we both said some hurtful things."

"I'm so sorry, Renée. Carter could be stubborn, but I know he loved you. He let me know every time you published a new book. He was very proud of you."

"Yes," she said, blubbering. "But because of that stupid argument, he never met his grandson."

She broke down in tears. When she'd gained control again, I asked her, "How old is your son now?"

"Just turned five," she said, taking deep breaths.

"Then think about this. Have your husband bring him out to the house there, so he can help you go through things. It would be a great way to let your son get to know his grandfather."

"Oh," she said, sniffling some more. "That's a good idea. Jay offered, but I just thought it was something I should do alone."

"I grew up without ever knowing my grandparents. It's something I have always felt badly about. As you go through things, it will spark memories and stories that he'll love to hear. And he might find something among Carter's things that will remind him of his grandfather."

"Thank you, Julia. I'll call Jay right away."

"And as soon as you're ready, Renée, let us know how to help. Angela, Ben, and I would all like to play a part in his service."

"Thank you. I'll call you."

I hung up and turned around and found that Ben had woken up. He was smiling at me from the recliner.

"You handled that beautifully."

"Thanks. How are you feeling?"

He tried to smile but came up short. "I'm okay, I guess. But I've lost the fire for finding out anything more on The Electi or Jack the Ripper. My best friend paid the ultimate price for my carelessness, and I'm not sure I can live with myself."

"How could you know these people were so scared of what others would think of them they were willing to kill to protect their names and reputations? I mean, it's ridiculous."

"But remember," he began, "it's all about power. They want to rule the world, or at least their own petty parts of it. Take their reputations away, and you take that away. They would just become ordinary people."

I couldn't help shaking my head in dismay. "The arrogance still overwhelms me. You heard Mae Beth say they had tried to recruit Graham. I guess it shouldn't surprise me. He'd be the perfect member."

"You should call him," Ben said. "He needs to talk to you, and not just Detective Abrams."

"I guess you're right. I'll go call him."

I pulled my phone out and dialed Graham's home phone, hoping against hope this time that Kitty wouldn't answer. Luck was shining on me because it was his deep voice that said, "Hey, Julia. How are you?"

"I'm fine. Ben's a little worse for wear," I said, sharing a look with my brother.

"That detective from the Mercer Island Police called."

"Our daughter is dating that detective, by the way."

"Oh? I didn't know that. He asked about what we should do with that box, and he wanted to update me. Why didn't you call me Julia? Maybe I could have helped."

I glanced out the window as a bird landed in the branches of one of the pine trees that lined my property. "There was nothing you could have done. They brought in the FBI. In the end, though, it was best friends and family that got us through it."

"Yes, Detective Abrams mentioned that, too. He said your friends got there just in time—." He stopped and paused. "Julia, you need to be more careful. I... I don't..." I heard him take a deep breath. "I don't know what I'd do if something happened to you."

A warmth spread throughout my body. "Thank you, Graham. By the way, Mae Beth was behind everything. Did Sean tell you that?"

"Yes."

"She told me last night they tried to recruit you to their secret society."

He let out an exasperated sigh. "Mae Beth talked to me about it a few times right after I'd won the governorship. She never gave the group a name, though, and I didn't know it was a secret society. She described it as more of a think tank. I had no idea it was the same thing you and Ben were talking about when you came to see me."

"Why didn't you join?"

"Because of you. She said the membership included some of the best thinkers in the country, and that they were shaping the future. She made it very clear, though, that they only considered certain people for membership, and I thought of you."

"Why? Because I wouldn't be invited to join?"

"Not at all. Because it sounded too elitist. Too exclusive. And I could hear you in my head saying, 'Remember, Graham, you're running to be governor for *all* the people.' Remember when you said that to me?"

"I do. The same day you told me you wanted a divorce."

"Ouch." He paused. "Yes, I guess it was. I just remember you being so proud of me and so encouraging. I often think of you saying that. It guides me, even today."

"I'm glad I still have some influence on your life."

"You have more than you know. Anyway, I'm glad you and Ben are both okay. Let me know when Carter's service is scheduled. I'd like to be there."

"I will. And thank you for your help, Graham. Do you know who you'll appoint to fill Clements' seat?"

"No. But too bad you're not a Republican."

"Very funny."

We hung up, and I went back out to the living room.

"Everything okay with Graham?" Ben asked.

"Yes. In fact, remarkably good."

"Speaking of phone calls, you haven't explained that supposed phone call from Mom last night."

His eyes betrayed his suspicion that it was all a hoax. I briefly contemplated saying that it was—that it had been Blair or Rudy, but then decided I couldn't lie to him.

"Look, Ben, I know this will be hard to believe, but she's been calling me off and on for the past year when she senses I'm in trouble. This time it was because she sensed *you* were in trouble."

He glanced out the window, processing what I'd just said. "I thought it was her. No one else calls me Bennie. And she has a distinctive voice," he said with a raffish smile.

A smile spread across my face. "She does that."

"But why didn't you tell me before? Why would you keep that a secret?"

I sat on the barstool to give myself a moment to consider my answer. "I guess I thought you'd think I was crazy. Sometimes I think I'm crazy."

"I already knew about the ghosts here at the Inn, though."

"Yeah, but you must admit that having your deceased mother call you on your cell phone is a stretch. Even if you believe in ghosts."

He chuckled and shook his head. "Julia, after spending this last week with you, I'd say your entire life is a stretch." His head tilted as if he'd heard something. "What's that noise?"

A clanking noise caught my attention as well.

"Oh no, it sounds like the dryer," I said. "I just had it serviced. Something must have come loose."

I hurried down the hallway to the rhythm of a metallic clink, clink, clink. I turned off the dryer and opened the door to a rush of hot air. As I tossed the warm clothes into the basket and pulled the last towel out, something fell back into the dryer bin, ringing metal against metal.

"What was it?" Ben asked from the end of the hall. "Do you need to call the repairman?"

"I hope not," I said as I reached into the dryer.

I stopped, staring at the culprit.

"What is it?" Ben asked.

"Apparently, Carter meant what he said in that note," I said with a shake of my head.

"What do you mean?"

I pulled out the perpetrator and held it up for Ben. His eyes widened as he stared at the ornate brass key in my hand.

CHAPTER THIRTY-FIVE

The next morning, we gathered back in the conference room at the police station to open the box. April had volunteered to stay behind once again to take care of breakfast for the guests.

"I'll let you do the honors," she said. "But I want a blow-by-blow account when you get back."

They had set the room up to videotape and record our actions. David returned from the Evidence Room holding the box gingerly between his gloved hands as if it were a bomb. He set it on the table.

"Chain of custody demands that one of us open it," he said. "Can I have the key?"

Ben's hand trembled as he handed over the key. David inserted it into the keyhole. With a muffled click, the clasp released. Ben and I exchanged a glance. *This was it. This was what Carter had died for.*

David carefully lifted the lid. Inside was the second box. It was made from the same dark wood, decorated with gold filigree around the edges. Inscribed on the top was the now familiar motto in Latin—*Limits don't exist.* Below that was the large letter *E* written in a gold script. And below that, in quotes, was the name 'Brothers of the Night' along with their motto, *quod capit*—or *do what it takes.*

A part of me wanted to smash the entire thing as some evil, twisted representation of all that is bad in this world. But another part of me screamed out to know who these people were. People arrogant enough to birth such a heinous idea. David carefully lifted out the second box. The sides of this box were carved into six panels. Each panel was further distinguished with gold lettering.

"What do they say?" Doe asked from across the table.

David handed the box to Ben, who had also donned gloves.

"This side," Ben said, rotating the box to the right, "holds the names of the six Brothers of the Night. Arthur Finley. Eustice Pembroke. Archibald Clemency. George Mountbatten, Alistair Bateman, and Frederick Alderidge." He turned the box around and paused, staring at what he saw. Finally, he said, "On this side are the six women killed by Jack the Ripper. Martha Tabram, Polly Nichols, Annie Chapman, Elizabeth Stride, Catherine Eddowes, and Mary Jane Kelly."

Gasps exploded around the table, and I glanced up at five very pale faces.

"I thought there were only five Ripper victims," Rudy said.

"That is what most Ripper scholars believe," Ben clarified. "However, there are a few who believe that Jack may have murdered two other women prior to Polly Nichols. Martha Tabram was one of those." Ben paused, staring at the names on each side of the box. "You know, for over a century, people have speculated about who Jack the Ripper was," he said quietly. "Some believed that he was a member of Parliament. Others thought for sure he was a doctor. There were those who thought he could have been a member of the royalty. Even butchers and famous artists were on the list. There has even been speculation that Jack the Ripper wasn't just one man, but more than one person working in tandem with others." He turned the box to focus on the names of Brothers of the Night. "It appears we could be on the verge of proving that particular theory correct."

"Are we going to open it?" I asked Detective Abrams.

"I guess that would be up to Ben. Do you know how?"

Rudy pointed to a long, tube-like metal combination lock affixed to the front of the inner box. "It looks like it needs that code Ben mentioned. But I thought you said it was a seven-digit code. That looks like a set of five double digit numbers."

"Now what?" Blair whined.

"I think I know what the code is. I think I've always known," Ben said.

"But if you get it wrong, it dies by acid, right?" I asked him.

"Right. But I get three tries." He looked over at me. "Everything I read has said that it was a code of seven."

"What does that mean?" Agent Glass asked.

"Remember that the men who created The Electi *and* Brothers of the Night felt they were the chosen ones. They were also very religious. And the number seven is one of the most important numbers in the Bible."

"Created in six days," Rudy muttered.

"Yes. And after creating the world, God rested on the seventh day," Ben said.

"And the seven-day week has been adopted by all human civilizations," Rudy added.

He looked over at her with appreciation. "Exactly. Many scholars believe the number seven represents perfection in all things."

"And with the *Electus*—the guy they kept in the shadows—there were seven Brothers of the Night," I added.

"Exactly," Ben replied.

"Shit," Blair whispered. "These guys saw themselves as God-like *and* as complete perfection?"

"No wonder they thought they should rule the world," David said.

Ben turned his attention back to the box and pulled a small piece of paper from his bag. On it was a series of numbers.

"Okay, here we go," he said.

He rotated the tarnished numbers in the following sequence: 19 5 22 5 14

Nothing happened. To the side of the combination was another small rotating calculator that had previously held the number 3. The moment Ben slid in his final number; the calculator rotated to number 2. It appeared the box kept track of the number of attempts to open it.

"Damn," Doe said.

Tension was so thick in the room, I had trouble breathing.

"Where did you get the numbers you used?" Doe asked.

"They represent the position in the alphabet for each letter in the word 'seven,'" he said.

"Wait!" Rudy exclaimed. "If you can input two digits in each position, wouldn't you have to put a 0 in front of the fives since they're single digit?"

"Are you sure?" Blair screeched. "This thing could blow up."

"Well, not exactly," I said. "It would just dissolve in acid."

She gave me a withering look.

"I think Rudy's right, though," Ben said. "It makes perfect sense."

"C'mon, Blair. It's worth a try," Doe said. "He'll still have one more try after that."

"Do it," I told Ben.

His hand was noticeably trembling this time. But he input the numbers 19 05 22 05 14. And the box clicked open, releasing not only the lock to the box but also the pent-up tension in the room.

Ben stared at the box and then carefully lifted the lid, expelling a heavy waft of sulfur, but, thankfully, no acid. Inside were two small leather-bound notebooks, a large ledger, and a stack of loose-leaf papers, many of them preserved in parchment envelopes. On the inside of the lid was a contraption that looked like the inside of a pocket watch, which butted against the underside of the combination lock. And next to that was a small, square glass container.

"I assume that holds the sulfuric acid," I said, pointing to the tiny glass container.

The glass was thick and yellowed with age.

"Probably," Ben said. "See that tiny lever?" He pointed to a small, sharply curved piece of metal at the bottom of the watch mechanism. "I think this piece hooked into the combination lock." He peered closely at the back of it. "See here," he said, pointing so that everyone could see. "I think this thing was spring loaded. Every time I put in a set of numbers; it rotated that lever to the right. On the third try, if I'd put in the wrong combination, the spring would have snapped, and it would have pierced the opening of the glass box, and the acid would have destroyed everything," he said, pointing to what looked like a small metal dot embedded into the glass box. "Since I put in the correct combination, it merely released the prong. Ingenious," he said as he expelled a breath.

"But look down there," I said, pointing into the box. "It looks like it might have leaked. A corner of the book was damaged, along with a few of the parchments."

Ben studied the glass box. "Yeah, it looks like you're right. I can see some residue on the glass."

"Well, let's see what's in there," Detective Abrams said impatiently. He gestured to an officer who hovered over Ben' shoulder with a video camera.

Ben pulled out the loose parchments first. A few were encased in paper envelopes that had yellowed over time but were in surprisingly good shape, considering their age. And several were in transparent envelopes.

"Someone made an attempt to preserve these, and obviously members have been curating them over the years," he said. "These are what's called polyester film pockets. Museums use them for archival documents. For instance, this looks like the original constitution of Brothers of the Night." Ben held up a large document covered in old script. "It includes the fundamental principles and rules of the club." He set it aside and grabbed another document. "And this looks like the same for The Electi."

He set that one down and picked up the larger notebook. On the cover, someone had written in a flowing script, *The Electi Ledger of Deeds*. Ben flipped it open. The paper inside was also parchment and more fragile than those encased in the film pockets. I knew enough about old documents to know that parchment would have been expensive for that time, but more durable. Ben skimmed the first few pages, written in beautiful script, while the rest of us held our breaths. All I could see were columns with names, dates, and numbers.

"Carter was right," he finally said. "This is The Electi membership roster. From the 1800s all the way to now. It includes the dates each person joined and a brief note on the secret they told, which allowed them to join."

Looking over his shoulder, I could only make out a few words, but the two that raised the hairs on the back of my neck were espionage and embezzlement. Obviously, two things someone would want to keep out of the public eye.

Ben pulled the second notebook out and the gold pin we'd just been discussing fell to the bottom of the box, again damaged by the acid.

"Well, there's the pin," Rudy said. "Guess it's not needed now."

Ben was scanning the notebook. He paled, and his breathing quickened.

"What is it?" Blair asked.

"I think the rest of you will want to hear this," he said, and read the first page.

This diary shall declare actions taken by myself and my brethren as members of Brothers of the Night whilst we strive to prevent further deterioration of the moral fabric of our great nation by the unrestrained wickedness purveyed by the devotees of grotesque and immoral acts. It matters but little that the courts would find fault against us and that upon confession we might fall to the shadows of the gallows, for we are rightful in this undertaking.

Let it be said that we contrived this idea when news of the death of Emma Smith was portrayed to the masses as that of a heinous act toward a poor castaway woman. This pathetic sentimentality cannot stand and was further reflected by our colleague who interns at London Hospital. By his account, Emma Smith was a drunkard and unrepentant prostitute who consumed valuable resources necessary to the health and well-being of more worthy individuals under care.

Such being the case, this strengthened our resolve that to fulfill the avowed purpose for which we believe we are intended, violent

*acts would be necessary and essential to ensure the future health of
our nation, especially in its role as a world leader as has been
assured to us by God.*

*Therefore, we six young gentlemen avow to be the executioners of
this most deadly of plans in the hopes we will inspire the permanent
eradication of said castaway women, robbers, vagabonds, and
others like them from the rookeries and streets of London.*

Archibald Clemency

No one said a word, until Rudy murmured, "And Archibald
Clemency is Walter Clements' ancestor, right?"

"Yes," Ben said solemnly. "He goes on to describe how he killed
Martha Tabram," he said, still skimming the page. He thumbed
through the next several pages. "And the next five pages mention the
names of the other five women and those of the young men who
dispensed with them and how," he said, fanning the pages.

"Shit," Detective Abrams said. "This is a bombshell."

"No kidding," I said. "But what do we do with it now?"

Detective Abrams shrugged. "My guess is that no one mentioned
in the book is alive now. Is that right?" he asked, nodding toward the
notebook.

Ben skimmed the pages again and then shook his head. "This
notebook holds only the entries from members of Brothers of the
Night back in the 1800s. But at least three of them are direct
descendants of people who hold positions of influence here in the
states. Clements, Bateman, and Mountbatten."

"Who is the descendant of Mountbatten?" Doe asked.

My face grew warm, and my pulse quickened. "I bet I know.
They wouldn't go by that now, would they?" I asked, staring at Ben.
"Like Clements, the Mountbattens changed their name. It became
Battenberg."

Blair sucked in a big breath. "Mae Beth," she uttered. "Mae Beth
Battenberg."

"Yes," Ben said. "I didn't know that until they abducted me. I had
never met her before. But I heard someone mention her last name,
and though groggy, I put the two together."

"Jeez," Rudy said. "Just our luck that three of the collective Jack
the Ripper's descendants would end up in the Seattle area."

"It could be because The Electi headquarters are here," I said.

"Or that as descendants of the Brothers of the Night splinter group, they are embedding themselves into leadership positions of The Electi," Ben said.

"What now?" Doe asked Ben. "Do you go on Oprah or something?"

Ben seemed stunned. "No. I don't want credit for this. In fact, I'm not sure I want anything to do with it."

"But..." I began. "You've spent so much time researching all of this. We wouldn't have found any of it if it hadn't been for you."

"And Carter wouldn't be dead if it wasn't for me!" he almost shouted. When I flinched away, he put his hand over mine. "I'm sorry. But don't you see, Julia? Clements, Trina Bateman, and Mae Beth are in jail. We don't know yet how much Tom Bateman knew, or if he had anything to do with it. But if he's innocent, this would change his life forever. His reputation gone. And there are three other extended families out there linked to the other three names in this book that will have to deal with the fallout if this comes to light."

"But who cares?" Rudy asked. "I mean, really. A lot of people are outed every day for dastardly deeds by themselves or people they know. You can't be judge and jury on this."

"And what about the Electus?" Doe asked. "Will we ever know who he was?"

Ben shifted in his chair.

"You know, don't you?" When he didn't answer, I said, "You never told us how you found the key to the box." He continued to stare at me. "It was the guy you interviewed in New York. He was the Electus, and he gave you the key."

"No," he replied. "He wasn't the Electus, but he knew who was. He said this person was known worldwide. Because of that, he would never reveal his name. Remember, I said the 5th Electus died suddenly, and the box disappeared. According to my source, other members of BOTiN swooped in and took the box, not knowing where the Electus kept the key. My source, however, did."

"And he gave it to you," I said.

"And that's how the box became separated from the key," Doe said.

"Yes," Ben confirmed. "He believed BOTiN had become a dangerous group of individuals, taking matters into their own hands, and committing wanton crimes to further their goals. While the 5th

Electus was a powerful individual and undoubtedly contributed to shaping world events, my source maintained he was an honorable man."

"Was he murdered?" David asked.

It was the first time David had said anything, reminding us we were at a police station.

"My source believed so, although he couldn't prove it. The man drowned in his own pool, even though he was an excellent swimmer. But my source believed BOTiN had gone off the rails, so to speak. He alluded to other suspicious deaths of individuals they wanted out of the way."

"Damn!" Blair said. "But he didn't have any proof?"

"No. But it's why he talked with me and handed over the key. He wanted them stopped."

"Isn't he in danger now?" I asked.

Ben dropped his head and expelled a breath. "He died three nights ago. I was following up on one of those leads I texted you about. I don't know whether it was from natural causes, though. And we'll probably never know. But his doctor had told him he had a good six months to live."

Detective Abrams got up. "What's his name? I'll call the local PD to launch an investigation."

Once again, Ben looked like a trapped lion. He clearly didn't want to give up the name of his source, but since the man was dead, I wasn't sure there was a reason not to.

"Jeremiah Reynolds. Judge Jeremiah Reynolds."

"Oh my God," Rudy whispered. "The last administration nominated him for the Supreme Court. It was pure politics that prevented him from getting in."

"I know," Ben said. He glanced up at Detective Abrams. "And since you now know that you should probably see this as well."

He pulled out a piece of parchment from a folder in his bag and laid it on the table. We crowded around to read a letter dated 1888.

Tuesday, September 18, 1888

My dearest Sir Edward Fernsby, the Honorable Duke of Exeter,

I hope this letter finds you well. I thought it my duty to acquaint you by letter to the concern I have for your well-being and the rest of The Electi. Therefore, I hope you will hold this letter in the greatest of confidences. I fear Archibald Clemency shall be the ruin of us. He and I had a drink at the Tipperary a fortnight ago, and he was most concerning in his boastfulness about Brothers of the Night and the creed they adopted when The Electi was temporarily disbanded.

You know how ruthless Archie can be in his pursuit of what he considers righteous power. He shared with me a memento gained from his latest escapade, a common button ripped from the crotch, he says, of the undergarment worn by one Mary Nichols. You may be acquainted with her name as reported lately by The Daily News and other papers.

His behavior is intolerable, and yet Archie shared with me the existence of a box in which he stored such mementos, along with the original Ledger of Deeds from The Electi. I believe we must rid ourselves of this box and its contents lest we come to ruin.

Arthur Finlay shared the drawings for the box with me, and it is a masterpiece of concealment. Suffice it to say that if we were to open it without the key, it would destroy everything inside. Since I am told you have the key, however, we have only to get the box away from Archibald to fully absolve ourselves of this sinful agenda.

I shall be in London on Thursday next and therefore desire that we should meet to discuss this unpleasantness further.

With the united compliments of my Father and Family, I remain Yours most sincerely,

Yours truly,

Philip Sallow III, Earl of Bath

So, the Electus back then was this Duke of Exeter," I said.

"Yes," Ben said. "Second cousin to Edward VII, King of England."

"And he may have helped to steer the Metropolitan Police away from Brothers of the Night as killers?" Doe asked.

"It seems so although no one could prove it," Ben said. He turned to Detective Abrams. "How much of this do you think will come out?"

"All of it," he said. "In order to prosecute these people, we'll have to use everything that's in that box and anything else you have. These people not only have the money to hire high-powered attorneys, but they also have the influence that can change verdicts. So, whether you want to take credit for finding the box or not, it's all going to come out."

"Besides, people have a right to know," Rudy said.

"Maybe," Ben said. "But the box needs to go back to Scotland Yard at some point. Or the British government."

"That'll probably be for a court to decide," David said. "Once the trials are over. And my guess is that with appeals, that could be many years from now."

CHAPTER THIRTY-SIX

The following Saturday, we set up for Carter's memorial service under a gray sky in Grieg Garden on the University of Washington campus. While the leaden hue to the sky above us matched my mood, the garden was a cozy little oasis surrounded by trees and colorful rhododendrons and azaleas. A small duck pond accented the park at one end with a large bronze bust of Norwegian composer Edvard Grieg at the other end. Although it was normally a thorough-fare for students, we had permission to cordon it off as a fitting place to pay homage to Carter.

Over one hundred people attended, including Graham and Kitty, the president of the university, the chair of European Studies, dozens of Carter's students, and even some of the maintenance staff who loved him, but hated cleaning his office.

"We were only allowed to vacuum the floor and wash the windows," one of the maintenance men told me. "If we even so much as moved something—a book, a photograph, or one of his silly toys, we never heard the end of it. And yet, every Christmas, he gave each one of us a bottle of Irish whiskey. He was one of a kind."

We heard lots of stories like that. One of his students, who had become a professor at Yale, spoke about how Carter would do random magic tricks in class. His story reminded me that Carter and Ben had practiced magic together when they were young. In fact, Carter had mentioned it in his note hidden in the casket. Ben was good at sleight-of-hand tricks and once stole a bad report card from a stack of mail on the counter in front of my mother. Carter got very good at picking pockets and making things appear out of thin air.

"This all just makes me want to cry again," I said to Blair, who was sitting next to me.

She had switched out her attire for the funeral. Instead of dressing so that every part of her body screamed for male attention, she looked like Audrey Hepburn auditioning for *Breakfast at Tiffany's*, dressed in a little black dress, and a big, floppy black hat that dipped down right in front of her face, obscuring her large sunglasses. All she was missing were Audrey Hepburn's signature big pearls. And yet, somehow, it worked.

Huge pictures of Carter flanked the small stage we'd set up. In one, he perched on the edge of the desk in his lecture hall with an enormous blackboard behind him. The other was a close-up of his laughing face. The pictures showed the two sides of him perfectly.

The president of the university, a hawkish-looking man, spoke first about how important Carter had been to the school for some thirty years. A colleague of his spoke next, telling humorous stories of how Carter had endeared himself to the brainiacs he worked with. A former student spoke after that, and then Renée took the stage, her face shadowed by grief. She talked about her father with her son, Josh, by her side.

And then it was Ben's turn.

He moved onto the stage with faltering steps, his face drawn and pale. Partly, I think, because of how sad he was. And partly because he felt responsible for why we were there.

He positioned himself behind the podium and took a breath. His face had mostly healed, although there were a couple of lingering bruises, and he still had trouble moving too quickly or taking deep breaths because of the broken ribs. He held the sheet of paper on which he'd written out his thoughts, but he stuffed it in his pants pocket at the last minute. Then he looked out at the crowd, took a breath, and began, "Carter Davis was my best friend since the time we were boys in Wisconsin..."

÷

Once the service ended, Graham and Kitty and their security detail left in a motorcade of big SUVs. His entire entourage had worn "Applegate for Governor" campaign pins. Graham and I had spoken only briefly, and maybe for the first time, he embraced Ben to tell him how sorry he was about Carter. It was a nice moment.

After they'd left, the girls and I joined Angela on the other side of the clearing, where we had set up several tables with food and beverages. Angela, April, and I had spent the day before making oodles of finger sandwiches, small cream-filled desserts, and cookies. Rudy and Doe had ordered the wine and soft drinks. And Blair had taken care of the flowers. We could have had it catered, but it was important for us to make this personal, and we wanted Renée to be free to greet the many people who had come to honor her father.

I was at the front of the table, moving desserts around to fill in spaces, when David sidled up to me.

"You know, we've both been so busy this week, we haven't had our intimate dinner. My apology is burning a hole in my throat."

A chuckle bubbled up as I looked at him. He had just consumed a cookie and wore crumbs around his mouth. I reached up and brushed them away.

"Well, we wouldn't want that to happen. I accept your apology."

He slipped his arm around my waist, leaned in, and kissed my forehead.

"I love you, you know," he murmured. "And I know how to solve my problem."

"*Your* problem?"

"Yes, *my* problem. Which is me getting upset when you get involved in my investigations. I say it's my problem because, well, it is. I'm the one that can't deal with it. Not you."

My eyebrows shot up. "Oh, dear, did I just hear a major shift in that cop brain of yours?"

He nuzzled my ear. "Yes. But don't rub it in."

"What's the big decision, though?" I said, pulling away to look at him. "You'll just lock me up next time? If there is a next time."

He grinned. "I have no doubt there will be a next time. Murder seems to follow you around like your wiener dogs."

"Then how do you plan to deal with it?"

He allowed a short dramatic pause to draw out before saying, "I'm going to retire."

Whatever I thought he was going to say, it wasn't that.

"But David, you love your job."

"I know. And I do. But I've been thinking of retiring for a long time. In fact, I could have retired at 55 with full benefits. But my wife was gone, and work had become my life. I was pretty good friends with the captain at the Mercer Island PD, and he offered to hire me. But look, I'm 66 now. I can easily live off my pension and do some fly-fishing and woodworking. You said yourself you'd like to have more birdhouses in your garden."

This time, the tears that formed in the corner of my eyes were from feelings of joy. "I did say that."

"And…" he said with emphasis. "What's to say I couldn't hang out a shingle as a private investigator? Maybe we could go into business together," he said with a grin.

"Oh!" I exclaimed. "That would be wonderful!"

I whirled around to tell Blair and smashed into a man behind me, holding a plate of lemon tarts. And just like in any chain reaction... his hand jerked up, sending his plate into the air and the ooey-gooey desserts directly into the face of the woman with him. She snapped her hand to the side, smacking a short bald man behind her in the back of the head. He jerked sideways, slamming into the president of the university, who then took a graceful header into the pond.

A hundred people stopped and stared—some mid-bite—while I had trouble breathing.

"Mom!" Angela said in shock.

As Blair, Doe, and Rudy stared at me and shook their heads, I shrugged my shoulders.

"Let's get out of here," David whispered in my ear. He grabbed my hand and dragged me away.

"But..."

"But what? You don't need to be here for this. Where's your purse?"

"Don't worry, Julia," Blair said with a wink. "We have your back. Go."

As two men rushed forward to help drag the university president from the pond, David and I escaped to my car and went home to celebrate his news in our own special way.

CHAPTER THIRTY-SEVEN

Ben stayed with me for almost a month to recuperate and help Renée clean out Carter's belongings. During that time, the university offered him a professorship, complete with annual sabbaticals to do his research. He accepted. In fact, he made Renée an offer to buy Carter's house.

One afternoon, as I was doing laundry, I spied Ben hiding something in the secret compartment of his briefcase. He did this, forgetting I knew how to open it. Later, while he was at Carter's house helping Renée, I looked inside to see what he was keeping from me. He's my brother, after all. And this reminded me too much of when we were kids, and he would hide things he didn't want me to see in the back of his underwear drawer. Which, clearly, I had discovered, but never let him know.

I snuck into his room and opened the secret compartment; nervous he might walk in at any moment. Inside was a small piece of old parchment. In small script, it mentioned a nobleman who had belonged to The Electi in its early days. This was the letter he had signed to join the society, admitting to something that would keep him forever quiet.

It was obvious Ben had done a sleight-of-hand trick and slipped the parchment into his bag when we were all preoccupied that day at the police station by what was in the box. I shook my head and smiled, thinking some things would never change.

My face flushed, though, as I read the brief document dated December 1887. A young boy named Thomas had written it. He was envious of his older brother, Roman, who would inherit his father's title and family property. In exquisite detail, Thomas explained how he had executed a plan to kill his brother. It was easy, he said, because his brother was a stargazer and liked to go up to the top terrace of their stately home at night to spend hours contemplating the constellations. Roman would often lean over the balcony to see the star's reflections on a lake a small distance away.

Over a period of several days, Thomas weakened the stone balustrade on the terrace and then waited patiently for the next time his brother would go up there to look at the stars. Roman did so two days later. As expected, he leaned over the weakened railing with his full weight and fell to his death.

I contemplated the letter and the fact that when Graham and I divorced, I had thought of going back to my maiden name of Brouwer. But Graham Applegate was my first real love and bearing his last name kept me close to him. Besides that, he was a powerhouse of a man destined for even greater things than the governorship of Washington State, perhaps even the White House.

So although the story of how Thomas had killed his brother was gut-wrenching, my stomach didn't sour at the cold-heartedness of the heinous act. Instead, my breath caught at the name of the young man himself—Thomas Allen Applegate.

THE END

FOLLOWING JACK THE RIPPER

The killer known as Jack the Ripper has become almost mythological and has always fascinated me. Partly because there has been so much speculation over the past hundred plus years about who he was and why he killed, and yet no one has really gotten close to identifying the man himself.

When the idea came to mind to use him as the reason someone close to Julia would get murdered, I studied up with a few books written about him and was spurred on by the TV series *Ripper Street*, which follows Detective Inspector Edmund Reid as he strives to maintain law and order in Whitechapel after failing to find Jack the Ripper. Reid was, in fact, one of the officers who hunted the killer back in 1888. The show is quite good, but if you don't have the stomach for violence, you'd best avoid it.

Anyway, I loved the idea of introducing a new character as Julia's brother, Ben, who was looking for the Lusk Letter, sent to the Whitechapel Vigilance Committee in 1888 by someone claiming to be the killer. It arrived in a box, which also contained half a human kidney. Someone described the letter as, "... the most disturbing and noteworthy of the three most prominent Jack the Ripper messages." This is largely because of the body part which accompanied the letter.

The result is, I hope, a satisfying read and at least a plausible theory as to who the real Jack the Ripper might have been.

The 'From Hell' Letter, also known as the Lusk Letter.

BROTHERS OF THE NIGHT DIARY ENTRIES FOR FREE

In my initial draft of *The Key to Murder*, I included several more pages from the Brothers of the Night's diary. Since I have already written them, I'm offering them to you for free if you will allow me to add you to my newsletter mailing list. You can always opt out later. Just go to my website at https://www.lynnbohart-author.com/ and click on the Contact page. Send me an email telling me you would like to receive the Brotherhood diary entries. If you're interested in reading the character profiles for either Julia Applegate or Detective Giorgio Salvatori, you may also request those. I will send them to you for your reading pleasure.

REVIEWS ARE IMPORTANT

Thank you for reading *The Key to Murder*. If you enjoyed it, you would honor me if you would take a few minutes to go back to Amazon and leave a review. Self-published authors live and die on the number of positive reviews our books receive. You can go here to leave a review: https://rb.gy/avvlus.

ACKNOWLEDGEMENTS

The list of people I depend on to bring these books to market seems to grow with each publication, and I am eternally grateful for all the help I receive. My go-to group for initial feedback is my writing critique group, who I have been with for over eight years. They methodically read each book two chapters at a time over a period of ten months and help to clarify the storyline and characters, challenge me on specific details, eliminate things that just don't work, and highlight internal 'gems' I didn't even know I had. Case in point: they liked Jake so much in *All Roads Lead to Murder* that I brought him back in this book. Special thanks to Tim McDaniel, Michael Manzer, Gary Larson, and Irma Fritz.

I also rely on a group of "beta" readers to give me honest feedback. They volunteer to read the book from cover-to-cover and not only catch mistakes, but identify inconsistencies in the storyline, things that might confuse the reader, or things that just don't make sense. This time around my thanks go to Karen Gilb, Rex Caldwell, Kitty Bucholtz, and my daughter, Jaynee Bohart. By the way, Rex Caldwell is my go-to expert on all things related to police matters.

A shout out goes to both my daughter, as well as my close friend Dakoda Mondragon for listening to me brainstorm endlessly about the storyline of this book. Creating a secret society and linking it to Jack the Ripper wasn't easy (but, oh so fun). And lastly, I would be lost without my friend and colleague, Liz Stewart, who edits my books. She is also very patient with me because she is forced to listen to more of my endless brainstorming whenever we have lunch.

I would also like to extend my sincere appreciation to Dakoda Mondragon for writing the music to the book trailer for *The Key to Murder*. He is a very talented music producer. You can listen to his music on Spotify: *Crystalskin*, *Lidocaine Lounge*, and *Android Visions*.

Once again, thanks to my friend, Mia Bradshaw, for another terrific cover. I decided long ago to keep the St. Claire Inn as the main focal point on every cover and only change things in the foreground to highlight the new storyline. Mia is very patient with me. She is a wonderful craftsperson and shows/sells her work in Seattle. Please check out her website at www.miayoshihara.com.

Finally, are members of my 'street team' who offered to help get the word out when the book launched: Karen Gild, Jaynee Bohart, Jaris English, Helene Boothroyd, Cindy Warden LaSance, Susy Gaffney, Christie Kathleen Michael Dimon, Adrienne Oliver, Venetia Vango, Terri Zura, Jenny Cabuag, Ann Nordquist, Charles Seil, and Anne Harbove.

ABOUT THE AUTHOR

Ms. Bohart spent 35+ years as a nonprofit executive for three different hospital foundations and then a regional community foundation. She holds a master's degree in theater, has published in Woman's World, and has a story in *Dead on Demand*, an anthology of ghost stories that remained on the Library Journals bestseller list for six months. She teaches writing through the Continuing Education Program at Green River College and has written for the *Renton Reporter*.

The Key to Murder is her ninth full-length novel and the fifth in the Old Maids of Mercer Island series. *Inn Keeping with Murder*, the first book in this series, remained in the top 100 ghost stories on Amazon for ten months.

You can check out her other books, including the Detective Giorgio Salvatori mysteries, on Amazon.com. The third book in that series, *The Essence of Murder,* takes Giorgio and Grosvenor, his faithful Basset hound, into the dark worlds of vampirism and dog-fighting rings.

If you would like more information about the author or would like to join Ms. Bohart's mailing list, please visit her website at: www.lynnbohart-author.com. You can let her know you'd like to be added to her newsletter list where you'll be notified of upcoming publications or events. You may also join her author page on Facebook.

OTHER BOOKS BY LYNN BOHART

OLD MAIDS OF MERCER ISLAND SERIES

Inn Keeping with Murder

A Candidate for Murder

A History of Murder

All Roads Lead to Murder

DETECTIVE GIORGIO SALVATOR SERIES

Mass Murder

Murder in the Past Tense

The Essence of Murder

STAND ALONE & SHORT STORY BOOKS

Grave Doubts (a novel)

Your Worst Nightmare (anthology of short stories)

Something Wicked (short story)

Read the first chapter in Mass Murder, the first book in the Detective Giorgio Salvatori mysteries.

FIRST CHAPTER OF MASS MURDER

A Giorgio Salvatori Murder Mystery

† CHAPTER ONE †

Premonitions were taken seriously in the Norville family.

When Syd Norville was six years old, his mother aborted a trip to Florida to celebrate the birth of her niece because of a dream she'd had the night before. In that dream, the plane crashed. The next day, the plane she would have been on did, in fact, crash on take-off because of a faulty suspension rig, killing all two hundred and forty passengers. When Syd was twelve, his older sister abandoned her millionaire husband-to-be at the altar because of a bad feeling about the honeymoon. The groom went on to Aruba alone. Two days later, his rented car flew off a cliff. When Syd was home on leave from the Navy, he'd been about to cross a downtown street when an inexplicable feeling made him retreat to the curb. A moment later, an old van barreled through the intersection followed by a police car, both passing within inches of where Syd stood.

Yes, the Norville family took premonitions seriously.

Syd's old Chevy truck pulled into the west parking lot of the massive Catholic monastery where he worked five nights a week as a janitor. He climbed down from the cab and let his right hand linger on the tattered steering wheel cover. A glance at the hazy moon peeking through a clump of trees at the south end of the property made him shudder. Something was wrong. He could feel it. And his impulse was to run.

He turned to listen, remembering the night several months earlier when a child's voice had sent him scurrying through the mammoth building looking for the source.

Since then, cold spots had stopped him in the middle of heated hallways and once, when a pair of invisible fingers slid across his forearm, he'd thought about finding another job. The acid pouring into his stomach now made him wish he had.

A penetrating breeze rising from the southern tip of the property sent shivers across his shoulders like a thousand sand crabs running for cover. It was five minutes to nine. He had to decide.

Syd grabbed his lunchbox from behind the seat and closed the battered truck door. He needed to ignore the voices in his head and get to work. His fingers flexed around the Rosary in his pocket for comfort. With a shake of his shoulders, he hurried toward the west door before he could change his mind.

Lights blazed in the banquet room, and the sound of laughter replaced thoughts of impending disaster. He eyed the white catering van still parked in the lot. The young Miss Fields would depart soon, leaving behind a small clean-up crew. These parties often lasted until well past midnight, so no telling when he'd have access to the banquet room, where his job was only to pick up the trash, vacuum, and spot clean the carpet.

He reached the back door of the kitchen when a car engine made him turn around. A pair of headlights flicked on in the parking lot, and a moment later, a familiar Toyota Camry pulled out.

Syd slipped inside the back door and turned down a short hallway towards the cleaning closet. He would start tonight at the other end of the building to avoid the party guests. He liked to mix up his routine, sometimes going through the building clockwise, sometimes counterclockwise, sometimes all out of order. It helped to relieve the boredom. Thirty years as a shop manager made this work meaningless, but the job helped to pay his wife's medical bills. After surgery to remove a kidney, her prognosis was good. The image of his plump little wife sitting at home watching her favorite T.V. show warmed his insides, helping to further reduce his jitters.

He stepped into the closet and flicked on the single 40-watt bulb that served as an overhead light. It illuminated the area next to the door, but Syd could have found his way around blind. He knew the closet that well.

His lungs inhaled the comforting sweetness of the powdered soap that sat in boxes on a shelf to his left, but an almost imperceptible tingling at the back of his neck made him think there was something more. It was an odor he didn't recognize, something dank among the aroma of pine and borax. With trembling fingers, he tucked his lunchbox under one arm and reached for the small flask he now carried in his pants pocket. He removed the cap with practiced ease and took a swig. The searing flow of whisky inflamed his throat.

Within moments, his muscles relaxed, and the tremors in his hands dissipated.

Now he had to get to work. He returned the flask to its hiding place and placed his lunchbox on an empty shelf, surprised to find one of the monk's wool blankets there. He reached for a handful of cleaning rags and then grabbed a spray bottle filled with his favorite cleaning solvent. A wire brush, rubber gloves, and a couple of old sponges completed his list of supplies. He stowed this all onto a large metal cart, loaded on the vacuum cleaner, and then stepped around a supporting column to grab the rolling mop bucket.

A small dark object sitting on the floor half in shadow caught his attention. Something had fallen off a shelf. Syd leaned down to pick it up and took a sharp breath. It was a woman's patent leather pump, looking incongruous in such functional surroundings. The shoe probably belonged to a party guest who had rendezvoused here with a male counterpart earlier in the evening. The thought disgusted him. He'd have to take the shoe to the kitchen. How was she walking around with only one shoe, anyway?

He reached down again to pick it up. The back of his hand bumped something just above it, causing whatever it was to swing back and forth in the dark. Surprised, Syd glanced up, peering into the shadows. When his eyes adjusted, a small cry escaped his lips.

He backed away with a jerk, knocking over a box of paper towels, stopping at the door, his lungs incapable of drawing breath.

He remained frozen like that, staring at the back wall. The premonition had been revealed. Just above the shoe dangled a slender foot encased in a black silk stocking, attached to the body of a dead woman.

You can find Mass Murder by going to Amazon.com.

FOLLOW MS. BOHART

Website: https://www.lynnbohart-author.com/
Twitter: @lbohart
Facebook: Facebook @ L.Bohart/author

Join my newsletter—

https://www.lynnbohart-   author.com/contact

Made in the USA
Las Vegas, NV
03 April 2022

46801725R00153